Praise for
New York Times
bestselling author

ELIZABETH LOWELL

"Elizabeth Lowell has long set a standard
of excellence for thrillers that never stint
on either romance or suspense . . ."

BookPage

"This author delivers pure,
undiluted excitement."

Jayne Ann Krentz

"Romantic suspense is her true forte."

Minneapolis Star-Tribune

"Lowell brilliantly mingles danger, deception,
and desire . . . romantic suspense at its best."

Booklist

By Elizabeth Lowell

ELIZABETH
LOWELL

Blue Smoke
and Murder

AVON
An Imprint of HarperCollinsPublishers

This book was originally published in hardcover June 2008 by William Morrow, an Imprint of HarperCollins Publishers

AVON BOOKS
An Imprint of HarperCollins*Publishers*
10 East 53rd Street
New York, New York 10022–5299

Copyright © 2008 by Two of a Kind, Inc.
ISBN 978–0–06–082986–5
www.avonbooks.com

First Avon Books paperback printing: April 2009
First William Morrow hardcover printing: June 2008

Avon Trademark Reg. U.S. Pat. Off. and in Other Countries, Marca Registrada, Hecho en U.S.A.
HarperCollins© is a registered trademark of HarperCollins Publishers.

Printed in the U.S.A.

10 9 8 7 6 5 4 3 2 1

For Evan,
my rock and my joy

Blue Smoke
and Murder

1

Northern Arizona
August
Midnight

Something was wrong.

Heart beating wildly, Modesty Breck sat up in bed. Listening over the pounding of her pulse, she tried to understand what had jerked her out of her sleep.

The wind blew hard, swirling around the old ranch house. She ignored the sound of rushing air. In the high, desolate reaches of Arizona's northern strip, the wind always blew.

The noise came again.

The front window groaned as someone pushed it up in the old wooden frame. Like her, groaning at every movement of her dry, brittle body. With fingers gnarled by arthritis, she found her glasses on the bedside table and shoved them into place, grateful that her hearing was still plenty good.

She fumbled under her narrow bed for the .22-caliber

snake gun that was older than she was. Its lever action jammed more often than it fired, but the prowler wouldn't know that.

When she struggled to her feet, the cold rose through the old wooden floor into her thick wool socks. Over the protests of stiff muscles and joints, she walked quietly to the bedroom door, her long flannel nightgown ragged where it touched the floor. The kitchen door was open, always, taking advantage of the residual heat from the oil stove.

A muffled thump came from the living room. Footsteps crossed the groaning wooden floor. Then a scuff when an old throw rug slipped underfoot.

Modesty smiled grimly. She didn't need any fancy burglar alarms when she was surrounded by an old house whose every creak was as familiar as her own breathing.

From beyond the house came the triumphant yowl of one of the barn cats parading a fresh kill in the moonlight. Like everything else living on the old ranch, the feral cats earned their keep.

Modesty waited, listening to the sounds of someone sneaking around her living room, opening old cupboards and drawers, closing them, moving on.

Finding nothing.

When the intruder headed into the kitchen, Modesty knew he wouldn't be able to see her. Quietly, avoiding the loose rugs and boards that creaked, she crept in the direction of the kitchen.

The intruder was a black shadow in the moonlight pouring through the window over the sink. The pantry door squeaked as he opened it.

She flipped on the kitchen light.

Score cursed and spun around. *Just my luck. The old lady has insomnia.*

"Black ski mask, just like in the news," Modesty said, her

voice as brittle as her bones. "Black coveralls and an itty-bitty flashlight. Where you from, boy?"

Score started for her.

She cocked the rifle. She would have levered in a round, but was afraid that it would jam, leaving the action open and the rifle useless except as a club.

"Go back where you came from," Modesty said.

Darkness stared at her from the openings in the ski mask. "Take it easy, Mrs. Breck. I'm not here to hurt you."

The voice, like the man, was low and thick. Though only a few inches taller than her five feet four inches, the man was muscular, stocky, easily twice her weight. None of it was paunch.

"That's Miss, not Mrs. Never cared for men. Nothing but trouble." Modesty gestured toward the back door with the rifle. "Git."

Score took another step forward, looked at the rifle and laughed coldly. "That old .22 is more likely to blow up in your face than hurt me."

Watching the weapon, Score came closer to Modesty without even appearing to move. He could tell by the blurred centers of the old lady's eyes that she was half-blind. Two more gliding steps and he'd have the rifle.

She tightened her crooked finger and the trigger. "I'll take my chances on it."

"Lady." Score's temper spiked. He pulled it in. Now wasn't the time to let his rage boil up. *Save it for the gym.* "You look like you could use some money. I've got five hundred on me. Tell me where the paintings are and it's yours."

Modesty felt like echoing the cat's yowl of triumph. *I knew those paintings were worth something. I'll be able to pay those back taxes without selling off the last of the stock.*

"Got all the money I need," she said. "Now git!"

She hadn't noticed the man moving, but suddenly the barrel of the rifle was pointed at the ceiling. With a wrench that made her hands ache, he yanked the gun out of her hands.

"Enough with the fun and games," Score said. He glanced at the breech and saw that the rifle had jammed. With a disgusted snarl he set the old weapon on the kitchen counter. "Where are the paintings?"

"Only pictures I have are family photos and such. What use are they to you?"

He stepped up so close she had to put a crick in her neck just to see the vague, blurred line of his mouth through the slit in the mask. If he had a neck, it was as thick as his upper arms.

"Don't make me hurt you," he warned. "Where are the paintings?"

"I'm near ninety. Pain doesn't scare me."

Score smiled slowly. "Yeah? How long will you be able to live here alone with every finger in your hands broken?"

Modesty made a small sound. Her greatest fear was being hauled off to some state institution to die with strangers puking and screaming around her.

I'll walk off a cliff first. But I'll go knowing that Jillian will be one Breck woman who won't have to depend on some damn man to survive.

Those paintings are her future.

"The only painting I have is the one I sent to an art dealer outside Salt Lake a month ago," Modesty said. "He wrote me the other week, said he sent it out for more opinions, and some fool lost it."

The man's mouth curled into a small smile. "You told the dealer there were twelve more paintings. Where are they?"

"I lied. Wanted him to think I'd give him more business."

"I don't believe you." More important, Score's client didn't believe her.

The grandfather clock in the living room chimed, marking off the hours.

"Last warning," he said. The surgical gloves he wore made his fists look huge, like pale bludgeons. "You're going to get hurt bad."

"Won't be the first time."

Score gave her an openhanded slap, not enough to knock her down but enough to make her ears ring. He caught her when she staggered. She winced when his fingers pressed tendon against bone.

"Listen," he said, "I don't get off hurting old ladies, but I do what I have to. Where are the paintings?"

"Who sent you?" she asked.

His smile was as thin as a razor. "If I told you, I'd have to kill you."

"Bet I can guess," she said.

"And if you guessed right, I'd still have to kill you," he said, laughing at the old joke. Then his voice hardened. He smacked her again, carefully, aware of her frail bones and his pumped-up strength. "So cut the crap and tell me where the paintings are."

"How do I know you won't kill me anyway?"

He stared at her for a long moment, eyes narrowed. "You'd bargain with the devil, wouldn't you?"

"I've lived my own life on my own terms," Modesty said, the words stronger than her thin voice, as strong as the fingers biting into her upper arms. "I'm not going to change now. And if you kill me, you'll never find those paintings."

"Now we're getting somewhere," Score said beneath his breath. "You admit they exist."

"This house was built by pioneers, people who lived alone and protected themselves. They built hidey-holes that even the Paiutes couldn't find."

"No problem. You're going to show them to me."

"The hell I am."

"Remember when you're screaming that I gave you a choice."

He released one of her arms and reached into the side pocket of his coveralls. When his hand came out, it held a strip of hard white plastic, like a short, thin belt with a tongue at one end and a locking catch at the other.

Modesty could see enough to recognize it. She used plastic cable ties on the ranch all the time. They were handy and strong, the modern version of baling wire. Real good at tying things together.

Like wrists.

Swallowing past the dryness in her mouth, she played her last card. "You'll never find the paintings."

But as she said it, she looked past him to the pantry he hadn't had time to search.

Score followed her glance. "Oh, I think I will."

Without another look at her, he turned his back and strode toward the pantry.

Modesty rushed to the counter and jerked open one of the drawers. She yanked out a wood-handled butcher knife that was as old as she was. The blade had been honed so many times that the steel was half its original width. And wicked sharp.

"What the—" Score began.

She lunged for him.

Automatically he threw up his forearm to block the knife. When he felt the burn of steel on flesh, his temper roared. He hit the old lady so hard she flew one way and the knife went the other. She reeled, staggered, tripped over a kitchen chair, and fell. Her head hit the edge of the old iron cookstove. She landed in a boneless sprawl.

She didn't move.

Swearing, Score looked at the red slash across his forearm. Blood was welling up, but not in spurts. A cut, that was all. Not even deep enough for stitches. Grappling with his temper, he looked at the old woman.

She seemed smaller, like a bundle of rags instead of a person.

He cursed steadily as he squatted beside her. He'd seen enough bodies to know what death looked like. A simple black-bag job on an old lady's house had turned into murder.

"What are you—stupid?" he snarled at her. "No way you were going to take me."

He eased his fingers underneath her head. She still had her glasses on, crookedly, but that no longer mattered. Her eyes were dim from more than cataracts. Beneath thinning white hair he felt a depression in her skull. She must have been dead a second after she hit, because there was no blood.

"Crazy old bitch," he said, standing up. "Why didn't you listen?"

With a final disgusted curse, he went to search the pantry.

He didn't find anything but canned goods and bags of rice and flour, sugar and beans. No trick shelves, no trapdoor, no false ceiling. Nothing but food.

He searched the rest of the house.

Nothing.

He went to the back porch and looked over at the sagging barn forty feet beyond the kitchen. The wind swirled around him, plucking at his coveralls with hard, impatient fingers, then racing away to batter the old barn.

He didn't have time to search the old building. He'd let the wind take care of it.

He picked up the can of fuel oil from the back porch and went back into the kitchen. It wasn't the first time he'd dressed a crime scene to look like an everyday accident.

If the paintings turned up, it wouldn't be the last time, either.

2

On the Colorado River
August 27
8:00 A.M.

oly shit," Lane Faroe said reverently.

The lanky teenager looked at Jillian Breck, grinned, then realized what he'd just said.

"Oops," he said. "Sorry."

"No problem." Jill smiled without looking away from the thunder and boil of a river narrowed to half its size by a bottleneck of basalt, a rock as hard as the water was determined to reach the sea. "That's what I say to myself every time I see Lava Falls."

And every time it's different.

That's why she loved it. The water flow from Lake Powell, two hundred miles upstream, changed from day to day. Rocks and boulders on the riverbank got undercut and tumbled into the current. Wherever they stuck, they piled waves in new ways, creating new currents, rips, holes, and eddies.

Running the Colorado was always different, yet always the same. Dangerous.

Exhilarating.

"Looks like a big chocolate snake somebody stepped on," Lane said.

Jill nodded. "A mean one."

That was the other thing she loved about the river. It tested her. She was going to miss river running when she gave it up, but she knew the time was coming. Soon. She had a restlessness that even the wild river couldn't cure.

Maybe she would turn the old Breck homestead into a dude ranch. Bring back horses and buy more cattle, dig a trout pond, organize camera and painting and hunting safaris, feed people from kitchen gardens watered by the old windmill.

Maybe she would keep on being a river bum, following the seasons down Western rivers, teaching kayaking and rafting and wilderness survival skills.

And maybe I should concentrate on this river in front of me. Lava Falls changed with the last monsoon rain. I'll need a slightly different approach.

Today she felt like an adrenaline ride, something for the tall, good-looking teenager to remember. Lava Falls would provide it. A hundred feet below her cliff overlook, rapids coiled and boomed and frothed. Whirlpools and back eddies hid behind the shoulders of huge rocks along the bank. The roar was constant, insistent, almost numbing.

The right side, she thought, nodding to herself. *Plenty of room today. Head for that big boulder sticking out from the bank like a house, let the power of the river turn the raft, dig in hard with the right oar, and shoot across to the other bank.*

Lane looked sideways at the river guide who was rowing him and his father Joe Faroe down the Colorado. Lane figured Jill was older than he was by at least a decade, but it didn't stop him from noticing how hot she was. She had the lean, smooth body of a gymnast, but she had hips and boobs, too. Since everybody wore sunscreen and not much else in the summer heat, he'd had plenty of time to enjoy the scenery around camp.

The problem with being a tall sixteen was that a lot of the women who looked really hot to him thought he was too young, and girls his age wanted older men.

Sometimes life just basically sucked.

But the view was great.

Jill turned and started back down the steep, ragged trail that had been worn dusty by river guides coming to check out one of the most dangerous rapids on a river famous for its risk. The Colorado claimed some lives each year, mostly the drunk or careless, but sometimes the dead were simply unlucky.

When Jill and Lane walked back down to the waiting rafts, Joe Faroe cocked an eyebrow at his son. "Are we walking or riding?"

"You can always walk around," Jill said before Lane answered. "The trail's about four miles. We'll wait for you downstream."

"I'm riding," Lane said to his dad. "I'm just wondering if a girl has enough strength to handle that water."

Faroe shook his head. Lane had an excellent brain, but he still had some things to learn about women. Jill had hiked the teenager into the ground at least twice on this trip, but he always came back with the guy-girl needle. He hadn't noticed how the other guides—female *and* male—deferred to Jill's judgment and skill.

"If it will make you feel better," Jill said innocently, "I'll let your daddy row. He's good and strong."

"No thanks," Faroe said. "I'll leave Lava Falls to the experts."

Lane grumbled. "Why him? You only let me row when the river is flat and the wind is against us."

Jill winked at Faroe. "What I lack in strength I make up for in smarts."

Faroe laughed and gave his son a one-armed hug. "She's got you there. She knows more about leverage than an unarmed combat teacher. And that's what running the river is about, leverage and smarts."

Combat, too, of a sort. But not the sort Faroe was used to. On the river he was happy to have someone else looking out for danger. That's what a vacation was all about—not having to figure out how to kill someone before he killed you.

"Huh," Lane said, but smiled at Jill. "You ever dump in Lava Falls?"

"Twice," she said, fingering the leather cord around her neck. It held a serrated folding knife with a hook on the tip. If she went over and got caught on something below the water, the blade was sharp enough to cut through the tough woven nylon flotation harness with a single stroke. She'd never had to use the knife. She hoped she never would. "You don't fight the water, you just float with it. That's why everyone wears the harness you're always complaining about."

"It's too narrow across the shoulders."

"Your dad's is worse, but you don't hear him complaining."

Faroe smiled. The float harness was more comfortable than body armor, but he wasn't going to point that out.

"Mom would have enjoyed this," Lane said, watching the river with eyes that were just like his father's.

"Not nearly nine months pregnant, she wouldn't," Faroe said dryly. "She was real clear on that. Wanted us to do the male bonding thing while she did the female gestating thing."

"Hope she waits to have it until we get home."

"She's not due for almost a month."

"She's huge."

"Don't tell her that," Faroe said.

They were the last raft in their party to take on Lava Falls. While the other rafts entered the current with whoops and shouts, Lane and Faroe followed Jill to their own small craft. They sat on the inflated gunwale and swished their feet in the water, making sure their gritty sandals were well rinsed before swinging their legs aboard. Then both passengers went to work on the straps securing their individual float harness.

"Ready?" Jill asked.

They answered with a thumbs-up.

Lane had the front of the raft, Faroe the back. Jill sat on the hard rowing bench in the center, facing forward, oars poised above the water. The rapids ahead was clearing of other rafters. She watched the river intently, correcting the angle of the raft as she entered the current. The approach to Lava Falls was crucial.

Do it right and get an adrenaline ride.

Do it wrong and suck rocks.

The current picked up, shoving the raft off to one side. She dipped her left oar and stroked once, correcting the line. The front of the raft started to buck gently as it picked up the first of the waves. She glanced quickly at her passengers, giving a last check to life vests. Sometimes Lane was careless about his. He resented the confinement.

The roar of the coming cataract was like a jet taking off.

"You buckled up, Lane?" she shouted.

He turned toward her, showing that he had pulled two of the three straps tight across his chest. The loose end of the third strap dangled free, eighteen inches of woven fabric ending with a tough plastic buckle.

"Fix it," she shouted, nodding toward the trailing strap.

He looked down, saw the problem, and took one hand off the safety grip to tuck the buckle up out of the way. The strap was stiff, and stubborn, which was how it had worked free in the first place.

The front of the raft plunged into the first hole in the water, then pitched up in the air like a rearing horse. Cold water sprayed Lane as the raft sideslipped. He gave a rebel yell of delight.

Grinning, Jill worked the oars, port ahead, starboard reverse, snapping the raft back into the correct line. The shift in direction and momentum caught Lane off balance. He slammed forward, bounced off the round, slick flotation tube, and was mostly airborne when the second swell caught the raft.

He shot over the side and into the roaring cataract.

Faroe leaned out and grabbed, but Lane's dark hair was snatched away from his grasp by the boiling current. The slick raft was faster than the leg-dragging swimmer.

"Float with it!" Jill shouted to Lane. "Don't fight it!"

She marked the spot where she'd seen him go in, then leaned hard on both oars, abandoning the carnival ride for a back eddy on the right-hand shore. The raft shot forward, angled off the current, and slowed as she caught the eddy behind a big bolder. She pinned the raft's nose against the back of the boulder and stared at the cataract upstream of them.

"There!" Faroe said, pointing.

Lane's red life vest winked against the frothing water. He lifted his hand and waved.

Jill let out a long breath.

The river sucked him under again for another white-washing.

Faroe kicked off his sandals, ready to go over the side of the raft after his son.

"No." Jill's command was sharp. "He's doing fine. I don't want two of you in there."

Lane bobbed back to the surface on an upwelling wave. He was moving swiftly with the current, bobbing merrily past them. Jill knew without looking that the other rafts would be standing by at the end of the rapids to pick him up.

Suddenly Lane stopped like a bronc snubbed off on a corral post. The current kept going, which dragged him down below the water. He struggled back to the surface for a breath before water dragged him under again.

And kept him there.

That damn loose strap!

But all Jill said aloud was "Take the oars."

She was in the river before Faroe could object.

Even as she hit the water, she knew she had to get rid of her life vest. It would push her quickly down the rapids and past Lane before she could help him. As the current caught her, she unsnapped catches and let the river whip the vest away. Treading water, she gauged the wild current, the jutting boulders, the holes that could suck people down and drown them. She slanted her body and swam hard at an angle so that the rapids would carry her to the place downstream where Lane had disappeared.

Lane flailed to the surface again, grabbing at air, getting water along with it, choking, disappearing again.

Jill rolled onto her back and slipped the cord holding the knife over her head, gripping the knife tightly in her right hand. She'd get only one chance to grab Lane. If she missed, the river would push her past him like a rocket.

She would probably survive.

Lane wouldn't.

With the current boiling wildly around her, she hooked the teenager underneath one arm as she was swept by. She dragged him up and yelled, "Breathe, then dead man's float!"

He took a gasping breath, hesitated, then went limp, facedown in the river. The current stretched his body out in the water, showing Jill where he was anchored against the torrent. She clung to Lane with her legs like a lover, inching down his torso until her right arm found the strap. She thumbed the blade open, felt it lock in place, and slashed across the strap.

They shot to the surface together. Lane flipped over onto his back, gasping and coughing. Jill kept her grip on him, letting his life vest keep both of them afloat. Suddenly she scissor-kicked hard, again and then again. Soon they were sliding into the back eddy where Joe was working the oars to keep the raft in place. Slick river rocks came up to meet their dangling feet.

Jill released Lane, watched him gain his feet, and felt a relief that made her lightheaded.

He looked down at the severed end of the strap dangling from his vest. Then he looked at the four-inch cut in his swim trunks. The nylon mesh of the built-in athletic supporter showed through the gash.

"Your—knife?" he asked, still panting and coughing.

Breathing hard, Jill nodded. She'd let go of the knife the instant Lane was free. Bouncing around in the rapids with a lethal blade wasn't smart.

"Sharp—sucker," Lane said. "Glad it—wasn't any—longer."

Jill threw back her head and laughed. Then she hugged him hard. He hugged her the same way.

Faroe watched and wished Lane was old enough for Jill. She was one of the good ones. Smart, quick, cool under pressure, strong in the best sense of the word. She reminded him in some ways of Mary, St. Kilda Consulting's long-gun expert.

He steadied the raft while Lane and Jill levered themselves aboard. Lane sprawled in the bow, coughing occasionally, but breathing just fine.

Before Jill took up the oars again, Faroe said simply, "Thank you."

She flashed him a smile. "Just trying to cut down on the paperwork. We hate losing clients."

Faroe smiled back. "My boss is the same way. Where's your waterproof ditty bag?"

Jill blinked at the change of subject. "Um, under my seat."

He unfastened the waterproof belly pack around his waist, searched for a few seconds, and pulled out a laminated business card. "Put this in it."

Automatically she took the card, glanced at it. A telephone number and a few words: ST. KILDA CONSULTING, JOE FAROE. She looked at him, puzzled.

"If you ever have a problem that worries you—*any* problem—call that number," Faroe said.

"Problem?"

"Stalkers, a pissed-off boyfriend, something that frightens you, no one to talk to, no money for bills. Anything, Jill. Any time. Call that number, ask for me. You'll get help immediately."

"Well, thank you, but . . ."

Faroe smiled at her confused look. "I know, you have everything under control. I used to feel the same way. Then I found out how many wicked curves life can throw. Keep the card with you always, and hope you never need it."

3

Hollywood
September 3
Late afternoon

Zachary Balfour tried not to look bored, which he was.

Or irritated.

Which he definitely was.

Nothing chapped him quite as much as a client who wanted to wear a "bodyguard" as an accessory when what she really needed was a muzzle and a rabies shot.

Not that he had any particular fondness for dodging bullets. He supposed he should be grateful this job could have been phoned in. But he wasn't thankful to be doing no-brain work at combat rates.

Seven days with DeeDee Breitling made a bullet look good.

You owe me for this one, Faroe. Little Ms. D-cup and dirt-for-brains might be the beloved niece of a D.C. official

St. Kilda Consulting wants to please, but she's wasting my time. The only stalker she has is in her dreams.

She needs me like a snake needs stilts.

The D.C. official knew it. The client had just wanted to have a tall, dark, and safe escort for her niece while DeeDee did Hollywood.

At least the gig would pay for a few weeks of roaming the West, looking for collectible old cars forgotten in even older barns or wrecking yards. That search was both Zach's passion and a way to keep food on the table, some of the time. The rest of the time he took contracts with St. Kilda.

But not as a nanny, for the love of God. What was Faroe thinking?

Maybe the boss was still sore about Zach cleaning him out in poker.

"Isn't that right, darling?" DeeDee Breitling asked.

She cooed, actually, but Zach was trying not to notice. Having four older sisters had taught him way too much about females for him to fall for this lip-licking idiot's act.

Too bad the surgeon didn't expand her brain along with her breasts. Or sew her mouth shut.

The idea made Zach smile.

DeeDee took that as agreement. She turned to the art dealer waiting expectantly. "It's perfect for my living room. Have it wrapped and sent to my Manhattan address."

Zach looked at the art she'd just bought and decided it was a match made in heaven. The two tiny gray splotches on the black background at the bottom left of the canvas represented her two brain cells groping for each other in the dark. The horse's butt outlined in gold in the upper right-hand corner of the frame needed no explanation. It represented the buyer.

At least the artist had a sense of humor, as well as a fine understanding of flow and line. Evoking an equine ass with a few spare strokes of the brush wasn't easy. Like creating a fine haiku, it took a lot of training, work, talent, and intelligence to pull off. Painting a whole horse and making it work took all that, plus technique.

Making the horse transcend the canvas took genius.

But DeeDee only liked the kind of art that other people told her she should. The great painters of the American West didn't have much traction in Manhattan. If you painted Paris scenes in the nineteenth and early twentieth centuries, it was art. If you painted Wild West scenes in America during the same time, it was called genre painting and generally ignored by East Coast museums and collectors. Thomas Moran—and lately, Frederic Remington—was the exception that proved the rule.

"Now, what about dinner?" she asked Zach.

What about it? Three leaves of lettuce and a carrot shaving doesn't take much discussion.

"This isn't Manhattan, of course," she said, frowning, "but there are still some decent restaurants."

"Sure you don't want to try Tommy's Burgers?" he asked hopefully. What was the point of getting close to L A if you didn't eat at the original Tommy's?

She shuddered. "No. I thought our last night in Hollywood should be special."

Zach told himself she was making a joke. But he knew DeeDee didn't have any sense of humor. He'd found that out within the first five minutes of his week-long assignment.

How do you owe me, Faroe? Let me count the ways.

4

Northern Arizona
September 11
Late afternoon

Jill drove past the ruins of the ranch house and the burned skeleton of the barn. She didn't stop. She would later, when she'd had more time to absorb the reality of her great-aunt's death. Modesty Breck had seemed to be one of those people who just got harder and leaner, not old so much as ageless. Like the land itself, spare and unrelenting. Something you always respected yet always took for granted.

No guilt trip, Jill told herself firmly. *After Mom died, the old witch barely put up with having me live in the original homestead cabin over the ridge from the ranch house.*

Modesty was a woman who liked her own space. A lot of it. Solitude and hard work were her chosen gods.

She died the way she wanted to live. Alone. So lose the guilt.

Easier said than done.

Dust and grit flew beneath the little Honda SUV's tires as the eight-year-old vehicle bounced and rattled over the rough dirt road. No one had been here since the last monsoon rains had pounded the dry land. There wasn't any other sign of life except for the occasional coyote and rabbit tracks preserved in dried mud on the road's low spots. Water had washed away everything else, even the tire tracks leading to the ranch house where Modesty had died.

When Jill topped the steep ridge, she saw the original homestead cabin lying sheltered in a small valley, built right on top of the spring that had attracted her Breck ancestors in the 1840s. When Jill and her mother had moved from—fled, actually—Utah, they had lived with Modesty in the "new" ranch house just long enough to fix up the homestead cabin.

As a young girl, Jill had loved climbing the red cliffs and spires that were the rear wall of the cabin. As an adult, she hadn't been back in six years.

The closer Jill drove to the cabin, the more relieved she felt.

At least I won't have to waste money on a motel while I take care of whatever needs to be done with Modesty's estate.

Some of the chinking had fallen out between the weathered logs and a shutter hung drunkenly over half of the kitchen window, but the rest looked just as she remembered—old, small, oddly comforting. A piece of history that had survived past its time.

All Modesty's lawyer had told Jill over the phone was that her great-aunt had died in the fire that burned the ranch house and outbuildings down to their rock foundations. Jill had stayed with her job on the river until she found a replacement guide. It had taken three weeks. The lawyer had assured her there was no reason to rush back. Modesty's remains had been cremated and scattered according to her will, and the stock didn't need tending because every last animal had been sold for back taxes. The lawyer had already filed for an exemption on further taxes due to the ranch house and barn burning down.

Taxes. God.

How much could an all-but-abandoned ranch be worth?

Jill parked in the overgrown yard, climbed out, and stretched before she went to wrestle with the old padlock that secured the front door. Not that there was much to steal—worn cowhide chairs, an old plank kitchen table, and bunk beds whose "springs" consisted of rope strung between two-by-fours.

Despite its rust-pitted appearance, the padlock opened easily to her key. Modesty must have oiled the lock recently. Or maybe she'd rented the cabin out to someone for a time. Cash was always welcome on a bare-bones Western ranch.

Inside, the cabin was surprisingly clean. Jill wouldn't have to camp out in the yard while she put the place in order. There was even a covered bucket of water near the ancient long-handled pump in the kitchen. She lifted the bucket to prime the pump, then stopped when she saw the neat rectangle of folded paper that had been tucked beneath.

Her name was written across the paper in Modesty's elegant, archaic handwriting.

Jill set the bucket aside and unfolded the paper. An odd sensation prickled over her arms.

She was reading a note from the dead.

GO TO YOUR OLD HIDING PLACE.
LIFE ISN'T AS SAFE AS IT SEEMS TO THE YOUNG.

"Well, that's weird," she said. "Wonder if the old bat was senile? God knows her sister was no model of sanity."

But Grandmother Justine was a long-dead family legend, and Great-aunt Modesty had always had a death grip on reality.

Jill tucked the paper into the hip pocket of her jeans, primed the pump, and smiled as clean water gushed into the old iron sink. With the supplies she had picked up in Page, she was set for several weeks. After that . . . well she'd worry about what came next when she knew how long she'd have to stay at the ranch. She didn't have any idea of what went into settling someone's estate.

With a sigh, she opened the cranky shutters on the east side of the two-room cabin, letting in the late-afternoon air while she unloaded the Honda and made coffee on the camp stove she'd brought. She took a mug of coffee into the front yard to enjoy the sound of the wind moving through the huge old cottonwood. The tree was one of the things she had truly missed after leaving the Arizona Strip.

The massive cottonwood had taken root near the spring long before any Brecks ever arrived in Arizona Territory. As a child, she had used the tree for a living ladder to climb partway up the cliff. The rest of the cliff she had climbed the hard way, when she was older.

"I suppose you'll die someday, too, old friend," Jill said, tracing one of the deep ridges in the cottonwood's bark with her fingertip. "I won't be alive to see it. You've got a few hundred more years in you than I do."

Modesty's note echoed back like a ghostly agreement.

Life isn't as safe as it seems to the young.

"Oh, all right," she said, annoyed by the cryptic message. "I'll do it."

Irritating people was something Modesty had raised to an art. Jill should be too old to have her buttons pushed so easily.

But she wasn't.

Muttering under her breath, she grabbed a flashlight from her backpack and looked around the cabin. There was an obvious root cellar outside. In the days before electricity came to the rural West, root cellars and springhouses had been as close to refrigeration as it got. Sometimes she had hidden in the root cellar.

But her favorite hideaway was inside the cabin, at the back of the pantry, where a handmade cupboard pulled away to reveal a rough opening. Behind the cupboard was a six-foot-square room. The space had been hammered from the sandstone cliff that was the back wall of the cabin. In the days before banks and police, when Indians and outlaws roamed the land freely, the hidey-hole had kept safe everything of value to the Brecks—including their own lives when raiders came.

She ran her fingers behind the third shelf, slid aside a concealed wooden bolt, and tugged on the edge of the cupboard. The tin-backed cupboard creaked and protested when the concealed door swung open. As a girl, Jill had always felt a delicious shiver of secrecy when she crawled into the small space and hid among the burlap bags of rice and beans and sugar.

She switched on the flashlight and looked inside. Instead of supplies, she found Grandmother Justine's ancient, battered steamer trunk. It was big enough to put a small pony inside. Once it had held her grandmother's art supplies.

Curious as to what the trunk held now, Jill tugged the lid open. The leather hinges were so old they were almost frayed through. She propped the lid against the rock wall and shined the light inside.

No crusted brushes or hardened oils or color-splotched palettes. Instead, there were six rectangular parcels, standing on their sides like giant filing cards. Each parcel was wrapped in oilcloth.

Jill felt a surprising sense of relief that everything hadn't turned to fire and ashes. Something remained of Modesty's heritage.

And her own.

I hope these packages are what I think they are. Even if they got me in some of the worst trouble of my life.

Modesty really smacked me when she found me looking at them. How old was I? Ten? Eleven?

Whatever, she was spitting mad.

Now Modesty was dead and the paintings were Jill's. She could look at them all she wanted. No more sneaking peeks at the forbidden fruit while Modesty and her mother were working cattle, mending fence, or opening and closing irrigation ditches for the little orchard, the big garden, and the pastures growing winter hay.

Carefully Jill took the packages out and leaned them against the stone wall. Only then did she notice the leather portfolio. She knew from the time before her mother died that the portfolio was filled with old photos and papers—the homestead filing, proof of water rights, wedding invitations, birth and death announcements. All the things that people collected on the way through life.

"Good. That should take care of any questions the lawyer might have."

Ignoring the portfolio, she eagerly took the large parcels inside the cabin. When she unwrapped the first, she found it was indeed two paintings. They were vivid, wild yet disciplined, intensely realized. Grinning, she unwrapped all the packages with the greed of a child at Christmas.

She hadn't seen the paintings since the time Modesty found her admiring them in a storage place in the attic of her great-aunt's house. She'd smacked Jill silly, smacked her some more, then marched her grandniece back to the homestead and told her mother that the child wasn't welcome at the ranch house anymore unless her mother was along.

"Years ago," Jill said with a bittersweet smile at how things had changed. She propped the paintings against the wall, marveling at their clean, unsentimental, yet profoundly emotional effect. "I wonder why Modesty didn't want me looking at them. But then, she was a quirky, cranky bitch."

It felt good to say it aloud. Her mother had always told Jill that she should be grateful that Modesty had taken them in when they had no other safe place to go.

Life isn't as safe as it seems to the young.

"Okay, can't argue that," Jill muttered. "But I was a kid, and I loved these paintings at first sight."

The Western landscapes were as big and wide and untamed as the land itself. The paintings captured the power of mountains, the bite of a snow wind, the sweep of the big sky, and the utter freedom of living on your own terms in a land that was rarely generous.

When she was a child, the paintings had enchanted her.

When she was an adult with degrees in art history and fine art, the paintings impressed her.

Now, as then, she felt a deep kinship with the painter, who had captured Jill's own spirit in oils. Maybe it was simply that all the landscapes had human figures in them—small in most cases, dwarfed in every case by the wild land—and somehow female.

Jill hadn't noticed that when she was a child. She did now, and wondered at it.

"Wait. Weren't there thirteen paintings?"

Frowning, she went back to the trunk. Nothing was left in it but the scarred leather portfolio. She pulled it out and looked inside. No painting, but there was a letter addressed to Modesty Breck. It had been postmarked a week before Modesty died, and bore the return address of an art gallery in Park City, Utah, outside of Salt Lake City. Apparently her great-aunt had felt the letter was worthy of being added to the family mementos.

Jill unfolded the heavy embossed stationery from the Art of the Historic West gallery and began reading.

Dear Ms. Breck:

Thank you for sending us the painting that you say has been in your family for so long. It is an interesting genre work. However, it is not signed. Therefore the painting cannot be attributed, despite your suggestion that it may be the work of a noted Western artist.

We are not able to agree with your suggestion that the painting has great monetary value, although we are sure that it has great sentimental value to your family. We have conferred with other experts on Western landscape painting and they share our belief that the work, while pleasing and well rendered, has only a limited resale value.

Under normal circumstances we would return the painting to you with this letter, but the canvas seems to have been misplaced. We believe it happened after it was in the custody of the second appraiser, and are earnestly endeavoring to locate and return it.

In the meantime, we have contacted their insurance carrier and our own and are awaiting instructions on how to proceed. We will contact you again as soon as we can resolve this matter. We are sorry for any minor inconvenience this may cause you.

Should you wish, we are presently prepared to make you an offer of cash compensation for what may be the permanent loss of the work. Judging by the limited market for unsigned landscapes with unproven provenance, of this approximate age, we believe the sum of $2,000 represents more than a fair settlement.

Please advise us if you are willing to accept this offer along with our sincere apologies and best wishes.

The letter was signed Ford Hillhouse. Jill read the letter again, this time translating the words into plain English.

Modesty had sent one of the canvases to a high-end art gallery for appraisal and got a polite sneer in return.

Jill knew enough about art and appraisals to recognize that when it came to putting a price on something, the lack of a painter's signature was usually crippling. Artists signed works. Anything unsigned was automatically suspect. Without a definitive way to identify the painter, the work became a kind of aesthetic orphan.

Or, in real English, barely worth the canvas it was painted on.

Jill remembered her mother saying that there was a long, unhappy story behind the paintings, which were the work of a great artist. Then her mother had said never, ever, to speak about the paintings again or Modesty would kick them off the ranch forever.

"Well, I kept up my silent end of the family bargain," Jill said to the paintings. "Why did Modesty suddenly decide to pull one of these out of the attic and shove it into the public light?"

The answer came as soon as the question was asked.

Money.

Those back taxes the lawyer mentioned. Modesty would have known that selling the breeding stock for tax money meant the end of the ranch.

Frowning, Jill thought about the gallery's letter.

Modesty sent one painting to an appraiser, who sent it to unnamed "others," and then she was told the unsigned painting was essentially worthless. And lost, by the way. So sorry.

Why would someone offer two thousand dollars for a worthless painting?

Simple. The painting isn't worthless.

Or is it just that the insurance people don't want a court hassle over a missing painting of problematic value?

"Probably a cheap way to avoid an expensive lawsuit," she told herself.

Or not.

Jill looked at the other paintings. She really didn't like what she was thinking.

Modesty wouldn't have lugged the paintings, the leather portfolio, and the old steamer trunk to the homestead cabin unless she was worried about the safety of the paintings.

Or she was crazy.

Life isn't as safe as it seems to the young.

Jill had a hard time thinking of her great-aunt as crazy. Snake mean? Sure. Hard as a whetstone? No problem. Man-hater? Definitely. Crazy?

Like a fox.

She looked at her watch. By the time she drove into town, the lawyer would have closed his office, the county records would be locked for the night, and the sheriff would be eating dinner at the Rimrock Café. He wouldn't take well to being interrupted by anything less urgent than life and death.

Modesty's death didn't qualify. It was yesterday's news.

"Looks like life isn't real safe for the old, either," Jill said to the paintings.

Silence answered.

Yet something had made Modesty move the paintings and family papers out of the ranch house. Within days or weeks of shifting the trunk, she'd died in a household accident while filling the old fuel stove in the middle of a cold night.

And the painting she'd sent out for appraisal was missing.

Unhappily, Jill looked from painting to painting, each breathtaking, each unsigned.

Why would a "great artist," according to my mother, not sign paintings?

Why did Modesty keep the paintings secret so long?

No matter how long Jill looked at the canvases, they didn't have answers for her. They simply murmured to her of the lonely grandeur of living in the demanding freedom of the West.

Modesty's life.

Modesty's death.

Jill looked at her watch again. She'd see the lawyer and sheriff in Blessing tomorrow. In fifteen minutes the rate on her costly satellite phone connection would go down, a reflection of local business hours.

She took her digital camera out of her backpack, hesitated over the paintings, and finally chose the three smallest. After taking several pictures, she pulled out her computer and downloaded the best images. Quickly she searched the Net for high-end Western art galleries within a day's drive. She chose Fine Western Arts in Snowbird, owned by Ramsey Worthington. Worthington had several galleries, all in high-end Western resorts. Plus he was the owner of the Best of the West, an auction house that was setting up to be the new Sotheby's.

If the ads could be believed.

After deliberating about who had the next-snottiest ad, she chose Vision Quest Gallery in Taos, owned by William Shilling. He'd been in business for thirty years at one location, which spoke well of his client list. She chose three more galleries almost at random. All of them were heavy on the Western theme, cowboys and Indians, hardships and manly hunts.

As for the Art of the Historic West gallery in Park City,

forget it. They had already lost one of her grandmother's paintings. That was why Jill was using the JPEGs instead of the paintings as her calling cards.

She didn't want any more of her heritage getting "misplaced."

5

When the buzzer rang on the front door of the Vision Quest Gallery, William Shilling glanced up and immediately pressed the door release. Mrs. Caitlin Crawford was the kind of client gallery owners loved to see at the door. She was beautiful in a classy way, discriminating, and the wife of an older man who could afford to drop seven figures on a painting without his pulse raising.

"Caitlin, what a pleasure," Shilling said, hurrying toward her. "May I get you some coffee? It's quite chilly out."

The door shut with a sound that suggested complex, durable locks.

"That would be lovely," Caitlin said, pulling off her black kid gloves and tucking them into a pocket of her black vicuna coat.

"No sugar, no cream, correct?" he asked as he helped her out of her cloud-soft black coat and went to the coffeepot.

"You're such a sweetheart to remember. And I'm sorry to give you so little notice. Talbert just decided to fly over and check on the new resort. Naturally, I couldn't pass up a chance to see you."

Shilling smiled and handed her a fine china cup. The smell of the specially blended roast made an earthy counterpoint to the gallery's restrained décor.

"You picked a good time," he said. "I have some paintings I was getting ready to e-mail you about. Really quite thrilling pieces."

"Dunstans?" she asked quickly.

His smile faded a bit. "Er, no, not really." Unsigned Dunstans weren't worth the canvas they were painted on. "There's a wonderful Blumenschein, a quite nice Sharp, and a small Russell, a lovely little gem. The owner is considering placing them in the Reno auction next year, as it's too late for proper publicity at the upcoming one in Las Vegas, but he's willing to consider—"

"No, thank you," Caitlin interrupted. "We'll be at the Las Vegas auction, of course. It's so rare that any Dunstans come on the market."

"And Talbert always buys them."

"But of course. As he tells me, what's the point of collecting if you can't have the best? All of it."

Shilling bit back a sigh. Talbert Crawford had become a legend along the Western art circuit. Only the crème de la crème for him.

All of it.

Thomas Dunstan was the best of the best. Unfortunately, the artist hadn't been the most stable of people. In fact, he'd been an alcoholic of the worst sort. Binge drinker, blackout drunk, and violent. He'd go years without showing a new painting to anybody. But at least he'd had the good sense to destroy his mediocre—or worse—paintings when he was sober. The paintings that survived had became iconic, the essence of the best of Western art.

Of the known Dunstans, Talbert Crawford owned thirteen. The rest were in museums or personal collections. Not for sale, in other words. And Tal had offered a lot of money. He'd even coaxed one out of the Dunstan family collection. Rumor said the cost was seven figures.

"Perhaps it might be time for both of you to expand your collecting horizons," Shilling said gently. "There are many fine Western painters who—"

"I'm afraid not," Caitlin murmured. "Not until we've bought all the available Dunstans. Talbert is quite firm on that." *Fanatical, in fact.* "Breadth in a collection is all very well and good, but depth is crucial."

"I don't know of any available Dunstans with unclouded provenance," Shilling said.

"But I keep hearing rumors of at least one new Dunstan. Perhaps as many as a dozen."

Silently Shilling condemned the gossip network of Western art collectors. "I've heard some rumors, myself." *Seen JPEGs, too. Unsigned canvases, every one.* "Naturally I called Ramsey Worthington. Neither one of us can pin down the rumor to a specific collector, curator, or anyone with credentials. It's like trying to capture smoke in your hands."

"I traced one rumor back to Park City, the Art of the Historic West gallery," Caitlin said.

Shilling rubbed a palm over his thinning hair. "Yes, I know of that rumor. The gallery supposedly sent the painting out to several people for appraisal." He shrugged. "The consensus was that it wasn't a Dunstan."

"Still, I'd like to see the painting myself."

"So would I. In fact, I requested at least a photo."

"And?" Caitlin said sharply.

"The painting has gone missing. Indeed, there's growing question whether it ever existed in the first place. The closer the big Vegas auction comes, the wilder the rumors. It happens almost every year. With barely a week to go, you have to expect things like this."

And Shilling had no intention of adding to rumors that undercut the sale of real, signed art.

Caitlin sipped coffee. A delicate frown line appeared between her dark, elegantly shaped eyebrows. "But this rumor had more substance. I was sure of it."

Shilling put a professional smile on his face. "Believe me, I had great hopes, too."

"You'll tell me if anything else comes along with Dunstan's name on it?"

"Of course. You and Talbert are always the first on my call list."

"Good." She smiled. "If I found out otherwise, I would be very hurt."

And Shilling would never see another dime of Crawford's millions.

Both of them knew it.

Neither of them was rude enough to say it out loud.

6

Blessing, Arizona
September 12
Late morning

Sheriff Ned Purcell rocked his high-backed chair away from the desk and stared at the ceiling.

"The fire was almost a month ago, Miss Breck. The ruling has already been made. Your great-aunt died in an unfortunate accident."

"I understand," Jill said evenly. "But considering her note to me, and the convenient loss of one of our family paintings, I feel we should look at things again."

"Miss . . ." He bit back an impatient word and looked out the window. The Breck women had been nothing but trouble for a century. Ornery to the bone. "In the big scheme of things, Modesty probably had a part in her own death. Old ladies who live alone shouldn't try to pour fuel oil into a stove that's already burning."

Jill straightened her back against the wooden chair on the other side of the sheriff's desk. She was real tired of hearing how women shouldn't be living without the protection and oversight of a man. That point of view was one of the biggest reasons she'd rarely looked back after leaving the Arizona Strip for a college scholarship in California.

"Great-aunt Modesty was born on that ranch," Jill said. "She lived with that stove her whole life. She was used to doing her own chores, including maintaining old engines and pouring fuel oil, branding and cutting and haying. Frankly, I was having a hard time accepting that she tripped and scattered burning fuel oil all over the kitchen. Then, when I found her note and the old trunk, I really felt the whole matter should be looked at again."

Purcell picked up the cream-colored Stetson that was as much a part of his uniform as the tooled leather belt with its gun, nightstick, handcuffs, and bullets.

Jill waited. She knew she was irritating the sheriff, but she couldn't just let all the questions go because the man believed at a gut level that a woman living alone would naturally come to a bad end.

"Maybe Modesty had just been lucky all these years," Purcell said bluntly. "A woman like her isn't supposed to live alone."

A combination of triumph and anger burned in Jill. She hated the assumption of every woman's inferiority to any man.

"I'm not sure I follow," she said.

Purcell leaned forward on his elbows. His face was clean-shaven, surprisingly pale for a man who spent so much time outdoors. His lips were thin and flat. He wore a white, pearl-buttoned Western shirt, jeans, cowboy boots, and a bolo tie. He was an elected rural lawman who ran for office every day of his term and dressed accordingly.

"Modesty Breck was a pain in the side to the folks around here," Purcell said. "She flaunted views that decent people in this county find offensive. More than one person came to me, saying that they thought she was incompetent, that she ought to have more supervision, particularly in her declining years."

"And there are those who thought she should have had more supervision, especially in her younger days," Jill shot back. "Some people can't abide the thought that a woman should choose never to marry, or worse, to leave a church-sanctified marriage and live on her own."

Red stained the sheriff's cheekbones. "Modesty Breck was a runaway bride."

"She never married," Jill said. "As far as I know, she never even agreed to an engagement."

"She led on several good men, making them believe she would marry them."

Jill held her tongue. If legend and gossip were true, Purcell's father had been one of those eager men. But in the end, Modesty had never found a man she couldn't live without.

Neither had Jill.

"Modesty's sister Justine was no better than a prostitute and an adulteress," Purcell said grimly. "Justine was a drunk who shot her *married* lover during an argument. My father brought them both in for drunk and disorderly. Justine's lover was a good man led astray by a flashy, easy woman. He felt so bad about it that he hanged himself in this jail the night they were arrested."

Jill's eyes widened. "What?"

"You don't believe me, I'll show you the arrest records, fingerprints and all. Purcells have been lawmen here since before Arizona was a state. We take pride in our work."

Jill didn't know what to say. She'd heard hints and whispers and speculations, but nothing as plain as Purcell's words.

"Justine's bastard daughter, your mother, was a runaway wife who divorced a good man, changed her name back to Breck and never entered a tabernacle again," Purcell said. "The Breck women are nothing but godless trouble-makers."

"It's a free country," Jill said, trying and failing to keep the bite out of her voice. "Including the freedom *not* to be religious."

Purcell scowled. He was an elder in the Mormon church. His authority as sheriff owed more to the church than to the badge clipped to his wide belt. Canyon County was a God-fearing place, one of the last frontiers of decency in an increasingly depraved nation.

"But the temple doesn't forgive a runaway woman," Jill said. "A male sinner, sure. A female? Never."

Purcell straightened his spine. "Spoken like a true Breck. But that's neither here nor there. You have a copy of the death certificate and the coroner's report. Modesty Breck tripped, broke her thick skull on the iron stove, dropped the fuel can, and caused the fire that burned down the old ranch house and spread to the barn."

For a long moment the room was silent except for the ticking of a grandfather clock in the corner. It had been keeping time in a lawman's office since before the Arizona Territory became an official state of the United States of America. And that lawman had probably been a Purcell.

Jill grimaced. *Too bad a lot of people in the rural West haven't caught on to statehood and the reality of the twenty-first century.*

"There's no motive, no reason for anybody to do anything to your great-aunt," Purcell said, looking at his watch. "Whatever insult the Breck women laid upon the church was a long time ago. These days, believers don't hold those kinds of grudges. Nobody around here wished Modesty any harm. Nobody thought about her at all unless some drifter was looking for work, and then we sent them out to the Breck ranch."

"What about the paintings?" Jill asked.

"What about them? That letter you showed me was pretty plain about the fact that they weren't worth anything. Take the insurance settlement they offered and consider yourself lucky."

"But why would Modesty suddenly move the paintings to my place and leave me a note saying life isn't as safe as I think?"

Purcell snorted. "I followed up with one of the appraisers your aunt tried to employ, a nice young man up near Salt Lake. He as good as said right out that the painting she sent him was a fake or a forgery. Maybe Modesty decided the other paintings were dangerous because she tried to pass them off as valuable. That's a crime, you know. Fraud."

"But—"

"I'd advise you to keep that in mind, Miss Breck," the sheriff cut in. "If you try to pass those paintings off as something they're not, you could end up in real trouble. The criminal kind."

Jill's strong hands gripped the arms of the chair. She stared at the lawman and counted to ten. Twenty.

Thirty.

Purcell leaned forward and smiled almost gently. "I know death is hard to accept, especially for an overeducated young woman like you. I just want you to understand that I have acted in good faith in this matter. If I didn't believe that Modesty's death was an accident, I'd pursue it to the limit of the law."

"But you believe that her death was accidental."

"Me, the fire chief, the coroner, and everyone else who looked at the facts. Modesty Breck was a stubborn old woman, hell-bent on living alone. We also know she was getting more frail. Did you ever think that she might have moved the paintings and papers to your cabin and then not so accidentally killed herself so she wouldn't be forcibly moved off that ranch for her own good?"

A chill went over Jill. "Are you saying that Modesty meant to die?"

Purcell shrugged. "Given what you told me, suicide is as much within the facts as the verdict of accidental death. If you insist, I'll reopen the case. But it sure would make collecting any life insurance more difficult. As the beneficiary, that's something you should think about."

It took Jill several silent moments to get a grip on her temper.

Purcell was everything she and the Breck women had hated about the Mormon West. If Jill wanted any answers to her questions, she'd have to find them herself.

She thought again of the card Joe Faroe had given her, then dismissed it. She wasn't being stalked. The only danger she was in was losing control and assaulting an officer of the law.

"Thank you for your time, Sheriff. I won't be bothering you again."

7

Ramsey Worthington frowned at his computer screen. It was a large screen, noted for showing the fine details of any properly prepared photographic file. As an auctioneer in high demand and the owner of several galleries selling fine Western art, Worthington frequently had to make judgments of fine art via electronics. If the piece interested him enough virtually, he would ask to see it physically before he made a decision whether to buy, trade, or represent the art in question.

"Something interesting?" John Cahill asked.

Worthington looked up at his manager and occasional lover. Cahill wasn't the jealous type. Neither was Worthington, at least not when it came to sex. As always, Cahill was dressed in a way that was neither too formal nor too casual, suggesting wealth and breeding without insisting on it. Not for the first time, Worthington wished that his wife had half of Cahill's understanding of style.

"I'm not sure," Worthington said. "The photo is obviously made by an amateur."

Cahill leaned over Worthington's shoulder to look at the screen. "Photo sucks, but the painting looks fabulous. How big is it?"

"She didn't say."

"She?"

"Jillian Breck."

"Oh, hell. Not that crackpot again," Cahill said, disappointed.

"No. Some relative of hers, apparently. Same last name, different first name. Supposedly the old woman died and Jillian Breck is the heir."

Worthington clicked to a second image. It was as powerful as the first.

Cahill made a disgusted sound. "Whoever is out there painting these 'Dunstans' should give it up and paint under his own name. He's good enough to make a decent living. With the right representation and some luck, he might even make an excellent living. He's quite powerful. Technique and intensity both. Not a common combination."

Worthington nodded.

A third image came up. Powerful, beautiful in its stark landscape and overwhelming sky.

"Did you send these to Lee Dunstan?" Cahill asked.

"Not yet. He was furious about the painting Ford Hillhouse sent. Sounded like Lee was going to stroke out over the phone."

"Why does something like this always happen before a big auction?" Cahill muttered.

Worthington shrugged. "Greed. Someone knows that big

money is out there attached to Dunstan's name. They want a piece of it."

"They should have done their homework," Cahill said.

Worthington nodded. "Yes, the human figures are unusual for Dunstan. Any forger would know it. Which means this one is either stupid—"

"Unlikely," Cahill cut in. "He knows his subject too well."

"—or these just might actually be Dunstan's work."

"They aren't Dunstans until Lee says they are," Cahill pointed out.

"Either way, I hope we can sit on them until after the auction," Worthington said. "The last thing we need is twelve excellent, probably fraudulent Dunstans circulating. Smaller things have taken the wind out of the market."

"What are you going to do?" Cahill asked.

"I'll think of something."

Cahill laughed quietly. "You always do."

8

Score was sweating hard, pumping iron in a controlled frenzy that kept him from punching a hole through the wall. It seemed that people just got stupider every day. He'd been lucky to leave the office before he took somebody's head off and shoved it up their dumb ass.

His cell phone went off. His private cell, the one that only a few people had the number for. He racked the weight and looked at the caller ID.

Blank.

"Score," he said briefly into the phone.

"I hope you're on the trail of those paintings."

"Like I told you." *About ten times already.* "Dead end. They burned." The only thing that kept Score's voice neutral was the really sweet yearly retainer this client paid.

But the more they paid, the more demanding they were.

"Then why is Jillian Breck asking galleries all over the West to look at JPEGs of three unsigned Dunstans?"

"So there were photos somewhere, sometime," Score said, wiping off his sweat with a big towel. "So what? I took care of the paintings, and the rest is bullshit and ashes."

"I'd like to believe that. I don't. Find those paintings or bring me proof that they don't exist. And do it before the auction!"

Score looked through his home gym's front window to the glittering panorama of lights that was the L.A. basin at night. "How can I prove something doesn't exist? Run the ashes through a spectrograph?"

"Whatever it takes. That's what you're paid for."

9

Arizona Strip
September 12
11:15 P.M.

J ill rolled over and tried to find a more comfortable position on the bunk. She couldn't.

*This bunk is softer than my usual bed on the rowing
bench of a raft. Relax, damn it!*

Eyes closed, she listened to the wind playing with the
cottonwood leaves. At the rate the temperature was falling,
the leaves soon would be turning sunshine yellow and flying
away.

What if Purcell is right? What if Modesty meant to die?

The wind blew harder.

Jill rolled over again.

What if she didn't?

With a word she rarely used in front of clients, Jill kicked
out of her sleeping bag.

"Never should have had that extra cup of coffee," she muttered, coming to her feet in a rush.

But she didn't have to pee and it wasn't caffeine keeping her awake. If she was up and prowling around, it was because she was too restless to lie still anymore.

"Maybe one of the galleries has sent me an e-mail."

And maybe not.

She thought of going to the hideout in the back of the pantry and looking at the paintings again, just to reassure herself that they were really real.

"It took you half an hour to wrap them and put them away. Do you really want to—"

The satellite phone rang, cutting across her words.

"Guess I'm not the only one awake." She picked up the bulky unit, looked at caller ID, and saw "private caller." Pretty much what she expected. Most cell phones didn't register on the land-based system, much less on the satellite phone.

She hated accepting unknown calls at satellite rates.

It rang again.

"It's got to be better than talking to myself. And the rates are real low right now." She punched a button, and said, "Hello?"

"Jillian Breck?" The voice was oddly thick, like someone with a plugged nose.

"Yes. Who are you?"

"Blanchard. I'm a Western art dealer. I understand that you have some paintings I'd be interested in seeing. That true?"

Jill frowned. She didn't remember sending an e-mail to anyone called Blanchard. But he easily could be working for one of the galleries she'd sent messages to.

"You have me at a disadvantage," she said slowly. "Are you sure you're calling the right number?"

"I understand a relative of yours tried to sell a canvas near Salt Lake City. That true?"

She shifted uneasily, remembering the sheriff's warning: *If you try to pass those paintings off as something they're not, you could end up in real trouble. The criminal kind.*

"Mr. Blankford—"

"Blanchard."

"Sorry. I think you've been misinformed."

"You don't know about a dozen Western landscapes that have been in the Breck family for a long time?"

Silently Jill absorbed that Blanchard knew more about the paintings than had been included in her e-mail to various galleries.

What she didn't know was if that was good or bad.

"My great-aunt submitted a canvas that had been in the family for appraisal," Jill said neutrally, "but I wasn't aware that she'd spoken to anyone about paintings other than the one she sent to Park City, not Salt Lake City."

"The Western art world is small and real close." The caller coughed hoarsely. "The canvas your relative sent made the rounds of a number of dealers. She hasn't answered my follow-up letter, so I'm trying you."

Jill's voice tightened. "Modesty Breck is dead."

"Huh. Sorry to hear it. Do you have the painting she sent out?"

"It was lost."

Blanchard made a sound that could have been a laugh or a smoker's cough or he could have been choking on something.

He cleared his throat. "What about the other paintings? They lost, too?"

Jill hesitated, then shrugged. She had put out lures in the shape of JPEGs, and someone had bitten.

"Which gallery are you with?" she asked.

"I work with several. Do you have any paintings like the first one your great-aunt sent out?"

"The paintings have been in the family so long nobody knows much about them. My great-aunt believed they were quite valuable."

"Your great-aunt must have watched too much *Antiques Roadshow,*" Blanchard said, impatience giving an edge to his hoarse voice. "We run into that a lot in this business. People look at a show on public television and get the idea that an old family trinket has huge value."

"If the pictures aren't valuable, why are you interested?"

The man blew his nose. " 'Scuse me. I'm just trying to save you some trouble. Any family paintings of yours might have historical value, maybe a few thousand dollars, but they're not by some great artist. If there are other paintings, you should be very careful with them. Passing counterfeits off as original works is called fraud."

Jill felt a chill, then exhilaration, like the sensation she experienced when she pushed off into the maelstrom of a big rapid. As a river runner, she knew what she was doing, and there was always an element of risk.

That's why she did it.

Blanchard, whoever and whatever he was, knew more about these paintings than she did.

And Modesty was dead.

"Funny thing," Jill said. "This is the second time today somebody has warned me about the paintings."

"Maybe we know more about the situation than you do."

"That wouldn't be hard," she said dryly. "That's why I'm asking questions of experts."

"You don't seem to like the answers."

"What I really don't like is the fact that the painting my great-aunt sent out is missing," she said.

"I heard something about that. Wasn't sure it was true, though."

"As you mentioned, you're a close community," Jill said. *As in closed.* "Even people I don't send JPEGs to hear about them."

He coughed again. " 'Scuse. Getting over a cold. I'm interested enough in those paintings to want to see them in the flesh, rather than electronically. How many did you say there were?"

"I didn't."

"You're a lot smarter than your great-aunt was. How about this? We'll set up a meet in a public place," Blanchard said. "You choose it."

"Where are you?"

"Anywhere you want me to be, any time, as long as you have those paintings with you. How about it?"

Jill hesitated the same way she did before nosing into the approach to Lava Falls.

I've chosen my course. Now I have to bail out or go with it.

She certainly didn't want to meet Blanchard at the Rimrock Café. She wanted a place where she didn't know anyone and no one knew her.

"Ms. Breck?" he asked.

She took a deep breath and headed toward the heart of the rapids. "Meet me tomorrow at 6:00 P.M. near Mesquite, Nevada, in the casino at the Eureka Hotel. I'll be at the penny slots wearing jeans, river sandals, and a black T-shirt that says Spawn Till You Die."

Blanchard gave a bark of laughter, coughed, and said, "I'm in east Texas now. Get a room in case I miss connections, okay? Weather's tricky at this time of year. And bring those paintings with you. I really can't tell what they're worth unless I actually see them."

He hung up before she could agree or disagree.

She punched out and stared at the phone. It was the first time she'd ever shoved off into bad rapids without getting a good look at the water. The adrenaline she was used to.

The fear was something new.

Again she thought of Joe Faroe and St. Kilda Consulting.

No. I'm not a little girl who needs her hand held in the dark by a big strong man. The casino is a public place with lots of money and therefore lots of guards and cameras.

I'll be safer than I am on the river.

10

Jill parked in the huge, dusty lot of the Eureka Hotel. She looked at the belly pack on the passenger seat, weighed the satellite phone in her hand, and decided to leave the expensive means of communication in the car. The throwaway cell phone she'd bought for emergencies worked just fine in this location. She stashed the satellite phone under the passenger seat, locked the car, and walked through the parking lot toward the lobby check-in.

The desert wind had painted a fine layer of grit over the long-haul trucks and RVs parked at the back of the lot, and the cars of the tourists who had been sucked off the highway by the promise of excitement.

She didn't understand the lure. The river took care of her adrenaline needs.

An inch beyond the parking lot and hotel, the desert waited, untouched and patient, knowing that wind, sun, and time would eventually grind down civilization and its sprawling greed.

She'd rather have walked into the desert. But she didn't. She went to the hotel. The moment she opened the front door, she got a dose of stale, smoky air. Yet the huge neon sign out front advertised smoke-free lodging.

It also advertised instant money, loose slots, and the best gambling in Nevada.

Living proof that you shouldn't believe everything you read.

"Sure doesn't smell smoke free," Jill said to the desk clerk.

The clerk wore makeup like she was still the showgirl she'd been twenty years and forty pounds ago.

"Rooms are smoke free," the clerk said. "In fact, there's a five-hundred-dollar room-cleaning charge if you smoke in your room. You want to smoke, go to the casino. It's allowed there."

"And the air-conditioning for the hotel and casino comes from a single central unit, right?"

"Yeah. Sign here, initial the notification of nonsmoking, the fine if you do, and length of stay," the woman said automatically. "Your room is through the casino to the elevators, fourth floor. Turn right and follow the room numbers."

Jill looked over the form, signed and initialed, and pushed the paper toward the clerk. "Any messages for me?"

The woman looked at the name on Jill's registration form and queried the computer. "No. Expecting someone?"

"A Mr. Blanchard might call. If he does, put him through to my room."

"Sure thing. Need help with your luggage?"

"No, thanks. Which part of the casino complex has penny slots?"

"The part that doesn't serve free drinks. North side. You get better odds on the dollar machines and the drinks are free."

"Thanks, I'll keep it in mind."

Jill set off through a casino whose machines flashed and beckoned at every step. She saw the distant neon sign that guaranteed penny slots and million-dollar payoffs. The stink of cigarettes smoldering unnoticed in flat tin ashtrays near "Nevada's loosest slots" almost covered the smell of anxiety and greed.

She grimaced and hurried through the casino. She might have problems with the sober, righteous Mormon patriarchy, but at least the air in Utah's public buildings was breathable.

When she walked into her room, the smell of air "freshener" made her feel like she was walking through the perfume aisle in a dollar store. She shut the door behind herself and threw the dead bolt. She didn't like hotels much, but it was more anonymous than the Rimrock Café.

She ordered a big salad and a hamburger from room service and settled in to wait.

11

Eureka Hotel
September 13
7:00 P.M.

When it was full dark, Score finally stirred from his observation post in the back of his minivan. Ms. Breck's dirt-bag SUV was where it had been for the past four hours, collecting dust.

He'd been collecting dust since dawn. He was used to the stakeout routine, but he didn't love it. Eating mini-mart snacks and pissing into Gatorade bottles got old real quick.

It had been especially hard to wait knowing that the paintings were locked in that tin-can SUV fifty feet away. She hadn't carried anything sizable inside, or sent the bellman out after any more luggage.

Score bit back a yawn, checked his watch, then looked for the guard whose boring job it was to drive through the hotel parking lot for eight hours, five days a week. The dude must have decided to save wear and tear on tires, because he'd parked his little golf cart and was drinking coffee, using one of the long-haul trucks for a windbreak.

When Score moved forward and opened the driver's door of his minivan, the wind nearly yanked the handle out of his hands. "Son of a bitch," he muttered.

The wind was as cold as it was strong. No wonder the guard wasn't driving around in the open golf cart.

If somebody told me to freeze in this wind for minimum wage, I'd tell them to jerk off.

Even though it was dark between the parking lot's widespread, sickly orange lights, Score pulled a toque over his head and down to his eyebrows. The result concealed the color of his hair and kept his ears warm. He stuffed a machete under his thigh-length leather jacket, taking care to keep the hooked end of the blade from notching his balls by mistake. His "slim jim" was already in its own special inside pocket, just itching to be used on a locked car.

He walked to the Breck SUV. As he'd guessed from the way she locked it up, the vehicle had a manual rather than an electronic lock.

Piece of cake.

He pulled out the slim jim, slid it down the driver's window, fished a bit, and yanked up the lock.

No alarm.

Nobody looking his way.

It took less than a minute to see that there weren't any paintings inside the SUV.

Hell, that would have been too easy.

But there was a satellite phone underneath the passenger seat that was as old as the car. Like the car, it still worked.

Tucking the satellite phone under his jacket, Score went back to his minivan. He opened the sliding door, ducked in, and closed it behind him. Both side walls of the van had custom racks that secured a multitude of metal suitcases, ranging from palm-size to big enough to hold an automatic rifle. He selected a case, turned on his penlight, and glanced quickly at the contents. Locaters and bugs of all sizes were stashed in their cut-out foam nests. He opened Jill's satellite phone, looked at the battery, and shook his head.

He pulled out a second metal suitcase. The bugs and locaters in this one came inside their own batteries.

Pricey bastards.

But it all goes on the client's tab.

One of the expensive bugs would work for Jill's phone. He popped out the old battery, put in the new and improved one, and opened up a special computer. He booted it up, checked the readout, and saw that the locater was hot. He muttered into the phone, checked that the bug was working just fine, and decided it was good to go. Unless she kept the phone five feet from her at all times, he doubted that he'd overhear much, but the voice-activated bug was part of the only locater/battery setup that fit her old sat phone.

If she's smart and bolts, then my client wasted some money. No problemo. Clients are made of the green stuff.

If she goes after the paintings, she'll give me the GPS coordinates.

In all, it would be more reliable and a whole lot less dangerous than beating the truth out of her.

He replaced all the suitcases in their niches, stashed the phone in his jacket, and went back to the little SUV. Just to be certain Ms. Breck hadn't hidden anything, he took out the SUV's overhead light and ripped up the seats with the machete.

Nothing.

More nothing under the spare tire, which he took bites out of with the machete.

He almost punched holes in the motor oil cans on the passenger side, but decided he didn't want to drip all the way back to his van.

Where are the paintings?

She didn't take them inside with her. Even rolled up, they wouldn't have fit in that little belly bag she wore.

And the fitted jacket she wore over her jeans didn't leave room for anything but the body beneath. Not a great rack, but she had a nice way of moving.

He checked the guard—still sucking on coffee. Moving quickly but not in a way that would attract attention, he went back to his van for a few more items, then returned to work on the SUV.

Stage setting. Jesus. I shoulda been a producer.

Even as he worked, he kept an eye on the parking lot. If the clever Ms. Breck decided to come out before he was done, well, shit happened.

And he had a load with her name all over it.

12

Eureka Hotel, Nevada
September 13
11:00 P.M.

Jill forced herself not to reach for the room phone and call
the desk again. They were as tired of telling her that she
had no messages as she was of hearing it. She'd used pay-
per-view to see a recent movie that interested her, lost a few
bucks and gotten her hands grimy playing the penny slots,
ordered another hamburger, and finally returned to her room
after three hours of perching on the deliberately uncomfortable stools in front of the cheap slot machines.

*I should have brought my dirty clothes. Bet there's a
laundry somewhere in the hotel. Then the trip wouldn't
have been a total waste of time, money, and gas.*

She watched the bedside clock crawl through a few more
minutes. How bad could connections be between east Texas
and Nevada? Was Blanchard hitchhiking?

She paced and then paced some more. After the physical activity of the river, her body wasn't used to hanging out in smoky rooms.

Screw this. I'm going for a walk.

She grabbed her jacket and the belly pack that doubled as her purse and headed for the elevator. Ignoring the relentless mechanical yammering of the slot machines in the casino, she strode toward the front doors.

After the air in the hotel, the wind was like diving into cold rushing water. For the freshness, she'd live with the flying grit. She paced the front of the hotel several times, wishing she was doing something useful.

Check the oil in your SUV. That's useful. Then you won't have to do it at dawn tomorrow, when you leave this place.

On the subject of oil, her vehicle could only be described as greedy. It had a quart-a-day habit.

Check the tires while you're at it.

Give the SUV a wax job.

Do something besides fidget.

She dodged a latecomer hurrying to the check-in, crossed the driveway to the parking lot, and headed for her aging SUV. The lot was partially full. Compressors on refrigerator trucks rumbled, waiting for drivers to bust out at the tables or stop hitting on waitresses. Some of the RVs had lights on inside, either night-lights or a beacon for bleary gamblers to stumble toward when they got tired of losing.

The guard's golf cart was idling at the entrance to the parking lot. A low conversation came on the wind, the guard telling a newbie where the overnight RV parking was. The mercury-vapor lamps cast a ghastly orange glow over everything, changing colors dramatically. If Jill hadn't known exactly where she was parked, she never would have recognized her vehicle. She cut through ranks of monster pickup trucks and SUVs the size of railroad cars. Finally she could see her own modest rig. It looker even smaller than she re-membered.

Then she realized that the left front tire was flat.

So was the left back tire.

She froze, listening for any sound, searching for any movement. All that came was the wind and the sound of voices headed toward the casino, away from her. Warily, keeping other vehicles between herself and her own car, she circled the SUV.

Four flat tires.

Front door ajar.

I locked it. I know I did.

When Jill was sure she was alone, she stood back and dug a tiny, powerful penlight from her waist pack. She sent the narrow beam over the interior of the car.

Nothing moved.

No one was inside, sleeping off a drunk or waiting for a victim.

The seats had been ripped apart. The dome light was bro-ken. There was a piece of paper stuck under the windshield wiper. What looked like ripped, coarse cloth jammed the open glove compartment.

She used the beam on nearby cars. Empty. Locked. Tires intact. No ads tucked under the windshield wipers. Whoever had trashed her ride had left the others alone.

Adrenaline lit up her blood like fireworks.

Gee, I feel really special.

Pissed off, too.

She looked around again, listened, heard nothing but wind and the growl of compressors keeping lettuce cold while drivers gambled the night away.

Quickly she closed the distance to her mutilated SUV. Nothing looked better up close. It looked worse.

She jerked the piece of paper out from under the wind-shield wiper. Block letters leaped into focus.

STAY OUT OF IT OR DIE

Adrenaline twisted into nausea.

She looked around the SUV again. Still alone. Still quiet. The guard was quartering a different part of the parking lot. She thought of calling him over, then thought of all the questions that the local cops would ask. Questions she really didn't want to answer.

With a hissing curse she went to the passenger side, opened the door, and reached under the seat. To her surprise her satellite phone was still there. She pulled it out and stashed it in her belly bag. Then she grabbed a fistful of whatever was choking the glove compartment.

As soon as her fingers touched the material, she knew.

Canvas.

Oil.

Anger burned away the faint nausea of fear.

That slime-sucking son of a bitch. The threat wasn't enough to make his point. He had to cut the missing painting to rags.

And it could just as easily have been her.

Manhattan
September 14
2:21 A.M.

As usual, Dwayne Taylor had night duty. He liked it that way. The calls were more interesting and the view from Ambassador Steele's office was one of the best in the city. Two of the office's six walls overlooked Manhattan. The odd sheen of the bulletproof glass only added to the dramatic color-and-black view of skyscrapers. Three other walls held screens with satellite views of places where St. Kilda had operatives and/or things were going to hell. The final wall held a door and various reference books.

Ambassador Steele sat in his high-tech wheelchair, talking through a headset, debriefing someone in Paraguay. Mission accomplished. International executive returned largely unharmed to his worried family.

The "hot" phone rang.

Steele covered his microphone. "Get that, will you?"

Dwayne switched the channel on his headset and picked up immediately. "St. Kilda Consulting. Who or what do you need?"

"This is Jillian Breck. Joe Faroe told me to call this number if I was ever in trouble."

Dwayne noted the tension in the woman's voice, typed his best-guess spelling of her name into the computer, and simultaneously asked, "Are you in danger at this moment?"

"Only of losing more money to the penny slots."

Dwayne smiled. "Not much danger, then."

"My car is cut to pieces. Someone put a note under the windshield that said go away or die."

Dwayne's smile vanished. Information on Jillian Breck began to roll up on his computer screen.

Highest priority.

Joe Faroe.

"Where are you now?" Dwayne's voice was a lot calmer than he was feeling. If Faroe said something was important, it was *important*.

"I'm in the Eureka Hotel, outside Mesquite, Nevada, in the casino. I figured it was safest here. Lots of guards."

"Excellent choice. Do you have a room?"

"Yes."

"Number, please."

Jill hesitated.

Dwayne waited for her to realize the obvious—if she didn't trust St. Kilda Consulting, why was she calling?

"Four-three-five," she said.

"Ask a guard to escort you to your room. Make sure the drapes are shut before he leaves. Lock the door, both dead bolt and chain. Joe Faroe will call you within fifteen minutes."

"Wait. I'm okay, just scared and mad. No need to wake him up. I'll just—"

"Get escorted to your room," Dwayne cut in firmly. His ruby signet ring glowed against his chocolate skin as he keyed instructions into the computer. "Fifteen minutes, Ms. Breck. If your room phone doesn't answer, Faroe will"—*have a shit-fit*—"be very concerned."

Silence.

"Ms. Breck? Are you all right?"

She made a tight sound that could have been a laugh. "Yes. I'm just not used to taking orders."

Dwayne almost chuckled. From what he was reading about her on the screen, he wasn't surprised. "Sorry. Let me make that a request. Please go to your—"

"I'm on my way to the elevator," she cut in.

"With a guard?"

"A bellman. I waved a ten and he appeared."

Not used to following orders, either, Dwayne thought. *Should make life interesting for whichever operative is assigned to her.*

A name came up on the screen. Zach Balfour was the op who was closest to Mesquite, Nevada. On vacation.

Not anymore, Dwayne thought.

He punched in Zach's number on line 4.

"I'll hold until you're safe in your room," Dwayne said to Jill.

"Really, there's no need for that. I feel foolish enough as it is."

"Better to feel foolish than be hurt."

"The bellman is really big," Jill said. "And I'm going to lose you in the elevator."

"Take the stairs."

"You sound like Joe Faroe."

"I'm much better looking," Dwayne assured her.

She laughed.

Steele finished debriefing the operative and glanced over

at the man who was his administrative assistant and right hand. Joe Faroe was his left. Grace Faroe was his alter ego in the field.

Dwayne gestured with his head toward Steele's desk and kept typing, transferring information into Joe Faroe's priority file, copy to Steele, while Jill and an increasingly breathless bellman climbed stairs to her fourth-floor room.

Line 4 dropped Dwayne into Zach's voice mail. Dwayne paused in his typing long enough to punch in the override code.

Jill's breathing didn't change during the climb. Dwayne heard a door opening, then closing, and the sound of a bolt going home, followed by the rattle of a chain.

"All safe and tight," Jill said into the phone.

"Stay there, please, until a St. Kilda operative knocks on your door. Don't open for anyone else, including room service, maids, hotel security personnel—"

"Or Santa and his busy elves," Jill cut in. "I get it. I'll wait for St. Kilda."

"We'll call and tell you which operator to expect."

When Dwayne switched his headset over to line 4, Steele said, "And?"

"The river guide who saved Lane's life just called. Someone gave her a screw-off-or-die note."

"Interesting. Where is she?"

"Mesquite, Nevada. Eureka Hotel casino when she called, now locked and bolted into her room, same hotel. Zach Balfour is our closest bullet catcher."

Steele's light, clear eyes absorbed information from his screen. Zach was St. Kilda's valued utility infielder and a man whose instinct for when an op was going south was legendary.

"Unhappy ex?" Steele asked, skimming Jill's file.

"She didn't say."

"Call Faroe."

"Just put in his number, line two. Zach Balfour hasn't picked up his—there you are, Zach. It's Dwayne. You've got a code two waiting in Mesquite, Nevada, Eureka Hotel, 435, Jillian Breck, death threat. You'll know more when we do. Move it."

Dwayne hung up in the middle of Zach's rant about bimbos and bullet catching.

14

San Diego, California
September 13
11:28 P.M.

Grace picked up Faroe's phone, saw who it was, and switched on the scrambler before putting the phone on speaker. "Grace, here. Joe's busy driving."

"How bad can traffic be at this time of night?" Steele asked, his voice crisp.

"It's not the traffic, it's the fact that she's having the baby!" Faroe said loudly. "Lane, how long since the last contraction?"

"Two minutes, twenty-eight seconds." Lane's voice was tight, deep. Like Faroe's. "How you doing, Mom?"

"Will you both shut up?" Grace asked pleasantly. "I can't hear the ambassador. And slow down unless you want a police escort."

Steele's surprisingly warm laughter came from the speaker. "I take it all is under control, Judge?"

"Yes, but you couldn't tell by talking to my men. My doctor is on the way in to the hospital, the staff is ready, and apparently so is the baby. What do you need?"

"Jillian Breck just called for Joe."

"What?" Lane said. "Is she all right? Is she hurt? Does—"

"Belt up, Lane," Faroe said. He knew his son had a crush on Jill—what healthy young man wouldn't?—but that wasn't the point. "Where is she?"

"Mesquite, Nevada. Eureka Hotel. Room 435. Safe enough for the moment. She's had a death threat."

"Craptastic," Faroe said, checking the intersection again as he accelerated through a yellow-going-red light. The Mercedes SUV gave a happy roar. "Never rains but it bloody pours."

Grace started to say something, then shut up as her abdomen clamped down back to front, hard and long, pushing the baby closer to the moment of birth.

"Time," she said to Lane between her teeth.

"Oh, god," Lane said, his voice thinning. "They're coming too close!"

Grace felt the same way herself. This baby was in one big hurry. She knew that for most women a second baby came faster than the first, but with a sixteen-year-gap between pregnancies, she hadn't expected the rule to apply to her.

"Zach Balfour is our closest free operative," Steele said. "Until we know the exact nature of the threat, we're going with an intelligent bullet catcher."

Faroe grunted. "Good. I like Zach's style. But the last time I talked to him, he was packing for a vacation. He change his mind?"

"No, I did. He was about forty miles from Mesquite, Nevada, heading south in the morning. Now he's heading north."

"Works for me."

"I doubt if it worked for him," Steele said dryly, "but he's on the way to Ms. Breck just the same."

Faroe almost smiled. "Did you get him out of bed?"

"He's recovering from babysitting DeeDee Breitling."

"Jesus. Give him double pay. Whatever. Just get him to Jill fast."

"I've seen the man drive," Steele said. "He'll be there fast."

Faroe slowed for another red light, scanned the intersection, gunned through it without stopping, and turned hard right. "We're almost at the emergency entrance to the hospital. Give me Jill's hotel phone. I'll call while they're checking Grace in."

"I could call her and—" Lane began.

"Time contractions!" Faroe and Grace said together.

Steele said Jill's number in a loud, precise voice.

"How long was that contraction?" Faroe asked, never looking away from the hospital rushing toward him.

"Not—done—yet," she said in a strained voice.

"Bloody hell," Steele said. "I'll talk to Jillian myself."

"No," Faroe said, leaning on the SUV's horn, summoning the emergency staff as he braked gently to a stop by the wide glass doors. "I owe her. This op is on me."

"It's on St. Kilda. I have plans for Lane," Steele shot back. "Now, just for the novelty of the experience, be reasonable. Grace needs you more than—"

"I can talk to Jill and tell Grace to push at the same time," Faroe cut in.

"You do and you'll need a surgeon to remove the phone from your ass," she shot back.

Steele almost laughed out loud.

Faroe did. "That's the delicate little flower I know and love. And here comes the med team. I'll call Jill."

He hung up, looked at Lane and the people hurrying close, and said, "Help your mother and answer their questions while I talk to Jill."

"Will do."

Faroe didn't answer. He was already punching in Jill's hotel number.

15

Eureka Hotel
September 14
12:17 A.M.

Zach Balfour knocked smartly on the door of 435, then
stepped back so that he was clearly visible in the room
door's peephole. Not that a view of his four-day stubble
would be reassuring, but he didn't give a damn. He was supposed to be on vacation, not catching imaginary bullets for
another bimbo.

"Who is it?" asked a woman.

The voice was low, slightly husky without being at all
breathless.

At least she doesn't sound like a squirrel on speed, he
told himself. *That's worth something.*

"Zach Balfour, St. Kilda Consulting."

"Slide your card under the door."

It wasn't a request.

His dark eyebrows climbed, but Zach dug out a St. Kilda card and pushed it as far as he could under the hotel room door.

A few moments later, the bolt clicked, the chain rattled, and the door opened.

"Come in," Jill said.

Zach didn't wait for a second invitation. He stepped into the room and watched while Jillian Breck closed, bolted, and chained the door again.

The room was pretty much what he expected. Against the far wall there was a double bed sporting a rumpled spread and a belly bag stuffed like a sausage. A small, butt-sprung couch that likely pulled out into another bed faced the TV. Neither clean nor dirty, the room was just a place to stash stuff between casino raids.

Jillian Breck wasn't what he'd expected. She wore jeans, a Ray Troll T-shirt, and beat-up river sandals. She had un-polished fingernails, minimal if any makeup, hair a casual auburn cap, nice breasts, trim butt, and a body that was both fit and unmistakably female.

Pale green eyes, steady and clear.

Real green, too, not contacts like the unadorable DeeDee.

Slowly Zach began to feel less homicidal toward St. Kilda Consulting. He held out his hand and said, "Pleased to meet you, Ms. Breck."

"Jill."

Her handshake was brief, surprisingly strong, with ridges of callus that came from rowing rafts down unruly rivers.

"Call me Zach. Have you had any more trouble since you first called St. Kilda?"

She blinked. "Well, that's blunt."

"Saves time."

She tilted her head and looked up, then down the long, lean man who stood in front of her. She'd worked with enough men on the river not to underestimate the power in his rangy body and wide shoulders, or the penetrating intelligence of his whiskey-colored eyes. A crop of black stubble did nothing to soften the hard planes of his face. He had equally black hair that was too rough to be well groomed, and too clean to be a collar-length gesture of contempt aimed at the civilized world. His clothes looked like he'd slept in them after a long day of hiking. Maybe several days.

"You're not what I expected," she said.

"No tuxedo, pistol, and martini, shaken not stirred?"

Her laugh was as real as the color of her eyes. "Sorry, I'm very new to this."

"Don't feel bad. Damn few people are used to death threats."

Her laughter vanished. Tight, pale lines appeared around the mouth that had been a soft, deep rose.

Nice going, Zach told himself with a sigh. *Turn the client into a net of twanging nerves with a few badly chosen words.*

DeeDee had never noticed.

Could be why he spent a lot of the time working with intel, not clients.

"My social skills need polish," he said. "Let's start all over again. Hi, I'm Zach. Joe Faroe wanted to come in my place but his wife is having a baby as we speak."

"Really?" Jill grinned. "I'll bet Lane is so excited he's bouncing in place. Not many boys his age would be, but he's really looking forward to having a crumb-crusher in the house."

Zach's smile surprised her as much as his beat-up hiking boots, dirty jeans, and clean hands.

"I hope he gets a brother," he said.

One of Jill's dark brown eyebrows rose. "You don't like women?"

"I have four sisters, all older than me by at least eight years. My dad died in a stock car race when I was twelve. I couldn't wait to live in an estrogen-free zone."

Jill smiled slightly. "I was raised by women in a militantly testosterone-free zone."

"Should be interesting."

"What?"

"The next few days."

Her smiled faded. "That's one way of putting it."

"Like I said, my social skills need some work. So why don't you do the talking? Tell me about everything that led up to my knock on your hotel room door."

"Everything?"

"If it has to do with the reason your little SUV got slashed, yes. You can leave out the boyfriend trashing, giggling sleepovers, brutal labor stories, and choices in gear for your monthlies."

Jill stared at him for a long moment. "Whew. You really meant it, didn't you? About the estrogen free."

"If I never again have to listen to a debate over the joys of pads versus tampons, it's fine by me. You can leave out the my-cramps-are-worse-than-yours contest, too."

"In return, you won't drool over big tits, pant over heart-shaped ass, and whine about not getting any. Deal?"

Zach smiled slowly, then laughed. This one definitely wasn't DeeDee. "Deal. Now tell me why you called St. Kilda Consulting instead of the cops."

"I trust Joe Faroe."

"And you don't trust cops?"

She shrugged. "Let's just say I'm not real impressed by the sheriff of Canyon County, Arizona. And he's even less impressed with me."

"Any particular reason?"

Jill took a deep breath and told Zach about her great-aunt,

the paintings, the gallery letter, the fire, the stiff-necked sheriff, and an art dealer called Blanchard from east Texas.

Zach might look scruffy, but he listened with an intensity and intelligence that reminded her of Joe Faroe. He asked questions, she answered with what information she had, he asked more, and she got frustrated by her lack of answers for basic data on her relatives.

"Hey, don't feel bad," he said. "Most people barely know their parents' birth dates, much less the grandparents' and grand-siblings'. I'm lucky to remember my sisters' birthdays. As for my herd of nieces and nephews, forget it. Don't worry, St. Kilda will fill in your family gaps. Beginning now."

Zach took out his cell phone, put it on speaker, and hit speed dial.

"Research," a woman's voice said.

"This is Zach Balfour. I need a run on an art dealer called Blanchard, male, may or may not be based in east Texas. A photo would be primo. I know that you probably won't find zilch, but you may get lucky."

"Hey, Zach. It's Shawna Singh. Steele told me to put you on the top of my list tonight. No guarantees about tomorrow, though."

Zach whistled softly. "I appreciate whatever time you can spare. I do like working with the best. If I'd known you were back from maternity leave, I'd have asked for you by name."

"Keep that in mind when you start chewing on me for not getting something from nothing. You know how useless a search based on a single name will be."

Zach grunted.

Jill smothered a laugh. She'd never met Shawna and already liked her.

"Anything better than Blanchard for me to handle?" the researcher continued.

"Modesty Breck," Zach said. "Normal spelling. DOB June 1922, '23, or '24, maybe '25, residence on Breck ranch outside of Blessing, Arizona. Sheriff Ned Purcell, Canyon County, Arizona. Justine née Breck, DOB . . ."

Pulled between curiosity and a feeling of unease, Jill listened while Zach ordered up research on her family. She wanted to ask if it was really necessary to pry into the lives of the dead, but didn't. She'd called for help, and she'd gotten it.

Now she had to live with it or walk away and go it alone.

Memories of the death threat, the trashed SUV, and the canvas rags jamming her belly pack along with her sat phone didn't make being alone look attractive to Jill.

Nature's violence was one thing.

Human violence was quite another.

"Then look at Ford Hillhouse, Art of the Historic West, Park City, Utah," Zach said. He knew a lot about Western art, but he'd been out of the art loop too long to take anything for granted. "Ramsey Worthington, Fine Western Arts, Snowbird, Utah. When I get more, you'll get more."

Zach answered a few questions, disconnected, saw his battery wasn't holding a charge worth a damn, and sighed. He doubted that any small Western towns sold the kind of goods he needed for his sleek sat/cell phone. He'd plug it in overnight and hope for the best.

He looked at his watch. "Two choices—sleep here or go get the paintings."

"Nobody but my great-aunt knows that I use the homestead cabin, so the paintings should be safe there. My mail comes to a P.O. box in Blessing."

Since St. Kilda's researchers hadn't mentioned the cabin, and it hadn't burned, Zach figured the art would be good overnight.

Besides, he'd been told to guard Jill Breck, not a bunch of paintings.

"I'll take the foldout bed," he said, looking at the butt-sprung couch facing the TV.

"What about my car?"

"Someone from St. Kilda will handle it. Just like they'll take care of the Chevelle I was hauling home when they called me."

Jill opened her mouth, closed it. "Just like that? They'll take care of my car?"

"Is that a problem?"

"I'm not used to other people taking care of things for me."

He smiled slightly. "Get used to it. It's what St. Kilda Consulting does best."

16

Reno, Nevada
September 14
8:00 A.M.

Lee Dunstan hung up the phone with a curse and wished he could have a whiskey with his breakfast eggs.

Damn doctors. Get a few fast heartbeats and they make you give up everything worth living for.

"What's wrong?" Betty asked.

Ken Dunstan looked at his father with concern. Lee was a stubborn old man who refused to slow down and let his son manage what was left of the family art appraisal/ reprographic business. Lee wouldn't have known an opportunity cost if it crawled up his leg. Hanging on to the Dunstan paintings for an extra quarter century had been foolish.

And then selling one to a single collector without soliciting other bids had been stupid.

"Whatever it is," Ken said, "take it easy. It's not worth getting a heart attack over."

"I'm not having any damn heart attack," Lee said, ignoring his wife. "You'll have to wait a long time for your inheritance."

Ken looked at the ceiling and shook his head. "Yeah, like I'm counting the days." *And like there will be anything left by then.*

"You should be," Lee retorted. "Only five days to the auction."

Under the table, Tiffany Dunstan put her hand on her husband's thigh, silently telling him to let his father's sniping go.

"Now, Daddy Dunstan," she said, "you know a few dollars will never replace you."

"Huh," was all Lee said.

Betty sighed, picked up the thermos beside Lee's plate, and poured another cup of decaf for her husband. She'd be lucky if he didn't throw the coffee into the fireplace. He hated decaf almost as much as he hated green vegetables, blood pressure meds, and getting old.

"That goddamn bitch!" Lee growled.

Nobody asked who the bitch was. In the Dunstan household, there was only one bitch that redlined Lee's temper in nothing flat.

Justine Breck.

"She's been dead for decades," Betty said, handing Lee the decaf. "You're alive. If that isn't revenge, what is?"

"Dead, but not buried. Not deep enough." He looked like he'd been chewing on bitterweed. "Troublemaking slut."

With that, Lee took a drink from the cup his wife handed him—and almost spit it back. He slammed the cup down and went to the kitchen for the other pot of coffee, the one everyone else drank from.

"Don't tell me that was her on the phone," Ken said dryly.

Tiffany gave him a look.

"Lee, you know what the doctor said about caffeine," Betty murmured.

"It's my life, damn it." Returning to the table, Lee took a swig of coffee and wished it was whiskey.

But he knew better than to start drinking when he was angry. Nothing good came of that, and a whole lot of bad.

He didn't want to end up like his father.

"The bitch ruined my daddy," Lee muttered.

Betty started to tune out. She'd heard enough about her father-in-law's old lover to last several lifetimes.

"He should have killed the bitch," Lee said.

Instead, Thomas Dunstan had killed himself.

Betty bit back a sigh. She was tired of the past getting in the way of the present. Real tired.

"So, who called?" Ken asked, wondering what had set his father off.

"Some gallery owner, wanting to know if I'd been approached about some new Dunstans." Lee's lip curled.

Ken didn't ask what that had to do with the bitch. He was just glad his father had switched the channel. The past couldn't be changed. The future could. He knew it even if his father didn't.

Tiffany got to her feet and hugged Lee. "I'm so sorry. Why can't galleries just accept that you and Mr. Crawford have all but two of the privately held Dunstan paintings? Why do unsavory people keep making trouble for you?"

Lee grunted and patted Tiffany's thin shoulder. "Don't you worry, sweetie. I know how to protect Ken's heritage."

Ken grimaced. If his father screwed this up the way he had everything in the past, there wouldn't be anything left to protect.

Tiffany smiled at Lee. "I'm sure you'll protect everything just fine."

Betty wished she was equally sure. "I'll be glad when this auction is over." She pushed her scrambled eggs around on her plate. "Most people in the West are land poor. We're art poor. It gets old."

Nobody said anything. It was the simple truth.

Lee drank more coffee. A retired teacher's pension, plus the occasional income from authenticating his father's paintings, didn't add up to the high life. But Tal Crawford was nobody's fool. At the end of the auction, Lee would be rolling in the kind of green cows didn't eat.

Assuming nothing went wrong.

Nothing will, Lee told himself. *Tal Crawford didn't get where he is by backing three-legged ponies.*

"You want diamonds, I'll get you diamonds," Lee said gruffly. "After the auction."

Betty pushed a few more yellow bits around her plate and didn't say a word of another simple truth ringing in her head.

In the closed world of Western art, nothing was a sure thing.

17

Zach put on his truck's parking brake, switched off the engine, and looked over at Jill. She was still asleep against the truck's hard door, using his leather jacket wrapped around her belly bag for a pillow. Obviously she hadn't slept real well last night with a strange man on her hotel couch a few feet away.

Or she'd still been shaken by the death threat.

Either way, Zach was in no hurry to wake her up. She looked peaceful, which she sure hadn't last night.

He lowered the window on his side. Nothing but wind, silence, and warm sunlight. As he'd thought, no one had bothered to follow them.

Perfect.

Or not.

Time would tell.

He reached back into the bench seat of the crew cab and fished out his laptop. He hadn't had time to check for new files before he and Jill left the hotel this morning. Might as well do it now. Jill could show him around the burned ranch house when she woke up.

No hurries, no worries.

No one was going to sneak up on them out here.

The Arizona Strip was a lonesome landscape. The only signs of civilization were distant jet contrails across the empty blue sky, and the singed line of old poplars that some long-ago Breck had planted as a windbreak next to the ranch house.

The rest was pretty much ashes and wind.

A bitter end to a pioneer family, Zach thought.

Jill stirred, sighed, but didn't wake up. Her hair burned copper and auburn in the sun coming through the closed window. Her breasts rose and fell beneath her dark T-shirt with every breath. Her lips were relaxed, pink, full.

Tempting.

No wonder Lane got himself a good case of puppy love. That's one intriguing woman. Strong without being butch, smart without strutting about it, and determined. The kind of woman who walked next to her man, made homes and babies, and settled the West.

He looked out at the blackened, skeletal remains of the barn, the old farm equipment scorched and rusting, the barbwire-fenced family graveyard near the pasture, and the bright run of springwater in the pasture ditches.

She's the last of the Brecks.

Alive but surrounded by death.

And I better keep her breathing, or Faroe will have my butt for kicking practice.

Zach booted up the computer, saw that the battery was

full—for once—and the signal strong. He typed in the code that would connect him via satellite to St. Kilda.

His black eyebrows rose. While he'd slept and then driven to Jill's ranch, St. Kilda had been busy. He downloaded files.

And downloaded.

And downloaded.

Shawna must have worked all night.

Now it was up to him to sort through all the facts and find the ones that might help him keep Jill alive. It was the sort of work he was used to. He was good at it. That's why St. Kilda paid him a retainer plus flat fee per op, just to make sure he didn't look at another employer.

The first file Zach found was Jill's. He opened it and began skimming documents with the speed of a man accustomed to sorting through mountains of information to find the few vital facts that could save lives.

Then his skimming slammed to a halt. The biggest files were dense JPEGs of Jill's paintings. Several of them hung in various rooms at Pomona College, a reminder to all fine arts students that talent could be honed, but it couldn't be taught. You either had it or you didn't.

Zach didn't.

Jill did.

The paintings were landscapes taken from her memory—cattle at the water tank, a horse with its butt to the snowy wind, a barbwire fence receding into nothingness against the wild immensity of the land. Zach could taste the snow, breathe the heady wind that had known only stone mountaintops, feel the thickness of the horse's winter coat turned against the cold.

Does Faroe know that she's an artist?

If he did, he hadn't said anything.

Zach finished skimming the files, then brooded over the

JPEGs of Jill's art, wishing he could see it more closely. But there was no time for a flying trip to Pomona and, hopefully, no need.

Silently he looked through the windshield and digested the raw data, turning it over and around in his mind, connecting facts and speculations, scattering question marks across his mental landscape. When he was done, he was back where he started: Jill was an unusual woman descended from a long line of unusual women.

Stubborn women.

Determined women.

Same thing, actually. Just viewed from another angle.

He looked over and saw her watching him with eyes the color of spring grass. Her hair burned with a soft fire that made him want to touch it.

"Morning," he said. "Well, afternoon, actually."

She looked at her watch. "I can't believe I slept while you were driving."

"I'm a good driver."

"You could be Jesus on wheels and I still wouldn't sleep."

Zach thought of her file. "A control thing."

She shrugged, then stretched. "Why did you stop here?"

"The road to the cabin looked rough enough to shake change out of my pockets."

Jill realized that he'd stopped so that she could keep on sleeping. The fact both amused and charmed her. She was used to hauling her own weight—and then some— when it came to any job. The men on the river had joked about it, but they were intimidated by her. She'd hiked, rowed, and worked every one of them into the ground.

It was the only way to get their respect.

"Thanks," Jill said. "But it wasn't necessary. I can do with very little sleep."

"No problem. It gave me time to go over some of Shawna's research. So tell me, what's a woman with degrees in computer science, art history, and art doing as a river guide?"

Jill's answer was a lifted eyebrow.

"You were home-schooled," Zach said, "went to Pomona College on a full-ride scholarship when you were seventeen, left four years later with three degrees, and went to work as a river guide—rafts and kayaks. I was just curious why you did that rather than teaching or selling art or making money in the tech sector."

"I like being outdoors." Then the last of the sleepy fuzz vanished from Jill's brain. She hadn't told Zach or Faroe that much about herself. "Did Shawna investigate me?"

It was more of an accusation than a question, but Zach answered anyway. "Of course."

"I asked for help, not an intrusion into my privacy."

He almost smiled. "Hard to have one without the other. But don't worry, everything so far has come from open sources. The *Canyon County Gazette* followed you like paparazzi. Big file of news clips. You smoked your SAT. Perfect score. Quite an accomplishment for anybody, much less a girl home-schooled on the Arizona Strip."

"Why did you investigate me?"

"Because you're in trouble. Hard to help if you don't know much about the person you're helping."

She chewed on that for a time. She didn't like it, but it made a sideways kind of sense.

"Mom worked out a deal with the satellite company," Jill said. "Kind of like a scholarship for bright, dirt-poor kids. Forty hours a week of free computer time."

"Most kids would have spent it playing games."

"I loved learning things as much as I loved working on the ranch. Freedom everywhere I looked."

"Freedom, huh?" Zach absorbed the fact. "Where did

you live before your mother came home and took back her maiden name?"

"What does that have to do with paintings and death threats?"

"Nothing. Everything. I won't know until you tell me."

"I lived in a place like Hildale," she said curtly. "I wasn't quite a Creeker, but close enough."

Jill watched Zach. His eyes were slightly narrowed, looking at a horizon she couldn't see.

"Creeker," Zach said after a moment, flipping through mental files. "Based on the days when Hildale and Colorado City were a single city on two sides of the creek. Fundamental Mormon community. Multiple wives required for a man to get into heaven. Bonnets, long sleeves and longer skirts, minimal education for girls, followed by real early marriages, usually to a much older man. Kids. Lots of them. Brings an entirely new meaning to the term 'blended family.' Midwives, not doctors. No birth certificates."

"Yeah," Jill said. "It makes it easier for the poofers to vanish and no questions asked."

"Poofers?"

"People—women, babies, or kids—who are here one day and gone the next. Dead and buried without ceremony or notice. Nobody ever says their name again or talks about how the poofers died."

The idea left a nasty taste in Zach's mouth, but all he said was "How many sister-wives did your father have?"

She flinched. "You didn't get that out of the *Canyon Gazette*. They avoid the whole subject of plural marriages, poofers, and anything else that might make the patriarchy frown. Then there are the Sons and Daughters of Perdition, the men and women who leave the church. My mother was a Daughter of Perdition."

"Are you?"

"Does it matter?"

"Not to me," Zach said. "As for knowing about fundamental Mormons, I soak up all kinds of learning from a variety of sources. No multiple degrees, though. Formal education didn't do it for me." *Between Garland Frost and working for the feds, I learned more than most people ever do, or ever want to.* "Is that why your mother left your father? She didn't want a sister-wife?"

"What does this have to do with—"

"The paintings came down through your family," Zach said neutrally. "That means your family is important to the investigation."

Jill hissed a word through her teeth. She hated talking about her so-called family. With impatient motions, she opened the door and got out of the truck. "I need to move around. I've done enough sitting."

Zach got out and followed her. She covered the ground easily, quickly, with the stride of someone used to hiking miles wearing a backpack. Smoke jumpers, the military special ops, and dedicated trekkers all had that walk.

None of them looked as good as Jill from the rear.

Deliberately he glanced away. Last thing he needed was an inconvenient lust for a client. Especially a client with an art and art history background who wasn't in any hurry to talk about the paintings that somebody cared enough about to cut up her car and threaten to kill her for.

I know you like her, Faroe, but it has to have occurred to you that Jill could have painted the things herself.

It sure has occurred to me.

And the more Zach saw of the Breck ranch—poverty central or he'd eat what was left of the barn—the more it seemed likely that Jill wouldn't mind having some money to play with.

She circled the black ruins and went to the untouched

metal windmill that was drawing water up for a ranch that no longer existed. She stared at the cool water pouring into the big tank, spilling over, filling ditches to irrigate pastures where stock no longer grazed.

Zach waited and watched Jill. It didn't take a detective to figure out that family life wasn't her favorite topic.

She stared at water flowing into the tank, ripples chasing across the shimmering surface, the liquid of life overflowing to run down irrigation ditches.

Just when Zach had decided that St. Kilda would have to dig up the family past for him, Jill started talking again.

"I have three full brothers," she said evenly. "Older. A lot older. Mom had a series of miscarriages in between and after the last son was born. When she went to the local midwife, she was told that she should pray more, it was God's will that she bear children. Mom nearly died trying to carry out God's will. Then she went to Salt Lake City and found a doctor who didn't put religion before his patient's needs."

Zach watched the expressions shifting over Jill's face like shadows over the landscape. He listened with an intensity that she didn't notice. She didn't like her past, but it was very much a part of her.

"Whatever the doctor gave her worked," Jill said. "No more miscarriages. No more babies, either. About that time my father became a fundamentalist. He moved everyone to New Eden, set up a house, married a sixteen-year-old, and had more children. He took a third wife. She was fifteen. Babies. A lot of them. Mom stuck with him."

Though Jill's voice was even, her eyes were narrow, her mouth flat. She didn't understand her mother. She didn't like her father.

She detested fundamental Mormonism.

I was raised by women in a militantly testosterone-free zone.

Now Zach knew why.

"Then Mom got pregnant with me," Jill said. "I suspect she thought she was safe from the baby mill—menopause and all that—and stopped whatever birth control the doctor had given her."

"That's how I came into the world," Zach said.

Jill smiled crookedly. "So you were an 'oops' baby, too."

"Pretty much."

She let out a long breath, and with it some of the tension that had come when she talked about the childhood she'd tried very hard to forget.

"Mom hung on to the pregnancy, had me, and gritted her teeth when her husband took a fourth, really young wife," Jill said. "At least I assume my mother gritted her teeth. Maybe she was relieved that he wasn't dogging her sheets anymore." Jill blew out another breath. "Whatever. She stuck with him until she overheard plans for my marriage to one of the elders. I was eight."

Zach's eyebrows shot up and he said something under his breath.

"Oh, the marriage wasn't supposed to be consummated until I started having periods," she said acidly. "You see, the elders were worried about me. I wasn't a good little fundamental wallflower. So they arranged for me to move in with some old man's extended family until I was ready to have babies. Then I'd be his fifth wife."

Zach didn't know he was angry until he felt the adrenaline lighting up his blood. "That's illegal."

"Not in fundamental Mormon country. The mainline church doesn't support plural wives, but it doesn't exactly sweat to exterminate it, either. It's an open secret in the Mormon West."

Zack watched while Jill bent over, picked up a rock, and sent it out over the pasture with a vicious snap of her arm.

"Anyway," she said, "Mom somehow got word to her aunt."

"Modesty Breck."

"Yes. A few days later Modesty came and brought us to the Breck ranch. I shed my polyg clothes—bonnet and long skirts—cut off my long braids with a kitchen knife. I learned to ride, rope, brand, handle hay bales, and mend fence."

"Your father just let your mother go?" Zach asked.

"Oh, he came to take us back. Once."

"What happened?"

Jill's smile was both real and cold. "Modesty ran him off with a snake gun. Told him if he ever walked on Breck land again, she'd kill him and bury him in the kitchen garden, because all he was good for was fertilizer."

Zach laughed. "I think I would have liked your great-aunt."

"She wouldn't have liked you. She didn't have any use for men. Mom took back her maiden name and changed mine, too. None of the Breck women have entered a tabernacle since."

"Yet you live in an overwhelmingly Mormon county."

"That's why I was home-schooled."

"No wonder you don't trust the sheriff," Zach said. "You don't trust anyone in civil authority."

"Not when the Latter-day Saints are involved. Ned Purcell is an elder in the church. Every elected official around here is publicly devout. More than a few of them have plural marriages, though nobody talks about it."

"School roll call must get monotonous," Zach said dryly.

"Oh, they're not stupid. Everybody but the first wife picks a last name out of a telephone book. Daddy is called uncle, except for the children of the first wife." Jill fired another rock into the pasture. "When it comes to women, this place is stuck in the 1850s."

"You'll be happy to know that St. Kilda Consulting is firmly grounded in the twenty-first century," Zach said.

"Joe Faroe certainly is. He respected my skill on the river. Actually, he enjoyed it. He really didn't care that a female was better at something physical than he was. That's pretty rare in a man, no matter what the year."

"You'd like his wife."

"I already like his son. There's nothing wrong with Lane that a few more years won't cure. He's going to be a good man."

"Full circle."

"What?" she asked.

"From your childhood to the river where you saved Lane's life to my knocking on your hotel room door because someone threatened to kill you. Funny thing . . ."

She raised an eyebrow.

Zach looked back at her. "You haven't mentioned the paintings once."

18

Hollywood
September 14
1:00 P.M.

No problemo," Score said into the telephone. "I've got the
kind of evidence you can't use in court, but he'll sweat
big bucks after you show him the airline manifest and
the photos from the kiddy whorehouse in Thailand. He'll not
only pay you alimony, he'll kiss your ass with gratitude for
not selling everything to the *Enquirer.*" He paused. "No, the
Enquirer won't pay more for the photos than he will. Trust
me on that."

Another phone rang. Someone in the front office picked
it up. Seconds later, a light blinked on his intercom, telling him that his next appointment was waiting. He wrapped
up his conversation, assured the client that the photos were
coming by special messenger to her lawyer, hung up, and hit
the intercom button.

"Send her in," Score said.

His door opened to one of his tech specialists. At the moment her hair was dyed black with green tips. The nose and lip studs were missing, but the tongue bell was still there.

Made him drool to think about it, so he didn't. She was one of his best techs. He didn't care if she showed up naked with pins stuck everywhere.

But she had a way of redlining his temper. No respect.

"Sit down," Score said. "What do you have?"

"Not much," Amy said. "I ran it through every electronic cleaner program we have. Still sounds like she packed the bug in a suitcase stuffed with clothes."

"Better than nothing."

Amy shrugged and handed over some pages of script.

A glance at the first page told Score what he already knew. The locater was alive and well. The subject was about twenty miles from the old lady's ranch. Heading home, because there sure wasn't anywhere else in that part of the world to go.

"Huh. Did she rent wheels?" he asked.

"If she did, the bug wasn't in range for the transaction. But the progress of the locater is right in line with what I'd expect from a car on the road."

"That's the trouble with satellite phones. Too expensive for most people to keep close like a cell phone. It's probably out of voice range a lot of the time."

"She hasn't used it," Amy agreed. "Maybe she bought a cell phone."

"Not from any carrier in Mesquite or Page."

Hacking into business records was Score's specialty. Cell phones, landlines, credit cards, airlines, hotels, restaurants, jewelry stores, state and federal government—if information was out there, so were Score's clever employees.

"Maybe the cell carrier hasn't registered her account in their main computer yet," Amy said.

"Or maybe she got smart and bought a throwaway," he said.

"That'll make it tough for us."

Score didn't answer. He was scanning the second page of the script. "Two voices? You sure?"

"One female, same pattern as you recorded when you called her," Amy said, scratching her head with a pencil. "One male, identity unknown."

Frowning, Score read the few verifiable words to come out of the mush of sound that the bug had sent to his computer. Then he swore under his breath. The word paintings had appeared more than once.

Is she talking about them being burned?

Is she selling them?

Does she really have them or were the JPEGs pre-burn files?

Is it all a scam?

Had the old lady's grandniece been in on it from the jump?

The garbled signal didn't have any answers. Neither did his own experience with Modesty and Jillian Breck. Modesty had died before she talked. Jill had been clever enough to avoid his trap altogether.

Even ducks know what to keep away from during hunting season. Dodging me in Mesquite didn't exactly require big smarts on her part.

But it irritated the hell out of him.

Score tossed the script aside with a curse. "Keep after it. And if that bug moves from its present location, tell me ASAP."

"How far? The government is dicking with the GPS again. Three-hundred-foot radius of error."

"Set up a one-mile guard perimeter. Tell me if or when she breaks that fence. Even ten feet beyond that mile. Got it?"

"Got it." Amy stood and headed for the door. The green tips of her hair bounced stiffly.

Score read the script again and again. Nothing new popped. Except his blood pressure. He really needed to hit the gym before someone stupid redlined his temper.

But more than a workout, he needed to find out what the Breck bitch was up to.

He looked at his calendar. He didn't have too many appointments in the next few days that couldn't be handled by other employees, but he had a few he should handle. He supposed he could assign another operative to Breck.

Not likely. Not with the old lady dead. Even if they busted it down to manslaughter, I'd do hard time.

This one I keep real close.

Silently he rubbed thumb against index finger, wondering if he should get closer to the Breck woman now or risk waiting.

If she had the paintings, yes, he should be closer.

If she didn't, no.

If. If. If.

He laughed out loud, the sound as reckless as he'd like to be. But he was too smart to be stupid.

I should cut back on the 'roids.

Not yet. It's too much fun twisting big guys' dicks.

He shook his head over the skinny runt he'd once been and went back to his calendar. If he had to, he could handle the Breck woman and not be missed from work.

He almost hoped she'd make him do it.

Reno
September 14
1:38 P.M.

Caitlin Crawford glanced up from the computer in her home office as her husband walked in. He looked out of place among the sleek modern furniture she loved. He was dressed like a weekend cowboy who'd never been on a horse. In the decade they had been married, she still hadn't gotten used to his wardrobe. But she'd learned to accept it.

A rich man was entitled to his oddities.

And it was really odd that Tal had taken her for his third wife solely because she came from an upper-crust Pasadena family who could no longer afford its good breeding. He'd acquired her like one of his paintings, enjoyed parading her "class" in front of his friends and business associates, and kept on wearing his hick cowboy boots and bolo ties.

And losing money.

He has a lot to lose, she reminded herself. *Anyone who can afford Pollock and Picasso has more money than he knows what to do with.*

Caitlin's mother hadn't raised any stupid daughters. Caitlin might not know about the intimate details of her husband's business transactions, but she had hired someone to keep tabs on all of his bank accounts. Cash was her bottom line. Being raised genteel and poor in a rich neighborhood had taught her what made the world go round.

It wasn't sex.

But her husband didn't make finding out about his accounts easy for her. Tal was old-fashioned about more than his wardrobe. She had a house account that he generously filled and never mentioned how business was, if she should spend less or more. If it weren't for whispers and rumors, she wouldn't have known that federal tax collectors had been taking a very hard, long look at some of his business write-offs. She didn't know why, or what, or how serious the government's case was. She only knew enough to be afraid.

If Tal went down, she'd go down with him.

"How did the meeting with Lee Dunstan go?" Caitlin asked. Her tone was upbeat, her smile warm, and her stomach tight with fear.

"I told you not to worry about a thing, baby. It's all taken care of. The IRS will be sniffing up someone else's butt real soon."

She managed not to curse out loud. Or scream. Eighteen months ago, the head of the accounting firm Tal used for business and personal record-keeping had been indicted, tried, and sent to jail for fraud, leaving behind a lot of financial wreckage for the IRS to sift through, searching for taxes owed on unreported profits.

"I'm glad to hear it," she said, smiling through her clenched teeth.

She just wished she believed it. But Tal never talked business with her, which left her dangling alone with her vicious fear of being poor again.

"Would you like to go over the guest list for the post-auction party?" she asked.

"I'd rather be whipped."

Caitlin had been expecting that response. Tal had married her to add a gloss to his home, his entertaining, and his reputation. Because she'd been raised to be a rich man's wife, she was good at gloss. Since she wasn't the type to count money that wasn't in her hand, she'd cut the guest list down to people who could do Tal's various business interests some good, and to hell with his freeloading shirtsleeve relatives and old acquaintances. He wouldn't miss them unless someone pointed out their absence.

The money saved would go to her own hidden bank account, along with everything she'd skimmed from the household account.

A woman married to an older man had to look out for herself. Though Tal would never admit it, he simply wasn't as quick as he'd been five years ago. Or even last year.

"Then I won't bother you with the details of the party," Caitlin said, smiling.

"You need any more money in the household account?"

"Don't I always?"

Tal laughed and pulled a checkbook out of his jeans pocket. "Fifty do it?"

"Sixty?"

"Hell, these parties just keep getting more expensive."

"And you keep getting more business from them."

Tal laughed. "You got me there. Sixty it is."

Smiling, he wrote his wife a check for sixty thousand dollars. She was a bargain at twice the price.

Class couldn't be bought, but it could be married.

20

Breck Ranch
September 14
1:49 P.M.

Jill drove up to the old cabin, put on the parking brake
of Zach's truck, and turned off the engine. She was still
rather surprised by him. When she'd said that the dirt
track leading to the old homestead was hard to find unless
you knew what you were looking for, he'd just handed her
the keys to his truck.

Altogether an intriguing man. Unexpected, too. She could
tell he liked the way she moved, but he hadn't even hinted at
a pass, much less made one.

Very intriguing.

Irritating, too. The longer she was with him, the more the
idea of a pass appealed.

"Home sweet home, such as it is," she said.

Zach closed the computer he'd been using. Silently he took

in the weathered old cabin backed up against a red sandstone cliff and tucked beneath a massive old cottonwood.

He whistled softly. "And here I thought *I* lived with pieces of history."

"What do you mean?"

"When I'm not on a contract for St. Kilda, I collect abandoned industrial art—old muscle cars of the '60s and early '70s—and restore them. Carcheology, as it were, relics of a time before OPEC ruled. But this cabin goes back to a time before internal combustion engines owned the world, a time when seeps of crude oil in Pennsylvania weren't worth the land they sat on."

Jill smiled. "I'd like to have lived then."

"You're one of the few people I've ever met who could actually do it."

The compliment surprised her. She glanced sideways at Zach. He was looking at the cabin, his light brown eyes like a hawk's, missing nothing.

Intriguing, irritating, intelligent. Sexy in a lean, easy-moving way.

She shook her head at the direction of her thoughts. She'd never jumped a man. She wasn't planning on starting now, no matter what her hormones were pushing for.

"What did St. Kilda say about Blanchard?" she asked, turning away from anything personal.

"There are art dealers in east Texas, and there are men with the last name of Blanchard in east Texas, but no man fits in both categories. Or woman."

"He could have been just visiting, or looking for art."

"He could have been a figment of his own imagination."

She smiled rather grimly. "Yeah, that occurred to me when I saw my trashed car."

Zach studied the weathered cabin with its thick, crooked shutters and rifle slits that had been filled in during a later, safer era. He'd seen the bones of pioneer cabins while he scoured the rural West for old muscle cars, but he'd never seen a place this old that people still occupied.

"The dude was hoping you'd bring the paintings with you," Zach said.

"I'd have to be dumb as road apples to do that."

Laughing, he turned and watched the sunlight burn gold and red in Jill's hair. "You'd be surprised how dumb people are."

"Actually, I wouldn't," she said. "I've had men refuse to get in my raft because—"

"—you're a girl," Zach cut in. "Stupid. Any man who looked at more than the usual places would see that you're an athlete."

"Usual places?"

"Tits and ass."

She snickered. "I think it comes with the Y gene."

"So Y gene equals stupid?"

"It can." She opened the truck door and slid out. "Ditto for XX. I've seen all kinds of stupid on the river."

Zach got out, looked once more at their back trail. No dust, no sign of watchers. The idea of her living here alone made him twitchy. No matter how fit she was, a professional with a knife or a gun—or a torch—would make short work of her.

But he wasn't dumb enough to say it aloud. She'd get mad, he'd get mad, and they'd get nowhere fast.

The wind picked up again, playing with the cottonwood leaves that had already fallen and tugging more free from the tree's broad crown.

Zach followed Jill into the cabin and through the small kitchen to the pantry. She fiddled at the back of one of the cabinets, it moved, and an opening into the sandstone appeared.

"Cool," Zach said, grinning. "My great-great-grandmother used to tell stories about living like this on a pioneer homestead in what became New Mexico. Never expected to see one of these old hiding places still in working order."

"We lived simply, but we lived on our own terms."

"That's the way my mother's family felt." He watched as Jill bent over and tugged at something. The much-used material of her jeans shaped a very nice ass. "Need any help?"

"Need? No. But I wouldn't mind."

In the name of duty, Zach crowded close to Jill until he could look into the opening. Her hips felt even better than they looked.

"The trunk?" he asked.

"Yeah."

He rubbed past her until he could reach a handle on the old steamer trunk. The leather was worn and brittle with age, but it held when he pulled on it.

Jill lifted her end of the trunk and staggered slightly, surprised. The trunk felt a lot lighter with him on the other end. After a few bumps and missteps, they got it into the kitchen.

"Was your great-aunt's note in here?" Zach asked.

"No. It was under the primer bucket at the sink."

"Smart. Only someone who planned to use the pump would lift the bucket."

"Modesty was smart. Hard, too. That's how she survived." She looked up at Zach. "And you're one of the few people in my generation who knows about hand pumps and primer buckets."

"That's me." He gave her a crooked smile. "Just an old-fashioned sort of guy."

"Got a bridge to sell me, too, right?"

"Any time you're in a buying kind of mood."

Jill hid her smile as she bent over and opened the trunk.

Zach was a lot of things, but she doubted that old-fashioned was one of them. Old-fashioned men were in a hurry to prove how strong they were. And the electronics he worked with so casually were as slick as any she'd seen. Part of her itched to get her hands on his computer. Most of her itched to get her hands on him.

With a muttered curse, she opened the trunk.

Zach saw a beaten-up leather portfolio and six rectangular packages of varying sizes. "What's that?" he asked, touching the portfolio.

"Family stuff—fading photos and old letters, legal documents, water rights, ranch boundaries, lease-lands, and whatever else somebody thought was worth keeping for the next generation. I went through them already. None of them has anything to do with the paintings."

"Okay. I'll put the portfolio on the bottom of my research list."

Right now he wanted to see the paintings that someone wanted bad enough to threaten Jill with death.

And maybe, just maybe, kill her great-aunt.

The timing of the death after the painting had been sent out for appraisal was a coincidence, to say the least. The missing, then destroyed, painting was another coincidence.

He didn't trust coincidences.

"Modesty inherited the trunk from her sister," Jill said, setting the tray aside. "My grandmother. She was a wannabe artist who was Thomas Dunstan's on-again, off-again lover."

Zach went still. *Thomas Dunstan.* No wonder some mystery man was trying to get his hands on those paintings.

"I know the name," Zach said neutrally, eyeing the rectangles stacked neatly in the big trunk. "Fine painter. Erratic output. I'll bet he's pretty pricey now."

"So I hear. There were thirteen paintings in this trunk.

Twelve, now. The dude who trashed my car ripped one of the paintings to ribbons. Just a small one, but . . ." Her clear eyes hardened. "It was a piece of beauty, of history, and now it's just scraps shoved into my belly bag."

Zach made a mental note to check out the bag when he went back to the truck. Garland Frost would whelp a litter of green lizards if a Dunstan had been destroyed.

"Twelve paintings." He whistled softly. "If they're Dunstans and can be documented, they're probably worth enough to pay taxes for the next century."

She paused in the unwrapping of the paintings. "Really?"

"Yeah. At a minimum."

"I know as much about the market for Western art as I do about finding, um, so-called industrial art in old junkyards," she said.

He grinned despite the adrenaline humming in his blood.

Twelve new Dunstans. Sweet God.

If they're real.

"I loved these paintings as a child," Jill said, pulling out a fat, carefully wrapped rectangle. "I used to sneak up into the attic, where Modesty had them hidden, and look at them. That stopped when Modesty caught me. She smacked me but good."

"And you sneaked back anyway."

She shook her head. "Mother told me Modesty would throw us out if she caught me in the attic again. I was a kid, but I'd learned how precious shelter was when we ran away from New Eden. I never saw the paintings again until my great-aunt was dead."

"Did Modesty say the paintings were valuable?"

"All she said about them was to stay away and never mention them again. To anyone."

Zach really wanted to peel off the wrapping and have a look at what Jill was holding, but made himself wait. One of many things he'd learned from Frost was patience.

Of a predatory kind.

"What do you think now that you've seen them?" Zach asked. "Valuable or trash?"

"I look at things as an artist, not as a merchant."

Ah, finally, he thought.

There was information about Jill in the files from St. Kilda, but he preferred to compare facts on file with what she willingly told him. He'd been real curious about some of those facts, given that one of Jill's three college majors was fine art.

Some of the best counterfeiters were frustrated fine artists.

"Do you paint?" he asked.

"I studied painting in college," she said. "I loved playing with oils, but making a living at it wasn't likely. So I went to my second love, the river."

He wondered what she wasn't saying. He didn't ask, hoping that she would keep talking. He needed her to trust him.

Part of the job, he told himself.

But he'd never been quite so determined to win a client's trust as he was with Jillian Breck.

"The more I learned about how to create certain effects with oils," she continued, "the more I began to wonder if these paintings weren't quite valuable. They're very good. In my opinion, anyway, which isn't worth a penny."

Zach wanted to rip the fat rectangle out of Jill's hands. But all he did was ask, "Didn't your great-aunt ever have the paintings appraised?"

Jill shook her head. "My grandmother never wanted the paintings seen by anyone. Modesty agreed, and kept that promise even after her sister died."

"That's odd."

She shrugged. "Modesty raised odd to an art."

"Then why did she finally send one of the paintings out to be appraised?"

"I'm guessing it was the taxes on the ranch. We're land poor. I just keep wondering . . ." Jill's voice faded.

"What?"

"If she would still be alive but for the tax bill. It's paid now, by the way. Back taxes, death taxes, the whole greasy tortilla. It took every head of stock she owned, plus the insurance settlement for the fire and accidental death. Next year . . ." Jill shook her head. "Next year the land will be on the market. Unless those paintings are worth something, I can't afford to keep the Breck ranch. And I'm damned if I'll hand it over to my fundamentalist brothers."

Zach looked out the cabin's open door, across the sloping bench of land the ranch sat on to the dry canyons and low ridges that ran all the way to the north rim of the Grand Canyon ten miles distant. The ranch was beautiful in the way of the arid West, the kind of spare, demanding beauty that most people couldn't see.

Jill could. Her eyes and her voice told Zach that she loved the land. She was hoping the paintings would allow her to keep the ranch.

"Art is a funny business," he said. "Getting funnier every day."

"From what I've gathered online, there's huge money in the art market."

"And no way to value a painting but its last auction price," he said. "Or the second-to-last price—that's the one two people were willing to pay."

"What do you mean?"

"Art is like everything else. It's worth what someone's willing to pay for it. Period. In order to make people pay more, much more, auctioneers and experts churn out a lot of blue smoke. The painting being flogged doesn't change from one decade to the next. Only the volume and quality of blue smoke varies. And the price of the art."

"You think my paintings are worthless?" she asked.

"I haven't seen them, have I?"

She smiled slowly. "Thought you'd never ask."

21

Hollywood
September 14
1:50 P.M.

S core had barely ushered a rich new client out of his office
before Amy strode in, all but slamming the door behind
her. The green tips of her hair quivered with anger.

"The next time you tell me ASAP," she said, "take my
calls."

He grabbed his temper before he decked her. He needed
Amy's head right where it was, on her shoulders. He'd always had a temper, but lately it was on a hair trigger.

'Roids.

*No. I do steroids, they don't do me. It's this damn Breck
case that's jerking me off.*

"The bug on subject Breck has moved about three miles
northeast from its initial site," she said.

"What's three miles away?"

"According to the map you gave me, a lot of nothing. It's Nowhere, Arizona."

Modesty's taunting words came back to Score.

This house was built by pioneers, people who lived alone and protected themselves. They built hidey-holes that even the Paiutes couldn't find.

"Anything on the phone bug?" he asked.

"No more than I already gave you. The subject must be away from her sat phone."

Score looked at his schedule, swore under his breath, and wished he knew what the Breck girl was up to.

He didn't want to leave Hollywood right now.

And he couldn't afford to boot the Breck case. That particular client was too important.

"Tell me if you get anything on the phone bug," Score said, "or if it leaves the ranch boundaries. And there's a bonus if you get anything solid out of the phone."

"Define solid."

"I'll know when you tell me."

22

Breck Ranch
September 14
1:58 P.M.

Without a word, Jill unwrapped more paintings and leaned them against the wall.

Zach was equally silent.

The paintings were riveting.

Holy hell. Frost would get hard looking at just one of them. Twelve is staggering.

The canvases ranged from eight-by-twelve to thirty-four-by-forty inches. Just canvas and stretchers, no frames. If they were Dunstans, they were worth the kind of money even smart people killed for.

"Modesty lived alone? No one else?" Zach finally managed.

"Not after my mom died and I left."

"Alone, and she hid these. That's crazy," he muttered.

"The wind out here can make you a little crazy sometimes."

He looked at the incredible paintings. "This is way past a little."

"Modesty didn't have time or patience for art. She was too busy surviving."

With that, Jill unwrapped the last two paintings and placed them against the wall.

"Holy, holy hell," Zach said on a long gust of breath. *If these are half as good as they look. . .*

Almost reverently he lifted one of the canvases at random and took it into the sunlight to study. The first impression was of fine brushwork and careful technique.

And that mind-blowing, indefinable something called greatness.

The painting showed the first tentacles of the modern West overtaking the Wild West. Tucked away against the base of a dry, rocky ridge, green bloomed, and with it a gas station that must have been startlingly new when the painting was made. Despite the intrusion of the new into the old—or perhaps because of it—the painting echoed with space and isolation and time. He turned the canvas over. IN-DIAN SPRINGS.

He picked up another painting at random. This one was a flawlessly executed Western landscape, basin and range country falling away from a lonely ridge. Below the ridge stood a cabin so small as to be insignificant against the sweep of the land. A human figure, a woman in a long red skirt and white blouse, carried a bucket of water from a spring.

The figure was suggested as much as drawn, a few brushstrokes added to the starkly beautiful land, brushstrokes that whispered of the human cost of pioneering the lonely, dry inter-mountain West.

"That's one fine painting," Zach said after a few minutes.

"Of course, my opinion isn't worth much more on the open market than yours."

"I was trained in fine art. Western genre painting was never mentioned."

"Yeah, I'll bet. Europe, modernism, minimalism, or nothing at all. Except Georgia O'Keeffe, maybe, if you cornered a professor and peeled off thin strips of skin until he or she begged for mercy."

"Sounds like you took my courses," Jill said.

"My education was more informal, but the teacher was first class." *And a real son of a bitch along with it.* Zach tilted the canvas so that sunlight raked over it from all angles, then flipped it over expertly to look at the back. "No signature. Again."

"None of them are signed."

He traded the canvas for another. A landscape again, just as technically brilliant and dynamic as the others, humming with time and space and distance, the thrill and exhilaration of testing yourself against an unknown, untamed land. Masculine long before Hemingway made a cult of it, and the hallmark of classic Western art.

This time a few spare brushstrokes evoked a woman with her pale skirt whipping in the wind, her back to the artist as she looked out over the empty land and endless sky. Again, the figure was very small in the context of the painting, yet without the woman the canvas would have been far less powerful. In a subtle way, she was the focus that made the picture transcend simple representation of a landscape.

Zach checked the back of the painting. A title had been painted in block letters on the canvas stretcher bar. ENDURING STRENGTH.

"Amen," he said softly.

Jill looked over his arm. "That's one of my favorites. The artist caught the heady isolation of this land perfectly."

"Are they all this good?" Zach asked, scanning the paintings against the far wall.

"I don't know what an expert would say, but I think so. They might not be to everybody's taste, but nothing is."

"There's taste and then there's insight."

He held the painting up and studied it from edge to edge, back to front, and all sides. No signature.

"I've seen a few Dunstans," Zach said. *Every day, day after day, but that was years ago.* Of all Frost's collection of fine Western art, and of all the paintings that had passed through his galleries, the Dunstans had most appealed to Zach. Frost, too. The old man wouldn't part with his two no matter what was offered.

"And?" she asked impatiently.

"These fit with my memories of Dunstan's work. I don't know how often he put figures in his landscapes, though." *Certainly not in the vast majority of them.* "The landscape is strong." *Try incredible.* "At the very least, this is the work of a gifted artist."

"Then it should be worth something."

"Like I said, art is a funny business." Zach shifted the canvas gently. "The lack of a signature makes it really difficult to attribute the paintings to anyone, much less to a cult icon like Dunstan. Did Modesty ever suggest that they were Dunstan's work? Maybe they were field studies for larger studio works. Lots of artists don't sign their studies."

"The most Modesty said about them was that her sister, Dunstan's lover, called them 'twenty-seven years of bad luck.'"

"Isn't that an old saying about broken mirrors, black cats, and such?"

"I always wondered if it was the amount of time Justine knew Dunstan," Jill said.

"Was your mother Dunstan's child?"

Jill shrugged. "Nothing shows in the family Bible. My mother is entered as Maureen Breck, daughter of Justine Breck. No father mentioned. From the few times Mother and Modesty talked about my grandmother, I gather that my mother could have had one of several fathers."

"A real modern relationship," Zach said dryly.

"More like whenever Justine and Dunstan had a big blowup, she took another artist-lover for a time. She always came back to Dunstan, though. Until the last fight, when they ended up in jail."

"Drunk and disorderly?"

"I'm told she tried to kill him."

Zach's dark eyebrows rose. "Never piss off a Breck woman, huh?"

"Keep it in mind," Jill said, smiling slightly. "After she got out of jail, Justine lived on the ranch with her much-younger sister and her daughter."

"I remember reading somewhere that Dunstan hung himself in jail," Zach said.

"Like I said, don't piss us off."

Zach smiled slightly. "You really do come from a long line of solitary, difficult women, don't you?"

Jill looked him in the eye. "You say that like it's a bad thing."

He glanced at the canvas in his hand. "I wonder how the artist who painted this would have described it."

"Breck women pretty much march to their own drummer, do their own thing, and otherwise don't take orders from anyone," she said. "But I've never minded being alone, at least not until the other night."

He put aside the painting and began pacing along the lineup of canvases against the cabin wall. Even on the third round, each painting was more striking than the last.

Incredible.

"Anything you left out when we talked last night?" he asked, still looking at the paintings. "Names, telephone numbers, gallery owners, lost lovers, someplace to start looking for the connection between you and the trash artist in Mesquite? Because as it is now, we have to go with investigating the galleries, owners, and art salesmen. If the threat is coming from somewhere else, we'll be barking up a whole forest of wrong trees."

Jill frowned at the paintings, thinking, then shook her head. "No help here."

"How about old boyfriends?"

"Nope."

"You never had a boyfriend?"

"I never had one who wasn't relieved to say good-bye. As you pointed out, Breck women don't take orders worth a damn."

"So it's whips and leather in bed for you?"

Her jaw dropped.

"Never mind," Zach said, trying not to laugh. "Question withdrawn. For now I'll go with the art connections. If nothing pops, I'll come back and question you some more."

"Come back?"

"Yeah. I'm going to put you in a St. Kilda safe house and—"

"No," she cut in. "They're my paintings. I'm staying with them."

"You're too inno—um, transparent," Zach amended quickly.

"Meaning?"

"I'm a better liar than you are."

"Well, that gives me all kinds of confidence," she said ironically.

"You don't care for liars?"

"No."

He nodded. "You make my case for me."

"What are you talking about?"

"You run rivers for a living. You don't like liars and don't lie well enough to fool anyone."

"So what?"

"So you're safer not being with a professional liar, because you'll have to lie right along with me." He smiled gently at her bewildered look. "Don't worry, you can trust St. Kilda with the paintings. We only lie to benefit our clients. Then we can churn out blue smoke with the best of 'em."

"Joe Faroe didn't say anything about keeping me locked away somewhere."

"He was a little busy at the time, remember? Wife having a baby?" Eyes narrowed, Zach studied Jill, measuring her determination to stay with the paintings. "That sort of thing makes a man a little scattered."

"You're an expert on having a wife give birth?"

"Hell, no. But I know how I'd feel in his place. You'll love the safe house. Good food, a swimming pool, all the amenities."

Pointedly, Zach picked up a painting and started examining it from all sides.

Discussion over.

Jill started to argue, then simply turned and walked out to the truck. She unwrapped his leather jacket from around her waist pack, yanked out her sat phone, and punched in the number she'd already memorized.

"Joe Faroe, please," she said crisply. "Jillian Breck calling."

23

Hollywood
September 14
2:03 P.M.

Score watched the intercom light flash at double speed.
Urgent.

Now what? Never get a minute to myself. What the hell is it now?

Score ignored the leap of his temper.

"Excuse me," he said to the frightened trust-fund baby sitting on the other side of the big desk. The dude was a coke-smoking gambler afraid of kneecap collectors. Not Score's favorite kind of client, but money was money. The kid's mother had a lot of it. "I'll just be a minute."

Without waiting for an answer, Score strode into the adjoining office where Amy was waiting, looking like someone who expected a pat on her spiky hair and a wad of money. He shut and locked the door behind him.

"This better be good," Score said harshly.

"The subject talked to St. Kilda Consulting. The man with her is a St. Kilda op."

"Huh." Score thought fast and hard. No matter how he looked at it, he didn't like it. St. Kilda was bad news. "Were the paintings mentioned?"

"Just once. From the context, I'd say the subject either has the paintings or knows where they are. She was objecting to the op's plan to stash her in a safe house while he pursued the death threat against her. No one said where the paintings were, but the implication is that the art is real and available."

Mother of all whores. How does a country girl know about, much less afford, St. Kilda Consulting?

Maybe Steele was betting on the paintings being worth St. Kilda's usual fee.

Worse and worse.

"You get the op's name?" Score demanded.

"Zach was all she called him."

"Don't know him." Which meant nothing. A lot of St. Kilda ops were contract workers rather than full time. "You have a script?"

"Coming up." She hurried to a nearby printer and scooped paper from the tray. "She talked to someone called Joe Faroe."

Faroe. Bad, bad news. This could be a real cluster.

Or not.

Some of St. Kilda's ops are straight bullet-catchers. Nothing fancy. Just one-on-one.

No problemo. I'll bend him into a pretzel and then take him apart.

The thought made Score's blood heat with something between anger and pleasure.

Score read while Amy waited, vibrating eagerness. All

he learned was what she'd already told him. The only good news was that the subject wasn't going to any safe house.

If Score had to, he could still get to Jill Breck. With her out of the picture, no one would get their act together in time to affect the auction.

His client would be happy.

Score would be happy.

Jill Breck would be history.

24

Breck Ranch
September 14
2:07 P.M.

Inside the house, Zach talked on his own phone to Grace
until Faroe was free. Grace's sympathy for Zach's position
ran over like a plugged toilet. There was laughter in her
voice.

". . . and from what I'm overhearing on Joe's end," she
said cheerfully, "Jill will walk if we try to tuck her away.
Joe's doing more listening than talking. Good for him. He
has a baby daughter now, so he'll have to learn to rein in his
protective impulses."

"Congratulations on the baby, and don't hold your breath
about Faroe backing off."

"Oh, I don't know. He's agreeing with Jill. She goes with
the paintings."

Zach told himself he was angry.

He lied.

And he knew it.

"Let me talk to Joe," Zach said.

"He won't change his mind."

"Ya think?" he said sarcastically.

Laughing, Grace exchanged phones with her husband.

"You want out?" Faroe asked Zach.

"No. You need me."

"Bullet-catchers aren't all that rare."

"Ones who learned about Western art at Garland Frost's knee are."

Silence. Then Faroe said, "So you like the paintings."

"A lot."

"Enough to kill for?"

"Me personally? No. Someone else? You bet. Provenance will be a bitch, though. If St. Kilda is counting on a piece of the paintings to pay for the op, you could end up with a double handful of nothing."

"Jill saved Lane's life on the river. Ask for whatever you need, whenever and wherever you need it. If St. Kilda has it, it's yours."

Smiling, Zach started making a list.

25

Hollywood
September 15
4:00 A.M.

Score woke up when the alarm on his computer went off.
Every hour on the hour. Slightly more often than the client called.

He'd stopped answering his phone. Even after a hard workout, he was afraid he'd lose his temper. This client was too important to scream at.

Rolling over, he eyed the computer on the bedside table. He hit refresh and waited for the computer to show a new readout. A red line and a blinking red arrow recorded Jill Breck's progress against a map of Arizona.

Still moving.

Damn. What are they doing—heading for dawn at the Grand Canyon?

Do they have the paintings? Or did they stash them in the same place the old lady did?

He sat up, reached out for a different computer, and hit the digital replay of the sat phone bug, selecting for certain words.

Thank god for computers. Nothing more butt-numbing than listening to a bug, waiting to hear something besides garbage.

With computers, he could cut to the good stuff.

Well, sometimes. Right now there was static . . . and classic country music playing in the background. Wherever Jill was keeping her sat phone, it wasn't close enough to do any good.

Or maybe she and the op weren't on speaking terms anymore.

If Score had been the St. Kilda op, he'd have been furious to have a client in his pocket, watching his every move. But it made Jill easier to get to, so Score wasn't going to complain.

All he had to do was keep a lid on those paintings until the auction was over.

Four days.

He yawned, wished he could go to back to sleep, knew he couldn't risk it. If Jill had those paintings with her—and he had to assume she did, because it was the worst-case scenario—he needed to steal or destroy them before the auction.

After another yawn, he called At Your Service's twenty-four-hour line and began spending thousands of the client's dollars chartering a plane out of Burbank.

He could always sleep in the air.

26

Outside Colorado City
September 15
6:00 A.M.

Zach drove to the edge of the small airport's paved strip
and parked. The plane he'd chartered should be on final
approach. He looked up.

No incoming lights.

He told himself to be patient. Headwinds, tailwinds, side-
winds, storms, and the rest of Mother Nature's bag of tricks
had the last word when it came to keeping schedules.

The small lounge near the tie-down area was dark. None
of the private planes waiting patiently in the light breeze
were being checked out for an early-morning joyride.

Beside him in the truck, Jill poured coffee from the thermos she'd filled at the ranch and handed him a cup. "You
still mad at me?"

"I wasn't mad at you to begin with, so there's no 'still'

about it," he said, searching the early-morning sky for signs of an incoming plane.

"I know you didn't want me to come along."

She looked at the side of his face, shadowed and modeled by the early-morning light. He looked unreasonably good. She wanted a taste.

She settled for coffee.

"Thanks," he said as he took the cup. "As for having you along, I just wanted to make sure you were on Faroe's karma, not mine."

"Well, that sounds reassuring."

"Your great-aunt is dead, your car is trashed, you have a death threat. You want reassuring? You'll find it in the dictionary between *real* and *stupid*."

She chewed on the words and swallowed them with coffee from the thermos. "I don't scare easily."

"More important, you don't lie worth a damn."

"We've been down this river before."

"And we'll go down it again," Zach finished the coffee and handed the cup back to her. "You stay with me and you play a role. Until further notice, I'm the sleaze job and you're the sweet young thing."

"I'm neither sweet, nor young, nor a thing." She lifted the thermos in silent toast and took another drink.

"The whole point of an undercover op is to make people believe you're something you aren't," he said.

"Like sweet, young, and thingy?"

He laughed and shook his head. "I'm beginning to appreciate what Faroe is up against with Grace. Of course, he gets some really nice side benefits."

"Intelligent conversation?" Jill asked blandly.

"I don't know anyone who made a baby just by talking about it."

She tried not to smile, failed, and just shook her head. "I'm beginning to sympathize with Grace. Truce?"

"We're not at war."

"Then what is it?"

"It's not a game," Zach said. "The only reason Faroe kept me with you is because I'm real good at making people believe I wrote the book on crooked. I also know enough about Western art to bullshit with the best of them."

Jill blinked. "Okay. You're a good liar. We've established that. And?"

"Lying is the best way to get down with the crooks who are running the scam."

"We're talking art?"

"And scams. Blue smoke, remember? That's how you separate the marks from their millions."

"We barely touched on fraud in my fine art classes," she said, frowning.

Zach scanned the sky that was getting brighter with each heartbeat. *Where is the damn plane?* He sipped coffee and went back to the education of Ms. Jillian Breck.

"A good forger can embrace today's art history bullshit, turn out the next missing Old Master from his grandmother's attic, and embarrass the shorts off the art establishment," Zach said. "No salesman, critic, or curator likes to talk about really good forgery with a mark. Raises too many questions about the nature of art and value. Worse, it makes the marks real nervous. He or she is trusting the experts to know good art and suddenly the experts are telling the buyer there ain't no such thing as certainty."

"Everyone who collects art isn't a mark."

He shrugged and sipped coffee. "Depends on your point of view. In China, old calligraphy sells for a lot of money. It's considered the highest form of art in a civilization that reveres art."

"Calligraphy? Really?"

"You make my point. You majored in fine arts and yet you've barely heard of Chinese calligraphy. It sells real well

among the wealthy Chinese, though. In art, context is everything."

Jill remembered Zach's care, expertise, and pure esthetic
enjoyment of her paintings. "Were you, um, blowing blue
smoke about my paintings?"

"No. That was personal. This is business." He held out
his empty cup and looked hopeful. "It's all about con artists
and marks."

She poured coffee carefully. "You sound like there's no
intrinsic, transcendent value in art."

He sipped coffee and almost sighed. Strong enough to
float horseshoes. Perfect.

"Before you lecture me about the transcendent nature of
true art," Zach said, "think about how well fine Chinese calligraphy sells in the U. S. of A."

"How well?"

"Outside of the overseas Chinese communities, it doesn't
sell worth a handful of spit. Cultural context makes the difference in value."

He scanned the sky again. Still empty.

"And context is another word for bullshit?" she asked.

"It can be. Especially when it comes to positional art."

"Positional art? Must be another thing we didn't cover in
my fine arts classes," Jill said, shaking her head.

"What do you do when you're the newest billionaire on
the block?" Zach asked, watching the sky. "You have the
mansions in trendy spots all over the world, you have enough
expensive cars for ten showrooms, you have a yacht bigger
than Monte Carlo; and so does every other billionaire. How
do you separate yourself from the herd?"

"Buy something the rest can't buy. One-of-a-kind art."

He turned and looked at her. "Have I mentioned how
much I like smart women? That's exactly what people do,
whether it's a Japanese corporation driving Impressionist

art out of the stratosphere to impress the Western world, or a tech billionaire outbidding everyone else for a Jackson Pollock. Positional art is a statement of importance that has damn little to do with love of art and everything to do with ego."

"A wealthy version of the old mine-is-bigger-than-yours game."

Zach laughed. "Yeah. In the context of an auction, you're buying the spotlight as well as the painting. Spend big bucks. Impress your business associates. Get known as an important collector. Get the red carpet treatment at high-end galleries. Don't give a hoot whether you personally like the art you buy or not. Welcome to the world of blue smoke and positional art."

"Interesting context," she said blandly.

"It leaves plenty of room for scams. At auctions, gallery owners have been known to front bidders on artists they represent and/or personally collect. Totally illegal, of course, but so are a lot of things that work. Suddenly your Unknown Artist is setting six-figure records. Gallery owner calls his favorite positional art suckers, churns out a butt-load of blue smoke, and sells the New Best Thing at a 200 or 300 percent markup."

"I'm beginning to think my education was wasted."

"Education is never wasted."

"You sound like you mean that."

"I do." Zach thought of Garland Frost. "And the education you resent the most teaches you the most." He hesitated, then shrugged. "That's the kind of education you're in for now."

"You think my paintings are forgeries?"

"I don't know what they are, besides really, really good. The point is, until we find out more, you're going to have to lie like a fine carpet when we meet some gallery owners. At least one of them likely will know a lot more than we do about shredded paintings and death threats."

She stiffened, then sighed. "I keep forgetting about that."

"I don't." *Ever.*

"What did you do before St. Kilda Consulting?"

"Intelligence."

Jill waited.

Zach sipped coffee and watched the sky. "The thing about positional art is that the more money you have looking for status, the higher the prices get in the art world."

Okaaay, she thought. *He can know all about my past, but his past is closed.*

For now, anyway. Later, though . . .

Jill didn't give up on the things that were important to her. She couldn't figure out why, but Zach was important.

"Given the money top art brings," he said, "no one should be surprised that the art trade attracts criminals. I've recovered stolen artworks by pretending to be a crooked museum curator. I've negotiated ransoms for kidnapped statues. I've passed myself off as the evil madman with a private gallery full of the world's stolen masterworks."

Jill didn't know whether she was intrigued or appalled. "You're going to laugh, but you seem so . . . straightforward . . . to me."

"With you, I am."

"I feel better. I think."

Zach gave her a sidelong look. He'd like to know how she felt. Literally. In the early-morning light she looked tousled and sexy, like she'd just come in from a hot night in someone's bed. He really wished it was his.

The distant hum of an airplane's engines penetrated the cab of the truck.

He sighed. Back to work.

Probably just as well. What I want to do with Jill doesn't come under the heading of good client relationships.

But I've got a feeling it would be really, really good.

A bright dot in the sky to the north grew quickly into a twin-engine plane. The aircraft flew over the runway, turned, and landed. It shot past the truck, turned smartly, and taxied back toward them.

"Someone you know?" Jill asked.

"One way or another."

Zach got out, stretched, and unlocked the hard metal top that covered the bed of the black pickup, protecting everything inside. He hadn't bothered hauling Jill's big trunk along. He'd wrapped the paintings in tarps—very carefully—and packed the documents and photos in a cardboard carton. Then he'd secured everything to the bed of the truck.

The plane pulled up on the strip near Zach's truck and shut down. One of the crew opened a door in the fuselage and let down a set of steps. He began unloading six large aluminum suitcases. Behind him, six slightly larger, hinged wooden boxes with dead-bolt locks waited to further protect the suitcases and their contents.

Zach talked to another of the crew, handed her the first package of two paintings, and watched. With great care she unwrapped the tarp, matched the paintings inside to the cutouts in one of the foam-lined aluminum cases, closed the case, and slid it into a plywood shipping box. She secured the dead bolt on the box and turned to receive the next package of paintings.

He nodded and returned to his truck, sure that the paintings were in the hands of people who knew what they were doing.

"Get out and stretch your legs," he said to Jill. "You'll be cooped up in the plane soon enough."

"I will?"

"Yeah."

"Where are we going?" she asked.

"Into the wild blue yonder."

Zach pulled his soft canvas duffel from the truck bed, followed by Jill's backpack. Her belly bag was looped through one of the backpack's many fasteners.

"You want your 'purse' with you or with the rest of the luggage?" he asked her.

"If it's with the luggage, can I get to it during the flight?"

"Not easily."

"Give it to me, then."

He unfastened the waist pack and tossed it toward her. Though stuffed to bursting, the pack didn't weigh much.

"Any special reason you're keeping the canvas scraps?" Zach asked. "Even if the rest of the paintings are solid gold, the shredded one isn't worth anything."

"When I want to strangle you, I think of the rags. My temper improves dramatically."

Zach smiled. "Good plan. Let's go."

He headed toward the plane.

"Where are we going?" she asked.

"Up, up, and away."

"Zach—"

"Try something new," he cut in. "Trust me."

"I'd rather count canvas rags," she shot back.

"And I'd rather be reconditioning the muscle car I left in the Eureka's parking lot. In or out, Jill. Your choice."

Without a word she headed for the plane.

27

Over California
September 15
6:30 A.M.

The small plane took a sudden downward swoop, then settled into a bouncy kind of stability as it cleared the Cajon
Pass and rushed toward the high desert country. Below,
a freeway unrolled in two wide, curving bands covered with
traffic.

Score woke up, rubbed his eyes, and booted up his computer. The first thing he opened was the latest script summary Amy had e-mailed. There were a few more words this
time, but paintings still weren't mentioned. Something about
scraps and rags, canvas and belly pack. He switched to the
GPS file.

They're on the move.

The subjects had stopped somewhere outside of Colorado City. Then suddenly they'd started making good time,

heading north to Utah, way too straight a travel line for a highway.

He turned on his microphone and asked the pilot, "Is there an airstrip near Colorado City?"

"Yeah. Not much to it, but it's there."

"Do you have to file a flight plan for it, coming and going?" Score asked.

"These days if you fart, you file a flight plan. Why?"

Score didn't answer. He switched to e-mail, sent a blast to his office, and waited.

He didn't have to wait long. Flight plans, no matter how small the strip, were of interest to Homeland Security and the FAA, and quite available on the public record.

"We need to file a new flight plan," Score said to the pilot.

"What?"

"We're going to Snowbird, Utah."

The pilot started to say something, then shrugged. If the wind cooperated, there was plenty of fuel to make Salt Lake City and still stay within safety regulations. If not, they could refuel in Las Vegas.

She entered the new destination into the onboard computer, filed the change, waited for the okay, and adjusted course.

"The additional cost will be added to your credit card," the pilot said.

"Just get me to Snowbird."

28

Over Utah
September 15
9:30 A.M.

Zach switched his headphone from sat/cell input to the
plane's passenger intercom. As he did, he frowned at the
battery reading on his sat/cell phone. No way to recharge
in the air. Hopefully, there wouldn't be any need.

Leaning over, he switched Jill's headphones from canned
music to passenger intercom. She glanced at him in silent
question.

"Nothing on Blanchard," he said.

"I'm shocked." She tried not to yawn.

"Ramsey Worthington is the new big thing on the Western fine arts circuit. He's planning to go public, turning himself into a kind of Western Sotheby's."

"Fascinating." She covered another yawn.

"No blots on Worthington's record. Not so much as a

speeding ticket. Big on the charity circuit, whether it's Mormon or Catholic or Hollywood."

"Hollywood is a religion?"

"Believe it," Zach said. "If you don't genuflect at the altar of Hollywood's latest cause du jour, you're dog food."

"Good thing I don't plan to be a movie star."

He smiled. "Yeah. No one has responded to your JPEG queries."

That got her attention. "I didn't give you my e-mail password."

"Looks like you're being ignored by the Western art literati."

"Zach, I didn't give you my—"

He kept talking. "A few months ago, one of Worthington's colleagues sold a Charles M. Russell oil. It was described as 'one of his better, but certainly not his best work.' It went for nearly seven million dollars."

Jill's lips moved but she was too shocked to say anything. Finally she managed, "I grew up with Russell's pictures from old feed-store calendars. He understood horses and wild animals, but . . ."

"So did everyone in the non-urban West," Zach said. "Most of the scenes we think of as 'Western' came from Russell and Frederic Remington art, or John Ford/John Wayne movies, arguably another kind of art."

"First you hack into my e-mail, then you talk about various genres of art."

"Utility infielder, that's me."

His off-center smile would have been charming if she hadn't noticed the piercing intelligence in his eyes.

But she did.

She was fascinated, not charmed.

She thought about pursuing the subject of having her e-mail hacked, then decided it wouldn't do any good. She'd asked for help. She'd got it, and its name was Zach Balfour.

Nobody said she had to like everything about it.

"Russell understood the West that was," she said, sticking to the relatively neutral topic of art, "from the land to the Indians, and the Europeans who replaced them. Nobody was a god. Nobody was a devil. Just people going about their lives."

"You'd get an argument from the modern critics who condemn Western art as bigotry on canvas."

She shrugged. "Beats being ignored."

Zach gave a crack of laughter. That was the beauty of a smart woman—she went right for the jugular while other folks were still trying to figure out what was happening.

"You're right," he said. "Some Western art is now accepted as world class, which means a whole new carcass to carve up for the folks with advanced educations and sharp academic knives. Plus new piles of money for art sellers."

"Still, nearly seven million dollars is way out there, isn't it?"

"When Gustav Klimt sells for an eighth of a *billion* dollars, everything on canvas starts heading up in price, even a painter once dismissed by Eastern critics as 'a mere illustrator.' Yesterday's stratospheric price is today's bargain."

Jill just shook her head. "So the cost of Western art rose because everything else did?"

"Partly. Mostly it was the simple fact of money moving west. The center of financial gravity shifted, and with it the idea of what is and what isn't art. Blue smoke billowed and high prices followed."

"Who bought the Russell?"

"I can guarantee that the new owner doesn't live full-time on the East Coast," Zach said dryly. "But there's a lot of money out west these days. New tech millionaires and billionaires with Western roots want to make statements about those roots and themselves. You have to decorate those second and third mansions, right?"

"So Western art has become positional art?"

"You learn fast. According to Ms. Singh, Worthington is the first dealer west of the Mississippi to have a vision of fine Western art as the new new thing in a world that is full of old old things. He's hoping to raise a few hundred million with his public offering."

"To buy art?" she asked.

"To create a big gallery and auction-house business specializing in fine arts, emphasis on the West."

For a time Jill was silent and motionless but for her fingers worrying a scrap of canvas that had crept free of her belly bag's straining zipper. "Sounds like a big money business."

"It is. A few years ago I worked on a case involving Russian art. Some high-end galleries in the West were importing container loads of Russian Impressionist art, trying to create a market for it here in the United States."

"Did it work?"

"The project is still under construction."

The ironic tone of Zach's voice made Jill wince.

"What happened?" she asked.

"The gallery importers ran up against the Russian *mafiya,* which was laundering money through Russian Impressionist art in its own American galleries. Those dudes don't play well with others. Transnational crime is a down-and-dirty business."

"God . . ." Jill let out a long breath. "Modesty had no idea what she was getting into. She just wanted to raise a few thousand for taxes. Instead, she raised a whirlwind and ended up dead."

"Oh, we do real well with our own homegrown thugs," Zach assured her. "The Russians are just some of the newer crooks at the international art money buffet."

"Blanchard? The good old American thug? Is he one of the pros?"

"Maybe. It's hard to tell the pros from the wannabes. A whole lot of kicking and gouging going on at this point."

"And the last one standing wins," she said unhappily.

"Pretty much." Zach stretched his shoulders and legs. Charter planes were better than cattle class on commercial flights, but the seats still weren't designed for long-legged people. "Research had some interesting things to say about Dunstan, too."

"Such as?"

"He was one of the few Western artists who actually came from the West."

She blinked. "Really? Where did the rest of them come from?"

"Moran and Bierstadt were Hudson River School. Easterners." Zach swirled coffee in his plastic cup, then drank the rest.

Jill waited.

"Most of the painters of the time were the same," he said, holding out his empty cup, looking expectant. "City boys. Paris trained, or learned at the knees of teachers who were schooled in Paris. The new kids on the block illustrated government surveys of the West and Eastern magazine articles to make a living. Or they taught."

"For someone who claims not to have a degree," she said, pouring the last of the coffee into his cup, "you sure know a lot about Western art."

He shrugged. "Like I said, I can bullshit with the best of 'em."

"It's more than that." She capped the empty thermos. "Why are you so prickly on the subject?"

Because I learned at the knee of one prickly son of a bitch. But all Zach said aloud was "Dunstan was Western born and bred. He specialized in what today is called the Basin and Range Country, with forays into Taos, Santa Fe, and the Colorado Plateau country for variety. Studied back east, came home to paint. But you probably already know that."

She shook her head. "Modesty never talked about her sister, much less her sister's lovers. And Mom . . . Mom was ashamed to be born outside of marriage. She rarely talked about her mother, and never said one word about the man who might or might not have been her father."

"Sounds like you had to stumble around some mighty big lumps under the family rug."

Jill smiled, surprising both of them. "You trip a few times and then you learn to walk around the lumps. It's called growing up."

"Not everyone gets around to it."

"You did, prickly and all."

"Thomas Dunstan didn't. He drank. He was born in Wyoming, son of a hard-luck rancher."

"There are a lot of hard-luck ranchers in the West," Jill said. "Fact of life in a dry land."

"No argument from me. My mother's family wasn't dirt poor, they were dust poor. Do you want to know more about your grandmother's sometimes lover?"

"I think it's past time I learned about him."

Zach handed Jill his half-full coffee cup. Then he opened the computer, selected the Dunstan file, and began reading parts of it to Jill, who might or might not be the granddaughter of the drunk who happened to be a fine painter when he was sober.

". . . regarded as a chronicler of the empty quarter of the West, a painter capable of capturing the majesty of land before the white man came and blah blah blah," Zach said, condensing what was in the file.

She snickered and sneaked a sip of his coffee.

He noticed, winked at her, and went back to picking facts from the computer file.

". . . painted and destroyed canvases until he produced one that he liked. Sometimes it was years between new canvases."

"Too bad more painters didn't cull their work before it went public," Jill said. "Picasso and Dalí come instantly to mind."

Zach laughed and kept picking out tidbits. "Sold well for the era, despite the scarcity of paintings. He drank. A lot. And this was noticed at a time and in a place where hard drinking wasn't remarkable."

"Sounds like the money he made from art went into booze."

"Back then, booze was cheap. Having a family and a mistress is expensive."

"Don't expect me to feel sorry for him."

"I don't. A man is born with two heads. Dunstan listened to his dumb one."

Jill almost choked on another stolen sip of coffee.

". . . sold for as much as ten thousand dollars a painting before he died," Zach continued blandly. "Back then, ten thousand was today's half million. Hell, maybe a million. Inflation happens."

She cleared her throat. "Does the file say who collected him?"

"In the beginning, mostly cattle barons and railroad tycoons, the kind of Western men who saw themselves as powerful enough to tame the wilderness. But lately . . ." Zach called up another file.

Jill waited, sipped more stolen coffee, and watched the dry land race by beneath the airplane's wings. She was having a hard time understanding that her wild-child grandmother's life had intersected with that of a man who became an iconic artist of the West.

A very expensive artist.

Zach's soft whistle came through the earphones, distracting her.

"What?" she asked.

He turned the computer screen so that she could see the record of Dunstan sales from the time of his death to the most recent sale a year ago.

Five hundred thousand dollars in the late twentieth century.

Four million dollars last year.

One painting.

Jill felt like the airplane had dropped out from under her. She swallowed hard. Then she turned to Zach, who was watching her with narrowed, intent eyes.

"Four. Million. Dollars?" she asked, her voice rough.

"Yes."

She shook her head sharply. "I'm having a tough time grabbing hold of this. I mean, I can't believe our family has twelve Dunstans, much less that they're wildly valuable."

"We don't know that they're Dunstans."

"Well, they sure got *someone's* attention," she said, thinking of her poor old car. And the slashed-to-ribbons painting. And Modesty Breck.

Dead.

Snowbird, Utah
September 15
10:04 A.M.

Ramsey Worthington waited with concealed impatience
while Cahill carefully, slowly, delicately opened a shipping container from the estate of a wealthy collector of
Western art. The paintings were among the stars of the upcoming auction.

As the owner of several galleries, and an auctioneer in
high demand, Worthington knew that he wasn't supposed
to have a favorite artist. Or at the very least, he shouldn't let
anybody know that he did.

Yet Cahill knew his boss was daffy about Nicolai Fechin's
paintings.

The "Tartar" painter might have been born in Russia,
but in the second quarter of the twentieth century he had
painted the Native Americans of the Southwest with an im-

pressionistic urgency and energy that was both personal and universal.

More than half a century after Fechin's death, his paintings were more valuable than ever, well over one hundred thousand dollars a canvas, and that was for the smaller works. Yet it wasn't the potential hundreds of thousands or millions of dollars the Fechin oils represented that lifted Worthington's pulse.

Quite simply, he wanted to be in the presence of greatness.

Worthington cleared his throat. He'd seen various representations of the Fechins in this dead collector's collection, but he hadn't seen them in the original.

Cahill hid his smile. Perhaps it was petty to tease Worthington by dragging out the process of opening the shipping container, but it certainly was enjoyable. Intellectually and fiscally, Cahill understood the importance of Fechin's portraits. Emotionally, they didn't lift his pulse. Give him the sweep and radiant grandeur of a Thomas Moran landscape any day. Now that was an artist to bring a man to his knees.

After a few more unnecessary flourishes, Cahill relented and removed a canvas from its carefully constructed nest.

Worthington made a sound that was between a sigh and a moan.

Cahill freed more paintings.

More rapturous noises came from Worthington.

"Stop it," Cahill said. "You're making me hard, and you have a luncheon appointment with your wife."

If Worthington heard, he didn't comment.

Cahill didn't bother to hide his smile. Worthington's relationship with his wife was a source of amusement to both men. She was clueless about her husband's cheerful bisexuality.

The phone rang in Worthington's office. His private line, reserved for his best clients. Or his most useful ones.

Worthington ignored the phone. He was lost in the vivid colors and insights of Nicolai Fechin.

Cahill strode over and picked up the call. "Fine Western Art, Jack Cahill speaking. How may I assist you?"

"This is Betty Dunstan. Is Ramsey available? It's about the auction."

"Betty! It's always good to hear from you." Cahill rolled his eyes. He didn't have to ask which auction. The one Worthington was overseeing in a few days was the most important thing on the Western art horizon. "How are you and Lee doing?"

"We're fine. Very anxious about the auction, of course. But I have some, um, concerns I'd like to talk about with Ramsey."

"Of course. Let me put you on hold while I pry him away from a client." Cahill punched the hold button and looked at Worthington. "Well?"

"You take it. I'm tired of holding her hand. And you have a monetary interest in the auction, too."

"Not as much as you do."

"I'm the auctioneer as well as the organizer," Worthington said. "Of course I'm better paid."

The hold button blinked like a red lightning bug.

"About her call . . ." Cahill said.

"Oh, hell. Give it to me. You don't understand women."

"Big *duh* on that one."

Worthington laughed. "Betty is a nice person, if a bit tightly wrapped. Don't know how she puts up with the pompous donkey she's married to."

Shaking his head, Cahill punched the hold button again and handed over the phone.

"Hello, Betty. Always a pleasure," Worthington said. "Sorry you had to wait for me. How may I help you?"

Cahill tuned out the one-sided conversation while he began tidying up the shipping/receiving room. As he worked, he kept looking at the Fechin oils, trying to understand their appeal emotionally as well as intellectually.

Maybe if he stopped thinking about the vermin situation during the time Fechin painted the natives, he'd appreciate the work more. But Cahill just couldn't get past the queasy certainty that many if not all of the models for Fechin's portraits likely had needed a good scrubbing down with lye. The thought of all the fleas and lice underneath the rustic costumes made him twitchy.

It was the same thing that had kept him from traveling in the poor places of the world. For him, hygiene wasn't a choice, it was a religion.

Give him Moran's elegantly wild landscapes any day.

". . . assure you," Worthington said evenly, though loudly, "if there were any loose Dunstans running about the Western art scene, I'd be the first to know."

He listened impatiently.

"Yes, yes, I know, the JPEGs," he said. "But JPEGs are simply electronic bits of nothing. Only the flesh and blood of canvas is real. The rest is—"

As Worthington listened to her interruption, his face flushed. His anger was visible if not audible.

"Betty, dear, you're working yourself up over nothing," he said, trying to sound soothing. "If any unknown Dunstans exist—and there is no proof that any do—Lee would still have the last word as to authenticity. As the author of Dunstan's catalogue raisonné, Lee's imprimatur is absolutely necessary to anyone wishing to sell *any* Dunstan canvas."

Cahill gave up pretending to be busy and listened. As Worthington had pointed out, Cahill had a financial interest in the outcome of the auction.

"Yes, I'm very certain," Worthington said. "Please don't worry. When the auction is over, you and Lee will be quite pleased. No unauthenticated Dunstans, assuming any exist, can prevent that."

Worthington shifted the phone to his other hand.

Cahill waited.

"No problem at all, my dear," Worthington said soothingly. "We're all excited about the upcoming auction. I'm glad I could put your mind at ease."

Worthington opened his mouth, closed it, and bit his tongue.

Cahill paced.

"I understand," Worthington said. "Of course, you would be the first to know if I see or hear anything substantial about the existence of unknown Dunstans."

Cahill pretended to look at Fechin's portrait of a young Pueblo Indian girl. Her black eyes were both innocent and already old, almost eerily so. *To hell with vermin,* he thought. The ancient understanding in the girl's eyes transcended her time and circumstances.

And vermin?

Cahill sighed. He simply couldn't get past reality to the art beneath.

Worthington hung up the phone and looked at Cahill.

"Still bothered by head lice?" Worthington asked sardonically.

"I almost got past it. Something about that girl's eyes. Remarkable. Riveting."

"The eyes are the living, breathing center of all Fechin paintings. That's what makes him such a brilliant portrait artist."

"True." *But not for me. Can't get past the creepy crawlies.* "I take it that Mrs. Dunstan is in a knot about the JPEGs."

Worthington grimaced. "Between her and Mrs. Crawford, I'll be ready for a straitjacket before the auction even opens."

"Lee Dunstan has bent my ear a time or three," Cahill said. "The man is obsessed with his father's former lover."

"Since Justine Breck was the cause of Thomas Dunstan's erratic output, I can understand Lee's ire. God only knows what that woman cost the world of Western fine art."

"Millions and millions, if the auction goes as planned."

"Of course," Worthington said almost impatiently, "but the loss of Dunstan's unique insight into the dying of the classic West is beyond price."

"Polishing your auction rhetoric?"

Worthington smiled. "People don't attend auctions merely to buy art. They come for the experience, the entertainment, the chance to be seen as a mover and shaker among their peers."

Laughing, Cahill shook his head. "Is our auction really going to be the slam dunk you described to Mrs. Dunstan?"

Worthington's smile vanished. "It better be."

30

J ill watched out the window while the plane landed at a small airport on the eastern edge of Salt Lake City. No sooner had the wheels touched the runway than a refueling tank truck headed toward the apron. Three people walked to the tie-down area and waited for the plane. The men were all casually dressed, yet they weren't lounging around. They looked alert in a way that reminded her of Zach.

As soon as the plane door opened, Zach went down the stairs. He spoke briefly to one of the men, who handed over a set of keys before he started giving orders to the other men. Zach flipped the keys on his palm as he turned back to Jill, who was standing at the top of the plane's metal stairway. She had changed into black jeans and a silky kind of green shirt that brought out the color of her eyes.

She looked way too edible for his peace of mind.

"Let's go," Zach said. "We don't have a lot of time to waste if we want to be in Taos before dinner. Leave everything on the plane."

"Taos? Dinner?"

Zach was already walking away. "It will take us about half an hour to get to Snowbird."

Jill turned back to the plane long enough to grab her belly bag, then ran down the stairs after Zach. No sooner had her butt hit the leather seat of the rental car than he started driving toward Snowbird with a disregard for local speed limits that made her blink.

Very quickly they were in the mountains. Sun poured over the soaring peaks. Aspen burned up the ravines and on the ridgetops like a golden autumn fire. She let down the window, took a deep breath, and then another. Yesterday's adrenaline roller coaster from fear to safety and back to fear seemed like a bad dream.

The black-haired, whiskey-eyed man who had almost enough stubble to be a beard was watching the road, not the scenery.

"It's so beautiful," Jill said.

Zach looked at the mountaintops without really seeing them. His mind was filled with plans he'd prioritized according to various reactions from gallery owners, plus the unhappy necessity of spending more time in the company of Garland Frost's arrogant, acid tongue.

"Yeah, it's real pretty," Zach said absently.

She thought about the plane. "Will the paintings be all right without us?"

He gave her a swift sideways glance.

"Never mind," she said. "Forget I asked. Control issues. St. Kilda rules and all that."

Zach smiled slightly and continued to push the new SUV. A discreet bumper sticker was the only indication that the car came from a local rental agency.

Jill inspected the interior of the car. Then she thought about the fast little plane and the three men who had spread out around it in a manner suggestive of sentries. She wondered if the men were armed.

Then she thought of Joe Faroe, Zach Balfour, and St. Kilda itself.

One way or another, the men were armed.

"Who's paying for all this?" she asked. "Cars, plane, sat/cell phone, research—"

"Take it up with Faroe," Zach cut in. "He's the one giving orders on this op."

"I thought you were."

"I'm the man on the ground. Faroe's the one learning how to hold a baby girl."

"A girl? Oh my." Jill laughed.

"Yeah, she'll be keeping Faroe up nights worrying for the next thirty years."

"Does she have a name?"

"Trouble."

Jill gave an eye-roll worthy of a teenager. "Somehow I doubt that."

"I don't. Faroe might have come late to parenthood, but he's one protective father."

"Late? Lane is sixteen."

"It's a long story."

Jill was curious, but she didn't ask. She came from a long line of long stories. She understood family privacy.

"Well, Joe can't be any worse than the father of one of my roommates in college," she said. "Sara's dad was a veterinarian. After she turned fifteen, he mounted a castrating knife on the front door. Claimed it would work just fine as a door-knocker."

Zach snickered. "She get many dates?"

"Not until she went away to college."

Shaking his head, Zach kept driving. Hard.

Jill would have been nervous, but nothing about the car or the man suggested that either was on the edge of losing the road. She settled back, relaxed as she rarely was when someone else was at the controls.

Coordinated, smooth, quick, thorough. Wonder what else he's good at?

She could think of a few things that would be fun test-driving with him. None of them had wheels.

Very quickly, wild mountain scenery gave way to chalets and chairlifts and empty slopes.

"Okay, time for your game face," Zach said. "You're the—"

"Sweet stupid thing," she cut in. "You're the kind of man Sara's father hung the castrating knife over the door to discourage."

Zach winced. "Not a happy visual."

"I'm sure it took the rut out of more than one young buck."

Privately Zach thought it wouldn't have worked over Jill's door, but he didn't say anything aloud. It was bad enough wanting her. Having her know it, and back away because of it, would turn a fairly straightforward op into Grade A goat-roping real quick.

How did Faroe manage to keep Grace alive when he was head over balls in lust with her?

But Zach hadn't asked his boss when he'd had the chance, and it was too late now.

He opened his mouth to go over the scenario for the gallery with Jill again. Then he thought better of it. She wasn't stupid. If he had to make adjustments to the game plan in midplay, she was quick enough to keep up with him.

If anything, he should worry about keeping up with her. The lady was too used to leading. Problem was, she could easily go through the wrong door while he was running to catch up. And Zach knew in his gut what Jill knew only intellectually.

Some doors were fatal.

Snowbird
September 15
11:03 A.M.

The first gallery Zach and Jill went to was housed in a fake
mountain chalet at the base of one of the ski lifts. The
slopes above the town were still summer-naked and dry,
not so much as a flake of snow anywhere. Finding a parking
place was easy.

"Western Light and Shadow, Ms. Joanna Waverly-Benet,"
Jill said, reading the sign. "This is one of the galleries I sent
JPEGs to."

Zach already knew that, but he nodded.

"If the big ones didn't want to bother, I thought maybe
a smaller, less-established gallery might be more eager to
work with me," Jill explained.

"Smart. Lucky, too."

"How so?"

"According to Shawna, Ms. Waverly-Benet is an up-and-comer on the Western art scene. Her specialty is painters of Dun-stan's era. In fact, I wouldn't be surprised if Hillhouse showed her Modesty's painting when he was testing the market."

"Well, she didn't answer my e-mail. But then, I haven't checked it since last night."

Zach pulled out his sat/cell phone, frowned at the level of the battery, and noticed that no new messages had come from St. Kilda.

"Ms. Waverly-Benet still hasn't answered your e-mail," he said. "Looks like even the little fish aren't taking the bait."

"Thanks so much for hacking my e-mail."

"St. Kilda lives to serve."

Jill got out of the big SUV, shut the door hard, and headed for the gallery. Automatically she touched her waist, check-ing the belly bag. Then she remembered she'd left it on the backseat. The bag's rough band had kept catching on her only good blouse.

Zach was one step behind her, then one step ahead. "I go through doors first, remember?" he asked curtly.

"And people say chivalry is dead."

"It was killed by rushing through doors first," he re-torted.

Large glass windows gave Zach a view inside the gallery. Clean, uncrowded, bright. Nothing unexpected. Everything in place, including a sleek brunette working on a computer just off the main showroom. She was just reaching for the telephone on her desk.

"Change of plans," Zach said. "I'm nice for this one."

"Should be a challenge."

He smiled and brushed the skin at the nape of her neck as he straightened the collar of her silky shirt.

She gave him a startled look. Then she smiled and smoothed down the collar of his black cotton shirt, taking care to slide her fingers into the opening of the neck.

Zach's eyelids lowered. "You're distracting me."

"Same goes." She smiled up at him, traced the pulse beating in his neck, and moved back.

His slow smile was a warning and a promise. He opened the door, stepped through while chimes sang a sweet welcome, and held the door open for Jill.

"I'll be right with you," the woman called out before she picked up her phone.

"No problem," Zach said, smiling.

The woman blinked, startled by the gentle voice and smile coming from a rough-looking man wearing enough stubble to make a movie villain envious. She smiled back at him, then began talking on the phone in a low voice.

Jill drifted off to look at a wall of Impressionist-style paintings. A few depicted the American West that no longer was. Most of the paintings showed Siberia in a storm, Paris in a spring rain, dancers stretching at the barre in the manner of Degas. Still other paintings offered the rural haystacks that Monet's many imitators had turned into a cliché.

She half expected to find a vase of sunflowers in homage to van Gogh.

Zach glanced at the paintings and then looked away with an attitude that said he'd seen them all before and hadn't been impressed that time either.

The woman's voice murmured in the background. Her low, cultured tones couldn't be overheard.

Curious, Jill looked at the cards that named the artists who clearly had been thoroughly schooled in classic Impressionism. Every name was Russian. Every painting was nineteenth or twentieth century.

The asking prices were all well into six figures.

No matter what the subject, the Russian painters had

flawless technique, rather like the superstars of ice, gymnastics, and ballet that the Soviet Union once had been famous for producing.

"You're frowning," Zach said to Jill. "Something wrong?"

"Nothing. That's the problem."

He raised an eyebrow. "It is?"

"The academics of these pictures are perfect. Light. Shadow. Color. Proportion. Brushstrokes. Everything."

"Makes you nervous, doesn't it?" he asked dryly.

"It makes me remember something you mentioned earlier about Russian Impressionism and"—she looked quickly at the woman, who was still talking—"the *mafyia*."

"Yeah, this kind of stuff has been flooding the market by the container load," Zach said heading for another wall, this one with scenes of the American West. "It's one way for the new Russian oligarchs to get cash out of the former Soviet Union."

"Amazing." Jill leaned closer to a painting.

"The prices?"

"That, too."

Zach's smile wasn't comforting. "The big problem is that nobody knows for sure which are historic paintings and which are being cranked out by painting factories in modern Russia."

"The Italians of Leonardo's day did the same sort of thing. One big name. A herd of 'student' painters doing the work." She moved on to the next painting, sunlight over water. "Really awesome technique."

"I like yours better."

Her head turned toward him so fast that her hair flew out. "My what?"

"Technique. The one you did of the horse with its rump to the wind really made me feel the bite of the desert winter—and that was just a JPEG I was looking at."

She tilted her head slightly. "Are you talking about the

painting at Pomona College?"

"You're too modest. They have six of your paintings hanging in various rooms. With a few breaks and a good handler, you could have a career in the commercial arts. If the critics fell in love with you, you'd become a 'fine' arts painter."

Jill shrugged. "Decent painters are as common as horse-flies. Check any fine arts department."

Zach shook his head. "You're one hell of an uncommon horsefly."

"Thanks. I think."

"Do you have more paintings around?" he asked casually, but his eyes were clear, hard.

"I used to," she said, studying—yes—a vase of sunflowers. "I gave them all to friends when I went back to the river."

"Landscapes?"

"Most of them. A few portraits." Then Jill went very still. "You're thinking that I painted Modesty's landscapes."

"It occurred to me."

It was foolish to feel angry, much less hurt, but Jill did. "Thanks for the vote of no confidence."

"If I hadn't investigated the possibility that you were the painter, I'd be working for some fast-food joint rather than St. Kilda. Never overlook the obvious is the oldest rule in the book."

"Good for you. As soon as I find a long nail and a hammer, I'll mount a gold star on your forehead."

"You didn't paint the canvases in Modesty's trunk," Zach said, ignoring Jill's sarcasm.

"Is that what Pomona College told St. Kilda?"

"That's what your paintings told me. You understand being alone, but not lonely."

"So did whoever painted what I found in the trunk."

"Yes and no," Zach said. "In those dozen paintings there's a corrosive kind of anger, a trapped animal's rage at whatever is keeping it from the freedom all around it. Your paintings don't have rage. You accept life and the land as it is. You're alone with the land, not alone *on* it."

"And you're a professional liar," she muttered, not wanting to be lured by the belief that Zach understood her paintings.

And her.

He ruffled her nerves enough on a physical level, without adding all the complications of intelligence into the mix.

"Sometimes I'm a liar," he agreed. "Right now isn't one of those times."

Jill blew out a hissing breath. "I keep thinking about the ruined painting and Ford Hillhouse's suggestion that it was all a fraud, but he'd pay Modesty a couple thousand to go away. How do you 'lose' a painting?"

"You send it out to three or four other dealers for their opinion, one of them has a foul-up in shipping, and a painting goes missing. It happens. That's why shipments are insured. Ask anyone in the trade."

"But—"

"I wouldn't be surprised if Hillhouse showed the painting to a few Dunstan collectors, just to see if one of them would be willing to roll the provenance dice."

"That's fraud."

Zach shook his head. "Not if both seller and buyer are aware that the painting hasn't been authenticated. Then it's just business."

"Then why did Hillhouse as good as call the painting a fraud?"

"That was one of the questions I was going to ask him," Zach said, "but he never took St. Kilda's calls, the painting is now a pile of scraps, and there's no point in wasting time nailing his balls to the wall. If anything in that equation changes, I'll get whatever answers I need from him, whenever I need them."

"But if he won't talk to you, how can you—" Her words stopped when she looked at Zach's eyes. She swallowed and reminded herself that just because people lived in civilization, they weren't always civilized.

"She's wrapping up her conversation," Zach said, indicating the woman.

"How can you tell?"

"Body language. You ready to play?"

"I'll never have a career in fine art," Jill muttered. "I can't paint and hold my nose, which is what I'd have to do to keep from smelling the bullshit that seems to be a big part of the scene."

"That's how you get blue smoke," Zach said. "You build piles of bullshit and set fire to them. Now lose the inner bitch and look pleasant for the nice saleslady."

Jill gritted her teeth. "It's a little hard to make nice with a stranger who won't answer e-mails and might have had a part in my great-aunt's death."

"Do it or take a walk. Now."

A single look told Jill that Zach wasn't kidding.

She forced her mouth into a smile and turned toward the elegant brunette who was approaching them.

32

Zach watched the woman as she walked up to him. She wore a cashmere sweater that showed discreet cleavage, painfully stylish high heels, and the kind of black wool slacks that cost more than most people made in a week. Her black pearl earrings and elegantly simple gold-and-pearl pin looked real, and really expensive.

"Hello, I'm Jo. I see you're admiring our Russian Impressionists. Their technique is—"

"Well known to dealers and consultants," Zach cut in, smiling to soften the words. "I'm here with Ms. Jillian Breck in regard to the unsigned Thomas Dunstan painting that you may have seen last month, and the JPEGs of unsigned paintings that were e-mailed to you recently."

At Dunstan's name, the woman's eyes widened and her hand went to her throat.

Zach saw the reaction for what it was—an involuntary effort to hide a strong emotional reaction. Fear, most likely.

Adrenaline slid sweetly into his veins.

It's about time someone noticed us.

"Is something wrong?" he asked, his expression and body language concerned.

"Wrong?" Waverly-Benet's voice was too high. She cleared her throat and lowered both her voice and her hand. "No. I just wish I'd never seen that particular canvas. I suspect it cost me a considerable commission, and tested the goodwill of people who are very important in the Western art market."

"I'm sorry to hear that," Zach said gently. "Professional jealousies are an unfortunate fact of life in the art business."

"So is fraud," she said in a flat voice.

Jill moved sharply.

Zach's casual stroke down her arm kept her quiet.

"I sent that painting to the definitive Dunstan expert," Waverly-Benet said, her body tight. "He sent me back the nastiest letter I have ever received. He called me 'obviously incompetent' for even considering that the painting might be a genuine Dunstan."

Zach whistled. "That's harsh, even in a business noted for its prima donnas. I saw that painting. It was a superior canvas, one that no one should be insulted for appreciating."

Ms. Waverly-Benet relaxed, warmed by Zach's understanding. "I thought so. Later I found out that the expert advised a prominent Western art collector not to place one of his canvases in my gallery for resale because I was an idiot."

Zach shook his head. "That sounds much more like a personal opinion than a professional one. In fact, it sounds legally actionable. I'm sorry you had to suffer it."

Jill tried not to stare at the gentle, reasonable, supportive, sympathetic alien who had taken over Zach's body.

"Unfortunately, this expert's opinion is the only one that

really counts," Waverly-Benet said bitterly. "It came from Olympus, so to speak."

"Are we talking about Lee Dunstan, the artist's son?" Zach asked.

"Yes, unfortunately."

"It's a shame the son isn't an artist," Zach said, "either by training or inclination."

Waverly-Benet sighed. "I agree. But Lee Dunstan controls the Dunstan droit moral, and that's that."

Jill frowned. "I know that it's common, especially in Europe, for a dead artist's family to retain the moral right to designate that artist's works as authentic. Without the family's stamp of approval, a work can be deemed a fake or, worse, a fraud."

Waverly-Benet flinched.

"Picasso's heirs have made a great living from droit moral," Zach said. "But it's much more rare in American art."

"Not lately," Waverly-Benet said, her body tight again. "The more famous the artist, the more likely you are to encounter some moral authority with the power of life and death over questioned pieces. If not a family member, then an academic or a curator or a critic who has made a lifetime study of an artist and produced that artist's catalogue raisonné."

"Ah, yes," Jill said. "Gathering piles and setting fire to them."

Zach fought a smile.

Waverly-Benet didn't have a smile to fight. Underneath the sleek exterior, she was angry and afraid. She pinned Jill with a dark glance and said, "If you're still trying to sell the painting I sent back to Hillhouse, you should be aware that you'll be courting serious legal problems."

"Modesty Breck sent the canvas out for appraisal, nothing more," Jill said. "The word 'sale' was never suggested."

"That so-called Dunstan was appraised and found wanting," Waverly-Benet said. "If that's what you came to me about, you're wasting my time and possibly harming my reputation."

"But you thought enough of the painting to—" Jill began.

"Obviously I was wrong," Waverly-Benet cut in. "I've had enough trouble over that canvas. I don't want anything more to do with it. Unless you have something else to talk about, please leave."

Jill started to say something.

Zach's hand settled over her forearm. And squeezed.

"Sorry to bother you," he said to Waverly-Benet. "We won't take any more of your time."

Jill allowed herself to be herded outside and into the SUV.

As soon as Zach started the engine, she said, "That was one scared woman."

"She's sitting on millions of dollars in inventory, her ski-resort rent would support a small third world country, and her reputation within art circles just took a hell of a hit. Damn straight she's scared."

"Still, she has no right to—"

"You should be scared, too," Zach continued relentlessly. "It's not your livelihood being threatened, it's your life."

33

This time I'm the hard case and you're the sympathetic one," Zach said as they walked up to the next gallery.

"Does that mean the sweet thing actually gets to speak?"

He gave her a sideways look. "Was I stepping on your lines back there?"

"What lines?"

"That's why I did most of the talking," he said blandly. "You don't know your lines."

"Really? I thought you'd been taken over by an astonishingly polite alien."

"Get ready for the rude alien."

"Nothing alien about that," she muttered under her breath.

"Aliens have excellent hearing."

She shut up and stared at the door buzzer, the locked door, and the very visible guard. "Looks like a bank."

"Fine art is portable and pricey, a combination that crooks

can't resist. Worthington is getting ready for the Las Vegas auction. Some really high-end canvas wealth is stashed in this gallery, waiting to be escorted to Vegas."

"But the auction is only four days away. Why is it here?"

"The hotel probably didn't want the insurance risk of storing the paintings until the auction. Or the individual insurers balked. I keep telling you, art is a business."

As Zach hit the buzzer by the door, he noticed that there was a bright new sign painted on the glass.

RAMSEY WORTHINGTON, FINE ARTS
Specialist in Western Works

"He's really making his move up," Zach said.

"What?"

"Worthington." Zach pointed to the sign. "He's not emphasizing Western art in his new sign."

"Hard to be the next Sotheby's wearing shit-kickers and a bolo tie," Jill said dryly.

Smiling, Zach hit the buzzer again.

"No one's hurrying out to greet us because you don't look like you fit in this place," Jill said quietly.

"That's the whole point."

"I don't look like I fit, either."

"Sure you do," he said. "West of the Rockies, a lot of very wealthy people prefer casual chic."

She gave him a sidelong look. "I've never had my go-to-town jeans referred to as chic."

"It's the whole package, not just the clothes." Zach looked at her and hoped his tongue wasn't hanging out. The blouse she wore wasn't cut low or tight, but the material clung to her breasts like a shadow. She wasn't wearing a bra.

It had been driving him nuts.

"You have a lot of confidence, physical and mental," he said, forcing himself to look at the gallery rather than what was beneath the silky blouse. "Subconsciously, people—especially smart salespeople—associate your kind of assurance with wealth. You set styles, you don't follow them. You have enough money to be a maverick, remember?"

"Then what am I doing hanging out with a rough-looking dude like you?"

"The usual."

"Which is?" she asked.

"Down-and-dirty sex."

Jill was still choking on Zach's answer when a young woman unlocked the door and smiled at them. The employee was a bright, cheerful blonde just past college age. She looked more like a marketing major than an art student. Her name tag said Christa Moore.

The front door guard didn't smile. He watched Zach.

Zach approved the guard's instincts.

"Welcome," Ms. Moore said warmly. "How may I assist you?"

"You can't, unless you're Ramsey Worthington in drag," Zach said.

Even though Jill was expecting it, she was surprised at the edge in his voice.

Ms. Moore looked over her shoulder reflexively. A door marked PRIVATE stood between a striking portrait of an Apache woman and a buffalo sculpture sniffing the breeze. The buffalo was motionless, yet explosively alive.

"Did you have an appointment with anyone in particular or—" she began.

"Ramsey Worthington," Zach cut in impatiently.

The woman blinked and automatically backed up a step or two. Jill moved into the opening, with Zach right on her heels.

The young woman made a humming sound of distress. "Oh, dear. Mr. Worthington didn't tell anyone that he had an appointment."

Zach shrugged and began glancing around at the gallery in the manner of someone who wasn't impressed by her problems or her workplace.

"Please tell Mr. Worthington that I want to look at what he has in the way of fine Western art," Jill said smoothly.

"Well, that's just it, I'm afraid," the woman said, turning to Jill, obviously relieved to be dealing with someone less rough-looking than Zach. "Mr. Worthington is in the midst of preparing for the auction in Las Vegas and he was very firm about not being disturbed. Why don't I get Mr. Cahill, the manager?"

"Why don't you get Worthington," Zach said without looking at the woman. "We've got a plane standing by to take us to Telluride. If the big man is too busy to sell us his goods, we'll find another gallery."

"Um, well, yes, of course," the woman said. "Excuse me while I conference with Mr. Worthington. It may take some time, especially if he is talking to one of his collectors about the upcoming auction."

"We'll either be here when he comes out or we won't," Zach said. His voice said that he didn't care much either way.

The young woman hurried off.

Jill glanced around, taking in the guard at a console. He was dividing his attention between Zach and the five closed-circuit TVs that displayed whatever was in view of the cameras scanning every inch of the gallery.

Just as the saleswoman opened the door marked PRIVATE, Zach said in a carrying voice, "Tell him it's the owner of the newly discovered Dunstan that was sent to him for an opinion."

Moore froze, then shot through the door like a housecat with a coyote on its heels.

"At least she knew what painting you were talking about," Jill said in a low voice.

"Yeah."

Finally.

Now all he had to do was pray that Ramsey Worthington took the bait.

"A t least this won't be a total waste of time," Zach said, glancing at his watch.

"Why?"

"Take a look behind you." He gestured toward a long wall hung with the kind of Western art that gave meaning to the word *fine*.

Jill turned, drew in a quick breath, and headed toward the wall without a backward look.

Zach enjoyed the view. Eagerness and impatience with all the game playing put something special in her walk.

Even the guard noticed.

Zach followed her toward the wall of art. Along the way, he picked a catalogue off the top of a stack. The pages of the catalogue, like the long wall, featured art from the upcoming auction in Las Vegas. Nearly all the paintings had traditional or modern gilt frames. Many of the canvases were big enough to fill the wall above the mantel of a trophy mansion in Vail or Telluride, Aspen or Taos.

Or a museum.

Jill did a quick turn down the long wall, then a much slower one. Either way, the results were the same.

"Incredible," Jill said when Zach came to stand beside her.

"No argument from me," he said. "There are some truly fine paintings here."

"Yet . . ."

Zach waited.

"I can't help thinking that Modesty's paintings are strong enough to hang here and not be put in the shade," Jill said. "Except for size. None of the paintings in the trunk are more than forty inches on a side."

"Dunstan didn't do a lot of big canvases," Zach said. "He wasn't painting for the museum trade. He didn't even keep a full-time studio at his home. He was truly a plein air painter. The great outdoors was his workplace."

She thought of the near-constant, always unpredictable wind of the Basin and Range country. "Out in the open, big canvases would be nearly impossible to paint. Especially in the wind. Like kites without tails."

"Most of the time, Dunstan got around on horseback or in an open wagon," Zach said, remembering what Garland Frost had told him. "Anything much bigger than forty inches on a side was too big to drag through the wilderness."

"Whoever painted Modesty's legacy didn't need a huge canvas to evoke a huge land," Jill said.

"That's part of their brilliance. Small paintings that expand your soul in a big way."

She glanced at him and saw that he was intent on the art in front of him. "You are the unlikeliest connoisseur of fine arts I've ever met."

"It's the beard stubble."

"It's the whole package. You look like an entirely physical man."

He gave her an entirely male look. "Any time you doubt it, I'll be glad to demonstrate."

"I don't think Ramsey Worthington would appreciate a live sex show," she said. "But thanks for the thought."

His smile flashed and vanished like lightning against a storm. He walked slowly along the wall.

"Any favorites?" she asked after a time.

"Albert Bierstadt and Thomas Moran are always worth spending time with," Zach said, pointing toward two of the biggest canvases. "Moran, especially. But I prefer his smaller canvases. Less theatrical, more real." He shrugged. "I'm in a minority."

"How about Charlie Russell and Frederic Remington?" Jill asked, walking toward two paintings.

"They're the men who led the charge of cowboys, Indians, and wilderness sojourners into the twentieth century." Zach looked at the two paintings. "The Russell is a fine example of the genre. The Remington has a signature."

She bit her lip against laughter. "Not one of his better efforts?"

"Even the best painters turn out ordinary canvases. Fact of life. But most people care more for the signatures than the art. The prestige factor disappears if no one knows the artist's name."

"You have a jaundiced view of art collectors."

"I was in the business for a few years," he said.

"I thought you were in intelligence."

"I was." *Still am, sometimes. Just for a different employer. One who understands that bad intel leads to really bad strategy.*

"What about the artists who aren't household names?" she asked, gesturing at the rest of the wall of art. "Some of these paintings are very skillful, both in technique and in evocation. And some of them are barely a step above old magazine illustrations."

"Some of these *were* magazine illustrations. Don't hold it against them. Western art is meant to be accessible. No scholarly explanations are required in order to enjoy it."

"My professors would call a lot of these sentimental and intellectually naive."

"Politics, not art," Zach said. "Used to be that the Church commissioned and explained art. Now it's the turn of secular priests selling modernism of some stripe to commission and explain. Same claim to moral power, different collection plate."

Jill watched Zach from the corner of her eye. He didn't notice. He was looking at each canvas with the eyes of a scholar and the body of a brawler.

If he'd been a painting, she'd have wrapped him up and taken him home.

But he wasn't, so she concentrated on a large canvas filled with colorful Indian braves and stalwart cavalrymen in blue coats and hats that had been tattered by weather and war.

"My professors would scream," she said, "but this painting really speaks to me. Guess I'm a natural-born plebe."

Zach glanced at the painting, then found its page in the catalog. Along with a brief biography of the artist, there was a price range the canvas was expected to bring.

"You're a plebe with great taste," he said. "That's a Howard Ruckelshaus. It's expected to bring between a million and a million-two. If there are some heavyweight Ruckelshaus collectors at the auction, I wouldn't be surprised to see the bidding blow right through a million and a half. That's what auctions are all about—excitement and record prices."

Jill stared at Zach, saw that he wasn't kidding, and went back to looking at the paintings. She spent a long time on a bigger-than-life portrait of a drenched, exhausted cowboy in a yellow slicker hauling a saddle in one hand and a bridle in the other. In the corral behind him, his weary horse had its head down, eating a freshly broken bale of hay.

"I've been there," Jill said. "So tired you see double. But the horse has to be fed, watered, and rubbed down before you crash."

"Code of the West?"

"Code of the ranch. Animals first, humans second."

The next painting that stopped her was an epic canvas, fresh and vivid, like it had just come from the artist. The canvas showed the driving of the golden spike that symbolically joined the transcontinental railway across the United States. Well-fed Anglo men were congratulating each other on completing an important job.

Yet the focus of the painting was not the successful men in business suits, but rather a large group of Chinese workmen who had been shunted off to one side. They were allowed to witness the event their sweat had made possible, but they weren't included in the congratulations.

Jill made a small sound and studied the workers. Their faces were individual, unique, subtly heroic, without the bland sameness of the businessmen. Like the cowboy's horse, the Chinese were bone-tired; unlike the horse, no one was going to see to their needs.

"Remarkable," she said. "The technique and composition are classical European, yet the Chinese men remind me of nothing so much as the clay army of Xian. Individually human and universal man at the same time."

"The artist is a Chinese immigrant. Lives in Tucson." Zach skimmed the catalogue. "Someday he'll be recognized as the great artist he is. Assuming galleries and collectors can get past a Chinese man painting the old West."

"That kind of bigotry is disgusting."

"So are a lot of things that are real. But don't feel too

bad—this canvas is expected to sell in the low six figures. Not bad for a dude who just turned forty."

Jill laughed softly.

"Something funny?" he asked.

"Just me," she said. "I have a fine arts degree from one of the most prestigious colleges in the United States, yet many of these paintings are utterly new to me. I hadn't realized how blatantly Eurocentric my fine arts education was. Most of my professors never got closer to America than Warhol's Campbell soup can and Jackson Pollock's premature ejaculations."

Zach made an odd sound. "I take it you're not a Pollock fan."

"I could give you chapter and verse on Pollock's importance to world art, his daring artistic vision, his slashing intellect, his blah blah blah. Yet his work never spoke to me on any level, including the intellectual. Neither did a lot of English pastoralists, but at least it was possible to admire their technique."

Zach started to say something, then sensed a person approaching behind them. He turned with startling swiftness and saw a tall, trim man with salt-and-pepper hair that brushed the collar of his dark blue blazer.

Ramsey Worthington had risen to the bait.

35

Snowbird
September 15
11:28 A.M.

'm Ramsey Worthington, and you are . . . ?" he asked.

Jill turned to face Worthington. He looked more European than American West. His voice was refined, carefully modulated, with just enough of a British accent to suggest high culture as defined by PBS.

He didn't offer his hand.

"Names aren't important," Zach drawled. "Isn't that what dealers always say? 'It's the quality of the art, not the name of the artist' that matters."

Worthington's blue eyes narrowed. "What is this about?"

"A Thomas Dunstan that was last in your custody before it was 'lost,' mutilated, and finally destroyed," Zach said.

Worthington's eyebrows shot up in what looked like genuine surprise. "Mutilated? Destroyed? What on earth are—"

"But the lost part doesn't surprise you, does it?" Zach cut in.

The door buzzer sounded.

"I don't know what you're talking about," Worthington said.

Christa Moore opened the door. Several people walked in. Their clothes ranged from shabby casual to casual chic. All of them had the bearing that said they could afford anything that took their fancy.

"I'll be real happy to explain," Zach said. "I'll even use little words and a loud voice. You want that here or in your office?"

Worthington looked at the newcomers. He knew them. High-level collectors giving a final review to some of the auction goods.

The collectors were also high-level gossips.

"My office," he said curtly.

The dealer's office was a sharp contrast to the spacious, neat gallery. Painting after painting was stacked in ranks against the walls and inside specially made cubbyholes. Shelves were buried beneath bronzes and carved marble.

Zach recognized an intricate Remington bronze of a cowboy astride a lunging horse. An original, numbered Remington was worth bragging about. The aged, bent cardboard tag attached to the statue by wire attested to the work's authenticity.

Jill's hands itched to pull out paintings and look at them. A single glance at Zach's face told her that wasn't going to happen. Worthington didn't look real outgoing, either.

"Now, what's this nonsense about a ruined Dunstan? All provenanced Dunstans are accounted for and in excellent condition."

Zach gave Jill a subtle signal.

Showtime.

"My great-aunt, Modesty Breck, sent out a canvas for appraisal. My adviser"—Jill nodded to Zach—"believes it found its way to you. The painting was reported as lost. Recently it was, ah, returned to me. In shreds."

Worthington frowned. "I remember the painting. Hillhouse sent it to me. I sent it back. I'm sure the receiving and shipping forms are filed, if it matters to you. As for the rest, it's neither my affair nor my responsibility."

"Forms can be filled out and filed by anyone with a seventh-grade education," Zach said. "They're worthless as proof of anything worth proving."

"You'll have to excuse him," Jill said earnestly to Worthington. "The destruction of the canvas really angered him."

Worthington gave Zach a wary glance.

Zach gave him two rows of hard white teeth.

"I came here because I wanted to know what you thought of the painting," Jill said.

"It's not my practice to discuss privately held paintings with anyone except the owner."

"No problem," Zach said. "Modesty Breck is dead. You're talking to her grandniece."

"I'm sorry for your loss," Worthington said automatically. "But that doesn't answer the question of ownership."

"I'm her heir," Jill said. "Would you like a letter from my lawyer? A death certificate from the coroner? Testimonial from an elder in—"

Zach spoke over her, "I know it upsets you to talk about it." He squeezed her shoulder—hard—and turned back to Worthington. "So what did you think of the painting?"

"Surprisingly good," Worthington said. "Reminiscent in many ways of Thomas Dunstan's work. But the lack of signature, plus other issues, made the painting an unlikely Dunstan. Very unlikely."

"Issues, huh?" Zach said. "Such as?"

Jill's smile asked Worthington to be more polite than Zach was being.

"Just how are you 'advising' Modesty Breck's heir?" Worthington asked.

"Any old way she wants it," Zach drawled. "She's real upset by her loss. You're real busy with your auction. The quickest way to get rid of us is to answer our questions."

It took Worthington about four seconds to come to the same conclusion.

"The historical record is the first issue," he said. "By comparison to other artists, Thomas Dunstan painted re-markably few works. So far as we know, every single one of those paintings has been authenticated and accounted for. His heirs have been very jealous of his reputation. They guard his heritage very closely."

"And make money doing it," Zach said.

"There is nothing unusual about paying for expertise."

"Since when has being someone's heir made the heir expert on anything?" Zach asked.

"It's called droit moral, and I have no time to explain it to you," Worthington said impatiently. "The second issue is that the subject of the painting is unlike anything in Dunstan's catalogue raisonné."

"More French words," Zach said.

"If you aren't familiar with them, you have no business advising anyone on fine art," Worthington said in a clipped voice.

"I understand French just fine," Jill said, hoping her anger wasn't coming through. "But the painting was a landscape, which is well within Dunstan's oeuvre."

Zach wanted to laugh, but it would have spoiled his bad-boy sex-toy act. He stroked her arm instead, fiddling with the silky edges of her sleeve.

"Dunstan seldom painted human figures into his work,"

Worthington said to Jill, ignoring Zach entirely. "Less than four percent of Dunstan's paintings had human figures. The figures were invariably male. Dunstan had an uncanny ability to paint landscapes that conveyed enormous masculine strength measured against the power of a raw, untamed land."

"I thought it was pretty well tamed by the time Dunstan was painting," Jill said.

"That's why Dunstan's work has always been so sought after by the very men who subdued the West," Worthington said, glancing at his watch. "His paintings were a tribute to the brute male power it took to survive in, much less to tame, the West."

Zach wondered how he would defuse the coming explosion. Jill wasn't about to take that kind of chauvinism without giving feedback. A lot of it. He squeezed her arm, reminding her that she was supposed to be the good cop in this duo.

Her muscles were tight.

He wondered if prayer would help.

Jill didn't give him time to find out.

"Are you saying that women didn't exhibit strength and courage in the old West?" she asked, wide-eyed. "I'd think that kind of bigotry would get you bounced from the national association of politically correct art critics *tout de suite, mon ami.*"

"You make my point for me," Worthington said, smiling without warmth. "Western art has been politically incorrect from its inception. For better and for worse, Western art is an almost exclusively male domain. Dunstan not only knew that, he celebrated it. His homage to male strength is the very core of his iconic status."

"Gee, and here I thought art was universal," Jill said, shaking her head. "Goes to show you what a college education is worth. Guess that's why I need an adviser."

And if that adviser doesn't stop petting me, I'm going to bite him.

Only question is where.

Worthington's smile warmed and he lied like the salesman he was. "In general, of course, art is universal and not gender specific."

"That's why there are so many famous women artists," Zach drawled, tracing the inside of Jill's arm. "Universal as all hell."

Worthington ignored him and concentrated on Jill. "The Old Masters of the West, and Dunstan most certainly was one of them, were true products of their age. They believed masculine power was the force that subdued the wilderness and created civilization. That is still a fundamental belief among the collectors of Western art. It is the very touchstone of authenticity in the genre."

Jill nodded like a good student. "So you're saying that you rejected my great-aunt's painting not on the basis of the artistic technique itself, but on the political subtext."

"Exactly," Worthington said. "All art is created in a historical context. That's every bit as important an element in judging the authenticity of a work as style and pigment selection, brushstrokes and types of oils."

Jill fought to look like a student rather than a well-educated woman who had just been patronized by a salesman.

Zach slid his fingers from her wrist to her elbow, and from there beneath the silky sleeve of her blouse. Caressing. Distracting.

Warning.

She let out a long breath. "I understand your point of view." *Arrogant, condescending, bigoted.*

"I'm sorry," Worthington said. "I know you must have had some high hopes about the value of the painting. Believe me, I would have loved to say the canvas was a Dunstan."

Jill tried to look like she cared. She must have succeeded, because Zach took his maddening fingers off her arm and opened up the auction catalogue.

"Not only would I have been introducing a new Dunstan to the art world," Worthington continued, "the painting would have been a stellar addition to the Las Vegas auction. Our showcase lot is comprised of some of the finest Dunstans ever put under the gavel."

"Really?" Jill asked, not having to act surprised. She was. "With such well-known names as Remington and Russell in your catalogue, I'm surprised that Dunstan would be the star."

"Among Western art cognoscenti, Thomas Dunstan is without peer. Setting the intrinsic value of the art aside," Worthington said, "Dunstan is a terribly attractive business investment. His worth has been rising sharply in the past few years."

Jill's attentive look encouraged Worthington.

"Frankly," he continued, "we expect to set a new sales record for a Dunstan canvas."

Zach looked up from the catalogue. "Good luck. You've got your Dunstans listed at between four and seven million right now."

She made a startled sound.

"That's conservative," Worthington said. "These are large canvases, for Dunstans. Last year, a smaller one brought four million. It was a private sale between a Dunstan family heir and a collector. Once the major collectors start bidding against each other in Las Vegas, the price could easily go to eight figures."

"Yeah? Who are the lucky collectors?" Zach asked.

"That's none of your business."

"Sure it is. I represent the owner of a dozen canvases that

can be attributed to Thomas Dunstan."

Worthington's eyes narrowed. He turned away from Zach and looked at Jill like she had just peed on his socks.

"I'm not in the business of offering free advice," Worthington said coldly, "but I can't let that preposterous statement go without comment."

Jill waited.

She didn't have to wait long.

"Your so-called adviser is leading you down a dangerous path," Worthington said in a clipped voice. "His claim that you have a dozen unprovenanced Dunstans is worthless and actionable. If you persist in this foolishness, you will find yourself arrested for fraud. Any number of well-known art experts will be pleased to work for the prosecuting attorney."

"I presume the chorus of naysayers will include you," Jill said, trying to look disappointed instead of furious.

"You bet he'll be there, probably singing lead," Zach said. "Nothing like the prospect of money to put a man in fine voice."

Worthington's face flushed with anger. "I have no monetary interest in Dunstan canvases. I don't own any."

"If two Dunstans sell at auction for seven million apiece, you'd make ten percent of fourteen million," Zach said. "If that isn't a monetary interest, what is?"

"This conversation is over," Worthington said through thin lips. "Leave immediately or I'll call the guard."

Zach laughed derisively. "That rent-a-cop? Get real."

Jill stroked Zach's arm and tugged him toward the office door. "Forget it, honey. If Mr. Worthington isn't interested in newly discovered Dunstans, it's his loss."

Without a word, Zach allowed himself to be led out of the gallery and back to the rental car. He tossed her the car key, got in the passenger side, and slammed the door hard.

"What's wrong?" Jill asked as she got in and started the

car. "I thought it went well."

Zach didn't answer.

"Didn't it?" she persisted. "We came here to scatter enough rumors to bring our buddy 'Blanchard' out of hiding. Once he finds out there are more paintings, that he missed them at the ranch and the casino, he's going to come sniffing around. So why are you angry?"

"He'll be sniffing right up your sweet backside."

"Isn't that what St. Kilda expected?"

"Yeah. But that doesn't mean I have to like it. Take us to the airport while I make some calls."

"What about the other galleries?"

"Not going to happen. I've had all the fun I can take putting your ass on the firing line."

Reno
September 15
1:00 P.M.

"Crawford residence, Caitlin speaking."

"Caitlin, this is Ramsey Worthington. Is Tal around?"

Caitlin closed her eyes for a second, murmured a prayer that nothing had gone wrong with the auction, and said, "Hello, Ramsey. Let me check." She hit the hold button, then the household intercom button. "Tal? If you can tear yourself away from the game, Ramsey would like to talk to you."

"I'm taking a crap. I'll call him back."

She winced at the coarseness that was as much a part of her husband as his bolo tie. And his money.

Unfortunately, money could be lost. Tal had done a lot of that in his life.

He always comes back richer than ever, she reminded herself.

He was younger then.
That doesn't matter.
She took a steadying breath.
Does it?

Fear crawled coldly through Caitlin's stomach. At forty she was too old to find another trophy husband looking for a trophy wife. She let out her breath in a long exhalation. When she was certain her voice would be calm, she picked up Worthington's call.

"Is it something I might help you with, Ramsey?"

There was a pause, then an impatient sound. "I just wanted to tell him that there are two scam artists peddling unsigned and almost certainly fraudulent Dunstans."

"What?" Caitlin knew her voice was too sharp, but there was nothing she could do about it, any more than she could control her suddenly frantic heartbeat.

Worthington was talking about her worst nightmare come true.

"A man and a woman," Worthington said, "I'd guess in their early thirties. I just wondered if they'd come to Tal with their dubious goods."

"No. He would have told me." *Wouldn't he?*

"Well, if anyone comes to Tal peddling previously unknown Dunstans, please ask him to contact me before he buys anything."

"He always does."

Worthington laughed. "Caitlin, you're beautiful and the soul of discretion, but we both know how single-minded Tal can be, especially when it comes to Thomas Dunstan's art."

Caitlin forced a light laugh. "You know my husband so well. But seriously, he hasn't said a word about any Dunstans except those coming up at auction in Las Vegas. We're so excited, the only reason we aren't in Las Vegas is the press announcement of the new museum in a few hours."

"Just what an auctioneer likes to hear. It's going to be an exciting time for everyone, especially once word of Tal's generosity hits the headlines."

An agreeable sound was all Caitlin could manage.

"I have a lot to do before the auction myself," Worthington said. "But if Tal hears anything, I'm never too busy to talk to him. Right now, I have to speak to Lee Dunstan."

Caitlin made polite good-byes, hung up, and stared at her clenched, bloodless hands.

37

core's fingers flew over his computer keyboard. He didn't need Amy's script to tell him that the Breck woman was on the move again. The locater he'd planted in her satellite phone was showing the kind of positional changes that only being in the air could bring.

Damn. Where is she getting the money to pay for all this?

He drummed his fingers impatiently on the side of the keyboard. Where she got her money wasn't his problem.

Keeping up with her was.

His fingers drummed while he waited for someone in the home office to get Breck's new flight plan.

When it finally came through, he cursed savagely. Then he put on his earphones and said, "We need to file a new flight plan."

"Where to?" The pilot's voice managed to sound curt and bored at the same time.

"Taos."

The pilot didn't require a computer to give her client the happy news. "We have to land in Salt Lake to refuel, as per our flight plan."

"What about Snowbird?" *Where the locater, and therefore Ms. Breck, spent some time.*

"No landing strip."

Figures. "Just get me to Taos the fastest way you can."

With a brutal motion Score yanked off the headphones and watched the blinking light of the locater slide away from him.

It would be a distinct pleasure to get his hands on the bitch who was causing him all this trouble.

38

Carson City, Nevada
September 15
5:00 P.M.

As Tal Crawford stood to one side of the governor of Nevada, he approved of his wife's unerring sense of style. Standing next to him, Caitlin was somehow relaxed and attentive at the same time, her eyes on the governor, seemingly unaware of the battery of cameras and microphones arrayed around the politician. Her hair was both sleek and casual, suggesting a woman completely at ease with herself. There was a gentle smile on her perfectly made-up mouth. The smile, like everything else about her from her stylish heels to her pastel jacket and matching skirt, was tasteful and camera-ready. Neither too fashionable nor too dated, simply classy.

Best investment I ever made.

The thought almost made Tal grin, but he kept his expression bland while he listened to the public theater that was so necessary to politics.

And politics were damned necessary to wealth.

"Ladies and gentlemen of the press," Governor Rollins said, "it is my pleasure to announce that one of our own native sons, Mr. Talbert Crawford, will soon donate to the great state of Nevada the most valuable collection of Western landscape paintings ever made available to the public."

The group of cultural mavens standing behind the governor clapped enthusiastically.

Tal tried to look like his new cowboy boots weren't pinching him. But they were.

Don't know how Caitlin puts up with those fancy shoes she wears. I'd be crippled in five steps.

"Now, I don't know much about art," the governor reassured the voters, "but I sure know what I like. And I really like the paintings of Thomas Dunstan, the single most important painter the West ever produced."

There was more applause.

"This day is truly momentous in the cultural history of our state," the governor continued.

The people behind the governor nodded and smiled eagerly, like children at Christmas. The excitement they felt was real, not camera-ready.

"With the donation of this magnificent collection, plus the Dunstans Tal plans to acquire at the upcoming Las Vegas auction, our fine state will possess fifteen of the major works of an artistic genius, clearly the most important man ever to paint our wild and beautiful state. That's a dozen more than any public museum or private collection now owns!"

Caitlin listened to the applause and prayed that everything would go as planned in Las Vegas.

It will.

It has to.

But none of her anxiety showed in her body language. A lady in public was always calm, gracious, and modest.

"With this collection," the governor said, "our state now has a claim on the cultural leadership of the West. The new state museum we're building will be a magnet for culturally aware people from all over our great nation."

Caitlin joined in the spattering of applause from the people gathered on and around the steps of the capitol.

Camera lights glared and flashed.

The governor smiled and turned to Tal. "In the name of the people of the great state of Nevada, I want to thank you for your generosity."

Cameras and microphone shifted to Crawford.

"My pleasure, Governor," Tal drawled. "God has seen fit to bless me with the means to repay just a small part of what I owe to our great nation. In addition to Governor Rollins, I want to thank Senator Pat Healy. He's been real helpful in pulling this all together. We're lucky to have him watching out for our interests in Washington." Tal smiled like a little boy caught snitching cookies. "Got to admit, if it wasn't for the efforts of these two great men, I'd never have been persuaded to part with my Dunstans, much less my whole collection of Western art."

Caitlin's smile froze in its gracious curve as she clapped and politicians smiled and camera lights flashed their blinding message of fame. She kept smiling while Tal went on to describe the unflagging public conscience of the governor and the senator, and how important Western art was becoming, the world finally recognizing the greatness that had always been in painters such as Thomas Dunstan.

There were no surprises in the speech for Caitlin. She had vetted every word, every action, every pause for reaction. Now all she had to do was pray that Tal didn't screw it up and act like the shit-kicker he was by birth and inclination.

"When this museum is completed and open to the public, millions of people will be able to enjoy the best of the paintings of Thomas Dunstan," Tal said. "And right here, right now, I want to challenge other Western art collectors to match my donation with works in their own collections. Competition is part of our great way of life, so come on down to the auction this Sunday in Las Vegas and see if you can go toe-to-toe with me for the only Thomas Dunstans to be offered for sale in decades. I promise you, we're going to make a name for Nevada and set new records for a great Western painter!"

The applause was really enthusiastic. Obviously, the cultured elite of Nevada had high hopes for Carson City's future as a mecca for Western art.

Tal grinned and stepped back, letting the governor take over again.

"Thank you, Tal," the governor said, then turned to face the barrage of cameras. "It is our responsibility and pleasure to make sure that our cultural heritage here in the West is protected and promoted in the same way our brothers from east of the Hudson River have promoted their regional artists. This day has been long overdue, but it's our turn, now. The great state of Nevada will be the leader of the new Western culture!"

The applause was loud and sustained.

Caitlin's smile brightened as she stood by Tal and applauded the crowd that was applauding him.

Almost over.

Almost.

She kept smiling and clapping and praying for the auction to be over.

39

A new Dodge Magnum was waiting for them at Taos Regional Airport. Very quickly Zach loaded the six wooden crates aboard. Even though the rental was about the size of a covered pickup truck, there wasn't much room left over behind the front seats for his duffel and Jill's backpack. He frowned.

"I'd feel better if St. Kilda had rented us an armored truck," he said as he slid into the driver's seat.

"Why? My paintings are just frauds," Jill said bitterly, getting into the passenger side and shutting the door hard. "Every Western art expert is certain of it."

"Uh-oh. Someone was brooding while I slept on the plane."

"Someone thinks this is all a waste of time and money."

"That's Faroe's call," Zach said. "Until we're sure that Blanchard's clock has been stopped, we play the game."

"I'm not sure I like the sound of that," she said.

"What? More game playing?"

"Stopping someone's clock. Sounds final."

Zach ignored her as he mixed with the early evening traffic. The daylight was slanting, rich, making everything look brushed with gold.

"What are we doing in Taos?" she asked bluntly.

"Seeing a Dunstan expert."

"Why didn't we phone it in? Everyone else seems to."

"Garland Frost isn't like everyone else," Zach said. "That's why we're here."

Jill watched while Zach skillfully found his way around on the short, unpredictable, and narrow Old Town streets. They were lined with time-worn adobe walls and ancient one- and two-story residences and businesses. Silently she looked at cottonwood trees as ancient as the one beside her ranch house and at windows whose glass was so old that its bubbles and ripples distorted the light pouring through.

Zach negotiated the narrow streets with the ease of long experience.

"Do you live here?" she asked.

"Not anymore."

"What made you leave?"

"Garland Frost."

"Then why are we here?" she asked.

"Garland Frost."

Zach's tone didn't encourage more questions. Jill thought about hammering on him just for the entertainment value, then decided against it. Instinct told her that an angry Zach Balfour wouldn't be entertaining.

The big Dodge turned onto a quiet street that ran alongside a head-high adobe wall. At the center of the block, a wide gate in the wall opened into a courtyard filled with cottonwood and evergreen trees. He stopped outside the front door of a sprawling adobe house and turned off the engine.

"Now what?" she asked.

"We see if we wasted jet fuel."

"Someday you'll give me a real answer."

"Wasting jet fuel is as real as it gets."

He opened the car's rear door, worked the hinged door on one of the crates, and pulled out a metal suitcase. The green wood of the crate grumbled and squeaked, but closed again. The plywood sides of the box concealed the fact that it was now empty.

As soon as Jill was out, he locked the car with the remote security key and went to the front door of the house. Ignoring the electronic doorbell in favor of the old bronze captain's bell, he rang it three times, hard.

And settled in to wait.

Nearly a minute later the door opened. A tall, silver-haired man in blue jeans, worn hiking boots, and a blue work shirt stood in the fading light. Lean, erect, fit, he had eyes as black as a night without stars.

He looked at Zach, then at Jill, then once more at Zach.

"So you came back after all," he said. His voice was raspy, neither deep nor high, just rough. "At least you brought somebody nice for me to look at, since I don't much care for the sight of you."

"Mutual," Zach said. "You going to let us in?"

The older man looked at Jill. He smiled and offered his hand. "I'm Garland Frost."

She blinked and found herself smiling in return. *Bet he was a real hottie when he was young. Even now, that smile could melt a glacier.* She took his hand and shook it briefly. "I'm Jill Breck, and I'm pleased to meet you even if Mr. Surly isn't."

Frost gave a bark of laughter. "He knows me."

"That's why I'm surly," Zach said.

"Come on in," Frost said to Jill. "I like you already."

"What about him?" she asked.

Frost looked at the silver suitcase in Zach's hand. "Did you bring me something?"

"Why else would I be here?"

Something flickered in the older man's eyes. It could have been anger, curiosity, hurt, impatience, or a combination of all four.

Jill didn't need her years of summing up clients on the river to see that whatever it was that lay between Frost and Zach, the emotion was as complex as it was painful.

"Why else indeed?" Frost said roughly. "I should shut the door in your ungrateful face."

"Then you'd never know what I brought you." Zach smiled, showing a lot of teeth. "And that would irritate the hell out of you."

Frost turned his back on Zach, took Jill's arm, and led her into the house. "Welcome to Taos. Amazing that such a good-looking young woman would put up with Zach Balfour."

Since Frost hadn't slammed the door in Zach's ungrateful face, he followed Jill inside.

He didn't hurry to catch up. He knew exactly where and how Frost was going to test Jill. The great room was great in more than space. If anyone wasn't fascinated by it, then Frost had no time to waste on that person.

Jill passed the test.

Silently she stared at Frost's great room. She hoped her jaw wasn't hanging open, but wouldn't have been surprised if it was.

In one corner a fire crackled in an unscreened fireplace. The scent of burning cedar infused the room with a clean, natural perfume. Dozens of paintings hung high on the pale plaster walls. Beneath them, at eye level, display cases filled with earthen pots, cowboy bronzes, and Indian artifacts stood shoulder to shoulder around the perimeter of the room.

From what she could see, everything inside the cases was of museum quality.

Library tables covered with stacks of books and partially assembled pots took up much of the rest of the floor space, except for a huge wood desk that looked out like an observation post. The desk was on a platform that was raised two steps above the floor of the great room.

"She likes it," Frost said to Zach. "Your taste in women has improved."

"She's a client," Zach replied. "I'm on assignment."

"Still with the government, then. Sorry to hear it. The contingent of bozos running the country doesn't deserve help."

"I left government work five years ago," Zach said. "Now I'm with St. Kilda Consulting."

Frost's silver eyebrows lifted. "I'm surprised Ambassador Steele would put up with you."

"He's a scholar and a gentleman. We get along just fine."

Unlike Frost and Zach.

Jill winced at the undercurrents, but hesitated to get between the two men. Besides, the room was fascinating. She itched to look in every drawer and cabinet.

"So you're back in the art business?" Frost asked, his expression still guarded.

Zach shrugged. "I'm here, aren't I? When I'm not out there, practicing carchaeology."

"What the hell is that?"

"Collectible muscle cars. But if you still have that old International Travel-All of yours, I'll give you five grand for it," Zach said.

"Why?"

"I know a man who is looking for one and will pay at least eight thousand."

"I don't believe you," Frost said. "What's his name?"

"Nobody you know," Zach said.

"I'll find out," Frost said. "There isn't anything in the world of collectibles that I can't discover in time."

"Yeah?" Zach asked. "Then find me a 1971 Plymouth Barracuda convertible with a 426 Hemi engine."

"I just might," Frost said curtly. "If I have time to waste."

"You'll need a lot of it," Zach said. "There were only nine of them made and eight have been found. Supposedly the last one was turned into scrap metal at a junkyard somewhere here in the Southwest, but I think that baby is still out there."

"So what? Cars aren't art."

"Tell that to the guy who paid two million and change for convertible number eight," Zach said.

"Two million dollars?"

"And change."

"I'll be damned," Frost said. "But it still isn't art."

"Matter of opinion."

"Quit baiting our host," Jill said to Zach without shifting her attention from the paintings on the far wall. "You know art when you see it. And I'm looking at some really fine art right now."

Zach and Frost both seemed surprised to be reminded that they weren't alone. They followed Jill's glance.

Eight Western landscapes flowed across the wall. All of them were beautifully presented with gilt museum frames and recessed illumination that brought out every bit of light and darkness in the canvases.

"Great Basin, western Rockies, Northwest coast, high plains, Southwest, every season and mood," she said, moving toward the paintings. "Incredible."

And two of the paintings were Dunstans.

40

A nything new?" Score barked into his headphone.

"Do you see anything new in your files?" Amy's voice said more than her words just how irritated she was. "I'm on a date and my phone keeps vibrating like a scared hamster. I've spent so much time in the women's can that Dave thinks I've got diarrhea."

"You're getting overtime."

"I'd rather get laid."

Score bit back a string of curses. The problem with hiring bright young computer techs was that they were younger than they were bright.

"There is nothing new on the phone bug," she said, spacing the words like Score was an idiot. "I said I'd call if there was."

"When was the last time you checked?"

"The last time you called. That would be four minutes and sixteen—no, seventeen—seconds ago."

"Where's your computer?"

"At the office, rigged to call the cell phone in my other pocket if something changes. I also have Steve babysitting my computer, in case something good pops. Why don't you just text-message him and cut out the middleman?"

With a disgusted sound, Score punched out of the conversation. He frowned at one of the computers he had with him. The pulsing light of the locater appeared over a street map of Taos.

The only good news was that the locater had finally stopped moving.

He zoomed in on the map until he had the address. Then he fed the information into his other computer and waited impatiently for directions to appear on the screen. While he waited, he watched the locater.

Still motionless.

"That's it, babe. Stay where you are. Papa's coming to get you."

And he really hoped the Breck bitch got in the way. Nothing personal. She was just more trouble than she was worth. Like her great-aunt. With a little luck, Ms. Breck would be talking to the old lady soon.

Assuming the dead talked.

41

Taos
September 15
6:21 P.M.

So you like Western landscapes," Frost said to Jill, breaking the long silence. "Especially the Dunstans. Why?"

She started, only then realizing she'd been wholly involved in the art, ignoring everyone in the room. "Sorry. Didn't mean to be rude."

"Not at all," Frost said. "Seeing your reaction reminds me of just how great those paintings are. I get so busy fitting pieces of pottery together that I forget to look up often enough."

Jill glance at Zach, silently asking him how much she should say to Garland Frost.

"Whatever is said doesn't leave the room," Zach said to Frost. "Agreed?"

Frost measured Zach with shrewd dark eyes. "Just like the old days."

Zach nodded.

"Agreed," Frost said. "What do you have?"

"Questions about twelve landscapes that have been in Jill's family for three generations," Zach said.

"Good paintings?"

"I like them," Zach said. "A lot."

Frost grunted and asked Jill, "Who bought the paintings?"

"I suspect they were a gift." *Or even a theft.* "I certainly didn't find any sales receipts in the family papers."

"Provenance?" Frost asked Zach.

"From Jill's grandmother, to her grandmother's younger sister, and then to Jill."

"There are plenty of experts and St. Kilda Consulting has a reciprocal agreement with Rarities Unlimited. Why come to me?" Frost asked.

"Until Thomas Dunstan killed himself, my grandmother was his on-again, off-again lover," Jill said before Zach could. "Originally there were thirteen paintings. When the land taxes were more than Modesty could afford, she sent the smallest canvas out to be appraised by a gallery in Park City, Utah. Somehow they 'lost' it."

Frost's eyes narrowed but he didn't say anything.

"Someone gave the painting back to me as a handful of canvas scraps," she said bitterly.

"Destroyed?" Frost demanded.

"Beyond repair," Zach answered. "The rags are in her belly bag. Don't ask me why. I told her they're worthless."

Jill shrugged, unsnapped the bag's strap, and threw the whole thing at him. "Then you get rid of them. I can't."

"Later." One-handed, Zach caught the bag and fired it toward the nearest sofa. The satellite phone gave the bag just enough heft to keep it aloft for the nine-foot flight. "The important thing is the death threat came with the scraps. That's when she called St. Kilda Consulting."

Frost looked at the metal suitcase Zach was still holding. "That better be one of the family paintings."

Zach put the case flat on the floor, unsnapped the catches, and opened it. When he removed the protective coverings, there were two canvases in perfectly cut foam nests, one canvas for each side of the case.

In complete silence, Frost stared at the paintings until Jill wanted to shake him.

"Take them out," Frost said. "Let me see them more closely."

Carefully Zach took the paintings out.

"Did you remove them from their frames?" Frost demanded.

"As far as I know, they were never framed," Jill said.

"Over here," was all Frost said.

He swept an arm across his desk, clearing a space big enough for both paintings. Art and archaeology magazines and papers fell unnoticed to the floor.

Zack put the canvases on the desk.

"Get the rest of them," Frost said without looking up from the paintings.

"I live to serve," Zach muttered.

"I'll help," Jill said quickly.

"Clear a space over there," Zack said, pointing to a library table littered with books. "I'll bring the paintings."

Frost ignored everything but the canvases in front of him. The intensity in his eyes was reflected in his silence. He didn't look up until Zach put out two more paintings. Frost went to them, his footsteps silent on the Persian carpet. When some of the books Jill was rearranging slid off onto the floor, he didn't notice.

Zach came back with another set of paintings.

Frost was looking at his own Dunstans. When Jill put the fifth and sixth canvases on the library table, he crossed quickly to them.

For the first time in her life, silence was driving Jill crazy. As Zach came back with numbers seven and eight, she lifted an eyebrow in silent question. He shook his head, closed the empty case, put it next to the others, and left.

Frost rearranged two of the canvases and said, "Light. The steel lamp near the potsherds."

Since Jill was the only other person in the room, she assumed he was giving the order to her. She went to a table halfway across the great room, unplugged the lamp, and carried it over to Frost.

He dumped more books on the floor to make room for the lamp's heavy base and long folding arm. Without being told, she plugged the cord into the nearest outlet.

If he treated Zach like this, it's no wonder the two of them didn't get along, she thought. *But I assume Frost's expertise equals his arrogance. If it didn't, Zach wouldn't have made the trip.*

She cleared books and Zach brought more paintings until all twelve were on the library table and six empty aluminum cases were lined up behind the door. The last painting on the table was her favorite—the landscape with a woman in a red skirt.

Frost studied it very closely. Then he picked up each canvas and searched it front to sides to back.

"Unsigned," Zach said. "All of them."

"I have eyes," Frost snapped.

The silence grew as he examined the last painting.

And grew.

Finally Frost looked up at Jill. "What horse's ass said these aren't Dunstans?"

42

The answer to that is complicated," Zach said. "One of the dealers was shut down hard by Lee Dunstan himself."

"When it comes to art, Lee doesn't know his butt from a warm rock," Frost said.

"Two words. Droit moral."

Frost's lips twisted in a sour line. "Like there's a gene for art that always gets passed on to the next generation."

Zach shrugged. "In the absence of provenance, the son has a lock on determining what is and isn't a Dunstan."

"Horseshit." Frost made an impatient gesture. "Yes, I know, that's the way it is. It's one of the reasons I got out of the art trade. Too many idiots." He turned to Jill. "So Lee Dunstan refused to certify your paintings?"

"I haven't sent him any. But if what he said to Jo Waverly-Benet is any sample, I'll save the postage."

"Which painting did he see?"

"The one that's now in rags," Jill said, gesturing to her belly bag across the room.

"*Son of a bitch.* Are you telling me that an unknown Dunstan actually has been destroyed?"

"All I know," she said carefully, "is that my great-aunt sent out the smallest of the thirteen paintings to be appraised. Now all I have are twelve paintings and a handful of rags."

Without a word Frost strode across the room, unzipped her belly bag, and dumped the contents on the sofa. When he saw the pieces of canvas, he began cursing under his breath, ugly words that he ordinarily wouldn't have spoken in a woman's presence.

He left everything on the sofa and turned away.

"Some days I despair for humanity," Frost said as he walked back to Jill. "This is one of those days."

"I despair on a more regular basis," Zach muttered.

Frost ignored him and asked Jill, "Who else didn't like the paintings?"

"Nobody but you and Zach has actually seen them. I sent JPEGs of three other paintings to various gallery owners in the West."

"Including Ramsey Worthington," Zach drawled.

"And?" Frost demanded impatiently.

"Worthington as good as told me I could be arrested for fraud," Jill said.

Frost's eyes narrowed. "Show me those JPEGs."

Zach went to his duffel, pulled out his computer, and booted up. He got the JPEGs on screen and handed it over to Frost.

The older man spent much less time with the JPEGs than he had on the canvases themselves. "No one even asked to see the paintings?"

"Only someone called Blanchard," Jill said, "after a fashion."

"Who doesn't exist under that name," Zach added.

"What did Blanchard say about the art?" Frost demanded.

"Not much. When he didn't find the paintings in Jill's car, he trashed it and left a death threat."

"And a ruined painting," Jill added.

"After our trip to Snowbird, I knew I wouldn't get any-where inside the Western art circuit," Zach said. "That's when I called your part-time cook and housekeeper, and told her that we'd be here for dinner."

"Well, that explains the quantity of food Lupita made," Frost said. "She always thought the sun shined out your back-side."

"Smart woman," Zach said blandly.

Jill snickered.

"We needed an honest opinion of the paintings," Zach said. "I came to you."

Frost's mouth softened into something close to a smile. "Well, at least you trust me that much."

"So give us your opinion," Zach said.

"If those paintings aren't by Thomas Dunstan, I'll eat my whole collection of Anasazi pots. But I don't have droit moral. I don't have Ramsey Worthington's stature in West-ern art circles. With my opinion and four hundred dollars, you could frame a small painting."

"Don't be too sure of that," Zach said. "Your kind of rep-utation doesn't disappear, it becomes legendary."

Frost looked at Zach the way he'd looked at the Dunstans. Then he nodded abruptly. "What can I do to help you?"

Jill sensed rather than saw the long breath Zach let out.

"Thank you," Zach said. "St. Kilda will be glad to pay for your—"

"Don't insult me," Frost interrupted curtly. "Get the ladder out of the garage and take down my Dunstans."

Zach started to bridle at the orders, then smiled slightly.

"Yessir."

Frost looked surprised, then almost smiled, too.

"I'll get the ladder," Jill said quickly.

"Never mind," Zach said. "I've played monkey for this man more times than either of us wants to remember."

"So stop yapping and get the ladder," Frost said. "I want those Dunstans side by side."

"Yours are bigger than mine," Jill said to Frost.

"No matter what a teenage boy tells you, bigger ain't better," Frost retorted.

Jill blinked, then laughed. Garland Frost wasn't an easy person, but she liked him in the same way that she preferred rapids to lazy, sweeping river curves.

Without a word, Frost disappeared into another room. Jill could see just enough of it to know that it was a library.

Zach reappeared, carrying a big aluminum ladder. He set it up beneath the two Dunstans and started climbing. He handed the first painting down to Jill.

"Get a good grip," he said. "It's heavier than it looks."

She took the weight without staggering. Rowing rivers was a great way to build upper body strength. "I have it. You can let go now."

"Lean it against the desk pedestal," Zach said.

Carefully she placed the painting by the desk and went back for the second one. By the time she put it next to the other one, Zach was beside her, looking at the paintings.

"One of them has a figure in it," she said. "Very small, but still there."

"Male," he said, examining the painting closely.

"Maybe. And maybe it's a woman in jeans. Women did wear pants back then. Working on a ranch, long skirts are worse than useless."

"The great icon of the masculine West painting a woman in or out of pants?" Zach asked dryly. "Worthington would dump a brick at the idea."

"I'd like to dump a brick on him."

"Frost's paintings are signed," Zach said.

"Lucky him." She hesitated. "Do you really think my twelve paintings are by Thomas Dunstan?"

"I'd bet a lot more on it now than I would have two hours ago."

"Frost is that good?"

"Yes. And he knows it."

"Does Ramsey Worthington?" Jill asked.

"Yeah." Zach grinned like a pirate. "Should be an interesting pissing contest."

Frost appeared with a large, rather thin book. He set it on the desk and opened it to a previously marked page.

"These are my Dunstans," he said. "*Canyon Dawn* and *Before the Storm.*"

Jill looked at the plates of the paintings, then at the front of the book. "Dunstan's catalogue raisonné. When did it come out?"

"Tal Crawford commissioned it eighteen months ago," Frost said, "about the time Dunstan's paintings started to soar in value. And I mean soar."

"Who is Crawford?" Jill asked.

"A major collector," Frost said. "I made a lot of money off him when I was in the gallery business. Heard he's been bidding on every Dunstan that comes on the market. He's been angling after my two paintings for years."

"Why?" Jill asked. "I mean, sure, I love Dunstan's paintings, but I don't feel a need to own every available one."

"You're not a collector," Frost and Zach said together.

"Different breed entirely," Frost continued.

"Amen," Zach said. "Like river rats."

"Gotcha," Jill said, smiling. "Crazy within predictable parameters."

Frost looked at her. "Thank God Zach's taste in women has improved."

"I'm a client," Jill reminded him.

Frost smiled. "You keep telling yourself that."

Zach changed the subject. "If anything, Jill's paintings are in better shape than yours. Brighter. More vivid."

"They were kept in a trunk in the attic," she said.

Frost winced. "Well, that's better than being stored in a barn. Have you hit them with the black light?"

"No," Zach said.

"Why not?"

"No black light," Zach said. "No time."

"Make time," Frost said. "Get mine. Second drawer, right side of the desk. Check the female figures in Jill's paintings. They could have been over-painted, added later, whatever."

Zach went to the desk and returned with what looked like a hand-held work light, except that the bulb was black rather than clear and it was battery operated. Jill watched over his shoulder as he turned on the light and aimed it at the first canvas. A purple glow spread across the landscape.

"Ultraviolet light," Zach said.

"Goth kids used them in raves," Jill said.

"I can't see you at a rave."

"Funny, I don't have that problem with you."

Zach's teeth flashed eerily in the backwash of the light. "When I'm not raving, I use UV to detect repairs or over-painting on canvases."

Jill looked at Frost. "Is that what you think happened? The female figures were added later?"

"It wouldn't be the first time," he said. "Was your great-aunt an artist?"

"No, but my grandmother was. From what my mother told me, Justine Breck did portraits of children and flowers."

"Female things," Frost said.

Jill bit her tongue.

Zach used the black light on each of the canvases in turn,

paying particular attention to the female figures in the pictures.

"Anything?" Frost asked impatiently.

"No. The figure is integral to each painting. Same for the gas station in *Indian Springs*. All painted at the same time as the landscape, and all necessary to the balance of the painting as a whole."

"I could have told you that," Jill said under her breath.

Frost ignored her. With easy expertise, he popped one of his paintings out of its frame and set the canvas among her paintings. He did the same with the second.

A chill prickled over Jill's skin. Without the frames, the signed Dunstans fit very well with the unsigned canvases. Speechless, she looked at Frost.

"Thank you," Frost said, but he was looking at Zach. "I haven't seen anything like these paintings in twenty years."

The two men faced each other for a long moment, each trying to say something that stuck between their minds and their tongues.

"You're welcome," Zach said finally. "I knew you would give an honest opinion, whether it was the one I wanted or not."

"Is it?" Frost asked.

"The one I wanted?"

Frost nodded.

"Part of me is doing backflips of delight," Zach said.

"And the rest of you?" Frost said.

"The rest of me is going to call St. Kilda and tell them that this assignment has just morphed into a grenade with the pin halfway out."

43

Taos
September 15
7:10 P.M.

S core sat in the back of the anonymous rental minivan.
He was parked close to a cutesy bed-and-breakfast sign.
That was the good news—a strange vehicle wouldn't
be noticed.

The bad news was that the B&B actually had some
guests, even though it was the lull between summer tourists
and winter skiers. But there wasn't enough foot traffic to get
in the way and the van's heavily tinted glass offered surprising privacy. He was rather comfortable as he stared across
the street and down the block at the iron gate and high adobe
walls of Garland Frost's home.

The really bad news was that nothing Score had learned
about Frost made him want to smile.

*Western art expert. Big reputation despite lack of de-
grees. Uncanny eye for good stuff. Retired.*

But not so retired that St. Kilda can't get to him.

At least Frost has a reputation for being arrogant. People spend a lot of time on their knees before they get his attention.

With any luck, the Breck bitch will piss him off.

The script from the bug in Breck's sat/cell was tantalizing, but hardly definitive. Amy was running it through various electronic cleaner programs. He should hear from her or Steve any minute.

He'd better.

Man, this is turning into a real cluster. I have to know if Frost is looking at JPEGs or the real thing or refusing to look at all.

And I have to know real soon.

The auction was breathing down his neck. The worst-case scenario told him that Frost was looking at the real paintings.

I can get over or through the gate. No problemo.

But the house?

Big problemo.

He'd bet real money that Garland Frost's house was wired for sound and pictures. Not like the old lady with her piece-of-crap rifle for security. Frost had a lot of valuable goods inside.

Score wasn't going to risk a black-bag job on that house unless he was certain there was no other way.

What really steamed him was that he couldn't even use his directional microphone to pick up conversation inside the house. Those adobe walls were a real sound sponge, and he couldn't get to any windows without exposing himself all over the place. Stalemate. His second computer beeped. He looked over, then activated the voice-calling feature. Steve's voice came out over the built-in speakers.

"Score?"

"No, it's the Easter Bugger. What do you have?"

"Definitely a third voice," Steve said.

Ya sure? Score thought sarcastically. *I could have told him that myself.*

"Dude's got a mouth like a sewer," Steve continued. "It's all in the transcript."

"Individual words or just the general direction of the conversation?"

"Words. Want me to read the script?" Steve asked.

"Not unless it's talking about paintings."

"Plural? Nope. Everything was really muffled, just like it has been," Steve said, "then suddenly it was clear. The new dude was on a rant about assholes who destroy art."

"Anything else?"

"The new voice faded into the other two voices, like the dude walked away from the bug. Things got soft again, but not like before."

Score came to a point like a hunting dog. "What's different?"

"Difference between turning the volume down and burying a speaker in mud. I've got a new sound-booster program that I'd like to try, but I didn't want to without ask—"

"Do it," Score interrupted curtly. "Get back to me soonest."

"It may be several hours. This program uses complex algorithms that take a lot of time, especially on my laptop."

"No matter how late, call me. And I mean call. Cell phone. Got it?"

"Got it."

"Then do it."

Score ended the voice program and stared out the window. All he could be certain of was that a painting had been destroyed. Since he'd been the one with the machete, he already knew that.

Why is it always the simple jobs that go from sugar to shit?

He went to the back of the van, opened a small silver

suitcase, and pulled out a semiautomatic pistol. He screwed the silencer on, checked the magazine, and went back to the front of the van.

When it was fully dark, he'd look around Frost's grounds. There might be a window where he could safely set up shop. From what he'd learned about the cargo at Taos Regional, six crates of goods had been unloaded from the plane St. Kilda chartered. It looked like the op was putting all his eggs in one basket.

Or maybe not.

If it walks like a duck, and talks like a duck . . .

It could be a red herring.

And Score knew just how to fry fish.

44

Taos
September 15
7:15 P.M.

The breakfast nook in Frost's big kitchen seated three. Barely.

The constant heat and flex of Zach's hard thigh pressed against Jill's was making her hotter than Lupita's tamales. Zach didn't seem to notice anything unusual. Except that with every motion, however small, he ended up closer to her.

It had to be accidental.

And chickens lay chocolate eggs, she thought, feeling the heat of a fit, big male body all the way from her ankle to her hip.

"I hear what you're saying," she said to Frost, "but I still don't understand the problem. Experts disagree all the time. Any lawyer can tell you that."

Zach leaned over to get more hot sauce. Coming and going, his arm slowly brushed against her breast. It was a good thing Frost was speaking, because right now Jill couldn't have said a word if her next breath depended on it.

"Experts can, and do, disagree," Frost said with a shrug. "I've seen litigation over attributions that go on for years, even in nineteenth- and twentieth-century Western art, which is relatively well documented."

Zach went for a second helping of hot sauce.

Or something.

"I've seen more money change hands in lawsuits over attribution than the art was worth in the first place," Frost said. "There's a case up in Montana right now, a picture I thought was a Charlie Russell and some others thought wasn't. One of the dealers went public with his doubts. The owner of the piece sued him for slander, defamation, and general idiocy for destroying the value of a five-million-dollar painting."

"What happened?" Zach asked, his voice low, husky.

Jill forced herself to breathe.

And reached across Zach for the stack of paper napkins on his right.

One good rub deserves another, she told herself.

Zach's breath came in swiftly. His thigh muscles flexed against hers.

"The good ol' boys on the Montana jury ruled in favor of the good ol' boy Montana expert," Frost said. "So the dealer turned around and sued the owner of the disputed Remington for malicious abuse of legal process. Another Montana jury awarded the Montana expert twenty million dollars or some such ridiculous amount. It's being appealed seven ways from Sunday. Going to be in court until hell won't have it."

"A lesson to us all," Zach said, breathing out when Jill's body finally settled back next to his, "but it's a good example of what can happen when you get wealthy collectors, lawyers, and art experts together. A real Mongolian goat-fu—er, roping."

"Does that mean you don't want to go public with your opinion of my paintings?" Jill asked Frost.

He laughed. "That's one of the joys of getting old and rich. I don't have to be afraid of anything or anybody."

"Like you ever were," Zach said.

Frost ignored him and spoke to Jill. "An expert pissing contest is only part of your problems. Another part is that, by comparison to the rest of Western art, the Dunstan market is thin and narrow."

Zach reached for more hot sauce. "I've seen recent sales prices that looked pretty good to me."

Jill got even by taking a deep breath. She knew her nipples were hard.

Now he did, too.

"Look behind the sales, boy," Frost said. "Things aren't always as real as they seem."

Zach coughed and cleared his throat, quite sure that everything he'd touched had been real. "What's that supposed to mean?"

"Dunstan had a low output," Frost said. "That can work against an artist."

"I thought that scarcity was the name of the game in positional art," Jill said.

"If there are several hundred canvases around, the competition gets spread a bit wider," Frost said, waving his fork for emphasis. "More people jump into an auction because there's more chance of picking something up." He stopped and looked at Zach. "You keep reaching for that hot sauce and you won't have any taste buds left when you're my age."

Zach ignored Frost and poured out a few more drops before putting the bottle back in the middle of the table. Slowly.

Frost shook his head. "For years there wasn't much call for Dunstans. The overall Western art market is fueled by Western money, mostly oil money, and cheap oil cut into the positional wealth of Dunstan fanciers."

"That hasn't been a problem lately," Jill said.

"No, but with art, you have to take a long view." Frost sipped his red wine, then held the glass up to the light and admired the rich color. "The collector impulse is a dark one. At the highest levels, it's more a competitive sport than anything else."

"Edging right into a blood sport," Zach agreed.

"At least I have the satisfaction of knowing that I paid for every piece in my various collections with money I made off other collectors." Frost smiled slightly. "Sometimes I think that collectors are trying to fill a black hole in their soul with all this stuff, but at least I've managed to make a living at it."

"I can see where Zach got his cynicism," Jill said.

"I did what I could for him," Frost agreed.

She rolled her eyes. "There's more to art than cynicism. Objects have an intrinsic as well as an extrinsic value. I suspect Zach has a highly refined aesthetic sense. And I *know* that you do," she told Frost.

"With that and four hundred—"

"—dollars you can frame a small painting," Zach finished.

Frost sent a hard look across the table.

Zach ignored it. Right now, the only hard thing that interested him was between his legs.

"Even among avid dealers and private collectors," Frost said, "Dunstan collectors are an odd lot. There are really only about ten of them, and most of the fifty canvases have been accumulated by them."

"Who?" Zach asked, looking up from his second enchilada.

"First and foremost, Tal Crawford," Frost said. "Billionaire. Oil magnate. Horse's ass."

"I thought he was a modernist," Zach said. "Didn't he pay a bunch of money for a Warhol about the time I left Taos?"

"That Warhol was for his office in Boston. The Picassos were for his Manhattan office. The Pollock went to his estate in Martha's Vineyard. Last I heard, he built a castle south of Reno, along with a cattle ranch that takes up most of the Carson Valley."

"So, naturally, he has to have some Western art for all those castle walls," Jill said.

"Billionaire and mega-millionaire art collectors are remarkably common," Frost said. "Nowadays they pretty much drive the art market, no matter what the genre. Positional art is sending prices sky-high across the board. More beer?" he asked her.

"What about me?" Zach didn't want one, but he couldn't pass up the chance to pull Frost's chain.

"You know where the refrigerator is," Frost said.

"None for me," Jill said.

"You sure?" Zach asked. "You can crawl over my lap to get out."

"You're such a Y gene," she said under her breath.

Grinning, he took a sip of his first and only beer.

Frost ignored them. "Actually, Tal might not be in the billionaire's club these days. Rumor is that in the last decade he's been real good at turning millions into thousands. Maybe that's why he's been concentrating on Western art in general and Dunstan in particular."

"Easy to make a big splash in a small pond?" Zach asked.

"Yes."

"If the Dunstans go for four mil and up, that's a pretty big pond," Jill said.

Frost shrugged, unimpressed. "Not really. From what I'm hearing, the Dunstans in Las Vegas will go for as high as ten million."

"It's all relative," Zach said. "Remember the Klimt?"

Jill drew in a breath, then let it out. "Yeah. Way more than ten million. It's just . . ." She shook her head. "That many zeros don't seem real to me."

"Crawford has been collecting for thirty years," Frost said. "One way or another, especially in the last few years, he's bought every Dunstan that came on the market, plus some right out of private collections. Word is he's the Bigfoot behind a Nevada state museum project that will house the best Dunstan collection in existence, mainly because it will be the only Dunstan collection in existence."

Jill glanced toward Frost's great room. "There are two unquestionably authentic Dunstans he won't own."

"Don't think I haven't been tempted by his offers," Frost said. "I could easily get seven million for my bigger Dunstan, but I can't afford to sell it."

"Why not?" Jill asked. "Besides your love of the painting, of course."

"Taxes," Frost said. "I'd have to shell out a huge amount of money on the difference between the purchase price and the appreciated price, and I'm damned if I think the government has earned it."

"I should have tax problems like that," Jill said.

"If we can authenticate your paintings, you will," Zach said.

"What?"

"Estate taxes," he said.

"Modesty Breck's estate is officially closed or paid out or whatever the lawyer's call it," Jill said.

Zach looked at Frost, who shrugged.

"It might fly," Frost said. "And it might not. Government always wants more money. It's how they buy votes."

"You mean I might have to sell half the paintings to pay estate taxes on the other half?" Jill asked.

"Or donate them to a museum and thereby hang on to the others for 'free,'" Frost said. "Donations are about saving taxes, not civic responsibility."

"Welcome to the wonderful world of taxes and family finances," Zach said. "And lotteries. No matter who wins, government always gets about half of the jackpot."

She reached for her beer and took a long swallow. "Remarkable. Why haven't we had a revolution?"

"Too few winners." Zach finished off a final bite of tamale and looked at Frost. "Do you have any way to get us in with Tal Crawford?"

Frost laughed. "It's easier to get a picture taken with the president."

"Maybe Steele knows someone who knows someone," Zach said.

"I could get to one of the dealers Crawford uses," Frost said, "but that's still a long way from Crawford. Besides, he's as likely to be in Africa or Venezuela as he is in Nevada or New Mexico."

"I'd like to see what his reaction is to a dozen new Dunstans," Zach said.

Frost slid out of the nook. "I'll call some people. If Crawford is west of the Mississippi, I'll find out. But only because I like you," he said to Jill. "If it were just for the cowboy you're traveling with . . ."

Zach watched Frost disappear from the kitchen, leaving him with the dirty dishes. It wasn't the first time that had happened. If Zach stayed, it wouldn't be the last.

And he didn't have much choice except to stay.

45

Taos
September 15
8:05 P.M.

Score eased open the side door of the van. The dome light didn't come on, because he'd smashed it. Streetlights were few and far between. Probably because the "sidewalk" was a strip of dirt along the narrow side street between what passed for a curb and the adobe walls of the houses. Despite the cheerful B&B, tourism hadn't really caught on in the neighborhood of high fences and iron gates.

Two streets over, traffic came and went along a strip of restaurants and galleries. No one turned down the narrow lane lined with thick adobe walls and inward-facing houses in the old Spanish style.

Time for a little recon.

His pistol rode uncomfortably in its belt holster. Silencers were always a pain. But they were a useful pain.

He really wished he didn't have a bad feeling about this op. Maybe it was just his natural paranoia. Maybe it was the six shipping cartons that had been driven to the house of a Western art expert.

Maybe it was the adobe walls closing in. Houses like fortresses lining dark lanes. Enough to make a man look over his shoulder.

Score shook off the uncomfortable feeling and concentrated on his work. Walking casually, like someone with every right to be where he was, he strolled down the dark, rough dirt path.

When he got to the gate, it was just the way it had looked through his binoculars. Closed. Locked. Good alarm, well installed. From the street side, the electronics that operated both gate and alarm were out of reach.

He turned to the adobe walls. If they had been meant to keep out intruders, they weren't very good for the job. Regularly spaced tile niches offered a fast way to the thick tree branches that overhung the walls.

Score went up.

No razor wire on top of the thick wall. No sensors. No broken glass. No bells or whistles. Nothing but dust and a few dead leaves.

Frost might as well put out welcome mats.

Score smiled. People that careless deserved whatever happened to them.

He dropped lightly down into the yard behind a tree trunk. After a few minutes of listening and watching, he glided up to the Dodge Magnum.

Locked.

Electronic security.

The St. Kilda op isn't careless, even if Frost is.

Since there was no light coming through any of the windows on the street side of the house, Score risked a quick flash of his penlight into the Magnum. Shipping cartons, just the way the man at the airport had described. Six of them. Closed up tight.

*Looks like Frost wasn't real eager to help out by apprais-
ing the paintings.*

*Assuming they're paintings in the cartons rather than
something to throw anyone who cares off the trail. St. Kilda
has more tricks than a school for magicians.*

Score turned off the penlight and faded back into the
cover of the tree trunk. He could steal the car, but that was
a fool's game. Even if he got through the gate security, this
close to the Mexican border a lot of the more expensive
rental jobs had a hidden locater built right into the vehicle.

Trying to take the shipping cartons out of the Dodge one
by one didn't appeal to Score. Six trips up and over the wall
with a crate was begging for trouble.

No matter what he decided to do, he'd have to wait until everyone inside the house was asleep. Or gone. There
was nothing to guarantee that the op and the Breck woman
wouldn't leave the house at any moment. Frost's reputation for
being a difficult bastard was part of his record. He was more
likely to throw out the op than he was to help St. Kilda.

Score smiled thinly. He'd wait and see what happened.
A motel parking lot would be a lot easier to work with than
Frost's driveway.

He went back over the wall as silently as he'd come.

Nobody noticed.

He eased back inside the van and resumed watching the
only vehicle entrance and exit to the old adobe house. If no
one in the house moved out by midnight, he'd leave long
enough to get some supplies from the 24/7 mini-mart/gas
stations near the edge of town. Then he'd come back, make
a commotion, and pick off anyone who was stupid enough
to run outside.

If nothing else, it should slow down the opposition long
enough for the auction to take place.

After that, he didn't care what happened.

T hat hasn't changed," Zach said, disgusted.

"What?"

"Lupita won't be in tomorrow and Garland will do anything to avoid dishes." Zach began collecting dirty plates. "Figures it's beneath him, I guess."

Jill laughed. "How long have you two been pretending to dislike each other?" she asked as she joined him in clearing the table.

"Pretending?"

"Pretending. You're not fooling anyone except yourselves."

Zach scraped plates into the garbage disposal and stacked them on the counter. Jill opened the dishwasher and began loading it.

"I went to work for Frost my last few years of college," Zach said. "Unpaid intern, and worth every cent, he used to say. I finally got a paycheck after six months. I stayed for five years. But . . ." He shrugged. "The place wasn't big enough for both of us."

"Two captains on a ship is one too many," she agreed. "First thing you learn on the river."

Smiling, Zach opened a drawer and pulled out an old brass key. "C'mon. I'll walk you to your room. I put your backpack in there earlier."

"What about my belly bag?"

"Stuffed in the backpack. You need it?"

"No."

She followed him into the crisp, high mountain air. A breeze shifted dead leaves across the Spanish tiles of the courtyard. The splash of a fountain was like soft laughter in the darkness.

Zach opened the door of a small cottage and stepped aside for Jill to enter. As she brushed by him, her warmth and subtle fragrance made his body tighten even more.

He shut the door behind him. The only light in the room came from a wall niche holding a small, ancient pottery cup.

"When I left Frost," Zach said, hanging the key on a nearby nail, "I wasn't planning on coming back. Ever. One of Frost's old business associates hired me on at the CIA, advising people on the international art market."

"I wouldn't think the CIA would have much use for art," Jill said, going to the fireplace.

"You'd be wrong. There's a lot of diplomacy and international intelligence work involved in the art trade. The Russians alone have laundered hundreds of millions of black dollars through high-end auction houses in London and New York."

A long match flared in the darkness. Jill touched flame to the dry tinder and small branches in the fireplace.

"Whatever happened to art for the sake of art?" she asked, straightening.

"Reality." Zach walked until he stood close to her and the graceful dance of flames. "But I wasn't any happier being a bureaucrat than I was as a gofer for an arrogant genius. So when Ambassador Steele made me an offer of contract work, I jumped."

Jill turned and looked at Zach. Really looked at him.

She liked what she saw.

"What?" he asked. "Is my nose on backward?"

"I didn't get to read your dossier, so I'm at a disadvantage."

His whiskey eyes were nearly gold with the reflection of fire. "You didn't miss anything worthwhile."

"For work, probably not. But for play . . . ?" She waited.

He went still. The tactile memory of her hard nipples was burning at the edges of his mind like fire.

"Ask away." His voice was too husky, but he could no more change that than he could the fit of his jeans, tighter with every heartbeat.

"Are you involved with anything other than St. Kilda and old muscle cars?" Jill asked.

"Like what?"

"A woman."

"No. You?"

"I prefer men."

"Plural?" he asked, deadpan.

"I think one of you is all I can handle." *Probably more than I can handle*, she admitted silently, *but finding out will be a wild ride.*

Just the way she liked it.

Zack wrapped his hand around the back of Jill's neck and drew her close, then closer still, until he could feel her from his mouth to his knees.

"Are you thinking what I hope you're thinking?" he asked.

"If your thoughts include two of us and one bed, yes."

"Bed, floor, wall, whatever. I'm easy."

"You're hard," she said against his neck, "which makes you easy." *And too tempting to pass up.*

The feel of her tongue lightly tasting him made Zach's breath break. "You're making me forget my lecture about the dangers of mixing business and pleasure."

"Running rivers is my passion and my work. Where's the downside?"

"Damned if I know."

Jill went up on tiptoe as his arms closed around her. The kiss was like Zach—strong, hot, hard, as exhilarating as the moment when the rapids took the raft.

All the anger and fear that Jill had been working to control since she'd found her vandalized car flashed into passion. The hunger that shook her was unlike anything she'd ever felt before. After her virginal curiosity had been satisfied in college, she'd rarely taken a lover. The river had been much more exciting than any man.

Until now.

Zach felt the passion trembling in Jill, heard her husky sound of hunger, and forgot everything but her taste, her heat, her skin sliding beneath his hands and tongue.

The bed was across the room.

Way too far.

He tossed her blouse over his shoulder and bent to the hard nipples that had been driving him crazy since dinner. Just as he sucked one of them into his mouth, he felt the cool breath of the room on his back as she peeled off his shirt and threw it aside.

The feel of her hands on the fly of his jeans made him flush with heat.

"Condom," he managed.

"Where?" she said against his bare chest, biting him with tiny little movements of her head.

"Back pocket."

"I was hoping for the front."

His laugh became a groan as one of her hands opened his fly and the other hand fished slowly for a condom in one of his back pockets.

"You're a tease," he said.

"You're worth teasing."

The approval in her voice and her hand stroking him almost made him lose it right there.

"Other pocket," he said hoarsely.

Her hand slid inside his underwear and emerged a few seconds later wrapped around him. He said something low and rough as her fingers and then her mouth caressed him.

"That's it," he said. "School's out."

A few seconds later Jill found herself naked and on her back next to the fire. Zach went to his knees between her legs, slid the condom into place, and tested her heat with his finger. Her liquid response and the scent of her arousal made him glad he was already on his knees, because sure as hell she would have brought him there. She was slick and hot and tight, her skin flushed with passion, her hips lifting to meet his touch.

He tried to push gently into her, but it was too late. She was way too hungry for any more play and so was he. He flexed his hips and entered her in a hard thrust, filling her.

Jill's breath came out in a throaty cry that made Zach go completely still.

"Too soon?" he asked through clenched teeth.

When she didn't answer, he started to withdraw. Then he felt the rhythmic contractions of her release around him, caressing him, taking him with her over the edge of passion. He thrust hard, deep, fast, then shuddered, pumping into her until the world went black.

Zach didn't know how long it was before he became aware of the fire crackling nearby, the feel of Jill's palms stroking his back, the softness and strength of her body beneath him.

"I'm crushing you," he said.

She laughed breathlessly. "Yeah, but I like it. Good thing, because there's a lot of you to like."

He nuzzled against her throat, then rolled onto his side, taking her with him, still buried inside her. "Sorry. Usually I'm not so quick off the mark."

"I rarely get off the mark at all," she said, stretching out against his chest with a sigh. "I'm still wondering what happened. And how to make it happen again."

Lazily he ran his fingertips down her spine and between her tight, sexy cheeks, then lower, where she was still hot and wet.

Her breath broke. "Zach?"

"Mmm?"

"Isn't it too soon?"

"Not for you."

She started to ask what he meant but found she couldn't breathe. She could only respond to the sleek probe of his fingers, the pressure, the rub and glide and tug, the fire burning up from his touch to consume her whole body.

He smiled at the feel of her climax. When she finally stilled and lay like a steamy rag against him, he slid slowly out of her.

She made a grumpy cat sound.

He laughed and hauled her to her feet. "Time for bed."

She yawned. "I like it here better."

"Come morning, you'll be thanking me."

"I'm thanking you all over the place right now."

Zach grabbed his jeans, scooped out more condoms, and looked at her. "Hope you're not too sleepy, because I've got some tasting and licking in mind."

Jill gave him a sideways, lazy kind of smile. "Where?"

"All over the place."

47

Garland Frost sat surrounded by paintings, brooding over the collection. Dunstan's catalogue raisonné was open on the desk. As comparisons went, the photos were nearly useless, but it was all he had to work with besides his own two paintings.

The more he looked at the unsigned canvases and the catalogue raisonné and his two Dunstans, the more convinced he was that Jill Breck's canvases were indeed Dunstan's work. Despite the female figures, despite the *Indian Springs* painting with its now-quaint gas station, despite the lack of signatures.

The paintings simply had to be Dunstan's work, or the work of a forger so brilliant that there was no meaningful difference between forgery and art.

An artist's true signature was in the brushstrokes, the energy, the choice of colors, the feel of space or the lack of it, the feel of peace or the lack of it, all the thousands of small artistic decisions that added up to one uniquely Dunstan canvas.

These were Thomas Dunstans.

All Frost had to do was prove it.

Exhilaration bubbled through him, giving him the kind of charge that he thought he'd lost to age. But it was all there, all waiting, needing only the introduction of something worthy of interest into a life that had slowly gone stale.

He felt like waking up Zach and hugging him. But he suspected Zach wouldn't welcome the interruption.

Smiling, Frost did what he'd done many times in the past few hours. He picked up each canvas in turn and examined it front, back, and sides. He was missing something important. He knew it.

He just didn't know what it was.

With an impatient sound he opened the laptop that he used for research. He scanned again the mentions he had found of Dunstan, the old photos of his work, the learned words describing the indescribable.

"Idiots and fools," Frost muttered. "Especially Lee Dunstan. Man no more knows art than horseshit knows heaven."

Absently Garland ran his fingertips lightly over the side of the *Indian Springs* canvas, thinking about Dunstan and art and life and the unknown. When he realized that his fingertips returned to the same spot on the canvas stretcher again and again, he stopped, then repeated the light movement, this time conscious of what he was doing.

Definitely a different texture.

He flipped the canvas so that it was bottom side up to look at what he'd felt. It could have been just an extra-thick bit of paint that intrigued his fingertips, but he couldn't be sure in this light. He took the canvas over to his desk, angled the bright light, and frowned over the bottom edge of the canvas wrapped around the stretcher, a part of the painting that wouldn't show after the canvas was framed.

He switched to black light and turned off the desk lamp. He looked at the result for a minute, then began going over the bottom edge of each painting with the black light.

Halfway through the examination, he was grinning. By the time he was done, he was laughing with the sheer exuberance of having discovered something fresh and wonderful at a time in his life when everything had seemed old and flat.

"Zach, my boy, you're going to kiss me on all four cheeks in the morning, and what's more, you'll thank me for the opportunity."

Still grinning, Frost started nailing down the truth with some online research.

48

core finished peeing into the empty bottle of Gatorade, capped it off, and set it next to the other one on the floor of the passenger side of the van. When he left town later tonight he'd do what long-distance truckers working on piece rates did—throw the urine-filled bottles out the window along the Interstate.

He checked his computers, found nothing useful on the Breck woman's phone bug, and decided it was time to go to work. Past time, actually.

The smell of gasoline was making him sick.

He slid out of the van, just one more shadow in the night. As he walked the block and a half to Frost's place, a spring-loaded sap made his jacket pocket sag and bang against his hip. His silenced pistol dug into the small of his back. The bottle of gasoline he carried in a paper bag did what it had been doing for the past hour—it stank. The shredded Presto log that cushioned the bottle inside the paper waited to help the party along.

Nobody noticed him go up and over the adobe wall.

He walked quickly to the Dodge, saw that the shipping boxes were still inside, and smiled. He gave the rear window a swift, expert smack with the sap. At the impact, safety glass crumbled to glittering pebbles, just as it had been designed to do. No sharp edges to cut flesh.

The alarm yelped in the few seconds it took to light the makeshift fuse on the gas bomb and throw bag and bottle inside the vehicle.

The flash of flame was so fast and so violent, it nearly burned his face.

Mother. Next time I won't use that much of the log.

But he'd wanted to be very sure that this fire caught and held. He stood beside the wall for a few more seconds, making certain that the flames wouldn't fizzle.

They burned with a ferocity that cast shadows like a small sun.

Suddenly the front door opened. Score saw a flash of silver hair, yanked out his pistol, and took aim.

Frost's pistol boomed an instant before Score fired.

49

Taos
September 16
1:11 A.M.

Zach had yanked on his jeans and was running for the guesthouse door before he consciously registered what had awakened him.

"Zach?" Jill asked, her voice husky from sleep.

"Stay here," he commanded on the way out the door. "Gunshots."

From the front of the compound, a car alarm barked urgently.

Zach shut the guestroom door and raced barefoot across the courtyard and through the house. His weapon was where he should have been—in the upstairs guestroom.

The front door stood open. Frost was down, red blood glistening in the hall light. A big revolver lay a few inches beyond his right hand.

Fire leaped in the driveway, engulfing the rental car and giving everything inside the adobe wall a hellish glow.

A bullet sang off the metal bell six inches from Zach's head.

Silencer.

Zach snapped off the lights as he went down hard on the floor next to Frost. With one hand Zach felt for a pulse.

Fast, but there.

He picked up Frost's revolver, took a two-handed grip, and aimed for a man-shadow that had paused at the top of the adobe wall.

Flames gleamed on dark metal in the shadow's hand.

The sound of Frost's gun thundered a second time, then a third, shattering the night. The revolver kicked hard against Zach's hands, but he'd been expecting it. Frost always said that a gun that didn't kick like a mule was for girls.

A cry, a curse, and the shadow disappeared over the wall.

Zach came to his feet in a rush and punched in the gate code. As he did, he heard bare feet running down the hall behind him, heard Jill yell his name.

"Call 911," he shouted over her voice. "Frost is hurt. Stay out of the light. Could be more than one shooter."

Zach ran to the gate, heard someone running away, and risked a fast look through the slowly opening gate.

A bullet screamed off the metal bars.

He dropped to his stomach and elbow-crawled forward just enough to see that the man was running again. Zach triggered two more closely spaced shots, a double explosion of sound.

A hesitation, then the shadow ran around the corner of the block and vanished.

Zach was on his feet and through the gate in a coordinated rush. Within three strides he was running flat out, chasing the deadly shadow.

50

As Zach disappeared through the open gate, Jill dropped to her knees next to Garland Frost. She wanted to scream at Zach to be careful, but it was too late. He was gone and all she could do was try to help Frost.

Even without street or porch lights, she could see that blood was spreading out from above and to one side of Frost's belt buckle, dripping onto the Navajo rug that warmed the tile floor.

Too much blood.

She snatched the cordless phone off the hall table, punched in 911, and tucked the phone between her ear and shoulder. Before it even rang, she was opening Frost's shirt, trying to see the extent of the damage. She barely noticed the rental car burning, the stink of plastic, paraffin, particleboard, and raw gasoline. She was wholly intent on Frost.

The operator answered in a calm male voice. "Taos 911. What is the nature of your emergency?"

"Gunshots fired, one man down, a car fire burning out of control," Jill said. "Garland Frost's house, Taos. We need an ambulance and we need it now. Fire truck, too. A friend is pursuing the shooter. Both men are armed. I don't know the address."

"We just got an alert from the alarm company at Garland Frost's address. Police units are on the way. Name and age of the victim?"

"Garland Frost, over seventy."

"Your name, please."

"Just get here," Jill said curtly. "I'll fill out forms later."

Without hanging up, she set the phone aside and concentrated on Frost. His eyes were open, glittering with reflected flame. His jaws were clenched against pain.

"Garland," she said in a clear voice as she ripped away his shirt. "Can you hear me?"

His head moved and his eyes focused on her for a few seconds. His mouth opened, but all that came out was a groan. His eyes closed and his body went slack.

One look at his wound told Jill that it was beyond her training. All she could do now was try to keep him from going into shock.

"Garland," she said calmly, clearly. "You have to help me. Stay with me here. *Look at me.*"

She stroked his cheek. When he didn't respond, she pinched firmly. His eyes opened and focused on her again.

"Do you hurt anywhere except your side?" she asked.

His head rolled to one side, then the other in a slow negative.

Relief swept through her. *Spinal cord isn't injured. Thank God.*

"Sh—shot," he said.

"I know. Help is on the way."

Sirens wailed in the distance. She devoutly hoped they were heading for Frost's house.

A gout of flame shot from the rear window of the car. If the gas tank blew, Frost would be right in the line of fire.

"Garland, I have to drag you farther inside. It will hurt. I'm sorry. I don't have any choice."

She hurried past him deeper into the house, picked up the far end of the tribal rug, and increased the pressure on it until the rug began inching away from the door.

Slowly, she told herself. *Don't make the injury worse. Gas tanks only explode in the movies.*

Bullshit. They explode whenever the conditions are right.

And only the gas tank knew when that would be.

Frost might have been in his seventies, but there was nothing fragile or birdlike about him. He was a solid weight on the rug. Jill's bare feet gripped the tiles as she eased backward. The phone came along with Frost. She wondered rather wildly if the blood dripping on it would short out something vital.

It seemed like forever, but it was only a few seconds before she had Frost safely down the hall. She ran for the front door and slammed it shut. Then she went back to Frost. He was sliding in and out of consciousness.

"Stay with me, Garland," she said firmly, picking up the phone. "Stay with me!" Ignoring the blood, she tucked the phone between her ear and her shoulder and felt for Frost's pulse. Still there.

He groaned weakly.

"My name is Jillian Breck," she said into the phone. "The patient is in and out of consciousness."

As she spoke, she stood and hurried to the small, old-fashioned parlor off the hall. She grabbed two fat sofa cushions and the decorative Navajo blanket that covered the back of the couch.

"Stand by one," the dispatcher said to Jill. "Med-techs are on the way."

As Jill returned to Frost, she heard the operator dispatching additional units and relaying information over a radio, warning the officers that one of the residents of the house was armed.

"Ma'am, tell the resident to put down his gun," the dispatcher said.

"I can't reach him and he wouldn't put the gun down anyway because someone is shooting at him. Whoever it is must be using a silencer, because I only heard one gun."

"There's a police unit less than a minute away," the dispatcher said. "Describe the good guy for me."

"He's barefoot without a shirt," Jill said as she elevated Garland's feet on the stacked cushions and wrapped the wool blanket around him. "Wearing jeans. Name is Zach Balfour. Over six feet, dark hair, built like rodeo rider." She kept as much pressure on the wound as she dared, hoping to slow the bleeding. "I have no idea what the other shooter looks like."

Jill heard Zach's voice calling her.

"In the hall," she yelled, covering the phone. "Police are on the way. You're supposed to put down the gun."

The front door opened and closed quickly.

"Might as well," Zach said, disgusted. "I'm out of bullets. Frost's old hog leg is big on noise and short on ammo."

"The resident is no longer armed," Jill said distinctly to the dispatcher. "Do you understand? Not armed."

"Copy. I'll tell the officers."

Sirens screamed closer.

When Jill looked up, the long, narrow windows on either side of the door framed Zach in the glowing, dancing reflection of flames.

"Do you think the gas tank will go?" she asked.

"Depends on how soon the fire truck gets here. How's Frost?"

"Alive."

Zach didn't ask any other questions. The strain in her voice said more than her words.

"When will the ambulance be here?" Jill asked the operator. "The patient is in shock. We don't have much time."

"Are you a doctor?" the dispatcher asked.

"I'm a professional river guide. I've been trained as a first responder."

"Tell them to send the fire truck to the front gate," Zach said, his voice loud enough to carry to the dispatcher. "That gas tank could blow any second. There's a pedestrian gate on the north side. It will be shielded from any blast. Send the med-techs in that way."

"Copy," the dispatcher said. "Gate, north side. Fire truck is less than a mile away. Police officers and med-techs will use north entrance."

"Last I saw of the shooter he was running south," Zach said. "I thought I heard a vehicle start up, but can't be certain. I didn't see any taillights or headlights."

"Copy," the dispatcher said. "Will inform the officers."

Zach put the revolver on the hall stand and looked at Jill. "I'll go open the north gate. Be back in less than a minute."

"Bring more blankets. What happened to the shooter?"

"I'm pretty sure I winged him, but he still flew. He's gone."

And then Zach was gone, too, running through the house barefoot, making no sound.

51

Taos
September 16
1:18 A.M.

One police unit stood off from the front gate and down the block. The siren was silent, but the blue-and-red light bar flashed a message of urgency. An officer with a bullhorn sent curious neighbors back inside their houses the instant they appeared.

A fire truck's big diesel engine revved as the driver switched power to the internal pumps. Behind a starburst of water from the hose, two firemen in turnout jackets and helmets advanced on the burning car. Water hissed on hot steel and vaporized, adding white steam to the roiling black smoke. Another fireman dashed forward with an axe and swung, shattering the safety glass in the side windows.

The flames began to die back, quenched by water. Very quickly the rental car became a sullen, hissing wreck. The air stank of chemicals and steam. Part of the fire still smoldered stubbornly.

Jill heard Zach leading med-techs through the house at a run. Since she had been working by the dying firelight, she flipped on the hall lights. Without the flames to give his skin color, Frost looked almost transparent. She stood and got out of the way of the med-techs.

The first tech, a woman, kneeled beside Frost to examine him. The second tech established a radio link with the hospital and began relaying vital signs as the first tech called them out.

For an instant Jill felt light-headed. Smoke, adrenaline, fear, or all three. Zach's arm came around her waist, steadying her.

"You okay?" he asked.

"Just taking a deep breath."

"You've got blood on you."

She looked at her hands and rubbed them absently against her jeans. "Frost has a lot more on him."

Zach led her down the hall and into the parlor. "The cops who are chasing the shooter will give up real quick and come back here to question us. If they're any good, they'll separate us to get our stories."

"So?"

"Tell them everything except what we believe about your paintings," he said softly. "We were just getting an appraisal from Frost. Got it? Just an appraisal. No St. Kilda, no death threat, no suspicions about your great-aunt's death, nothing but paintings and an expert appraiser."

A woman's voice called from the hall, "Are either of you this man's family?"

Zach went back into the hall. "He has a daughter in Santa Fe, last I heard. I'm an old friend. What do you need?"

"The patient is weak, but he wants to talk to you," the woman said. "Better do it before we move him."

Zach understood what the woman wasn't saying. This could be his last chance to talk to Garland Frost.

As Jill came out to the hall, she saw Zach kneel at Frost's side. The older man reached out with a feeble motion. An oxygen cannula rested beneath his nose and partially covered his mouth. His lips were moving.

Zach took the shockingly cool fingers between his warm palms. He leaned over and placed his ear close to Frost's mouth.

". . . stn . . . um . . . nt . . . on . . . tm."

Frost repeated the sounds again and again. His hand twitched inside Zach's palms.

Zach felt Frost's thumb poke at him weakly. He released Frost's hand. The older man's hand shook as he thrust his thumb up beneath Zach's nose.

"Are you saying you're okay?" Zach asked.

Frost's head rolled in a negative. He mouthed a word.

"More oxygen?" Jill guessed.

Again the painful negative movement of his head. Groaning, he jabbed upward with his thumb, staring into Zach's eyes like he wanted Zach to read his mind.

Suddenly Frost went slack.

"No," breathed Zach. "Damn it, no!"

He put his fingers over Frost's jugular and felt a pulse. Weak, but it was there.

"Get him to the hospital," Zach said to the med-tech. *"Now."*

No sooner had he spoken than the second med-tech called out to the firemen. Two men leaped for the truck and ran toward the house, litter basket at the ready. They loaded Frost aboard and took him past the ruined car to the ambulance.

"We'll go to Holy Cross Hospital," the female med-tech said. "If you can find the daughter, tell her to get over there quick."

Zach's lips flattened with what hadn't been said. "I'll do that."

"We'd like to ask a few questions about this shooting," said a cop as he walked in the open front door.

"Talk to her first," Zach said, jerking his thumb at Jill. "I've got to call the next of kin."

52

Taos
September 16
2:30 A.M.

Zach started up Frost's old Travel-All. The engine fired with a smooth rumble. Frost still kept his vehicles in good repair.

"Do you think the cops believed us?" Jill asked.

It was the first time they'd been alone since the guesthouse.

"Close enough," he said.

"I got real tired of repeating the same answers to the same cop, over and over again."

"Standard. The cops have a shooting and an arson to solve." *Maybe a murder, too. But, God, I hope not.* "A prominent citizen is involved. Until Frost corroborates our story, we're as close to a suspect as the cops have."

"Why would we call them if one of us shot Frost?"

"Why wouldn't we?"

Jill opened her mouth, then closed it with a sigh. "Forget I asked. My brain isn't in top form."

He lifted his right hand and ran it down her cheek. "You did fine, Jill. Better than I had a right to expect of a civilian. You kept your head and helped instead of getting in the way."

"With that and four hundred dollars . . ." She made a sound that could have been laughter, but probably wasn't. "Do you think Frost will make it?"

"He's tough." *Way too much blood. Damn near bled out in the hall.* "If they get blood into him quick enough, he'll be up and swearing in no time."

"What did his daughter say?"

"She's on her way. It will be two hours, maybe more."

Jill watched streetlights slide by either side of the windshield. There were few people out, and fewer still were sober.

"Why?" Jill asked after a minute.

Zach knew what she was asking. "It wasn't a hot prowl gone wrong. The car was the target, which meant the shooter was after the paintings."

"They're in the house."

"The shipping cartons were in the car. Add paraffin, gasoline, and light it off. Step back before it explodes in your face."

"But why shoot Garland Frost?"

"He was home," Zach said grimly. "And he's a maverick. The thought of Lee Dunstan pissing all over his appraisals wouldn't bother Frost a bit. Hell, he'd enjoy it."

"Then you think Frost was actually the target?" Jill asked, her voice strained.

"I'll ask the shooter just as soon as I get his neck between my hands."

She looked at Zach's profile. In the random illumination of streetlights and dashboard lights, he looked like a bleak stone carving. He might have argued a lot with Garland Frost, but he still cared about him.

"How did the shooter know we were here?" she asked.

"That's the problem with flight plans and rental cars. You leave a paper or electronic trail that any decent computer hacker can follow."

"All the way to Frost's house?"

"That's what I said to Faroe. He's trying to get through to the rental company, find out if our rental had a locater beacon in it, and if so, was it active."

"Why would they—never mind, Mexico."

"Yeah. A short run to the border and the thief is several thousand bucks richer."

"You think the shooter is still around here?" she asked uneasily.

She didn't like thinking about how close Frost and Zach had come to dying a few hours ago.

"We've got guards on Frost. And I'm going to stay with him until his daughter gets here. I want you with me."

He turned into the hospital parking lot and stopped close to the emergency entrance.

Jill saw two patrol cars and hoped the questions wouldn't start all over again. She didn't know if she had the patience for it.

When Zach saw the plainclothes unit next to the patrol cars, he wondered who had been assigned the case. The answer came as soon as he and Jill walked through the automatic doors into the hard-shelled sterile waiting room. Three uniformed officers were conferring with a tall, redheaded man in jeans, boots, and a hooded sweatshirt.

"Well, there's a break," Zach said under his breath. "Alton Corrigan is still in town."

The redheaded man turned and looked at them, then shook his head wearily. He crossed the waiting room, hands in the belly pocket of his sweatshirt.

"Zach, you should have stopped by to say hello before you got yourself involved in a shooting," Corrigan said. "It would have saved me a lot of trouble. Now I can't even shake your hand until my men have cleared you."

Zach nodded. "Sorry about that. How's Frost doing?"

"Surgery," Corrigan said. "One of the nurses came out a minute ago to tell us that the bullet nicked an artery. If you hadn't gotten him here quick, he would have died."

"That's her doing," Zach said, nodding toward Jill. He introduced her and added, "Alton used to be chief detective, but if he's talking about 'my men,' I'm guessing he made chief of police."

Corrigan looked hard at Jill, then back at Zach. "You two are both friends of Frost?"

"She's my client," Zach said. "We were researching some family paintings she owns. Frost was an obvious place to start."

"First time you're back in, what, five years?" he asked, looking at Zach.

"Something like that."

"And Frost didn't kick your ass right out on the street?" Corrigan shook his head. "Must be pretty special pictures you brought him."

"That's what we were trying to find out," Zach said.

"Are those pictures related to the fire-bombing of your car?"

"One minute I was asleep and the next I heard a gunshot and was up and running," Zach said. "That's all I know for sure."

"Why do I feel like you aren't telling me everything?" Corrigan asked.

Zach's smile was as weary as it was real. "Because I'm not. I'm working as an investigator for an attorney named Grace Silva Faroe. Ms. Breck is Judge Silva Faroe's client, so there's privilege attached to some of this."

Corrigan grunted.

"I've told the cops everything I know for a fact," Zach said.

"What do you suspect?" Corrigan shot back.

"Last time I checked, New Mexico law doesn't require that I tell you any or all of my speculations. But I can guarantee that I want to find out who shot Garland Frost even more than you do."

"I don't much care for it," Corrigan said bluntly, "any more than I care for hard-assing you or Ms. Breck. But if I have to, I will."

"No news there."

"Do you really think you shot the perp?" Corrigan asked.

"Not enough to send him to a hospital."

Corrigan grunted again. Then with a curt nod to Jill, he went back to his men.

53

Hollywood
September 16
8:00 A.M.

T hat's right," Score said into the phone. "The six shipping cartons are charcoal, and so is anything that was inside them."

"Stay with them anyway."

Score bit down hard on his temper. He really didn't have the patience for stakeouts, short sleep, and twitchy clients.

"How long?" he asked through clenched teeth.

"Until after the auction."

"It's your money."

"Keep that in mind."

He looked at the dead phone and slammed it into the cradle in disgust.

"Yo, boss," a voice said from outside his locked office door.

Score hit the button to release the lock. "Get in here."

"You look like hell," Amy said as she walked in. She tossed a printout on his desk.

I should fire the mouthy bitch.

"I work hard on it," Score snapped.

But not as hard as Amy did. Today her hair was pink and silver.

Score tried not to notice. He was used to the studs and rings she wore in painful places, but the ever-changing hair colors still threw him. It was like employing a chameleon.

"I was up all night with a client." He rubbed grainy eyes and tried not to wince. His right biceps felt like he'd been branded. Nothing burned like a kiss from a bullet.

Wish that auction was over. I haven't had a decent night's sleep since the bloody JPEGs went out.

He flicked a finger at the printout. "Anything good?"

"Something went down at the other end of the bug. Heard sirens, shouting, what sounded like gunfire."

Score swallowed a yawn. "Yeah? Anyone hurt?"

"Either it's real cold there or a dude named Frost bit the big one. The name came up a lot."

"Huh. He die?"

Amy didn't bother to hide her yawn. "The last time I heard anything, the female subject was on the way back from the hospital. Frost was stable, but drugged to the max. It's all in the printout."

Left-handed, Score flipped through the printout. "Looks like the bug is picking up more than it did before."

"Yeah. Must have taken the phone out of whatever was wrapped around it. But it's on and off. The subject doesn't exactly wear her sat phone as a fashion statement." Amy yawned again. "Oh, there was some talk about being followed."

Score's hand hesitated, then resumed flipping through the printout. "Who?"

"They don't know. Or if they had any ideas, they didn't discuss it in range of the bug. All they talked about was how easy it is to get flight plans and if the rental car had some kind of locater system since New Mexico is so close to that great chop shop south of the border."

Score read the section, frowned, read it again, and decided that Amy was right. So far nothing had happened to the subject that couldn't be explained by something other than a personal bug.

"Okay," he said.

"Does that mean I get some time off?"

"I'll let you know after I talk to the client. Until then, stay with the bug."

"Hell."

"It could be worse," Score said.

"How?"

"You could be looking for a job in a traveling freak show."

54

Taos
September 16
9:00 A.M.

Even though the last cops were gone, Garland Frost's circular driveway remained off limits. The arson investigators wanted to work with a "clean" scene. Zack looked out the front door of the house and was grateful the paintings hadn't been inside the rental car. It looked even worse in daylight.

He heard the back door open.

"Zach?" Jill called.

He shut the front door. "I'll meet you in the kitchen. Coffee should be ready by now."

"There is a God."

Zach smiled and rubbed at the beard that had overtaken his face. *I really should have shaved before I got in bed with Jill.*

But she hadn't complained. In fact, she'd enjoyed rubbing her palms against his cheeks. And other parts.

When he got to the kitchen, Jill was yawning and rummaging in the cupboards for coffee mugs. Her cheeks looked chapped. Her neck looked nibbled.

"Any word on Frost?" she asked.

"Same old same old." Zach got the mugs, poured the dark, lethal brew, and handed one over to her. "I wish I knew what he was trying to tell me."

"You can ask him when he wakes up." She took a sip, said "Hoo-yah!" and took a bigger swallow. "Now, that's coffee."

Zach smiled slightly. "According to the procedure the docs outlined, Frost won't wake up until the auction is over. They're pretty much keeping him in a coma."

"He survived a nicked artery, the random damage of a bullet in his midriff and a long surgery," Jill said. "Not many men his age would have made it."

"Silencer."

"What?"

"A silencer slows down the velocity of the bullet when it leaves the muzzle," Zach explained. "That's why Frost survived a hit from a 9 millimeter."

Jill shivered.

"Cold?" Zach asked. "I could light the fire."

"This coffee is better than any fire." She noticed the open computer on the kitchen table. "Working already?"

"Just checking in. Where's your sat phone?"

"In the guesthouse. Did yours finally die?"

"Thinking about it," he said. "Singh checked yesterday's flight plans on all charters out of Salt Lake to Taos."

"Good news?"

"Depends on your definition of good. Somebody took off from Salt Lake about an hour after we did and landed at Taos about eighty minutes after we did."

Jill's eyes narrowed. "Are you saying we were followed?"

"Not like a tail," he said. "They were too far back. Our flight plan was easy enough to get. The car is on a rental agency's computer, which sure can be hacked. Faroe's checking to see if the rental has a locater unit aboard. This close to the border, it's pretty common."

"I . . ." Her voice died. "I'm not used to a road with this many switchbacks."

"Yeah, some real neck twisters. And the fun would really get started if somehow, someway, we've been bugged. On the other hand, it could be a real break."

"Bugged?"

"Yeah. If we have one, and we can find it, we turn it into an asset."

"How?"

He rubbed his chin thoughtfully. "Faroe and I are arguing about that."

"Who's winning?"

"I am, and he's not liking it," Zach said.

She looked at the computer he'd been working on. The screen showed a muddy version of a Dunstan landscape.

"You need a screen with more pixels," she said. "Like Frost's."

"I'm not appraising," he said. "I'm just exploring the Dunstan art market in view of what we learned from Frost. I'd have St. Kilda do it, but they're running an unusual number of ops right now. Research is crying. So unless it's life-or-death urgent, I'm not kicking in their door."

She stared at the computer screen. "So Thomas Dunstan has his own Web site?"

"Yeah, but this one belongs to Worthington's Las Vegas auction. I've been looking at the online catalogue."

"Lousy reproduction."

"Only on my machine. Besides, the interesting thing isn't the art, it's the prices."

She bent over and tilted the screen. Immediately the picture sharpened. *Ruby Marsh* was the name of the painting. The scene was of thrusting mountains, clean blue sky, and a marshy valley turned gold with autumn. The dimensions of the canvas were huge, definitely museum size.

The price was six to eight million dollars.

Zach watched Jill's eyes widen and knew that she'd reached the bottom line.

"That painting is one of the centerpieces of the Las Vegas Auction of Fine Western Art," he said.

"Wow."

"That's one word for it. Worthington has pulled out all the stops on this one. Russell, Remington, Howard Terpning, Joseph Sharp, Blumenschein. If you believe the hype, this will be some of the best Western art in a generation to go under the gavel."

"Does Whatshisname—the big Dunstan collector—own this?" she asked, pointing to the painting called *Ruby Marsh*.

"Talbert Crawford?"

"Yes."

"No, this belongs to Dunstan's son."

"The one who savaged Waverly-Benet's reputation?"

"The same," Zach said.

"The one who said my paintings were frauds?"

"Yeah."

"Jerk," she said.

"Probably." Zach leaned over her and scrolled back through some Web pages on the computer. "Take a look at this."

Jill sat at the table, angled the computer screen again, and began reading an article with a Carson City logo and yesterday's date.

Leading figures in the State's art community
are expected to announce major donations
to the collection of paintings that will be
showcased in a new wing of the Museum of
Nevada and the West in Carson City.

Announcements planned for later in the
week will involve contributions by such
well-known collectors as Tal Crawford, prominent investor and owner of a large ranch
east of the Carson Valley.

Crawford has been engaged in discussions
with state arts officials about his plans to
contribute a number of major works to the
museum.

A spokesman for Crawford would not confirm
specific donations but did acknowledge that
the collector has accumulated "probably the
biggest collection of Western art in the
state, particularly a large number of works
by Thomas Dunstan, who is regarded as one
of the most important landscape painters in
the West.

"Mr. Crawford has always prided himself
on sharing these important works with the
rest of the world," the spokesman said.

Sources in the governor's office said they
hope to have an announcement regarding the
exact donation by next week.

"So that's what Frost meant by Bigfoot," Jill said, looking
at Zach. "Saturday. That's the auction, isn't it?" she asked.

"Day after tomorrow," he agreed absently, his mind on
Crawford, Western paintings, politics, and auctions.

"I keep thinking that what Frost was trying to tell us had
something to do with the paintings."

"A thumbs-up for authenticity?"

She frowned. "Maybe. Or maybe it had to do with the
auction itself. Got any more coffee?"

"I've been meaning to speak to you about your caffeine habit," Zach said, reaching for the pot.

"Yeah, I know. I really should drink more coffee. Beginning now." She held out her empty mug.

Smiling, Zach refilled it. "I don't think Frost gave me a thumbs-up for the authenticity of the paintings."

"Why?"

"As long as I knew Frost, he never used that particular gesture. He'd spent too much time in Australia, where it means something entirely different."

"Really? What?"

"Up your arse."

Jill sputtered, swallowed hard, and cleared her throat. "I'd like a spew alert when I'm having morning coffee."

Zach smiled, kissed her slowly, and rubbed his bristly chin. "I'll let you drink in peace. I'm going to call Faroe and have him put something on research's pile. Then I'm going to do what I should have yesterday."

"What?"

"Shave."

"Itchy?" she asked.

"How'd you guess?"

"Guys on the Colorado always complain about grow-out itch. But not as much as they whine about monkey butt."

He paused before he took a final drink of coffee. "Monkey butt?"

"You ever been to the zoo and seen the butts on female baboons when they're in heat?"

He nodded warily.

"You sit on a rowing bench in a swimsuit, rubbing back and forth as you go down the river, getting doused with gritty water at the rapids," she said, "and pretty soon you have monkey butt."

"Bright red and tender as hell?"

She nodded.

"Shaving doesn't help?"

She cringed. "Don't even think it."

"Okay. I'll go shave my monkey face." Zach started to leave, then stopped when he saw Jill eyeing his computer. "If you want to play, use Frost's computer. Mine has some tiger traps built in."

"Tiger traps and monkey butt. We're quite the pair."

Zach's whiskey-colored eyes met hers. He smiled, but his eyes were very serious. "Yeah, we are."

55

Lane Silva Faroe watched his tiny baby sister sleeping in the antique cradle next to a bank of high-tech computers. His father was talking in one phone, had a second on hold, and was participating in a conference with Ambassador Steele via computer.

His mother was up to her ears in legal texts at a nearby desk. Something about the rights of foreigners in Zimbabwe. Or maybe it was Venezuela.

And every time his little sister twitched, his parents looked at her.

Must be some kind of built-in parental radar, Lane decided.

As much as he enjoyed having a new baby sister, he was getting restless. With everyone around him so overwhelmed by work, he felt useless.

Like a baby.

Faroe hung up one phone, picked up the other, listened, and said, "I'll add it to the pile at Research, Zach. But since it isn't a code three, don't hold your breath." He hung up and made a note.

"Dad?" Lane said.

"Yeah?" Faroe answered without looking away from his notepad.

"I'm done with my homework, I've wrapped up my special project, and I want to help with the Jill Breck, uh, project."

"How?"

"Well, I heard you telling Zach that Research was jammed up and he'd have to get in line unless it was a balls-to-the-wall code three."

Faroe's mouth curved in a small smile. "Did I say that? Hope little Annalise was asleep."

"All she does is sleep and poop. And eat."

"Living is a full-time job for a baby."

"I could swarm Zach's topic."

Faroe blinked and turned toward his son. Like him, Lane was long and lanky. Unlike him, Lane hadn't grown into his frame.

Or his patience.

"Run that by me again in English," Faroe said.

"Whatever Zach wants to find out about is a topic," Lane said with exaggerated patience. "Swarming is getting together with a bunch of other key jockeys and researching a topic using all the different search engines."

"Swarming."

"Yeah. Can I? All I need is some search words."

"Give it to him," Grace said without looking up from the legal reference she was reading. "He wants to help the lady who saved his life."

Faroe checked the computer screen again. Nothing new. He looked at the notes he'd taken from Zach, then ripped off the piece of paper and handed it to his son.

"Swarm on," Faroe said.

Lane snatched the piece of paper and ran back to his room, mentally listing the online buddies he could get to help him. He knew five for sure. And each of them probably knew four or five.

And each of them. . .

Swarming.

56

Taos
September 16
9:14 A.M.

Jill gave up on the paintings and the black light. No matter how hard or long or where she looked, she didn't see anything exciting. She glanced toward Frost's computer. It was either shut down or sleeping. The screen was dark.

Maybe it wasn't something he found in the paintings.

Maybe it was something he found online.

She went to Frost's computer. Unlike Zach's, this was a Mac, the kind she owned. Except this one was twice as big. The screen was huge. But the OS was the same. She could use it with her eyes closed.

A tap on the enter key woke up the computer.

So he was using it last night.

Or he's one of those people who never shut down.

She sat at the desk and pulled the computer closer. The

screen showed the same Web site that Zach's had, but a different Dunstan painting.

Once more, Jill fell under the spell of a landscape that was both evocative and precisely detailed. Dunstan had a grasp of perspective—and an ability to execute his inner vision—that made the artist in Jill frankly envious. Dunstan's works captured the broad sweep of the West in a way that was both nineteenth-century romanticism and twentieth-century hardheaded realism.

She sighed, hesitated, and told herself that she wasn't invading someone's privacy. She just needed to find out what Frost had tried to say before he went into shock. If the computer could help her, then she had every right to use it. Too many people had been hurt since Modesty had sent the first painting out for appraisal.

It still didn't feel right to snoop in Frost's computer.

"Maybe I should wait for Zach," she said under her breath. "And maybe I should just sit in a corner and whine. Life isn't fair, much less polite. Get over it."

She went to the browser's pull-down menu and opened the "history" file. A list of the Web sites that Frost had viewed recently appeared.

Even better, there was a memory cache on the computer that gave her a choice of searching sites that had been viewed in the past hours, days, and weeks.

Again, some of the sites were ones that Zach had visited. The same, yet there was a difference she couldn't put her finger on. Not surprising. A search was as individual as the person and/or search engine that initiated it.

Web addresses for Thomas Moran dominated Frost's search. Granted, Moran was the artist Dunstan was frequently compared to, especially in terms of emotional impact, but some of the other artists Frost had viewed ran the gamut from modern to post-modern to thin slices of the art world that she'd never studied.

Then she noticed that the word *fingerprint* was in bold type at all the sites.

The kitchen door opened and closed. "Jill?"

"In the great room," she called out.

Freshly shaved and showered, Zach strode into the room. A mug of coffee steamed in his hand. He looked at her bent over the computer like a miser counting gold. Her body language was a study in intensity.

"Find anything useful?" he asked.

"I don't know."

Something in her voice made adrenaline slide into his blood, more potent than any caffeine. "What do you have?"

"After we went to bed, Frost was on the computer."

Zach smiled with hot memories. "Hope it was good for him, too."

Jill snickered, but didn't look up from the list of sites. "He was searching for fingerprints."

Zach paused in the act of drinking coffee. "Keep talking."

She gave him the highlights of the sites she'd hit so far. "In the second half of the twentieth century, it was fairly common for artists to authenticate their paintings with more than a signature. Finger- or thumbprints, mostly thumbprints."

"Too bad Dunstan was dead by then."

"So was Thomas Moran, and he used a thumbprint."

Zach came to a point. "Yeah?"

"Moran started out signing his name just like everyone else," Jill said, reading quickly from the notes she'd made. "In the middle of his life, he added a *Y* as a middle initial after art critics called him Yosemite Moran because he painted so many canvases there."

Zach wanted to tear the computer out of her hands, but restrained himself. Barely. "Anything else?"

"Then, early in the 1900s, Moran began to sign his canvases *and* leave a thumbprint along the edge of the canvas that was rolled—pulled—over the stretcher. A lot of modern artists make that part of the canvas a continuation of the painting itself. Kind of a self-frame."

Zach made a sound that said he was listening.

She read from the computer and paraphrased quickly. "One of Moran's brothers tried to cash in on the master's reputation by creating spectacularly inferior canvases and signing them 'Moran.'"

"Cheesed off old Tom, did it?"

"Sure did. Thomas Moran began to use his unique thumbprint to prove that there was only one Moran worth owning."

"Not a thumbs-up after all," Zach said, heading for the Dunstan canvases leaning against the wall. "A thumb*print*." He reached for the first canvas. "Which side?"

"Could be anywhere, even in the painting itself. Moran put it on the part of the painting that wrapped around the stretcher. That way it didn't disturb the elements of the painting. But Dunstan's paintings are more textured, so it could be anywhere and not stick out like a—"

"Don't say it."

"Sore thumb?" she asked innocently.

Zach smiled but his eyes were fierce as he examined the canvas. *Indian Springs* was certainly textured. He flipped it over and looked at the canvas wrapped around the stretcher frame.

"Right," he said. "No one could see it if canvas was framed." *And I'm not seeing it now.*

He moved to better light.

Jill picked up another canvas and held it a few inches away from her eyes, examining its surface. She saw nothing but brushstrokes and blocks of color. Then she remembered the reference to Moran's placement of his trademark on the wrapped edge of the canvas.

"Black light," Zach muttered.

"What?" she asked, caught in her own examination of a painting.

"Frost left it on," he said, holding out the lamp, pointing to the switch, which was in the "on" position.

"So?"

"So he was using it after we went to bed, and forgot to turn it off. Batteries are dead."

Zach went to the kitchen, banged around in drawers, and found batteries. He popped out the light's old batteries and replaced them. Purple light glimmered.

"Bring a painting," he said, grabbing a Dunstan at random.

Jill followed him into the walk-in vault that stored some of Frost's most valuable pieces of ancient and more recent art.

"Shut the door and turn off the light," Zack said.

As soon as she did, black light blossomed. The painting glowed in eerie transformation. All colors changed. Forms became almost three-dimensional. Brushstrokes took on an even deeper, very distinct texture. Thin spots in the coverage of the canvas and places where the artist had laid down extra pigment for esthetic effect were as clear as black print on a white page.

"Do you see anything in the painting itself?" she asked.

"Not at first glance."

"Try the edges."

He shifted the canvas in his grip, turning it so that the top edge was within the black light's magic sphere.

"See anything?" she asked.

"Paint."

He flipped the canvas at a ninety-degree angle.

Both of them stared at the new strip of canvas.

"Nothing but paint," she said.

"Yeah. Hope we don't have to go over the face of the

canvas itself," he said, turning the painting another ninety degrees. "It could take for—" His voice cut off like a switch had been thrown.

"Toward me, just a little," Jill said, her voice husky with excitement.

He tilted the painting very slightly, throwing the textures into higher relief.

"Is that what I think it is?" she said, touching the canvas lightly.

"Yeah, it is." He flipped the painting again. "On the bottom edge of the stretcher. No mistaking those ridges and whorls. Give me the canvas you have."

Jill turned the painting she carried upside down, presenting the bottom edge of the stretched canvas to the black light.

"I will be damned," Zach breathed. "Another thumbprint. Same place."

"How can you tell it's a thumb rather than a finger?"

"Experience."

"So Dunstan 'signed' even his unsigned canvases?"

"Looks like it. I'll get Frost's paintings."

Jill took the black light he handed her and tried to wait patiently for him to return with the other Dunstans.

She would have paced, but the vault was too small.

It got even smaller when Zach returned with the two larger canvases. He turned them bottom side up and leaned them against a case of ancient red and black pottery. He tilted the black light.

Jill stared at the strips of canvas. "There, a few inches from the corner."

"Just like the other ones."

Frost's second canvas had a thumbprint as well.

"I'll get the rest of my paintings," she said.

Very quickly the vault was lined with upside-down paintings.

All of them had a thumbprint along the bottom edge of the stretcher, a few inches in from the right side.

"You're frowning," Jill said. "You should be grinning and giving me high fives."

"I'm just wondering how unknown thumbprints will stack up in court against droit moral and the entire Western art establishment."

"*Unknown* thumbprints? Don't you think it stretches credulity to believe that someone other than Dunstan put his thumbprint on all these canvases?"

"Lawyers live to stretch credulity. It's how they make money." Zach said something under his breath. "If only Dunstan had lived twenty years later, his fingerprints would be on file somewhere."

"They might be."

Zach's head snapped around toward her. "Where?"

"Canyon County jail in Blessing. That's where he hung himself."

"They took fingerprints?"

"All the lawmen in the Purcell family were medieval in their views of women," Jill said, "but the men prided themselves on being on the cutting edge of law enforcement."

"Polygamy excepted?"

"There's no polygamy in the Mormon West," she said sardonically. "That's just a figment of prurient media imagination. Doesn't exist."

"Makes it a lot easier not to find something if you aren't looking for it."

"Is your middle name Purcell?"

"God, I hope not." He grabbed her, kissed her soundly, then released her slowly. "We've got too much to do for what I really want to do."

She took a deep breath. "Right. What comes first?"

"I call St. Kilda and start spending money."

"Start? You've been doing that since we met."

"You ain't seen nothing yet. Framing pictures costs as much as chartering planes."

"Why are you framing pictures?"

"First thing Frost taught me was that when it comes to selling art, presentation is all." Zach pulled his sat phone out of his back pocket and looked at the battery indicator. Deader than Kelsey's nuts. "Where's your sat phone?"

"Cell is cheaper."

"St. Kilda will pay."

"I'll get it."

Zach started making lists in his mind. When Jill returned, he took the phone and punched in some numbers. Then he punched in more numbers. Finally he talked to someone long enough to get transferred to Joe Faroe.

"Faroe here. How's Frost doing and what happened to your phone?"

"As well as can be expected and the battery died," Zach said. "I'm running barefoot, so listen up. I need the same cargo experts I had for yesterday's flight, and I need them now. Make sure they come ready to party. Have them bring an extra car. And another airplane card. Mine's about done and I need it for at least one flight immediately."

"How's your own party gear?" Faroe asked.

Zach felt the weight of the pistol in the holster digging into the small of his back. "Ready, willing, and waiting for an invitation to dance."

"Hold."

He waited with outward patience while Faroe called logistics and got everything in order.

"Bet Faroe is regretting the day he insisted on running this whole op himself," Zach said to Jill. "I outright love giving that man gofer orders."

"Have I mentioned that you're a real Y gene?"

"You didn't complain about it after dinner."

She smiled slowly. "Sometimes Y genes have a place."

"Yeah, and it's right between—" Zach broke off and listened.

"You'll have what you need in half an hour," Faroe said. "And you'll have a new sat/cell phone, too. Try not to kill it before the op is over. What's your destination?"

Zach thought quickly and then shrugged. They had to file flight plans, and flight plans were public. "Closest airport to Blessing, Arizona, and a car on that end."

"Hold."

Faroe was gone for only a few moments. "Go to the All West charter agency. A plane will be waiting for you. There will be a car on the other end. Where do you want the cargo to go?"

"I'll tell you when I'm not running barefoot."

"I'll be waiting for your call."

Faroe punched out before Zach could.

57

Blessing, Arizona
September 16
2:30 P.M.

Sheriff Ned Purcell made Jill and Zach wait for twenty minutes in his outer office. They sat side by side on two straight-backed wooden chairs, like truants waiting for the vice principal.

Zach shifted on the hard chair and looked over at the receptionist, who also ran the sheriff's communications center. The desk nameplate announced that she was Margaret Kingston.

"Would things go a little faster if we told you we chartered a jet to get here?" Jill asked.

Her voice was sharp. She was the designated bad guy for this duo. Zach hadn't trusted her to hide her irritation with Purcell's patriarchal Latter-day Saints approach to civil law.

The receptionist held up a hand, asking for a moment,

then continued toggling switches back and forth, checking records and relaying text messages to units in the field.

"I told the sheriff that you were out here with a man," the receptionist said finally, "and that you wanted to talk about your grandmother, who died a long time ago. Not exactly a life-or-death emergency."

With that the woman gave her attention back to situations that were more urgent than something that had happened before she was born.

"All we really want is to go through some of the old jail records," Jill said.

"Still need the sheriff," the receptionist said.

"Why?" Zach asked.

"That's the way it's done around here," the receptionist said as she picked up a ringing telephone.

Zach started to tell her what a waste of everyone's time that was, remembered that he was the clean-shaved good guy, and shut up.

The door to the inner office opened. Ned Purcell stuck out his head and gave them the kind of look a plumber gives an overflowing toilet. He jerked his head toward his office, then turned to the receptionist. "Hold my calls for a few minutes, honey."

"Yes, sir."

Jill looked at the sheriff walking back into his office and then at the receptionist. "*Honey*? In the real world, that's called demeaning at best, sexual harassment at worst. Unless, of course, you're one of his very own honeys?"

Kingston ignored her.

So did the sheriff.

"Ease up, darling," Zach said calmly. "The sheriff didn't mean anything disrespectful."

Jill bit off what she wanted to say and gave Zach an adoring look. "I'm sure you're right, sugar-buns."

"Close the door behind you," was all the sheriff said.

He settled down in his high-backed leather chair, reached for a can of Diet Coke that sweated on the leather blotter, and took a drink.

Zach looked at Jill. "Diet Coke? I thought you said the sheriff was an elder in the Church of the Latter-day Saints."

"They call Diet Coke 'Mormon tea,'" she said. "It wasn't around when Joseph Smith got the good word about coffee and tea being evil, so a lot of Mormons figure soda is okay."

Zach closed the door. "Learn something new every day."

"You want something from me, or are you just polishing a comedy act?" Purcell asked.

Zach knew the sheriff would prefer to do business with another man, but he was real tempted to give Jill her head anyway, just for the sport of it. He'd known many men in Purcell's generation who just hadn't gotten the message that women were people. Men like the sheriff weren't necessarily stupid or corrupt—they were just set in their ways. Like old concrete.

"The last time Jill was here," Zach said easily, "you told her that you had records from a time when her grandmother Justine Breck and Thomas Dunstan were brought in. Drunk and disorderly, I believe."

Purcell nodded, looking both official and bored—yet he watched Zach with the direct, hard eyes of a man used to summing up other men. He took another swig of Diet Coke.

"Do you still have the record of the arrest?" Zach asked.

"It turned out to be more than D & D," Purcell said. "Justine had a .22 rifle. Said her lover was threatening her, so she shot him. He claims that she was the one doing the threatening. She was too drunk to aim good, thank the Lord. Sure did take the starch out of him, though. Bullet burns do that to a man." He set down the soda. "Anything else? I'm busy."

"Were charges brought?" Zach asked.

"Darn right they were," Purcell said. "Can't have a woman shooting a man right on the main street of Blessing."

"Might give the other women ideas," Jill said sweetly.

Zach quickly asked, "Was Justine Breck kept in the jail here?"

"The old jail, actually," the sheriff said. One-handed he crushed the soda can and tossed it into the wastebasket. "We used it for females after the new jail was built. Didn't have but one or two of them. Women were too busy taking care of families to get into trouble."

Jill said something under her breath.

"What kind of booking procedure was used in those days?" Zach asked, ignoring her comment about sister-wives with the fertility of rabbits and the intelligence of dirt.

"The best available at the time," Purcell said. "The men in my family have always been forward thinkers. Photographs, fingerprints, defense lawyers, speedy trials, everything they have back East, we have in Blessing. We might be at the end of the map, but we're not stupid about the law."

Zach nodded and squeezed Jill's shoulder in warning. They needed the records and the sheriff was the gate-keeper.

"Yes," Zach agreed. "I've heard good things about this county. Probably comes from having a long line of sheriffs who were raised to do the job right."

Jill bit her tongue hard enough to leave skid marks.

Purcell nodded. His posture relaxed. "We take our obligations seriously. That's not something a lot of city folks understand."

"Did Justine Breck go on trial?" Zach asked.

The sheriff grimaced. "Breck's lawyer was too smart to

go for a jury trial. The judge was an outsider, new to the job. He felt sorry for Justine, because her lover up and hung himself, so he went against my father's advice and let the Breck woman go after a few weeks. But the judge did tell her if he ever saw her in court again, he'd throw the book at her. For a wonder, she listened. We never had trouble with her again."

"We'd like to see the booking records," Zach said.

"Why?"

"Zach's boss was once a federal judge and is now a high-powered lawyer," Jill said. "She assured me that such records are public. If you don't agree with her, she'll have a warrant here before you can say Mormon tea."

"She?" Purcell said, sighing.

"Yeah, what's the world coming to," Zach said sympathetically. "Women lawyers and judges. Next thing you know, process servers and sheriffs will be women."

"Want to place a bet on the gender of the person who shows up with a warrant for the records?" Jill asked.

"Slow down, darling," Zach said. "The sheriff is just doing his job. It's not an easy one. Some days the citizens are worse than the crooks."

Purcell looked at Zach for the space of a long breath. Whatever he saw tipped the balance. Zach wasn't bluffing and he wasn't insulting a small-town sheriff.

Best of all, Zach was keeping the pushy Breck woman in line.

"Hope you do better with her than other men have done with Breck women," Purcell said as he reached for the telephone and hit the intercom to the receptionist. "Call the records department and tell them two people are coming by to get dusty."

58

Hollywood
September 16
2:25 P.M.

As soon as the outer door opened, Amy leaped to her feet. "It's about time you got back from lunch."

"My office, now," Score said.

He was in a pisser of a mood.

The way this case keeps eating up my time, you'd think I had only one client.

A really important one.

"Shut the door," Score said. He sat down at his desk and fought against the kind of burp that made his eyes water.

Goat cheese. Who decided that men should eat that stuff on a pizza and be polite about it?

But what really had given him indigestion was the client, a Hollywood mover and shaker who was getting shaken down by someone and wanted to kick some ass in return.

When will they learn to leave underage boys alone?

Not that Score was complaining. Much. When people turned into saints, he'd be out of a job.

"Well?" he said to Amy.

"She's on the move again. Back to good old Blessing, Arizona."

"Huh." He found a roll of stomach mints and crunched up three of them. "What for?"

"She's talking to the sheriff."

"About what?"

"Her grandmother's arrest."

What does that have to do with the paintings? Score thought. "So?"

"Well, except for one call, she wasn't close to the bug, so I couldn't hear anything until they left for the airport from Taos." Absently Amy tested the holding power of her hair gel with her fingertips. Starting to droop. So was she. She'd worked through lunch.

"What call?" Score demanded.

She flipped to the next page of the printout. "The op reported in to St. Kilda, using the subject's sat phone."

"What'd he say?"

"Asked for the same cargo handlers as yesterday and—"

"I told you to get in touch with me ASAP if paintings were mentioned," Score cut in.

The bite in his voice made Amy flinch.

"Nobody said anything about paintings," she said quickly. "Is that what the cargo was?"

Score didn't know the answer to that question, but was afraid that the word "cargo" would cover twelve paintings quite nicely.

They must have been in the house, not the car.

There was nothing he could do about it right now. Except swallow hard, keep his temper, and chew up some more stomach mints.

"When did this happen?" he asked.

Amy winced. When Score got that tone in his voice, pink slips started arriving on desks. She didn't want hers to be one of them.

"The conversation took place at 9:42," she said.

"Any talk about where the cargo is going?" Score asked.

"No."

Score went still. His stomach clenched, sending goat cheese on a burning return trip. "Anything else?"

"The subject has already landed in Blessing, Arizona. The bug must be close because it's real clear."

"What about the cargo? Is it with them?"

"No. All the op said to her was that it was in a safe place."

Damn St. Kilda anyway. What are they doing involved in a totally domestic op?

Goat cheese kept trying to claw its way back up Score's throat. He fought it to a draw and snarled, "Cut to the chase."

"They went to see the Canyon County sheriff in Blessing," Amy said, summarizing the transcript of the bug. "Wanted to look at Justine Breck's arrest report."

"Huh. Why would they care? It happened a long time ago."

Amy shrugged. "I don't know. Apparently the grandmother and some dude had the kind of drunken shouting match that ended up with him being shot and both of them in jail."

"Him who? Did they say?"

"Not by name. All I know is that he was her lover. And he hung himself in jail."

Score drummed his fingers on his desk and wondered what St. Kilda was up to now. This case had been nothing but one screw-up after another. He was getting real close to losing his temper and beating the crap out of the first person he got his hands on.

It would feel so good.

"Anything else?" he asked.

"They're going to look at the records. And the bug is working real clear."

"No mention of paintings?"

"No. Just some comments about the Frost guy and the fact that he won't be talking to anyone for a few days. Something about a coma."

Well, at least that worked, Score consoled himself. *About time I caught a break. Now if only I could be certain that those paintings had burned.*

Or certain that they hadn't.

Worst case scenario: They didn't burn and St. Kilda has them now. Which means this op is well and truly in the shitter.

I should have shot the bitch instead of the old man. She's the one causing all the trouble.

Score belched and swore never to eat goat cheese again, no matter who the client was. "I want to know where they go after Blessing. Stay with it until Steve gets here."

"When will that be?"

"When he taps you on the shoulder. If you hear anything about paintings—"

"Tell you ASAP," Amy cut in. "Got it the first ten times you told me."

She made it out the door before Score lost it and started kicking the desk.

59

San Diego
September 16
2:29 P.M.

Grace picked up the phone. "Zach? Faroe's tied up."

"How about you?" Zach said.

"Make it quick."

"Can St. Kilda have a warrant for public records regarding the arrest of Justine Breck and Thomas Dunstan in Canyon County, Arizona in . . ."

Grace shifted the baby to her other arm and started writing. "Did you get photos of the thumbprints on Jill's paintings?"

"Yeah, but only for insurance. A fingerprint expert will need better photos. The thumbprint is hard to see except with black light. Dunstan used a lot of texture, plus the frames on Frost's paintings added a certain amount of wear."

"But the thumbprints on each canvas looked the same to you?"

"Sure did. That makes it damn near certain that Dunstan painted Jill's canvases."

"Then they're worth a lot of money."

"Multimillions, according to the estimates in the auction catalogue. But if all her paintings come on the market at the same time, it could lower the price," Zach said. "Or maybe it would create a feeding frenzy. Who knows? Collectors are a screwy lot."

"We'll be real careful to get good photos of her paintings," Grace said. "Any idea how much paper we're talking about for the warrant?"

"I'll tell you as soon as we know." At the other end of the line, Zach heard a very young baby's fretful cry. "Feeding time at the zoo?"

"She'll last another few seconds. When do you want the records picked up?"

"Yesterday. Too many things have burned, if you know what I mean."

"Just make sure Jill isn't one of them."

"She's within reach at all times," Zach assured her.

Grace smiled. "*All* times?"

He cleared his throat. "I'll call when we need something else."

"How's the new sat/cell working?"

"So far so good."

Faroe hung up just as Grace did.

"Anything wrong?" Faroe asked.

"Not with the new phone. So far."

"That man has a weird electrical field. Goes through batteries—even the rechargeable kind—like grass through a goose. What did he want?"

"A warrant for public records."

Faroe's eyebrows lifted. "If they're public, why bother?"

"Zach says too many things have burned so far."

"He has a point."

The fretful cries became more urgent.

Faroe said, "Give her to me. I'll change her while you do the legal stuff."

"You can change her after she eats." Grace opened her blouse and began nursing the baby. "I can write one-handed. Has anybody heard from Ambassador Steele on the Brazilian money-laundering payoff?"

"Accounting is depositing our percentage of the finder's fee as we speak."

"Good. At the rate Zach's spending money, we'll need an infusion of cash. Where is our closest fingerprint expert?"

Faroe bent over his computer, punched keys, waited. "She's in L.A."

"Put her on standby notice as of now."

60

Score picked up the phone with a snarled "Yeah?"

"It's Amy. You better get over here quick. They're talking paintings and fingerprints and—"

Score hung up and headed for the basement cubbyhole that was Amy's office.

As he closed his office door behind him, his phone rang.

He didn't even hesitate.

"It's—" began his receptionist.

"Take a message," he interrupted curtly.

He shut the outer door, leaving the receptionist to handle an unhappy client.

Score didn't care. He had his own problems.

The paintings are safe. Mother of all screw-ups.

Damage control would be a bitch.

61

Blessing, Arizona
September 16
2:33 P.M.

The boxes were coated with a red-brown dust that came from decades in the desert. Despite the looks of the boxes, the contents were mostly in order, filed by date and name. Sometimes the files were done by department, then date, then name. Sometimes by category of crime. Sometimes by a personal filing system that made little sense to someone else.

After a series of trials and errors based on various combinations of name, date, and department, Jill came up with police reports and trial exhibits of all ten criminal proceedings that had taken place the year Justine Breck decided to shoot Thomas Dunstan.

"Got it," Jill said, then sneezed.

"Bless you," Zach said. "What do you have?"

"*State* v. *Justine Breck*." She waved an oak-tag accordion file and fought back another sneeze. "This place has less ventilation than a cellar." She reached into her belly bag and scrounged around until she found a tissue that was almost as old as she was.

Zach took the files while she wiped her nose. He walked away, smacked the file against his thigh to get rid of some dust, and handed the whole thing back to her.

"Your family, your file," he said.

Jill untied the bow knot in the cord that held the file closed. As the cord came undone, she spread the file wide and went through it quickly, looking for the kind of cards that held fingerprints.

It didn't take long.

"Well, bless the sheriff's upright old heart," she said, pulling out two half-sheets of thick paper.

Zach managed not to grab them from her.

"Justine Meredith Breck and Thomas Langley Dunstan," she said. "Arrested for D&D, ADW, and other bad choices. And yes, we have thumbprints!"

She held the papers out to Zach. The top of each half sheet was a form detailing name, age, date of birth, booking date, and all the other minutiae required for proper jail records. The bottom of each sheet was divided into a grid, five squares across and two down.

Each square of the grid was marked with a smudge of black ink.

Zach took the fingerprint cards and held them so that the light from the narrow basement window fell across them. "Score a few for the good guys."

"You can use them?"

"Oh yeah. Hold the cards while I photograph them."

"Both cards?"

"Before the case ever gets to court," he said, "the lawyer

in me wants to put paid to the argument that it might be the framer's—or a lover's—sticky thumbprints on the paintings."

"Reasonable doubt?"

"Not really," Zach said, pulling a camera out of his back pocket, "but who says people—especially juries—are reasonable? Think O.J. Simpson."

"I'd rather not, thanks. Want me to hold the sheets?"

"Yes. Over there. I'll use the macro setting and as much natural light as possible."

"Why the photos?" Jill asked. "I thought St. Kilda was sending someone with a warrant to pick up the originals."

"Think of it as fire insurance."

The door opened and Sheriff Purcell walked in. "What's this about fire?"

"Just an observation on how easily old papers burn," Zach said.

"That's why the sign says No Smoking." Purcell shifted and looked at the file Jill was holding protectively. "See you figured out the filing system."

No thanks to you, she thought grimly, *or the dragon at the front desk.* "It has a few odd kicks to its gallop," Jill said, "but we figured it out."

"What are you doing with those papers?" he asked Zach.

"Taking pictures." Zach's voice was pleasant, matter-of-fact.

Purcell frowned. "You didn't say anything about pictures."

"We didn't want to go through the red tape for a full copy of the file," Zach said. "Your people have better things to do than chase old paper for us. Don't worry, we're being very careful with the originals."

"There's a public copy machine on the first floor. Dime a sheet," the sheriff said.

"Thanks for the offer," Zach said, "but we can do it faster with a digital camera, and with less potential harm to the originals."

Purcell watched for a few minutes in silence. "Mind telling me what this is about?"

"I'm afraid that comes under the heading of privilege," Zach said easily, "and right now we don't have any reason to think you're involved in our research for this case." He turned to Jill. "Just hit the high spots, darling. We can always come back if we need to."

"No problem, sugar-buns," she said, spreading out the documents she'd chosen on top of dusty cartons. "High spots and no detours."

Purcell started to say something, then shrugged and walked out.

"Can you hold that letter real flat for me?" Zach asked. "Handwriting is tricky."

Jill went to Zach's side, carefully straightened and held down an old piece of paper, then waited until he told her to turn it over. Working as a team, they copied the documents in the file folder. Then they replaced everything, photographed the file back in its box, and photographed the dates on the outside of the carton.

Fire insurance.

62

Blessing, Arizona
September 16
2:56 P.M.

Y ou drive," Zach said, getting into the passenger side of
the too-small rental car. Last-minute reservations were a
pain in the butt. Literally.

Jill took off her belly bag and threw it in the backseat.
The car had been designed for a planet where people's legs
were shorter than their arms.

"Where are we going?" she asked.

"Same airport we came from."

"And then?"

"Depends on what I find in the files."

While Jill left the town of Blessing in her rearview mir-
ror, Zach transferred photos from his camera to the computer. Before he opened the first file, he copied everything
and sent it to St. Kilda.

More fire insurance.

Then he began to read.

"Hello?" Jill said after a while. "I'm part of this dynamic duo, remember?"

Zach looked at her. "So far it's just Breck family history. I figured you already knew it."

"You figured wrong."

Smiling slightly, he went back to the first document and began summarizing for Jill.

"Your grandmother, Justine Breck, and Thomas Dunstan were arrested by Deputy Joel Purcell near the City Tavern."

"Where's that?"

"Just outside Blessing city limits," Zach said.

"Figures. It's called the Watering Hole now. Canyon County is dry. Technically it's a private club, because private clubs are allowed to sell booze. In the real world the entry fee you pay at the door is called a cover charge."

He snickered. "Can't figure out which chaps you the most—hypocrisy or patriarchy."

"I'll let you know when I decide."

"Seems like your grandmother and Dunstan had been celebrating the Fourth of July, but things went south."

"What happened?" Jill asked.

"Well, according to the bartender—can you believe his name was Truly Nolan?"

"Unfortunately, yes."

Zach shook his head. "Anyway, the bartender heard Justine and Dunstan arguing. A real shouting match."

"Over what?"

"Didn't make sense to anyone listening, but that's the way it goes with a lot of drunken brawls. According to the bartender, Dunstan 'took it' for a bit. Then he hauled off and backhanded Justine across the mouth."

Jill's hands flexed on the steering wheel. "Sweet guy."

"You know how those artists are. Real sensitive. He hit her so hard her chair fell over backward and she was tossed into another table's drinks. Then he jumped on top of her and tried to strangle her. Things got real lively after that."

"Strangle her?"

"Yeah. He lost it, big-time. This was in the days before air-conditioning, and something tells me it gets real hot around Blessing on the Fourth of July," Zach drawled.

"Well over a hundred degrees. And that doesn't include the wind, dry as sandpaper and hot as hell," Jill said. "Wonder what they were doing in Blessing?"

"Besides drinking and fighting? Painting. At least that's what Dunstan said, and his clothes had the stains to prove it. Seems he loved to paint the area around the Breck ranch, from Blessing to the canyon rim, Indian Springs to the places where sagebrush died and creosote took over."

"Is that in the report?" Jill asked, surprised.

"It's called reading between the lines. And some research I did while we were waiting to see if Frost would make it out of surgery."

"Dunstan's catalogue raisonné. You were reading it like it held the secret of life or death."

Or maybe just sanity.

All Zach said was "Good old Truly Nolan broke up the brawl with the ax handle he kept under the bar. When the dust settled, Justine was gone. Dunstan took off after her. He was about fifty feet inside the city limits when she started yelling, 'You'll never hit me again, you son of a bitch!' Then she shot him with a .22 rifle."

"The Breck family snake gun," Jill said. "Modesty still used it—when it didn't jam, which was most of the time."

"It didn't jam that night. Justine fired and kept on firing until she ran out of bullets."

"Or it jammed."

"Other than burning Dunstan's butt with a shot, she missed," Zach said.

"Pity. If I'd been around, I would have given her my Colt Woodsman. Or I'd have shot the bastard myself."

He slanted her a sideways look. "Remind me never to piss you off."

"Don't worry. The family snake gun didn't survive the fire."

"It's your Woodsman I'm worried about."

She smiled crookedly. "I pawned it to get money for school books."

He wanted to hug her. Instead, he kept talking. "Once Justine ran out of ammo—"

"—or the rifle jammed," Jill said.

"—the deputy arrested her and hauled her off in cuffs."

"What about Dunstan?" Jill demanded. "He was the one trying to strangle her."

"Oh, they got around to arresting him, too," Zach said. "Just as soon as the local doc finished pouring whiskey over the bullet burn and bandaging Dunstan's butt."

"Then what?"

"The patriarchy you know and love kicked in."

"Meaning?"

"Justine was charged with attempted murder. Dunstan went down for public drunkenness. He got a night in the cooler."

The knuckles on Jill's hands showed white on the wheel, but all she said was "Strangling doesn't count as attempted murder?"

"Not when she was a mouthy bitch who had it coming." Zach's lips twisted into something a lot colder than a smile.

"You sound like you agree with Dunstan," she said.

"More like I've read one too many domestic disturbance reports. Makes me wish I had a time machine."

"Why?"

"I'd finish what Justine started. I have no patience for a man who belts women around."

The very neutrality of Zach's voice made Jill's stomach clench. She hoped he never used that tone on her.

She let out a long breath. "Sorry. I was taking out what I was feeling on you."

The back of his fingers skimmed over her jaw. "It's okay. I don't wilt if a woman gets mad."

"A lifetime of older sisters?"

"Real good training," he agreed. He stroked her again, then went back to the computer. "When the deputy checked on Dunstan at breakfast, he was dead. Hung himself with his belt."

"A great painter and a miserable human being," Jill said. "R.I.P."

There was silence while Zach read more documents.

When he finished with all the court papers he said, "Nothing new. Just bureaucracy at work. Justine pleaded self-defense. The judge slapped her wrist for public drunkenness and discharging a firearm within city limits, and limited the punishment to time already served, plus a year of probation, blah blah blah."

"Like Sheriff Purcell told us—the judge was new to Canyon County. Is that all that was in the file? What about the handwritten letter?"

"It was listed under Dunstan's property. Must have had it on him when he was arrested."

"So read it to me," Jill said.

"Handwriting is spidery. The light wasn't real good when I took the picture. Ink is faded."

"Meaning you can't read it?"

"Meaning I'll have to PhotoShop it." Zach called up another program, ran the JPEGs of the letter through the works, and came out with something that was close to read-able. "Okay, here we go. It's dated about two weeks before Dunstan died."

Jill let out a long breath. And waited.

And waited.

She glanced over. Zach was reading with an expression of shock on his face.

"What is it?" she demanded.

"If it's what I think it is, the last half of the pin just came out of the grenade."

"What are you talking about?"

"Be glad you're sitting down. The letter is from Justine to Dunstan." Zach started reading aloud. "'By the time you read this, I will be gone. My mother and grandmother both had husbands who raised their fists to their wives. Even if you were my husband, I would not take your beating with folded hands and pleas for mercy from you or your God.'"

Jill muttered something and flexed her fingers. "I wish she'd shot him in the balls."

"Way too small a target." Zach continued reading, "'Whatever we had is as dead as yesterday's fire. I should never have taken you as a lover. Not because it was a sin against God and society, but because you are a liar and a cheat. You used me for your own ends; then you beat me be-cause your pride was humbled by my talent. We both know the truth, even if we never spoke it aloud. Without me, your fame as an artist is at an end, for I am far more than your Scarlet Muse.'"

Jill made an odd sound.

Zach kept reading aloud. "'To paint honestly I must live honestly. Do not think to write me and tell me how much you love me. Do not think to beg forgiveness for something you will surely do again if I permit it. It is not within me to forgive any more than it is within you to leave your loveless, respectable marriage.'" Zach shook his head. "It's signed Justine."

"Now what?" Jill asked.

Instead of answering, Zach went back to the computer, opened files, compared JPEGs from the arrest with the best photos he'd taken of the bottom edge of Frost's Dunstan paintings. Frowning, Zach zoomed in and compared some more. He was no expert, but it looked to him like a match.

He started laughing softly.

"What?" Jill asked.

"Just thinking of Worthington and his oration about the essence of masculinity and Duncan's iconic status in Western art. Guess Justine must have clanged when she walked."

"Are you saying . . . ?"

"I sure am. Justine wasn't Dunstan's Scarlet Muse," Zach said. "The thumbprints on the paintings are hers, not his. She was the artist. All he did was put a man's name on the finished canvas."

"That's why the family paintings weren't signed by Dunstan," Jill said "But they're as much a Dunstan as anything he did sign. What is the going rate for 'Dunstans' in the auction catalogue?"

"Enough to make murder real profitable."

63

Hollywood
September 16
3:35 P.M.

Score read the transcript, reread it, and then read it a third time. Though his face was flushed, his hand was fairly steady as he set the transcript aside and looked at his eager employee.

"Well, that wraps it up," he said, forcing a smile. "You earned yourself a few days off. See you next Monday."

"Yes!" Amy said with a force that made her hair bounce.

She rushed out of his office, shutting the door hard behind her in case her boss changed his mind.

Score fisted his hands and glared at the door like a man hoping for . . . something.

Anything.

Just not what he already had.

There weren't many options left. St. Kilda had the paintings, which meant that it would take a truck bomb to destroy them. He didn't fancy his chances of walking away from that kind of op free, much less alive.

At least Frost is out of the picture, Score thought angrily. *Hurray for our side.*

The Breck bitch is a lot easier to get to. Take her out of the game, and the game's over.

And there's just one op with her.

He sat in the chair for a long time, vibrating with anger, thinking about ways and means of "accidental" death.

Fire was his personal favorite, but he wasn't inclined to use it again. Kidnapping and disposal was an option. Unfortunately, it would take more than one person to do it right. Another person was a potential witness for the prosecution.

Or a potential blackmailer.

Drowning was good, but the targets were a long way from deep water. Car crashes worked only if the local coroner had the brains of a flea. Otherwise an autopsy would prove that the victims were dead before the crash. A robbery gone wrong was an old favorite, but not his first or even his second choice.

He really didn't want St. Kilda crawling up his ass. Word on the street was that if a St. Kilda op died on the job, Ambassador Steele got even. Always.

No matter how long it took.

But only if there's a trail of blame to follow.

Score thought about calling the client and saying, *Sorry, no can do. Here's my bill.*

It might be the smart thing to do.

And it would be really dumb for business. When word got out that he'd turned a straightforward black-bag job into a gigantic goat roping, he'd lose his high-end clients real quick.

When the reputation that kept him in business was part of the ante, busting out of the game wasn't an option.

Motionless but for the pulse beating hard in his neck, Score went through everything again, thinking through the probable fallout from each course of action, all the ways of clouding the blame trail, leaving someone else to take the fall with St. Kilda or the law.

Then he went through the options all over again, searching for anything that he might have overlooked the first time through. When his temper was riding him, he had to be extra careful.

He read the transcript a fourth time. After a few more minutes of thinking, he put the sheets through the cross-shredder, along with every other piece of paper from this case. When the confetti machine finally fell silent, he was a little calmer. He keyed his way into the mainframe computer, accessed Amy and Steve's machines, and erased everything to do with the case.

Then he wiped the master files.

And the hard disks that had held them.

Score had used enough computer files in court to know that they were a double-edged sword. He didn't want anything coming back on this case to bite his ass.

When he was sure he'd cleaned up all traces of the case in the business computers, he reached for the phone. Blowing smoke was a long chance, but it was the best chance he had of winning the game.

And he *would* win.

They didn't call him Score for nothing.

64

Snowbird
September 16
4:10 P.M.

Ramsey, you better take this," Cahill said. "Lee Dunstan calling from Las Vegas."

Irritably Worthington looked up from overseeing the last of the auction's paintings being loaded into a van for the trip to the airport. "What's his problem?"

"Something you don't want me yelling across a crowded room."

With a hissed word, Worthington turned to the people loading the van. "All right, you have your instructions. I expect to see every one of these paintings and sculptures fully and completely intact when I get to the Golden Fleece tonight."

"Yes, sir," the boss said. She turned and called over her shoulder at a young man who'd stumbled on the loading ramp, "Slow down, Murphy. You're not at UPS anymore. Nobody's holding a stopwatch on you."

Worthington turned and stalked through the back entrance of the gallery, where Cahill was waiting.

"I don't have time to hold Lee's hand," Worthington said savagely.

"You have time for him on this. Trust me."

Worthington disengaged the hold button and said with false cheer, "Hello, Lee. Getting excited about the auction?"

"You could say that." At the other end of the line, Lee gave his wife a defiant salute with a half-empty whiskey glass and took an eye-watering swallow. "Ramsey, old buddy, we have a problem. The bitch is back."

"Are you drunk?" Worthington asked in a clipped voice.

"Getting there. So will you when the auction blows up in your face on Sunday. The ten million a painting that everyone is counting on will be lucky to be half that."

"Sweet Jesus." Worthington tried for patience. The closest he got was "I don't have time to listen to your drunken blather."

"Too bad." Lee smiled grimly. He hadn't allowed himself a tear-down-the-town drunk in a long time. He was looking forward to it. Maybe he'd never wake up. "You've got less than two days to prove that Justine Breck didn't paint what Thomas Dunstan signed."

Worthington looked at the ceiling, but there weren't any answers. "Is Betty there?"

Lee looked at the pale, strained face of his wife. She was dressed in the worn jeans and faded work shirt of the rancher's daughter she once had been.

"She ain't the bitch I'm talking about," Lee said.

With a silent curse, Worthington covered the phone pickup and snarled at Cahill. "What the hell is happening?"

"All I know is that Lee Dunstan is saying that his daddy didn't paint the Thomas Dunstans we'll be auctioning off Sunday," Cahill said. "Justine Breck did."

"Ridiculous," Worthington snapped. He took his hand off the phone. "I don't have time for this nonsense. Put Betty on the line."

"Sure. I need another whiskey anyway." Lee motioned to his wife. "He wants to talk to you."

Betty watched her husband walk toward the hotel's liquor cabinet. He wasn't staggering yet, but he would be soon.

I knew it was too good to be true, she thought bitterly. *Five million a painting was outrageous. Ten million was just plain greedy.*

She picked up the phone. "I'm sorry, Ramsey. Tal just called and was screaming at Lee so hard I heard him clear across the room. So Lee called you."

Worthington dug his thumb into the skin between his eyebrows, trying to shut down the headache that had come out of nowhere. "What the hell is going on?"

"His wife picked up a blind call warning that someone was going to try to sink the auction by claiming our paintings were done by Justine Breck, not Thomas Dunstan."

"Betty, Betty." Worthington's thumb dug in deep enough to leave a crescent mark from his nail. "It would take far more than an unsubstantiated rumor to convince someone of any artistic sophistication at all that the Dunstans aren't exactly what we know they are—paintings by one of our greatest Western artists. A competitor is simply trying to cause trouble before the auction. A tempest in a teapot, that's all." *Or a bit of extortion. Hardly the first time—or the last.*

"But what about the thumbprint?" she asked.

Worthington wondered how Betty knew that he was trying to dig a hole in his forehead with his thumb. "What thumbprint?"

"The ones on the Dunstan paintings that belong to Justine, not to Thomas Dunstan."

"Betty." Worthington took a better grip on the phone and his exasperation. *It's always something before a big auction, and it's always at the worst possible time.* "Even if his lover's fingerprints were all over the canvases, all it would prove is that Justine was with Dunstan when the paintings were created. Since Dunstan didn't paint unless his Scarlet Muse was with him, finding her fingerprints on the canvas would hardly be earth-shattering. Even if the identity of the owner of the purported fingerprints could be proved, which is highly doubtful."

"But Tal was so upset."

"I'll call Tal and straighten things out. Are you in Las Vegas now?"

"Yes."

"Keep a lid on Lee. The less said, the better."

Betty looked at the man pouring whiskey into a tumbler and sighed. "I'll do what I can." She hesitated. "This will make the paintings less valuable, won't it?"

"Don't worry," Worthington said. "And keep Lee away from the public until he's sober. If you get a call from anyone offering to sell new Dunstans to you, pass the call on to me."

"Why would anyone want to sell us Dunstan paintings? We don't have that kind of money."

Extortion, you silly twit. What else? Worthington's thumb ached almost as much as his head. *Lee verifies fake paintings and everything is sweet—except Crawford will have my balls if I don't generate enough auction excitement to support a minimum of eight million dollars per Dunstan. Ten is what Crawford really wants. That will make the kind of waves that nobody can question, not even the IRS.*

Worthington was, in his own way, as eager as Crawford to make a huge splash. It would bring his new auction house to the attention of the big players in the art world in a dazzling way. But that would be hard to pull off with a dozen dubious Dunstans coming out of the woodwork at the last moment.

Crawford didn't have the money to soak up twelve new paintings at four million each, much less at ten. And if the new paintings went for less, they would devalue the ones Crawford already owned.

"Don't worry about anything except keeping a lid on Lee and calling me if someone contacts you about the paintings," Worthington said. "Do you understand?"

Betty sighed. "I don't understand anything, but I'll do what you say."

Worthington hung up and dialed Crawford's cell phone number from memory.

Answer, you bastard. Time is running out.

65

D ad?" Lane asked, sticking his head out of the bedroom
doorway. "Where are you?"

"In our office," Faroe called out, "burping the eating
machine."

"I didn't know if you wanted all this on the St. Kilda network, so I thought I'd give you what I have so far."

Computer under his arm, Lane walked into his parents'
office. He took the locked gun cabinet and the wall of electronics for granted, but he always loved seeing the array of
computers. Working for St. Kilda Consulting meant not only
that his parents had great equipment but that he got to use
it sometimes.

His idea of heaven.

The baby tucked against Faroe's shoulder gave a belch
that Lane would have been proud of.

"Is that a round-two burp?" Lane asked.

Faroe blinked. "A what?"

"You know. You're full and then you give a big belch and you're ready for—"

"Round two," Faroe said, shaking his head. "Gotcha."

Grace looked up from her computer and held out her arms for little Annalise. "I have a new search running on the Moorcroft case."

"Anything?" Faroe asked.

"I'll know in a few hours. Or days. Depends on how many levels I have to go through to strike gold."

"We've got to hire some more researchers," Faroe said.

"Steele said he's vetting them as fast as he can."

"He's worse than the government when it comes to background checks."

"Good thing, too," Grace said dryly. "St. Kilda is a lot more demanding than good old Uncle Sam."

"Steele has me," Lane said, smiling and opening his computer. "Look at this. I don't understand half the language, but there are a lot of zeros to the left of the decimal."

"Drag a chair over," Faroe said, settling into his own office chair, "and show me what your swarm found."

"This is only preliminary," Lane said. "We haven't had much—"

"Gimme," Faroe cut in. "No researcher ever has enough time."

Lane sat and scooted a rolling office chair across the Spanish tile floor. Faroe stuck out a long leg and cushioned the impact of his son's landing.

"I'm not sure where to begin," Lane said.

"At the bottom line," Faroe said.

"Which one," Lane said under his breath.

"You always say that."

"You always give me a reason." Lane frowned at the computer. "Okay, most recent hits first. I shunted all the general Western art stuff into a separate file if—"

"Bottom line," Faroe said ruthlessly.

"Right. Recent Dunstan hits. Governor of Nevada, one of the state senators, a congressional representative, and a rich dude called Talbert 'Tal' Crawford congratulated themselves at a press conference called because Crawford is making a big contribution to something called the Museum of the West. He's donating his entire collection of Western art, including whatever he buys at the Vegas auction on Sunday."

Faroe watched his son with steady eyes that were more green than hazel, intelligent, and fierce in their intensity. "Generous man."

"Yeah. It's his first big charitable contribution, too, and he has megabucks. Has had it for years. Oil, mostly."

"Interesting."

"I thought so," Lane said. "You always say to look for the pattern, then look where it isn't followed."

Faroe's smile made him look deceptively gentle.

"I've got a bunch of stuff on Crawford from the financial angle," Lane said.

"Let's stick with Dunstan for now."

"There's not much to stick with. All the really recent hits have to do with the museum. Most of the other recent hits on the Dunstan name have to do with the upcoming auction. The art bloggers are all over it like a cat covering—" Lane glanced up, saw his mother nursing the baby, and cleared his throat. "All over it like a cat in a sandbox."

Faroe bit back a smile. Lane was really trying to keep his language clean around his baby sister.

So was Dad.

"A month or so ago there was a thread on some art blogs that some new Dunstans had been discovered," Lane said, "but nothing came of it that got posted on the Internet. Other blogs said anything new by Dunstan would be a fraud or a scam of some sort."

"Copy the blogs to me," Faroe said.

"Already did."

"Despite what you sometimes think," Grace said without looking up from her computer or the baby, "your son actually listens to you. Sometimes."

Lane snickered. "The blogs are saying that the four to six million dollars per Dunstan is low end, because he comes on the market so rarely that there's a lot of demand. The figure ten million dollars keeps coming up again and again in the really recent hits. Some serious buzz going down."

"Good news for the art business," Faroe said.

"Bad news for Uncle Sam," Lane said, "according to one source."

"Yeah?" Faroe asked. "In my experience, the government always gets its cut of the action."

"Something to do with taxes," Lane said.

"Are we talking Crawford?"

"Yeah, but you said you wanted to talk about Dunstan."

"Do you have anything else on Dunstan?" Faroe asked.

"Just secondary and tertiary sources quoting primary sources and then each other. For example—"

"Quit jerking Joe's chain," Grace cut in. "He may be in the mood for it but I'm not. Bottom-line time."

Lane started to defend himself, then thought better of it. He knew he was yanking his dad's chain, but only in a sideways, sort of buddy kind of way. Nothing serious.

"About two years ago," Lane said, drawing up a new document on the computer, "Crawford's business manager was busted on some bad tax shelters. He got bail on appeal, then hopped a plane to Paraguay with two showgirls and a lot of money in offshore accounts. Turns out that some of the deals he cut for Crawford weren't what they looked like on the surface. Certainly not when it came to claiming federal tax deductions on losses."

"Bottom—" Faroe said.

"—line," Lane finished. "Crawford owes over a hundred million in taxes and penalties to our favorite uncle. He's fighting it, but he's lost two appeals already. The third one is still in the works."

Faroe's soft whistle was all the reward Lane needed.

"I don't really understand a lot of this," Lane continued, "but one of the swarmers has real financial smarts. She said that a cheap way to pay taxes is to give away stuff you already own to charity and take its value off your taxes."

"Stuff?" Faroe asked.

"You know. Art, jewelry, property, that sort of thing. Stuff. Give it to a charity or a public trust."

"Or a museum," Faroe said. "Good job, Lane."

His son grinned.

"Giving away 'stuff' works especially well if you can somehow inflate the cost of the donation," Grace said, turning away from her computer without disturbing little Annalise. "That way you never paid full price, but you're taking a full-price deduction. Or the sale price says one thing, but the buyer pays only a fraction. Under the table, of course. Deductions all around."

"Nothing like auction fever for raising prices," Faroe said. "Or plain old bid-rigging works, too."

"Does Crawford own any other art?" Grace asked Lane. "Or just Western art?"

"I came across something about a really important Picasso or two, plus some Warhols and a huge painting by the splatter dude."

"Jackson Pollock?" Grace guessed.

"Yeah. Him," Lane said.

"Why wouldn't Crawford sell or donate those?" Grace

asked. "Modern art is at an all-time high. No need for inflating prices, artificial or real."

"Yeah," Lane agreed. "Can you imagine paying over a hundred *million* dollars for a picture of a guy kissing a girl?"

"Depends on the artist," Faroe said.

"Some dude called Klimt."

"Pass," Faroe said. He looked at Grace. "I like my women to look like women."

Grace smiled at the heat in Faroe's eyes. If Lane hadn't been a few feet away, she would have given her husband the kind of kiss they both loved.

"But Lane has a good point," she said. "Why go to the trouble of inflating prices on relatively unknown art when you have much better known art you can give away with less hassle?"

"Vanity," Faroe suggested. "Bet his name ends up on Nevada's museum building. A Warhol wouldn't get it done."

"Maybe he actually likes that modern cra—er, stuff," Lane said, looking at his little sister. "So he's keeping it."

"Or his best-known art could already be tied up," Grace said.

"How?" Lane asked.

"Collateral on loans," his mother answered.

"Huh?"

"Think of it as a high-class pawnshop," Grace said. "You hand over the paintings to a bank vault, and the bank hands over the loan to you. It's done all the time when there's a cash crunch among the really rich. Very quiet. Very discreet. Nobody knows that the paintings are temporarily held hostage by the bank."

"They loan at full value?" Faroe asked.

"Banks aren't stupid," Grace said. "With that kind of collateral, you get maybe fifty percent of retail price, usually less."

"That's still a lot of zeros to the left of the decimal," Faroe said. He leaned toward his son. "How much did your swarmers get on Crawford's finances in the last five years?"

"Not as much as I could if you'd let me hack into a few private databases," Lane said eagerly.

"Give me what you have. If that's not enough, we'll talk about hacking."

Grace rolled her eyes. "First we have Ambassador Steele home-schooling Lane on the reality versus the media coverage of world politics. Now we have Joe Faroe teaching his son the cutting edge of computer ethics. What's next? Mary teaching applied physics by showing Lane how to drop a man with a sniper's rifle at eight hundred yards?"

"Good idea," Faroe said. "I'll put it in the lesson plan."

Hiding a smile, Lane started researching Talbert Crawford's finances in open sources.

If he was a really good boy, the closed sources would come later.

66

Las Vegas
September 16
5:07 P.M.

Zach looked at the crowded lobby of the Golden Fleece.
The huge tank of water with circulating gold dust was a
big draw. People stood around watching a monster sheep
fleece straining gold from the water until the fleece gleamed
like its fabled namesake. It was a method of recovering
gold dust that was as old as the legend. From the look of the
fleece, it was nearly at the end of its collection cycle.

The hotel was booked wall-to-wall, and had been from
the day it opened. One of the upsides to contract work for St.
Kilda Consulting was that they could get a room almost anywhere, at any time, from a flophouse to a penthouse. Someone always knew someone who knew someone.

In this case the someone at the end of the chain of favors
was Shane Tannahill, the owner of the golden-glass and

black-steel monument called the Golden Fleece. And it was Tannahill's name that had convinced someone in the auction bureaucracy to allow the hotel owner's personal guests to see some of the paintings before the official preview tomorrow.

Thomas Dunstan's paintings, to be precise.

No big deal. The paintings were, after all, there to be previewed. It was a necessary part of every auction protocol. Zach was just being certain that no one got in the way before they examined the stretcher edges of the paintings.

He didn't have a good feeling about this op.

He kept telling himself it was because he was personally involved with the client, and therefore more edgy, but he wasn't buying it.

Somewhere, somehow, in that great flusher in the sky, this op was going south.

He knew it.

He just couldn't nail down how, who, where, or when.

Faroe's call hadn't helped. The idea that so many millions were at play for a man as politically powerful as Tal Crawford just made Zach jumpier. When the zeros started rolling up, people got crazy.

"What's 'the usual bodyguard arrangement'?" Jill asked, sitting next to Zach in the lobby.

"Two rooms, connecting door." *Only one of the beds will be used, unless we mess it up too much. Then we'll use the other.*

But thinking about that was stupid. He needed his mind on his op, not his crotch.

"I take it the connecting door gets left open?" she said.

"Always." He looked at his watch. "Hope this auction dude gets here soon. I'm too old to live on junk food forever. No matter what the ads say, sugar, salt, and grease aren't food groups."

Jill opened the auction catalogue and looked through it

again. Like Zach, she hoped it wouldn't be long until they saw the paintings.

She kept wondering if she was dreaming.

"I still don't believe it," she said in a low voice. "Five to eight million dollars. Each."

"Remember what Frost said—the buzz on the art circuit is ten million bucks for the big ones. Each."

"Is that common?" she asked.

"What?"

"To have a lot of rumors that basically fix the price of some paintings at a higher cost than the auction catalogue indicates."

"It's called excitement, and the more the better. The catalogue is nothing but a guesstimate of future bidding." Zach's stomach growled. Living out of mini-marts and fast-food outlets was a great way to starve.

"You heard those two back there," she said, indicating the registration desk of the Golden Fleece, where guests waited twelve deep for the opportunity to check into the most luxurious hotel-casino-shopping megaplex in Las Vegas. "They were talking about ten million per Dunstan at Sunday's auction like it was a done deal."

"In good times, paintings can blow through the top of their range," Zach said.

"Are times that good right now?"

"I could argue either side of the question." He frowned, thinking back on the conversations he'd overheard while they waited in line to register. A lot of the people were here for the art auction, not the casino action. "But you're right. Nearly everyone is talking ten million for the Dunstans. It makes me wonder."

"About what?"

Zach kept watching the people milling in the lobby. The plainclothes guards were well dressed and invisible to anyone who didn't know that in Vegas, armed guards were always around. A whole lot of those Bluetooth receivers plugged into men's ears weren't what they seemed.

It was easy to separate the hopeful buyers from the hopeful sellers. The sellers didn't clutch heavily earmarked catalogues. But seller or buyer, the undercurrent of excitement, of being at the place where art history will be made, was unmistakable.

It made the back of Zach's neck itch.

"What's wrong?" Jill asked in a low voice.

"I'm wondering how big a fix is in on the auction."

"That's just one more subject my fine art education lacked," she said wryly.

"What?"

"Fixing auctions."

"Any auction can be fixed," he said, thinking of Faroe's conversation about Lane's swarming. "Hidden floors for some goods is a favorite."

"Translation?"

"Say that the auctioneer and the owner of some paintings have made an agreement that no paintings from that owner will sell under, oh, five million. Or a buyer and an auctioneer have an agreement on a minimum price. Normally a floor is put right out there for everyone to see. If the floor isn't met, the painting or whatever is withdrawn. That's open and legal."

"And when the floor is hidden?" she asked.

"It's illegal," Zach said. "It could involve straw bidders in the crowd, or bogus signals from the phone banks, or winning bidders who quietly fail to follow through and take delivery after the headlines about a painting's record price are made—any or all of the above can be used to be sure the floor is reached, and probably surpassed."

Jill frowned. "I can see why the seller would want a big

price. Where's the benefit to the buyer if he's the one doing the rigging?"

"Tax deductions. The bigger the sale price of the object, the bigger the deduction if the work is donated. When everyone is in on the fix, the seller gets enough of a kickback to pay capital gains on his art 'profit,' which he never really sees but still has to pay taxes on. Or the seller donates other paintings at the inflated price and ends up not having to pay taxes on his gains for the paintings he did sell."

"You're giving me a headache," Jill said.

He shrugged. "Those are just a few of the ways to rig sales numbers. When St. Kilda's researchers get some breathing space, they'll go through the records and see just how much real money Dunstan owners have tied up in their paintings. I'm betting that at least one of them doesn't have a tenth of the upcoming auction's price into his Dunstans. The rest is blue smoke and auction fever. There are plenty of ways to juice the numbers, especially at an auction."

"Is it common?" she asked.

"You mean like dirt? No. Common like something you should always be aware of in any auction? Oh, yeah. Millions of bucks change hands on the tip of a paddle or the lift of an eyebrow. A smart auctioneer or a savvy floor man can cover a multitude of backstage tricks. Sometimes the whole auction isn't rigged, just certain lots in the auction. Real hard to prove and it all adds to everyone's bottom line."

"So a dozen new Dunstan paintings wouldn't be very welcome if the game is already scripted."

Zach smiled thinly. "About as welcome as a snake in a henhouse."

A young man wearing an expensive suit and a harried expression crossed toward them.

"Here we go," Zach said in a low voice. "Remember,

we're front people for a potential bidder, nothing more. Mr. and Mrs. Arlington."

"Another charade. Craptastic."

"You want to wait in the suite? I can take care of this."

"I thought you were worried about me being alone."

"You wouldn't be," Zach said, watching the crowd. "St. Kilda has ops in town, so if someone whispers St. Kilda in your ear, or Faroe's name, do whatever they tell you to, including hit the door or the floor."

She took a deep breath, steadying herself for a run down unfamiliar rapids. "I'll follow your lying lead."

"Pretext, not lie. You're hurting my delicate feelings."

Her laugh turned into a cough as the young man stopped in front of them. "Mr. Arlington? I'm Jase Wheeler. I'm very pressed for time, as you can well imagine." He gave them a harried smile. "As you were told, the paintings aren't really set up for public viewing at this—"

"No problem," Zach interrupted, smiling easily. "My partner and I are used to artists' studios. Nothing messier."

Jase tried again. "You really would have a better opportunity to examine the works tomorrow, when we move across the hall to the Grand Ballroom."

"Unless we like what we see today, we won't be here tomorrow, because our client won't be bidding," Zach said. His smile had a lot more teeth than Jase's.

"I see." Jase straightened his suit-coat. "Your client was particularly interested in the Dunstans, I believe?"

"Yes," Jill said. Her smile, too, was more teeth than good fellowship. She was getting tired of being transparent to salespeople when Zach was around.

"I hope your client has a great deal of money," Jase said to Zach. "The excitement about those particular canvases is very intense."

"Our client never worries about money," Jill said, "just about getting what he wants."

"And he wants Dunstans, but only if they're top quality," Zach said.

"I don't recall a financial disclosure form being filled out for any client represented by you," Jase said.

"There won't be any need of financial disclosure unless we like what we see today," Zach said gently. "Or is a financial vetting required simply to preview the works?"

"Uh, no, of course not," Jase said.

Zach waited.

Jase gave in and guided them down a long narrow hall to a meeting room that was crowded with dozens of easels containing artworks.

"Only two of the Dunstans are on the floor right now," Jase said. "The others are still, uh, being uncrated."

"If you're lucky, we'll see something interesting in what you already have out," Jill said coolly. "Otherwise, you might want to expedite the uncrating of the other two."

Jase's shoulders tightened, but he didn't say a word.

67

Las Vegas
September 16
5:13 P.M.

At the front of the room, two Dunstans waited in gilt frames that had been secured to large, sturdy easels.

Zach stopped twenty feet away and studied the paintings carefully for a full two minutes. The first painting was a Great Basin landscape that glowed with its own internal light, the magic moments of late afternoon sunlight captured forever in oils. The other painting was much more fierce, a winter storm slashing down across a dry lake bed that could have been in Nevada or east of the Sierras in California.

"Remarkable, aren't they?" Jase said. "No one manages to catch raking light like Dunstan did."

Jill made a sound that said she was too busy absorbing the paintings to waste time restating the obvious.

Zach walked up to the two paintings, examining them

from a few feet away, looking pointedly at all four corners and the edges. Then he turned toward Jase.

"The corners look like they could be damaged," Zach said.

Jill took the cue and came to stand closer, staring at the corners of each painting.

"Very doubtful," Jase said. "These are some of the finest Dunstans in the world. They came directly from the family collection. They've never been offered to the public before."

"Yeah?" Zach said. His voice said he wasn't buying what Jase was selling. "So the Dunstans are peddling their heritage—or are they just editing the family collection?"

Jill bit back a smile. *Editing* was art-speak for culling inferior works from a museum or individual collector's holdings.

"Not at all," Jase said instantly. "It's simply that there comes a time in a man's life where art like this is simply too precious to keep in the home. The costs of insurance alone are staggering. Lee Dunstan is a simple man with simple needs."

"At four million apiece, the paintings could take care of a lot of simple needs," Jill said.

Jase ignored her. "Lee wanted his father's work to be in a place where it could receive top-level care and display. The new museum in Carson City is just such a place. Lee will donate two of the four Dunstans to the museum. Those are the paintings that haven't been uncrated, because technically, they aren't part of the auction."

"They won't be sold?" Jill asked.

"No. As I said, Mr. Dunstan will donate them at the end of the auction."

"What's he waiting for?" Jill asked.

Jase kept ignoring her and talked to Zach. "Your client

should know that four million is the bottom level of accept-
able bidding. We expect the paintings to go as high as ten
million, perhaps higher. Talbert Crawford will be at the
auction in person. He is the foremost collector of Thomas
Dunstan, although there are at least three others who will be
hoping to outbid him. It's very rare that Dunstan's work is
offered at a public auction."

"Did Crawford have to fill out a financial qualification
form?" Jill asked.

"Of course," Jase said. "Every bidder must. No excep-
tions."

"If we still care, my client's personal banker will call you
tomorrow morning," Zach said casually. "She'll answer your
questions."

"What kinds of art does your client already own?" Jase
asked.

"Whatever he wants. He's new to the Western art market. He wants to start at the top. Saves all the kicking and
gouging."

Jase blinked. "Well, a major Dunstan canvas certainly
would be a tremendous place to start."

"Depends on the Dunstan," Zach said. "Before I give my
okay to the client, I want to black-light these. You have a
place where I can do that?"

"Certainly," Jase said. It was something any serious collector would want done with an expensive painting before
the bidding began. The fact that Zach was being thorough
was reassuring, underlining the earnest intentions of his client. "I'll have the boys bring the paintings to a back room."

"Unframed," Zach said.

Jill held her breath.

"My client never buys a painting until I see it without
its frame," Zach added calmly. "It's like marrying a woman
before you see her without makeup and designer clothes."

Jase almost smiled. Seeing the paintings naked, as it were, was another common demand, especially if the potential buyer was concerned about the condition of the canvas or stretchers. Framing could—and did—hide or minimize defects.

A snap of Jase's fingers brought two young men trotting over. Under his supervision, they popped the canvases out of their frames and stood by, waiting for more orders.

"Follow me," Jase said.

Zach and Jill fell in behind the young men with the canvases. They went down another hallway to a narrow back room where paintings were uncrated and cleaned, repaired, even reframed if necessary. As with real estate and used cars, curbside appeal was all-important to selling art.

If it looked dingy, it sold at a dingy price.

An armed guard sat on a folding chair just inside the door. He nodded to Jase and ignored everyone else.

Easels were scattered throughout the room. Two other people were examining various unframed paintings. One of them was using a battery-driven black light. When she set it aside and left with her companion, Jase picked up the light and handed it to Zach.

"Excuse the rudimentary conditions," Jase said to Zach.

"Like I said. We're used to artists' studios."

Jase nodded at his two helpers. Each placed a painting on an empty easel and stood close by, waiting to be needed.

"Either shut the door or kill the hall lights," Zach said.

One of the helpers leaped to a dimmer switch on the wall behind the guard. Artificial twilight descended.

Zach turned on the black light and moved it across the front of one painting.

On the first pass the surface was uniform, constant, as it would be if all the paint had been laid down at the same time.

"Back here," Jill said.

Zach retraced the painting with the black light until he and Jill could examine several areas where the artist had sketched landforms with extra layers of oil, blending blue and black and green to evoke the rich, earthy colors of a Western landscape.

"Looks clean," Jill said. "No variation in style, just texture."

"Signature is normal, painted after the canvas was dry," Zach said.

"After the artist gave up on achieving perfection," she said softly, "and went on to a new challenge."

"Been there, done that?" he asked.

"Every time I picked up a brush."

Smiling, Zach examined the top and side edges of each canvas. There was wear at the corners and a slight loosening of the canvas itself on the stretchers. Nothing critical, just the natural aging process that began the instant an artist finished a canvas.

"Turn each canvas so that I can examine the bottom edge of the rolled canvas," Zach said.

The two young men duly flipped each canvas.

Zach moved the light slowly along the bottom edge. Once. Twice. Three times. He looked at Jill.

No thumbprint.

68

Very lightly Zack ran his fingertips along the bottom edge of the painting. Jill took a deep breath, let it out, then took another breath, sniffing the bottom corner of the second painting.

"Black light," she said.

Zach gave her the light. She held it at an oblique angle to the edge of the stretcher.

"See it?" she asked.

"Looks like it was added after the paint dried," Zach said.

"Well after," she said. "It still smells faintly of oil. The modern, quick-dry kind, complete with modern, quick-dry sealant."

Once discovered, the over-painting leaped out like a scab on otherwise smooth skin.

Jase crowded in on the painting and stared. "You're right, the repair seems new. But it has no significance."

"Really?" Jill said skeptically.

"Probably the original frame was put on before the canvas had completely dried," Jase explained. "When the frame was recently removed for the canvas to be re-stretched, some paint came with it. Thus the repair. It certainly doesn't matter to the value of the painting as a whole. I doubt if you would even notice it without the black light. Once the canvas is back in its frame, the over-painting will be invisible."

"Looks like the canvas might have been damaged," Zach said. "That would affect the price."

"If it was true, yes. The documents from Lee Dunstan didn't indicate any such damage," Jase said.

Zach shrugged. "Then you won't mind if I record this for my client?"

"Record?"

Zach produced the little digital camera.

"No images," Jase said immediately. "All reprographic rights remain with the artist's estate."

"I'm not going for the front of the painting," Zach said. "Just the part that will be hidden by the frame at the auction."

Jase hesitated, glanced at his watch, and said, "Please be quick about it. I have another appointment in two minutes."

Zach bent over the canvas and recorded the over-painting under various lighting conditions.

The pager on Jase's belt went off. He looked at the code and frowned.

"We can find our way out," Jill said. "Don't be late on account of us."

"If you need to shift a canvas, one of my helpers will do it," Jase said. "Insurance, you understand. We can't have anyone touching the art."

"Of course," Jill said. "Thank you for your time. I assure you that our client will be very interested in these paintings. Nothing like a new, extremely wealthy collector to spice up an auction, is there?"

It was every auctioneer's wet dream, and Jase knew it. "All qualified bidders are welcome." He smiled. "If you'll excuse me . . ."

While Jase hurried out of the room, Zach went to the other canvas. The black light flashed over his face. His grin looked demonic in the purple glow.

When Jill would have said something, he bent and kissed her swiftly, then breathed in her ear, "Not one word about thumbprints."

Like the other canvas, this one must have been put into the frame before it fully dried, because there was more over-painting near the bottom corner.

Jill leaned in, breathed deep, and said, "Same as the other."

"Yeah. What do you want to bet it has the same cause?" Zach asked mildly.

"I wouldn't bet against it," she said, flinching when the camera's built-in flash went off.

"Not even in Vegas?"

"Especially not in Vegas."

"Smart woman."

"Keep it in mind," she said.

"Always," he promised.

As soon as Zach was finished, they thanked the helpers and headed out of the room. When Jill was certain no one could overhear, she turned to Zach.

"How did someone know to—"

He stopped her words with a hard kiss.

"But when—" she began as soon as he lifted his head.

"Not until we're in the shower. Naked."

69

Lee Dunstan staggered slightly, then righted himself by leaning against the plush sofa.

Can't hold liquor the way I used to.

But he wanted another drink anyway.

When he went to get it, he found Betty pouring the rest of the bottle into the bathroom sink.

With an angry cry, Lee lunged toward her, knocking her and the empty bottle against the glassed-in shower enclosure. The shower's heavy glass banged, vibrated, and held. The bottle shattered.

Betty slid down to the floor and put her face in her hands.

Lee turned on his heel and went to the room phone to order another bottle. Before he could pick up the receiver, the phone rang.

"What?" he snarled into the receiver.

"Ah, Mr. Dunstan?"

"Who the hell are you?"

"Jase Wheeler, with the auction. I just wanted to share some very good news with you."

Lee took a deep breath. The room spun. He took another breath. Things settled down.

Mostly.

"I'm listening," Lee said.

"The advisers for an unknown, extremely wealthy mystery bidder showed up to look at your Dunstans. They inspected them very thoroughly. They floated the idea that some damage had been done to the canvas because there were spots of over-painting on the bottom edges of the stretched canvas, but I—"

"Edges? *Edges!* Those paintings are in frames!" Lee shouted.

"Of course. We took them out. It's quite common for potential buyers to inspect—"

"Tal Crawford is the only buyer that matters," Lee cut in, "and he's looked at my paintings all he needs to. What is this bullshit?"

Behind Lee, shards of glass clinked into the trash as Betty began cleaning up after him.

"Obviously I've caught you at a bad time," Jase said smoothly. "I apologize. I just thought you would be pleased to know that, from all the buzz that's going on, it appears that your paintings could be worth every bit of their high-end estimate. If you have any questions or would like to know any more, please feel free to call me at your convenience."

Lee looked at the dead phone and slammed it back into the cradle so hard it hurt his hand.

Cursing steadily, he punched in Tal Crawford's cell number. When it was picked up he said harshly, "Tal, old buddy, we got ourselves a problem."

70

ike Zach, Jill was freshly washed, wearing new clothes from the skin out, and feeling like a well-scrubbed vegetable. Unless the devices were smaller than anything St. Kilda had heard of, they weren't carrying bugs.

Anywhere.

They had left everything in their suite, where one of the hotel's security officers was going over the place for bugs. The new, certified bug-free clothes and electronic sweep were compliments of Shane Tannahill, who really hated devices that weren't part of his own casino security network.

"Hungry?" Zach asked, massaging the nape of Jill's neck absently as he sat next to her in a plush booth and looked around the luxurious restaurant.

The Golden Fleece had one five-star and three four-star

restaurants on the premises. Foodie heaven. And tonight's meal was on St. Kilda.

Five stars all the way.

Jill gave him a sidelong look. "I'm hungry. Are you on the menu?"

He smiled. "You are. Dessert."

She smiled and tried not to think about how much fun their shower had been. Zach in a playful mood was mind blowing.

A beautifully groomed young woman stopped by their table. "Hello, I'm Lia Maitland. Mr. Tannahill asked me to give you a message. May I join you for a moment?"

Jill waved her hand at the opposite side of the booth, which was empty, as she and Zach were sitting thigh to thigh.

"Thank you." Lia slid into the booth and continued speaking in her low, discreet voice. "Your suite was clean. Your apparel was clean. So was your duffel and backpack. As you suspected, the satellite phone in the belly bag has a locater and an eavesdropping bug."

Jill blinked. *As who suspected?* She looked at Zach.

He was watching Lia.

"The bugs are probably integrated into the satellite phone's battery," she continued, "but since we were told only to identify, not to neutralize, any bugs, I left the phone intact. The locater is broadcasting on a frequency anyone could pick up. The bug is voice-activated. We attempted to trace it. It's shielded. Given enough time, we could break the security. If we can't do it, Shane Tannahill can."

"Not necessary," Zach said. "We'll handle it on our end."

Lia nodded. "Will there be anything else you require?"

"I'd appreciate it if you could relay your message to St. Kilda Consulting through the same coded channel they used to reach you," Zach said.

"Of course."

"And thank Mr. Tannahill for us," Jill added.

Lia nodded, slid out of the booth, and vanished.

"What made you suspect my satellite phone was bugged?" Jill asked in a low voice.

"I was wondering before the thumbprints got covered over," Zach said, leaning close to Jill. "Then I was sure."

"Why?"

"Flight plans are only good for airports, yet someone found us at Frost's house."

"Did we mention Frost on the plane to Taos?" Jill asked.

"No. I was thinking and you were mad. We didn't talk much."

"But someone knew about the thumbprints in time to cover them on the Dunstan family paintings."

Zach nodded. "The only way I could have been bugged was if someone knew I would be assigned to this op. No one knew that until it happened, including yours truly."

"You were on vacation anyway."

"Yeah. Somebody could have sold out St. Kilda and bugged my phone," Zach said, "but that's not my first choice. Faroe is very, very careful who he employees. Steele is even worse. Everybody who works for St. Kilda gets the kind of vetting that makes sure secrets stay that way. Individual clearances are updated frequently and randomly."

"So you decided it was probably me," Jill said.

"Yeah, but I was damned if I could figure out how or where you were bugged. You came straight from the river to your ranch and then to Mesquite."

"Blanchard," she said bitterly. "While I was in my hotel, I left the satellite phone in my car, shoved under the passenger seat."

"That was my next question—if your sat phone had ever been in a vulnerable place."

"Now what?" she asked.

"We eat the first decent meal we've had since we met."

"But—" she began.

"And we talk about options."

Zach was hoping they'd come up with one that didn't include putting Jill on the firing line, but he didn't expect it.

Her sat phone was their only connection to whoever had shot Frost.

71

Las Vegas
September 17
12:31 A.M.

The sound of a satellite phone ringing in the next room brought Zach to full wakefulness. Automatically he started to get up, then realized it was Jill's phone, not his. He turned on the bedside lamp and reached over to wake her.

Her eyes were open, clear, watching him.

"Do I answer?" she asked softly.

Zach wanted to say no. He nodded his head.

She fought her way through the luxurious pillows surrounding her like a flock of sleeping swans and walked toward the adjoining room.

He watched her push open the door and wished she wasn't walking closer to danger with every step.

Maybe it's a wrong number.

But Zach's gut knew it wasn't. He kicked clear of the pillows and went to stand next to Jill.

"Hello," she said, angling the phone so that Zach could hear.

"Ms. Breck?"

The voice had an odd tone that told Zach it was being filtered. No voiceprints would be useful for making a case in court.

"Who is this?" Jill asked.

"I'm an art dealer. I represent a private collector who wants to remain anonymous. My client is very interested in some paintings you have. Are you alone?"

Zach's dark eyebrows lifted.

"What does that have to do with my paintings?" she asked.

"My client heard that you hired a renegade private security organization named St. Kilda Consulting. If it's true, my client would refuse to deal with you."

"Let me make sure I have this right," Jill said. "Your client doesn't like who is representing me, so he won't deal with me?"

"Did you know that St. Kilda was involved in a gun battle that cost the lives of several people and left a federally protected government witness close to death?"

"Really?" Jill said, looking at Zach.

He shrugged. Old news.

"The principals in that matter were Grace Silva, a discredited former federal judge, and Joe Faroe, an ex-convict with a long history of violence."

Jill looked at Zach.

His smile wasn't the kind that comforted people. He walked toward the desk and found a notepad and pen with the hotel's logo on them.

"I didn't know that," she said slowly. "It makes St. Kilda sound, well, sort of shady."

"St. Kilda Consulting has been put on the watch list of every government agency in the United States," the caller said. "It's a mercenary corporation, a private military company, and as such is required to register with the State Department because of its many questionable overseas contracts."

Zach returned with a hotel note tablet that said GO WITH IT.

She gave him a *well, duh* look.

"You're making me very uneasy," she said into the phone. "That's not at all what I thought St. Kilda was."

"Sorry to be the one bringing bad news," the caller said smoothly. "The good news is that we can do some profitable business, but only if you get rid of St. Kilda. My client simply refuses to have any part of such an organization."

"Well, that's reassuring," she said, trying not to laugh. "How did your client learn about the paintings?"

"The world is full of wealthy, anonymous collectors. At the high end, art is best conducted on a private basis. Many collectors are afraid that publicity will draw the attention of thieves and extortionists. As long as you're with St. Kilda, my client thinks that you might be, at best, an extortionist. After all, that's what St. Kilda Consulting is noted for."

"Extortion?"

"In a word," the caller agreed.

"Frankly, I'm just a woman alone who finds herself in a very strange, sometimes dangerous world," Jill said. "I didn't ask for any of this, but I've got it just the same. And . . ."—she sighed—"I've become uneasy with St. Kilda."

Go, babe! Zach nodded, silently encouraging her. *Base the lies on truth. So much more convincing that way.*

"Then we have a basis for the deal," the caller said.

"What is your client willing to pay for the paintings?" Jill asked.

"If the paintings are all similar to the one that was trafficked around Salt Lake City—"

"They're better," she cut in. "Bigger." She looked at Zach and smiled. "Size does matter, you know."

He bit back laughter.

"I could offer you a million dollars for your paintings," the caller said.

"A million?" She made a scornful sound. "How about ten million? Do you know what Dunstans are selling for on the market today?"

"Not a chance," the caller said. "Your paintings aren't signed Dunstans, and no one who matters will authenticate them. Considering that, a million is very generous."

"What if the paintings could be authenticated?" she insisted.

"That's the ten-million-dollar question, isn't it?" The caller's voice roughened. "There's no historical record of the paintings other than your unsupported word they were in your family. Even if you found, say, a thumbprint in place of a signature, there's no way to prove that the thumbprint belonged to the artist."

Zach was writing busily.

"Really? But fingerprints are accepted in—" she began.

The man kept talking. "A lot of people could handle paintings before they're dry. Friends, fellow artists, groupies, a hasty framer. Considering that fingerprints as a whole, like DNA evidence, have become an area of controversy in criminal cases, you'd be stupid to front those paintings as Dunstans. Unless you have the resources for a prolonged legal battle . . . ?"

Zach shoved the notepad under Jill's nose.

"Three million dollars," she said, reading quickly, her voice hard and her eyes shocked. "Cash. Used, nonsequential bills. Nothing smaller than fifties or larger than hundreds."

"Two million," the caller said.

She looked at Zach.

He nodded.

"All right," she said. "Two million."

"Where are the paintings now?"

"Safe," she said quickly. "Don't you worry about them. I nearly lost them twice to fire. Not taking that chance again."

"Can you get to the paintings or does St. Kilda have them?" the caller asked.

She looked at Zach.

He pointed at her.

"I can get to the paintings," she said.

"Fire St. Kilda," said the man. "Check out of your hotel. Pick up the paintings and drive north out of Las Vegas. Be prepared to drive all the way to Reno if you have to. You'll be contacted along the way and given instructions on how to proceed."

"You need your meds adjusted," she said without looking at Zach, who was writing rapidly. "I'm not bringing the paintings with me."

"Then we don't have a deal."

"Let me think a minute," she said.

Zach wrote faster.

"I'll leave the paintings with a concierge at a Vegas hotel," she said, reading upside down. "I'll give the storage receipt to a friend of mine."

He turned the tablet and held it out to her.

"This friend will wait for my call," she said, reading quickly. "After you give me the money, I'll get in my car and call my friend, who will be waiting in the lobby of a Vegas hotel. She'll hand over the storage receipt and tell your people which hotel has the paintings."

"You must watch a lot of television," the man retorted.

"Listen, dude," Jill said, using her river-captain voice, "I learned a lot about structuring a safe deal when I was selling date-rape drugs to USC frat boys. Just because I spent a lot of time on the river doesn't mean I don't know city ways."

There was a long pause, then a laugh before the caller asked, "Can you arrange all of this by early tomorrow?"

She looked at Zach.

He nodded.

"Yeah," she said. "When do we meet?"

Zach made a stretch-it-out motion with his hands.

"I'll call," the man said.

"So when do you want me to start driving north?"

"In time to reach the Idaho border before sunset, even if you take a few side trips along the way."

Zach nodded.

"Okay," Jill said. "I'll leave in the morning."

"Bring half the paintings with you or the deal is off," the caller said.

"But—"

"Not negotiable," the caller said, talking over Jill. "Fire St. Kilda. Keep the phone you're talking on with you at all times. I won't call a different number or accept your call from a different number. No phone, no deal. No six paintings, no deal. Come with company, no deal. Get it?"

Zach's smile was as thin as the cutting edge of a knife.

"Got it," Jill said. "When are you calling?"

"You'll be the second to know, while you're driving somewhere north of Las Vegas on Highway 93, tomorrow afternoon. But don't count on staying on 93, and have a full tank of gas."

The caller broke the connection.

Jill hit the caller-ID function. The number was blocked.

Surprise, surprise.

Muttering under her breath, she threw the phone at the top of the unused bed, where it sank out of sight in soft piles of pillows.

Zach dragged her through the connecting doorway. Silently he eased the door shut. He led her into the far bathroom and turned on the shower, but didn't get into it.

"Okay," she said, drawing a deep breath. "I need a friend in Vegas I can trust with the paintings."

"You'll have one. Male or female?"

"Female. But this guy doesn't play nice. His friends are probably the same."

"No worries." Zach grinned. "We have some very competent females at St. Kilda Consulting. The paintings are going straight into Shane Tannahill's casino vault."

"I won't get away with that on my end," Jill said. "I'll have to have six real paintings for the show-and-tell."

Zach wanted to argue but didn't. He could already hear Grace. *We can't prove anything unless the paintings are real, the money is real, and the exchange is made.*

That was the downside of employing judges. They had such firm ideas about what would and would not fly in court.

"And I'll have to be alone," Jill said tightly.

"No way. Forget it."

She didn't like it, but she didn't see any way around it.

Sometimes rapids couldn't be finessed. They had to be ridden.

"I'm not going to waste time arguing about this," Jill said. "Where's your phone?"

"Why do you need it?"

"I'm calling Grace Silva Faroe. Then I'm going back next door and firing St. Kilda over my sat phone."

72

Faroe picked up the phone, listened, and glanced toward the rocking chair where Grace was nursing Annalise.

"She's busy," Faroe said. "Talk to me."

"Who is it?" Grace asked.

"Jill, on Zach's phone."

"I can lactate and think at the same time," Grace said, holding out her hand for the phone.

Faroe got out of bed and walked over to Grace. Naked.

"Get some pants on," she said, trying to ignore the eye-level view as she reached for the phone. "I'm going blind."

He smiled. "The phone is on speaker, *amada*."

"Hello, Jill," Grace said, taking the phone and telling herself she was too old to blush. "Are you calling me from a shower for the usual reason?"

"Um, what's the usual reason?" Jill asked.

"Bugs," Zach said into the phone.

"Right. Bugs," Jill said. "My sat phone is in the other room and the door is closed, but Zach is being paranoid."

"Cautious," Zach said.

"Am I necessary to this conversation?" Grace asked.

Faroe reached for the phone.

Grace handed him the baby to burp.

"Let Zach summarize," Faroe said. "Then everyone can argue."

"The opposition called Jill's sat phone about five minutes ago," Zach said. "She's supposed to fire St. Kilda, leave half the paintings with a friend in Vegas, drive north alone with half the paintings, and wait for the nice arsonist/shooter to call again and give her a meeting place to exchange paintings and information on the other six paintings with said nice arsonist/shooter for two million, cash."

"Bullshit," Faroe said.

"Took the word right out of my mouth," Zach said.

"Thank you for your input," Grace said ironically. "Does anyone have a better plan for getting our hands on Mr. Nice before he burns down or shoots up the whole world?"

Silence.

Followed by a baby's lusty burp.

"Ah, intelligence at last," Grace said. "Shooter Mary is practicing with the military outside of Las Vegas. She'll be the contact, assuming Mr. Nice is so stupid as to show up and ask for the second half of the paintings."

With that, Grace handed Faroe the phone, picked up another phone, and punched in Mary's cell number.

"Who's Shooter Mary?" Jill asked.

"Our long-arms specialist," Faroe said. He smiled thinly. "She fights real good up close and personal, too."

"She's put me in the dirt a few times," Zach agreed. "But I still don't want Jill to go alone in the car."

"Nobody wants her to go alone," Faroe said. "That isn't the point."

"You won't do her any good riding in the trunk," Grace said clearly. "And you can be sure she'll be vetted for company along the way before anything else happens."

Zach made a growling sound of frustration that told everyone what they already knew—he'd lost the battle.

But not the war.

"I have a plan," Zach said.

"I'm listening," Faroe said.

"First, we've got to get Jill a BlackBerry," Zach said. "She can text-message me without tipping off the dude listening to the bug."

"Done," Faroe said.

"Second, get me a Cessna Skymaster and a really good pilot," Zach said.

"How soon?" Faroe asked.

"In time to keep up with Jill when she leaves tomorrow at, say, an hour or so before noon. It might be later, but I want to have everything in place well before she leaves."

Faroe grunted. "I'll get back to you."

"No Skymaster, no op," Zach said flatly. "I'll tie Jill up and take her into the desert until the auction is over."

"I'll get the Skymaster if we have to steal it," Faroe said. "Then what? Cold convoy?"

"Yes. I'll have her six o'clock, ten thousand feet up, pretty much invisible to anything but radar. The Skymaster can float along almost as slow as she can drive, and it has enough range to go from Vegas to stateline."

"What will you do if Jill gets into trouble along a lonely stretch of Nevada road?" Faroe asked. "Parachute down?"

"That's where the good pilot comes in," Zach said. "I need

one who is used to taking off and landing on short strips, like the ones in the Middle East."

"Not a problem. We have more than one good pilot on tap."

"I'll need some chase cars and a motor home on the road, behind Jill or in front," Zach said. "Bodies with guns."

"Mary can help with that," Grace said. "The men she's training with right now are technically civilians. They'd love the exercise."

"We'll see," Faroe said. "Men with guns aren't that hard to find."

"Smart ones are," Grace said.

"Agreed," Faroe said. "Assuming it goes down the way Zach outlined, are you sure this is what you want, Jill? You're going to be bait and you're going to be alone. Are you okay with that?"

"Okay? As in happy-happy? No," Jill said. "But being alone is the only way to get the job done, so that's how I'm going to do it."

"You could take the paintings and disappear," Faroe said. "I'm betting that it's the auction driving this. Once it's over, you'll be safe."

"So will the man who shot Garland Frost and probably killed my great-aunt," Jill said. "That's not good enough. I don't want this wacko loose to kill other innocent people when I could have stopped him. I can't live with that."

Faroe wanted to argue, but didn't. He felt the same way himself. So he tried a different approach. "You do realize that the caller could be setting you up to take a fall as an extortionist?"

"That's what I told her," Zach said.

"How can it be extortion when the paintings are real?" Jill asked impatiently.

"I didn't say it *was* extortion," Faroe said, "only that it could be made to look like a shakedown long enough for the local law to arrest you and keep you away from the auction."

"That's what I'd do," Zach said.

"So would I," Faroe said before Jill could speak. "Tal Crawford of Crawford International is the biggest Bigfoot expected in the Vegas auction. If he's behind your problems, you'll be bucking the local law as well as your bug artist. CI has its hooks into law enforcement in Nevada. Crawford is a big man in the state. We know the governor is kindly disposed toward him to the tune of a couple hundred thousand in campaign contributions. That could easily mean that the state police would rather listen to Crawford's version of events than yours."

"Were they legal contributions?" Zach asked.

"Grace vetted the filings. There's nothing improper about them."

"Too bad," Zach said.

"Yeah."

"So Crawford is clean?" Zach asked.

Faroe smiled thinly. "He hasn't buried any bodies where St. Kilda can dig them up. Yet. His lawyers are the best money can buy."

"Ditto the politicians," Zach said sarcastically.

"We don't have time to play Oh, Ain't It Awful," Jill said. "I'm supposed to call Faroe on my sat phone and fire St. Kilda. What's my new girlfriend's name again?"

"Mary," Faroe said.

"Mary what?"

"When you're near the bug, just call her Mary," Faroe said.

"Good," Grace agreed. "I'm briefing her as I listen to you waste time."

"Let Mary take Jill's place," Zach said.

"Too risky," Jill said instantly. "Whoever is tracking us must know what I look like."

Zach hissed a word but didn't disagree. There were pictures of Jill scattered all over the public record.

Faroe said something too low to catch. He knew just how Zach felt.

"Last chance, Jill," Faroe said. "Are you certain you want to put yourself in danger over this?"

"Yes," Jill said. "Besides, if things get dicey, Zach will be only a few minutes away, right?"

And it only takes a few seconds to kill someone.

Everyone knew it, but no one said it aloud.

73

Hollywood
September 17
1:04 A.M.

core listened to the bug on Jill Breck's sat phone and laughed out loud. St. Kilda didn't like being fired.

"*Listen, Joe,*" the Breck woman said for the third time. "*This just isn't working. You're spending all kinds of money and not getting anywhere. I want the paintings back as soon as possible. And it better be possible by tomorrow morning.*"

"*Going off alone at this stage isn't smart,*" Faroe said.

"*And staying with St. Kilda is dumb. My paintings. My choice.*"

Silence, then a sigh. "*Whatever you say, Ms. Breck. When you sign off on the paintings tomorrow morning, your relationship with St. Kilda is at an end.*"

"*Good. And don't bother calling me, hoping to change my mind. I'm going downstairs to try my luck at the tables.*"

The connection ended.

Smiling, Score leaned back in his chair and mentally reviewed the players and their positions on the chessboard of the op. He loved an op like this. Any mope with a gun could kill someone, but it was the mental game that separated the players from the wannabes.

Score was a player.

Now that St. Kilda was off the board, arranging the downfall of the clever Ms. Breck would be a pure pleasure.

74

Las Vegas
September 17
2:15 A.M.

Jill lay with Zach, sweat gleaming, pleasure burning. With whispered words and interlocked bodies, they climbed a long slope of sensation to the cliff at the top of the world. Then they went over, freefalling through fire, landing in a tangle of sheets and one another.

When they no longer trembled and breathed brokenly, he kissed her with a gentleness that made her eyes sting.

"You have to go," he said in a low voice. "Now."

Her body tightened around him. "We have hours yet."

"You need to sleep or you won't be ready for whatever happens."

"I can run on less sleep than this."

"If you don't leave now," Zach said, "I'll keep you here and to hell with the op."

Jill stared into his eyes and knew that he meant it. Temptation went through her in a shivering wave that had nothing to do with passion. Then she closed her eyes and untangled from him slowly, reluctantly.

"Tell me that after tomorrow," she said as she eased to her feet.

Zach started to tell her that tomorrow was an expectation, not a guarantee. The look on her face said she already knew that.

"After tomorrow," he said.

His words could have been a warning, an agreement, or a vow. She didn't know which.

She did know better than to ask.

Quietly she walked from their shared room to the empty one. She closed the connecting door very softly. Her sat phone was right where she'd left it, drowned by a flock of large, fluffy pillows.

It will work out, she told herself.

There will be a time after tomorrow.

Won't there?

When she got into bed, the sheets were as cold as her fear.

75

"That's right," Jill said into the room phone, "I'd like to rent something big enough for a lot of luggage, but not so big it's like driving an elephant on ice."

"One of our guests just asked me to return a Cadillac Escalade to the airport for him," the concierge said. "Would that vehicle be satisfactory?"

Jill wouldn't have known a Cadillac Escalade if it left tire prints up her back, but since St. Kilda had rented the vehicle and left it to be "returned," she knew that half of the paintings would fit into the cargo area.

"Works for me," she said. "Will the hotel be able to accommodate three pieces of very valuable luggage in a secure place?"

"Of course. The receipts for three suitcases will be with your car rental agreement."

"I'd rather you kept them until a friend arrives to pick them up. She'll present her ID to Mr. Tannahill's head of security."

"As you wish," the concierge said smoothly. "I'll deal with the rental company for you. The rental papers will be at the concierge desk for you to sign. Please bring your driver's license."

"Of course," Jill said. "Thank you for the trouble."

"For a personal guest of Mr. Tannahill, it's no trouble at all. Please let me know if you need any further assistance."

After Jill hung up, she looked at the sat phone lying two feet away from her on the nightstand. She wondered who was listening, if it was the same person who had killed her great-aunt and burned the old house down around her dead body.

Unease rippled through Jill, leaving a chill in its wake. Zach had already checked out. She was alone.

Being alone wasn't new to her.

The loneliness she felt was.

So was the reality of a shooter and arsonist listening to her every breath, the flush of the toilet, the rustle of her clothes when she dressed.

It flat creeped her out.

You asked for it. You got it. Now suck it up and get the job done.

A knock on the door made her jump.

Dial back, she told herself harshly. *If you rev too hard now, you won't have anything left for the real rapids.*

And she knew those rapids were coming. She just didn't know when or how.

The knock came again.

"Who is it?" Jill said loudly.

"Quincy Johnston from St. Kilda."

She checked the peephole. A gray-haired man with a

plush walrus mustache and a leather briefcase stood in the hallway. Behind him, two bellmen waited beside luggage carts that held three large aluminum suitcases apiece.

She took a deep breath and unlocked the door. "Bring them in."

The bellmen maneuvered the carts into her room.

"Sign here," Johnston said.

"Not until I see the paintings," Jill retorted.

Without a word Johnston noisily opened each of the six cases, then closed them. "Satisfied?"

With Zach gone? Not likely.

"Yes," was all Jill said aloud. "Take those three suitcases to the concierge's secured storage area," she told one bellman. "Leave the claim tickets with the concierge."

"Yes, ma'am," he said.

"When I call the concierge, the head of security will release the three suitcases to the person I name. But only when I call. Do you understand?"

"Yes, ma'am," the young bellman said again.

"If you have any questions, I'll brief the concierge on my way out."

"Yes, ma'am."

Johnston gave the bellman two twenties.

The young man smiled and left.

The second bellman accepted his own hefty tip and walked out, leaving both luggage and cart, shutting the door behind him.

As soon as they were alone, Johnston opened his briefcase and handed her some papers.

"Read carefully before you sign," he said. "We don't want you flip-flopping on us again. When I walk out of here, St. Kilda walks, too. You'll be on your own."

"That's the whole point of firing St. Kilda," Jill said. "I work better alone."

"Your choice." Johnston sounded bored.

She took the papers and rustled them, making enough noise for the bugged phone to pick up. Then she started reading.

Johnston opened his briefcase, put his finger to his lips, and handed her a leather portfolio.

She almost dropped it. "Heavy words, here."

"One of the partners in St. Kilda is a judge," Johnston said. "If you require translation of any legal jargon, please let me know."

"So far, so good."

She opened the portfolio, saw a BlackBerry, a Colt Woodsman, two loaded magazines, and five one-hundred-dollar bills. She raised her eyebrows.

"Explain clause three, paragraph two," she said.

As Johnston began a long ad-lib, she checked the weapon quickly, carefully, knowing that his voice would cover any noise she might make.

How did Zach know this was the right gun for me? Jill asked silently. *Was it in my file? Did I tell him?*

Can he read my mind?

Who cares? she told herself. *The gun is here and I can operate it with my eyes closed.*

"Okay, I get it now," Jill said, carefully laying the unloaded gun, two magazines, the BlackBerry, and the money on the bed. "I'll never darken St. Kilda's doorstep again, and vice versa." She handed over the empty portfolio. "You have a pen I can use?"

"Of course."

She signed, he countersigned, and the deal was done.

"Here's your copy," Johnston said, handing her two papers instead of one. "Good luck, Ms. Breck," he added, opening the door. "Without St. Kilda, you'll need it."

The door closed firmly behind him.

Jill looked at the flat, long-barreled semiautomatic pistol and two loaded magazines lying on the peach sheets of the bed. She hoped that was all the "luck" she needed.

"Where did I leave that TV remote?" she asked aloud. "It should come with a leash."

She started throwing pillows around until her sat phone was covered up.

"Ah, there it is."

She turned on the TV to a twenty-four-hour weather station, ramped up the volume, and went back to the bed. She eased one of the magazines into the butt of the pistol but didn't cycle the action. She slipped the extra magazine, the pistol, and the money into her belly bag. On the way out of the hotel, she'd carry her sat phone in her hand, like someone anxious to call or be called. After that, the phone could live on the passenger seat.

The BlackBerry PDA was familiar. Some of the rafting outfits she worked for used them.

She folded the copy of her severance agreement with St. Kilda and put it into her belly bag. The second piece of paper was more interesting. She sat on the bed to read the typed message.

Jill,

Zach told me you used a pistol like this before you went to college. The bullets are .22-caliber long rifle hollow points. The opposition shouldn't be surprised you're carrying. If they are, they're seriously stupid.

Give a hundred to the concierge. Use the rest for gas and food on the road.

The alert function on the PDA is muted. Do visual checks every ten minutes or so. If you have local cellular service, you can text-message me. My IM is the first address stored. Zach's is second. The BlackBerry is bugged—locater and voice activated, just like the opposition's bug on your satellite phone.

If things really head south, scream.

Mary is wired in as your friend/contact on your sat phone. Use my number, then hit #. The call will be forwarded to her. Be sure to use the protocol you and Zach talked about last night.

Jill smiled, remembering what else they had done while discussing "protocol."

Check in at least every two hours on the sat phone. Every hour would be better. They'll be listening, but they expect you to use some kind of cut-out to release the second half of the paintings.

We'll be with you all the way. Zach will be above, the others will be on the ground no more than four minutes away.

When the opposition makes contact, message me if you can. Or talk to yourself near the BlackBerry. Either will work.

Drop this paper in the toilet and flush. Remember, the opposition may be watching you from the moment you leave your room, so stay in role.

—JF

Jill reread the note and dropped it in the toilet. The paper melted like the water was acid. She flushed and went to finish packing.

When she was done, she checked the PDA. No messages had arrived. Quickly she finished filling her backpack, eased the gun and spare magazine into her belly bag, added the BlackBerry, and was ready to go.

Or as ready as she ever would be.

Same as the river. You watch, you weigh, you decide. You like the adrenaline, remember?

Yeah, but only when I'm the one on the oars. Right now I'm up a dirty river and there's not an oar in sight.

She didn't like the feeling.

And there was nothing she could do about it except quit.

She wasn't a quitter.

Taking a deep, slow breath, she put the sat phone on the luggage cart before she wheeled it out the door and into an elevator. A moment later she was in front of the concierge's desk. The desk was run by a handsome man whose name tag said EDUARDO and listed his hometown as Bogotá, Colombia.

"Do you have a piece of paper, a pen, and an envelope I can seal?" she asked.

"But of course."

"Thank you."

She wrote quickly on the paper, stuffed it into the envelope, sealed it, and gave it to the concierge. "This is for the head of security."

Eduardo nodded.

"You look like you handle requests like this all the time," Jill said.

He gave the liquid shrug of a man born well south of the Mexican border. "In my homeland, such precautions are business as usual."

"Seems as if the world really is getting smaller every day," she said with a feral smile.

"The receipts for your luggage are already in the hands of the Golden Fleece's head of security," the concierge said.

"Good. When I call, the person I describe in this"—she tapped the envelope in his hand—"will present credentials to the head of security, and the cases will be turned over. Nothing happens until I call."

Eduardo nodded.

"If I call you and tell you to change the plans in any way," she said, "hang up immediately and call the Las Vegas police."

"Of course. If you could fill in your driver's license number and sign the rental agreement, all will be in order."

She took her thin cloth wallet out of her belly bag, found her license, filled in the number, and signed.

"Thank you, Ms. Breck," he said, handing over the rental agreement. "Your car is in front, waiting for you. Would you like assistance with your luggage?"

"No, thanks." She pulled a hundred-dollar bill from her belly bag and said, "I appreciate your trouble."

"It is no trouble at all," Eduardo said, smiling and pocketing the bill. "Have a safe trip."

Jill laughed, a hard sound that owed nothing to humor. "Yeah, that would be nice."

But she didn't expect it would turn out that way.

76

Over Nevada
September 17
6:15 P.M.

Zach sat in the right-hand seat of the orbiting aircraft, binoculars against his eyes. Ten thousand feet below, he saw the glint of water and slash of green that was the Indian Springs oasis. The glare of slanting sunlight on the metal roof of the gas station was like a fire.

The pilot had taken up station about a mile west of the highway and was trying to more or less match the speed of the Cadillac on the desert floor. It was tricky. The opposition had Jill running back and forth and around like a hamster on a bent wheel.

The only good news was that she was a Western driver—eighty miles per hour unless she hit a straightaway, then up to ninety.

Talk about going nowhere fast. Zach shook his head and told himself to be patient.

The Escalade sat beside the front door of the gas station. Through the binoculars, he followed Jill as she came out of the station and stood beside the car, sat phone in one hand, BlackBerry in her belly bag. He could hear her end of any conversation.

"Now what," she said impatiently into her sat phone.

Silence.

"Yes, I'm filling up on gas at a price that makes the paintings look cheap."

More silence while she listened.

"Again? I'm getting tired of that stretch of highway. Yeah, yeah. Whatever."

Zach wondered when and where the opposition was going to stop playing games. The sun was already sliding down the sky, heading toward the western horizon and the dark velvet twilight of a summer desert evening.

His sat/cell vibrated. He hit the connect button, read the caller ID, and said, "Nothing new."

Faroe wasn't any happier than he was. "They've had enough chance to vet Jill and everyone else on the highway. Are they waiting for dark?"

"Wouldn't you?"

"Craptastic."

"I'll take that as a yes," Zach said. "The good news is that it will make it easier for her to escape, if it comes to that."

"The bad news is that in the dark, you'll have to tighten up the chase units. Actually, that's good. We've switched chase vehicles four times. Won't need to worry as much about being made after dark."

"This has to be hard on Jill's nerves," Zach said.

"Worry about your own. She's solid. Steele is already making noises about signing her up as an op."

"Is that good or bad?" Zach shot back.

"Not our choice, is it?"

Faroe broke the connection.

Zach wanted to put his fist through the thin aluminum skin of the airplane. Instead he took a few slow breaths and turned hot impatience into the cold stillness of a predator. He wouldn't be any good for Jill if he was on the breaking edge of frustration.

Quick playing jerk-around, you bastard. It's time to party.

77

Indian Springs, Nevada
September 17
6:16 P.M.

Jill leaned against the car and let the gas feed in through the battered metal nozzle. The long, straight highway just beyond the gas station cut across an alluvial fan that spread gracefully down the mountains to the desert floor. Just the sight of the dry ridges and shadowed ravines of the mountains loosened her tension. She knew that the desert was frightening to some people, boring to others. To her the desert was clean, spare, whispering of endless space for the mind and soul to run free.

She itched to paint the land almost as much as she itched to touch Zach again. She didn't know if that was good or bad. She only knew it was as real as the metal towers marching away over the dry land, their arms holding lines that hummed with power.

The highway itself was an intrusion, but not as much as the heavy lines draped from steel towers. She looked through them, beyond them, to the majestic wild, lonely landscape that Thomas Dunstan—or her grandmother—had captured so indelibly.

To the right of the Cadillac, a knot of cottonwoods swept the wind with restless leaves. Their fluttering green announced the presence of water in a dry land. The cottonwoods had been here when the Indian Springs canvas had been painted. The trees were still there, still restless, still shouting of cool water in a dry, relentless wilderness.

Jill let her glance roam the landscape, seeing with the eyes of her grandmother. Take away the power lines, and the area had changed very little since *Indian Springs* had been painted. The gas station had evolved from a ramshackle frame building with two antique pumps into a sand- and sun-blasted metal structure with four pumps out front, but the trees and the fault line of little springs running along the base of the mountains looked the same.

Where are you, Zach?

Ten thousand feet overhead.

Somewhere.

Out of reach.

What's the big deal? I've spent a lot of my life alone.

But death threats took a little more time to get used to.

Shaking off the edgy feeling, Jill went into the station, used the bathroom, bought several liters of water, and paid for everything. The old man who took her money wasn't feeling chatty. Neither was she.

While the man slowly, painfully, counted out her change, she looked behind the counter at the faded black-and-white print of the gas station with a ribbon proclaiming the date and the GRAND OPENING of the station. The photo had been taken a long time ago, when cars in the rugged land were an adventure, not a necessity, back when the frail man counting pennies over the counter had been a little boy yearning to be old enough to break broncs and chase lean cattle through sagebrush valleys.

Jill looked from the photo to the man whose fingers were arthritic from winters spent chasing stubborn cows out of nameless ravines.

Were things really simpler then?

Or does it just seem that way now?

She put the change in her belly bag, went to the car, pulled back onto the road, and settled in for an unknown time of driving before her sat phone rang with new instructions.

She'd no more reached cruising speed when her phone came alive. She eased off the gas and answered.

"What?" she demanded.

"A sheriff's car will stop you. Do what the deputy says."

The connection ended.

"O frabjous day," she said bitterly. "The local cops are friends with the other guys."

Silence answered.

It was all she'd expected.

San Diego
September 17
6:18 P.M.

Grace had watched and listened while her husband peeled away layers of bureaucracy until he got to the man in charge. She stayed silent, because the phone was on speaker.

Besides, she'd already done her part by calling a retired federal judge and having him talk to the sheriff's secretary.

"So what you're saying, Sheriff, is that you won't tell me why your deputy singled out that particular young woman and told her to follow him?" Faroe's voice was mild, gentle.

Grace winced. She'd learned that when her husband sounded most gentle, he was the most dangerous.

The sheriff might have to learn, too.

Faroe's hand gripped the phone hard. He wished it was the sheriff's balls.

"No, I won't tell you," the sheriff said impatiently. "None

of your business, no matter how many retired judges your wife knows."

"Then I'll guess why your deputy decided to pull the woman over," Faroe said. "My teenage son did a quick database check of contributions to your last election. You received thirty thousand dollars and change in campaign contributions from a group of law-abiding folks up in Carson City."

"What does—"

Faroe kept talking. Gently. "That's a lot of money in a little county like yours, so I asked my son to check out those Carson City names. It took him maybe thirty seconds to find links between five of the ten contributors. Seems like they're all members of the same law firm. Are you following me okay, Sheriff?"

"You're wasting my—"

"My kid could start a court-records search on one of the proprietary databases that covers your state," Faroe continued gently, relentlessly. "But I'm betting he'll find that the law firm has only one real client, and more digging would prove that single client is the source of your campaign funds. Do you want me to name that client?"

Silence, then a sigh. The sound of papers being stacked. The click of high heels on tile as some woman came and went from his office.

"What do you want?" the sheriff asked.

"St. Kilda Consulting is engaged in a murder, arson, and robbery investigation on behalf of the young woman who is presently being intimidated by your deputy, acting on behalf of your big-time donor," Faroe said.

"I don't know anything about that."

"Just doing a favor for a big man, huh?"

"Nothing illegal about it," the sheriff said. "The deputy has to patrol the area around Beaver Tail Ranch anyway."

Quickly Grace typed the destination into her mapping program.

"Odd name for a ranch in the desert," Faroe said, watching Grace.

"We have some odd ranches here. Again, nothing illegal."

The printer spat out a piece of paper. Grace handed it to Faroe.

"You keep telling yourself that, Sheriff. Then you listen real good when I tell you that you're in danger of becoming accessory after the fact to murder."

"That's a load of BS," the sheriff shot back. "There haven't been any murders in my county in nine months."

"If you want to keep your record clean," Faroe said, "you'll get on the radio to your deputy and tell him to call in as soon as he leads Ms. Breck to her destination. Then you'll tell your deputy to haul his ass back out to Highway 93 and drive north to"—he looked at the map Grace had printed out—"milepost marker 418. Should I repeat that?"

"No."

"Tell your deputy to stop at marker 418, turn on the light bar, and block all southbound traffic for the next ten minutes."

"What for?"

"Road hazard," Faroe said. "A small private aircraft will touch down south of him and let off a passenger. As soon as the plane takes off again, your deputy can turn off his light bar and head north."

"Why north?"

"Because you want to keep your job. And if you let your *good, rich friend* know what's happening, I will guarantee that you won't be able to get work anywhere, including picking up trash at a downscale cathouse."

"If you're wrong—"

"I'm not."

Faroe punched out.

"Will he do it?" Grace asked.

Faroe let out a long breath. "Zach will be the first to know."

79

Contact continues," Zach said into the microphone that went to the men on the ground who were shadowing Jill, front and rear. "White sheriff's car with blue-and-red light bar is still behind Jill, about a quarter mile back. He may be looking for company. Keep giving him a lot of space."

The sound of microphones popping in agreement came through the small headset Zach wore.

He looked out through the aircraft's windscreen at the road ahead, straight and black to the far horizon. Trucks and a few RVs were most of what little traffic there was.

"What's out here for the next hundred miles?" Zach asked the pilot.

"Sand, rock, and rabbitbrush. And maybe a half-dozen whorehouses."

"Whorehouses? Out in the middle of nowhere?"

"Roger that," the pilot drawled. "There are thirty accredited brothels in the state of Nevada. I think at least half of them are along Highway 93. Chances are, if you see a settlement beside the road, it will have a name like 'The Lobster Ranch' or 'Kangaroo Court.'"

"Lobster Ranch?"

The pilot grinned. "Yeah. Like the sign says, 'Not too many lobsters but a whole lot of tail.'"

"Maybe that's why I never chased classic cars down there," Zach said, sweeping the landscape with his binoculars. "I thought there weren't enough people to leave behind junkyards. But from up here, I've noticed several small ones off the highway."

"Probably old ranches. Everybody down there now is dead or driving through. Truckers, mostly."

"Hence the tail ranches."

"They're state-regulated," the pilot said, glancing automatically at the control panel. "All the girls get checked once a week. Newspapers carry the results in the public notices, just like restaurant inspection reports."

Zach laughed out loud at the thought of government-inspected tail. "Nevada. Gamble with your money, not your health. Gotta love it."

He kept the binoculars on the patrol car.

It kept the same interval behind Jill for five miles.

Zach switched the headphones to his sat/cell and punched in a number. A St. Kilda communications specialist answered instantly.

"Balfour in Nevada," Zach said. "We're still in contact. Still an open tail, county sheriff's car, quarter mile behind the Caddy."

"Roger."

"Get ready to coordinate communications if I have to set down."

"Standing by."

Zach popped the microphone in answer and switched over to the BlackBerry's bug frequency just in time to hear Jill talking to Mary.

"The patrol car will lead me to the meeting," Jill said.

He couldn't hear what Mary said.

"Hopefully the next call I make will be the one you're waiting for."

A pause.

"Stay close to the phone," Jill said.

Zach's sat/cell vibrated. He switched over to it. "What?"

"The destination may be Beaver Tail Ranch," Faroe said. "If the sheriff is smart, the deputy will drop her there and head for milepost 418. He'll stop traffic southbound. We'll stop it northbound. Once the deputy turns on his light bar, land ASAP and get to the car that will be waiting by the road. I don't want to lose this client."

"I'm not real happy with the idea myself," Zach said. "And I'm less happy about seeing the cops on the opposition's side."

Faroe grunted. "Money talks. Crawford has it. After I had a little come-to-Jesus talk with the sheriff, he agreed to stay out of our way."

"You sure of this?" Zach asked.

"No."

"Hold." He turned to the pilot. "Is there a Beaver Tail Ranch close by?"

The pilot looked at the land and pointed into the distance. "Up ahead where the dead trees are."

Zach went back to the phone. "I trust somebody at St. Kilda took apart the state of Nevada to see where Crawford put the fix in?"

"The governor owes Crawford," Faroe said. "So does a state senator and a few odd congressmen. So does the sheriff."

"Since when are corrupt politicians odd?" Zach asked.

"The sheriff thought he was doing a favor for a wealthy man who supports the local law. Nothing unusual about that, in Nevada or anywhere else."

Zach swept the ground with the binoculars. The shabby ranch surrounded by dead or dying trees came into focus at extreme distance. "Have you heard anything about Garland Frost?"

"He's improving much faster than they thought he would," Faroe said. "He's even trying to give orders."

Zach smiled. "Good for him. He can be a real son of a bitch, but he didn't deserve what happened."

"Child," Faroe said, "since when has 'deserving' entered into life's equation?"

"Since—hold it." Zach saw the light bar on the patrol car flash to life. "Cop car just lit up. It's going down at the Beaver Tail."

"Keep her alive."

Easier said than done.

Nevada
September 17
6:24 P.M.

Hi, Mary," Jill said into her sat phone. "I wanted to make sure you were still awake."

"Working on it. How's it on your end?"

"Just got a wake-up call from the cop behind me. I'm slowing down and pulling over. I'll leave the connection open."

"Watch yourself," Mary said. "Friends are hard to find."

"Same goes."

Jill laid the phone aside. Now that it was happening, she wished she had more time. Something had been bugging her since the service station at Indian Springs, but she couldn't pin it down.

Later, she promised herself.

The wheel bucked in her hands when the two tires on the

right side of the Escalade hit rough gravel at the edge of the pavement.

The cop pulled even, matched speeds, and used the loud-speaker in the car's grill. *"Follow me!"*

The voice sounded like Halloween in hell, but she signaled agreement and eased back onto the highway.

"Okay, I'm not pulling over," Jill said into the sat phone. "I'm back on the highway. He wants me to play Follow the Leader."

"Keep me in the loop," Mary said.

"Don't worry. I'm feeling real talkative right now."

Jill picked up her speed again to match the officer's. Two miles later, his brake lights flashed once in warning. She slowed as he did.

The cop's left turn signal came on.

"We're turning left," Jill said. "Old gravel road, mostly dirt and weeds now. Buildings about a half mile away. Dead trees around. Could have been a ranch once. Or a resort. Or—"

Her voice died as she focused on a battered, sun-faded sign next to the dirt road.

"Okay, this is weird," Jill said into the sat phone. "It's a cathouse. Or was. The sign reads 'Beaver Tail Ranch, Lots of Both Right Here. Y'all Come.' The place looks like it's been a long time between lube jobs."

Mary choked off laughter. "Anybody there?"

"So far, all I see is me and the cop. Why don't I feel good about that?"

"Because you're smart."

"Yeah?" Jill asked. "Then why am I here?"

Mary didn't answer.

Jill didn't expect her to.

81

Beaver Tail Ranch
September 17
6:25 P.M.

Score watched the deputy park at the end of a row of rickety cottages whose doors opened onto the dried, rocky area surrounding an equally dry swimming pool. The pale, curving body of the pool was pocked by dark holes where tiles had fallen out. The dying light gave the cement a creamy glow.

"Alert the ops in the barn," Score called over his shoulder.

A voice from another room called, "Yo."

Score watched the deputy go to the Escalade and circle his finger, silently telling the Breck woman to lower her window. Her words carried clearly from the bug to the headset he wore.

"I don't like this, Mary," Jill said. *"It looks deserted. And the deputy wants me to roll down the window."*

"Your call."

"I wish."

Score grinned. He knew it was his call all the way.

The deputy was a middle-aged man with buzz-cut hair beneath his uniform hat. He hitched his utility belt up over his belly, leaned in, and spoke through the partially open window.

"The man you wanted to meet is in the fourth cottage down the row," the deputy said, pointing.

"Who's with him?" she asked.

He shrugged. *"I was told to bring you here. I've done it. That's all I know."*

"That's right, you dumb putz," Score said in a low voice. "Now go back and sit in your car until we call and tell you to arrest Ms. Breck on extortion charges."

The deputy got in his car, made a U-turn, and sped back down the gravel road to the highway.

"What the hell?" Score said. "Dumb as a brick. Can't remember even simple orders." He hissed through his teeth. When the time came, he could get the deputy back here quick.

Through the partly open window, a surge of wind shifted dust into the Escalade.

"C'mon, babe," Score said in a low voice, pulling a black ski mask over his face. "Come and get it."

82

Beaver Tail Ranch
September 17
6:26 P.M.

'm going in," Jill said to Mary. "I'll call you once I check the money."

"Be safe. If that doesn't work, be matte-black bad."

Jill almost smiled. Someday she'd like to meet Mary. "Same goes."

She hung up and tossed the phone in back with the aluminum suitcases. It banged and clattered.

Hope your ears are ringing, whoever and wherever you are.

She picked up the BlackBerry and put it in one of the cargo pockets of her hiking pants. The belly bag hung around her waist. She opened the top zipper, shifted the pistol so that she could reach it with one grab, and checked the safety.

Matte-black bad.

And the mother of all rapids is just ahead.

The idea of rowing with a black pistol was unnerving.

It can't be any worse than my first trip alone down a class-five rapids.

Can it?

Jill got out of the car and looked at the cribs arrayed around the dusty pool. The "cottages" looked shabby, abandoned.

Looks like the sex business isn't real good out here.

Beyond the ranks of cottages, more than half a mile down the rutted road, several sagging barns and outbuildings silently stated that once this had been a working ranch, rather than a working girls' ranch. The distant buildings were even more beaten down by time and sun than the cribs, where sex had come with time limits and a price list.

The door in the fourth cottage away from her banged open with more than the force of the wind. There was a flickering blue light showing inside. Somebody was watching TV.

Got bored waiting, did you? she thought with grim satisfaction. *Too bad. I'm tired of being your puppet.*

Besides, she didn't know how much time it would take St. Kilda's people to close in on the ranch. She wanted to give them every second she could.

Slowly, like a woman with all the time in the world, Jill stretched, loosening muscles that had been confined too long in a car. The stretch felt so good that she repeated it, held it, and did it all over again a third time, breathing in the fading heat and exhaling clammy manacles of fear.

She could fairly taste the impatience radiating out of the fourth cabin.

You can just wait for it, dude, she thought. *I certainly have.*

Ignoring the primitive unease that slid down her spine from her nape to the bottom of her hips, she pressed down on part of the key fob. The Escalade's cargo area opened. She pulled out one suitcase and locked the vehicle again, leaving two cases inside. No way was she going to be shuffling three suitcases when she needed a hand free for the pistol.

The open door on the fourth cottage banged in the wind again. Despite the nerves jumping in her stomach, Jill didn't flinch at the sound. Wind rattling around old buildings was as familiar to her as her childhood.

Neither fast nor foot-dragging, she walked toward the open cottage.

And wished she was somewhere else.

Anywhere.

Zach, I sure hope you aren't far away. This isn't the kind of river I know how to run alone.

83

ake one quiet orbit close enough for me to read the serial numbers on the helo in back of the barn," Zach said to the pilot. "Do it fast."

The plane began shedding altitude. It hit the layer of air where the heat of day met the coming chill of night. The plane jumped around, a drop of water in a searing skillet.

Even with motion-compensated binoculars, getting numbers wasn't easy. He stared through the lenses and memorized the numbers on the helo.

"Got it," Zach said. "Take us up again."

The plane began to climb back into twilight while Zach punched number one on his speed dial.

"Faroe," said a deep voice.

"We've got trouble," Zach said. "There's a Jet Ranger

parked behind the whorehouse barn, which is about three thousand feet from the cribs. Two black Suburbans are parked with the helo. Looks to me like somebody brought in another security outfit."

"Who?"

"Trace these helo serial numbers," Zach said, speaking distinctly as he repeated what he'd seen through the binoculars.

"I'll get back to you," Faroe said.

Zach switched to the pilot's frequency. "We're going to land."

"Where?"

"On the highway."

"What about traffic?" the pilot asked.

"It's taken care of."

The pilot took the plane higher.

"I told you to land," Zach said.

"Do you want to walk away from it?"

"Yes."

"Then shut up and let me do my job."

Zach switched back to his sat/cell. "Come on, come on," he muttered. "How long can it take to run the numbers on a—"

His sat/cell rang. "Who are they?" Zach demanded.

"Red Hill International," Faroe said.

"The high-ticket security outfit out of Las Vegas?"

"The same."

"They have a pretty good rep," Zach said. "What are they doing working for an arsonist and shooter?"

"Best guess? They're getting hosed by a lying client."

"God knows that never happens in this business," Zach said sarcastically. "The really bad news is that friendly fire kills just as dead as the other kind."

"The ambassador is talking to General Meyer of Red Hill as we speak."

"Screw talking. I'm taking this bird down," Zach said. "Jill isn't armed to go up against Red Hill."

"Neither are you."

"Tell me something I don't know." Zach disconnected and switched frequencies to talk to the pilot. "Take me down."

"Which part of the highway?"

"The cop car with the flashing lights is the upwind end of the runway." Zach pulled his duffel from behind the seat and took out a long-barreled pistol and spare magazines. "The downwind end is behind us, where the RV is parked across the highway. From the dust I've seen in the headlights, I'm guessing we'll get occasional gusts of wind from southwest to northeast."

Not good news for a landing.

"I've noticed." The pilot's voice was flat.

He turned the plane into the wind and lined up with the highway. He dropped into a zone where the air wasn't quite as bumpy.

But it was still a long way from smooth.

"I'm glad St. Kilda will be the one explaining this to the FAA," the pilot said.

"Engine trouble, what can I tell you?" Zach said. "Put me as close as you can to the ranch entrance."

That meant a really short landing. The pilot hissed a word not approved by the FAA.

"Can you do it?" Zach asked.

"Tighten your harness" was all the pilot said.

Zach looked at the buildings coming closer with every second. Jill wasn't anywhere in sight.

She'd already gone in.

Be smart, Jill, Zach prayed silently. *Turn around and run like hell to the Escalade.*

But he knew she wouldn't. Worse, he knew it wouldn't make any difference if she did.

Red Hill wasn't a bunch of amateurs.

84

The gaping door of the fourth cottage opened into a room that looked cheap and hard-used. Jill stood to one side of the doorway and glanced around. The carpet was faded and stained, but the coffee table had been dusted recently. Two cheap cast-iron chairs huddled around an equally cheap ice-cream table. The TV was on, picture only. The sex tape that was running showed Tab-A-to-Slot-B graphics for the sexually stupid.

Despite the lack of landscaping and the dry pool, it looked like the room was still being used by working girls. The bed was made. The table and the TV had been dusted. The electricity was on.

A half-wall across the rear of the room partially concealed an oversize spa tub. The tub was full, but unoccupied.

The jets were off. The sharp, unmistakable smell of chlorine hung in the air.

Maybe the women make their tricks sluice off in bleach before they climb on.

She certainly would.

"Anybody here?" Jill called out.

In the bathroom, Score wanted to laugh. He finally had the bitch within reach. He'd been waiting for this moment for a long time.

Too long.

"Come on in," he snarled. "Close the door."

Jill thought the voice was almost familiar. *Blanchard without the cold? The mysterious caller without the filter?*

"Do you understand that there are people who know exactly where I am?" Jill asked, not entering.

"Just get your ass in here," Score said, scratching his face through a ski mask. "You're wasting my time."

Like you haven't wasted mine? Jill thought.

Slowly she stepped just inside the room. One of her hands was around the suitcase handle. The other was very close to the unzipped belly bag. Her heart was trying to crawl up her throat, but her stomach kept getting in the way.

"I said, close the door," Score said roughly. "You have a problem with your hearing?"

Jill's adrenaline turned into anger. "You want it closed, you close it."

Score stepped out of the bathroom. "You didn't learn much in Mesquite, did you?"

"Much what?"

"Fear."

"If you want to scare me, take off the mask. I bet I'll be terrified."

Score came around the half-wall and stood close to her. He was about her height, twice her weight, and three times her muscle. He glared at the single suitcase in her hand.

"Where are the rest?" he demanded.

"I have two paintings with me. You can inspect them, but only if you show me the money first."

"You think you clang when you walk?" Score asked.

Jill struggled with an unholy cocktail of fear, adrenaline, and anger.

She lost.

"Is that what happened to Modesty?" she taunted. "You didn't like listening to her clang?"

Score laughed despite the rage sleeting through his blood. "She was stupid. She jumped me, fell, and knocked herself right into the next world. You feeling that kind of stupid?"

The man's casual summary of her great-aunt's death was like a bucket of ice water in Jill's face.

"No," she said. "I'm feeling like getting this done and getting on the road."

"Don't want to play, huh?" He licked his lips slowly.

His tongue looked thick and wet in the slit of the black mask. She simply stared at him, suspended between adrenaline and disgust.

Score laughed, knowing he was scaring her. He went to the closet, yanked out a briefcase, and walked over to stand close to her.

Real close.

Jill wanted to back up. She didn't.

Ski Mask knows I'm sickened by him. He's using it to intimidate me.

She took the briefcase and handed over the suitcase, not even flinching when his latex-gloved fingers slowly stroked over her hand.

"Stay here," he said. "Count your money. Throw it on the bed and get off on it. Just don't try to leave before I tell you to. You'll get hurt. I'll enjoy that, but you won't."

"Where are you going?"

"To make sure the paintings are real."

The instant the door closed behind him, Jill raced to the window and pulled the heavy, faded curtain aside just enough to peek through.

The man stripped off his mask, walked toward the crib two doors down, knocked, and entered.

But not before she memorized his face in the last cool gasp of sunlight.

The angle of view she had was tight, but she could see another man step out of the other cottage into the dying day. The second man was well groomed, freshly shaved, dressed in black slacks, charcoal shirt, and no tie. His loafers screamed of city sidewalks and money, a lot of money.

He had the self-assurance to go with it.

Art buyer? Lawyer? Sleazy millionaire?

Whatever, he wasn't wearing exam gloves, which might put him a step out of Ski Mask's gutter. Then again, maybe not. The biggest thieves hired the most expensive lawyers.

The man in the exam gloves signaled toward the barn. She caught a flash of movement—sun on glass or metal—in the hayloft.

She brought out the BlackBerry and spoke clearly. "I'm in the number four cottage, no names exchanged. There's a well-dressed lawyer or art buyer or city millionaire waiting two doors down. The muscle-bound thug who met me in a ski mask is talking to him. There are more men out in the barn. I don't know how many. Whoever the opposition is, he has money to spend."

Jill let go of the curtain. "I'm alone right now. I'm checking to see if there's a back way out."

No such luck.

Above eye level, over the toilet, there was a sliding

frosted glass panel. Jill stepped up onto the lid of the toilet and eased the panel open.

"No back door, but there's a small window over the head. I see a barn and—" Her voice broke. She swallowed. "There are two really big black SUVs, smoked windows, waiting in the barn doorway. And what looks like the rotor of a helicopter. Are you listening, St. Kilda? *This is a trap.*"

And she couldn't see a way out.

85

Beaver Tail Ranch
September 17
6:34 P.M.

A white Lincoln Navigator wheeled up beside the Sky-master almost before the plane stopped. Zach flung off his seat harness, shoved open the door and leaped out, duffel in hand.

All the windows of the Navigator were rolled down. You could shoot into a car with closed windows, but it was hell to shoot back that way.

A man bailed from the front seat and pushed into the already full backseat, making room for Zach next to the driver.

Zach jumped in front and slammed the door. He didn't recognize anyone, and didn't need to. Their weapons were clean and carried professionally. Body armor bulked up their clothes.

Zach wished he and Jill were wearing some. But he hadn't taken his on the vacation that had become a job, and Jill probably didn't even know what body armor looked like.

The Navigator turned onto the ranch road and accelerated, its headlights looking frail against the dusk.

"Red Hill still in place?" Zach asked the driver.

"Last I heard," she said.

"Craptastic."

"That's what Faroe said."

"Anything new?" Zach asked.

"The client—"

"Jill," Zach cut in. "Her name is Jill."

The driver gave him a sideways glance. "The BlackBerry bug on her works fine. She spotted the Red Hill vehicles and helo and described them. She's in the fourth cottage on the right. She looked for a back way out. Didn't find one. There's an extra com rig for you in the glove compartment."

Zach opened it, put on the familiar lightweight headset, and adjusted the voice pickup. Now he could communicate with the rest of the team, as well as with St. Kilda.

"Any idea who hired Red Hill?" Zach asked.

"If Faroe knows, he isn't sharing."

"Then he doesn't know," Zach said.

The Navigator hit a rough patch and shuddered hard.

The driver kept the accelerator halfway to the floor.

Jill's voice whispered through Zach's earpiece. *"Ski Mask is coming back toward me. His body language is all about rage. So is the gun in his hand. Whatever happened in the sixth cabin really punched his buttons."*

"Faster," Zach snarled.

The accelerator slammed to the floor and the Navigator surged forward.

Zach had a cold feeling in his gut that it wouldn't be fast enough.

86

Beaver Tail Ranch
September 17
6:35 P.M.

Score yanked the ski mask back over his face and stalked toward the fourth cottage. Rage surged through him at being chewed out by some candy-ass lawyer half his age who thought a private investigator was another name for dumbshit errand boy.

Stupid lawyer about wet his pants when he saw my gun. Does he think the world is run by big words in his lying mouth?

The lawyer was a mistake.

Score figured he'd have to be the one to fix it. The thought made him smile.

A million bucks and South America was looking better every second. He'd eaten enough crap from way too many smart-mouthed suits.

He opened the door on cabin number 4 hard enough to bang it back on its hinges. Part of him was worried that his temper was slipping out of control.

The rest of him just wanted to bring it on.

The gloves are finally off. Any more shit goes around, I'll be the one sending it.

Jill looked up from the briefcase full of bundled, used hundred-dollar bills. She didn't know how much money was there, but she doubted it was two million. Even in hundreds, two million bucks was a lot of bills.

Twenty thousand, to be precise.

"Where are the rest of the paintings?" Score demanded.

"Where's the rest of the money?"

"You'll see it when I see the rest of the paintings."

Jill didn't know whether to be relieved or worried that she'd been right about the short money.

"Give me the keys to your car," he said curtly.

"Why?"

"Fuck it," he said, turning on his heel. "I'll just trash it and burn what's left."

"Wait!" Jill reached into her belly bag. The gun felt cold, unreal against her fingertips. The keys felt ordinary. She launched them toward him. "Catch."

Score nailed the keys with a vicious swipe of his hand.

Somewhere out back, an engine started up. Then another. The whine of a helicopter engine winding up drowned out the sound of the cars.

What the hell? Score thought. *First the deputy bags it, and now Red Hill is getting restless.*

He looked out the door just as a black Suburban accelerated toward the cottages and the dirt road leading back to the highway. Following the first Suburban was another, equally black, equally intent on leaving. The second vehicle stopped for men who swarmed up out of the desert, covered in dust and camouflage gear, weapons slung for travel.

With a vicious curse, Score pointed his gun toward Jill. "Go back to counting money, bitch. If you leave, you're dead."

Jill froze.

The front door slammed shut.

She grabbed the BlackBerry and ran to the front window.

"Something's happening," she said quickly into the bug. "The men in the Suburbans look like they're leaving. Ski Mask blew out of here with the mask in one hand and a gun in the other. From what I can see, he's totally lost it. Yelling at the sixth cabin, waving the gun around. Even in the dim light, his face looks flushed. Can't make out the words. Now the well-dressed dude is trotting over. He's got his cell phone against his ear and is yelling at Ski Mask. The helicopter is revving up. The Suburbans are driving toward the highway, ignoring the—"

Jill's voice cut off in shock as a pistol barked once. The well-dressed man spun sideways, then went down hard.

"Ski Mask shot him," she said numbly. "He just shot him. My God."

The gun barked again. A head shot this time. The body twitched and went utterly slack.

Ski Mask looked down at the body, spat, then turned away.

The BlackBerry fell from Jill's numb fingers. Something had gone terribly wrong.

And now the murderer was heading right for her.

She ran for the bathroom, grabbing the briefcase full of money and one of the wrought-iron chairs along the way. Once inside the bathroom, she locked the door, tilted the chair on two legs, and wedged it under the handle.

I'm safe for now, she thought, holding the briefcase like armor against her chest.

And trapped. Did I mention trapped?

The door creaked when someone kicked it hard. The next

kick sent cracks screaming through the cheap wood. The man outside was cursing steadily, savagely.

Jill stepped onto the toilet seat and wrenched the sliding window off its tracks. She didn't know if she could make it through the small opening.

She knew she had to try.

She grabbed the gun from her belly bag, banged it against the window frame, pointed the muzzle at the door, and pulled the trigger three times. Sound echoed around the small bathroom.

If Ski Mask had been standing in front of the door, he was badly hurt or dead.

A man screamed curses and returned fire. Bullets smashed through the door at waist level and below, screaming off porcelain.

Ski Mask hadn't been standing in front of the door. And now he was going to kick down the door and shoot her until she didn't move again. Ever.

87

Beaver Tail Ranch
September 17
6:38 P.M.

Gunshots sounded above the SUV's racing engine. Zach recognized the sound of the Colt Woodsman. The return fire was from a bigger caliber pistol.

"Faroe!" Zach said urgently. "Is Jill on the air?"

"No. We heard shots fired over Jill's bug, but Red Hill had already agreed to withdraw. What's happening?"

"Does Red Hill have her?"

"Negative."

Something burned like ice in Zach's chest, in his gut. "Jill could be down, hurt. Tell Red Hill to get the hell out of my way."

"The general has already done that. Jill's last known position was cabin four."

"Go!" Zach said to the driver.

The driver didn't bother to point out that she couldn't go any faster.

A set of headlights appeared, coming down the one-lane dirt road at them. Dust and grit boiled up in the lights.

"Don't slow down and don't give way," Zach said.

Jill, talk to me. Tell me you're alive.

You've got to be alive.

Silence came through his earphones.

"They're not giving way," the driver said.

"Put 'em in the ditch," Zach said.

The driver flipped on the emergency-blinker and kept the accelerator pinned, hurtling through the dusk.

The onrushing Red Hill vehicle held its course until the last possible instant, then veered off into the sage and scrub. There was a loud grinding as something metal slammed into rock. The Red Hill SUV caught air, slammed down, veered back onto the road behind Zach, and raced for the highway.

"There's a second vehicle somewhere," the driver said.

"Ignore it unless it gets in your way," Zach said.

"And if it does?"

"Ram it."

The driver waited, but Faroe didn't override Zach's command.

"Zach, you don't have body armor," Grace's voice said. *"Let the other ops take care of it."*

Zach didn't answer.

"Zach?"

The driver looked sideways at her passenger's face, then looked away. Zach was in the kind of mental space where she never wanted to go.

Headlights flared near the ranch. The second Red Hill SUV didn't even try to play chicken—it just took off into the desert, cutting a wide arc around the St. Kilda vehicle before getting back on the dirt road and speeding toward the highway.

An executive helicopter lifted and banked away, lights blinking, climbing fast, heading toward Las Vegas.

The driver put the Navigator into a power slide that ended at cabin number four. While the SUV was still moving, Zach opened the door and bailed out in a hail of rocks and sand. He hit the ground running, gun at the ready.

A shot rang out from number four. Then another.

The scream of pain was female.

A bulky male figure dashed out of number four and turned the corner, heading toward the back of the cottage, running hard. The gun in his hand had a surly gleam in the headlights. He held the weapon one-handed, fired the same way.

Like the shooter in Taos.

Bullets gouged dirt inches from Zach. He stopped and fired two closely spaced shots.

The man jerked, reeled, and scrambled around the back of the cabin. As he ran, he dropped a spent magazine and slammed another one into the butt of his pistol.

Zach went low through the front door of the fourth cabin, sweeping the room over his gun, remembering the driver's words.

She looked for a back way out. Didn't find one.

"Jill!" he called. "It's Zach!"

Silence answered.

Gun at the ready, Zach took three gliding steps and saw the bathroom door. The breaks streaking through the cheap paint and the bullet holes like black eyes made his stomach clench.

One kick finished what somebody else had started. The door screamed and broke away from its handle, taking the ice cream chair with it.

The bathroom was empty.

The toilet window gaped. Khaki shreds hung from it.

Jill was alive.

And so was the killer chasing her.

88

Beaver Tail Ranch
September 17
6:40 P.M.

Pain was a living, wild creature clawing at Jill.

She accepted it and kept running, long legs driving hard, as wild and alive as the pain itself.

The blood flowing down her right arm made the briefcase handle slippery and sticky at the same time. She switched hands. She thought about the gun in her belly bag.

Not now.

Later.

If I'm trapped again.

The first thing her great-aunt had taught Jill was not to waste bullets on a target she couldn't hit. Sprinting flat out the way she was, her right hand bloody from a wicked cut, she would be lucky not to shoot herself.

Don't look over my shoulder.

He's either behind me or he isn't.

A shot screamed off a nearby boulder. She flinched at the spray of rock chips.

He's behind me.

She kept running, turning unpredictably every few steps, like a rabbit chased by a coyote. Pain was a whip forcing her body to hold the sprint that was her best chance of saving her own life.

She'd hoped that the other shots she'd heard had been St. Kilda arriving and taking down Ski Mask. She'd hoped, but she hadn't expected. Even though it felt like she'd been running forever, she knew it had been only a few minutes. Three at most. Quite probably only two.

St. Kilda hadn't had time to arrive.

You're on your own.

Keep running.

Her heart felt like it was going to hammer out of her chest, her breath was starting to burn, but she didn't slow down her headlong sprint. She didn't take her concentration off the dusk-shrouded desert in front of her and the shoulder-high, brittle brush.

The lay of the land told her there was a ravine ahead. She didn't know where or how far.

She only knew that that ravine was her best chance of survival.

89

Beaver Tail Ranch
September 17
6:41 P.M.

Zach turned and raced for the front door of the cabin, blowing through the St. Kilda ops that had followed him inside.

"Stay here," ordered a male op. "You don't have body armor."

"Neither does she," Zach snarled, shouldering the op aside.

An op in the bathroom yelled, "Two people, running east. Client is first. Target is second. Too far for pistols. Bad light getting worse. Pass that rifle up here!"

Zach kept going, increasing his stride. In the dusk-to-darkness, a rifle wasn't going to do much good. Jill was doing the smart thing and running for cover.

So was the killer behind her.

From beyond the cabin, the sound of man-made thunder rolled through the twilight. Someone was shooting.

It wasn't a Colt Woodsman.

The op behind Zach began shouting orders to the others.

He ran hard, away from the back of the cabin, careful to stay just off the path of the target in case the op with the rifle got lucky. In his mind he replayed the few seconds he'd had the shooter in range.

I hit him, but he didn't go down.

Son of a bitch is wearing body armor.

A head shot would be the only fast way of killing him. And a head shot was a tough target when the man was running.

No problem. I'll just get close enough to shove the barrel up his ass.

But that would take time.

Time Jill didn't have.

90

Beaver Tail Ranch
September 17
6:42 P.M.

Jill was running hard through raking, dry, shoulder-high brush when she hit the edge of the ravine. She shifted her balance in midair, twisted, and landed with a jolting roll that made her hurt arm scream. The soft, sandy bottom of the dry creek absorbed some of the shock of her landing. The rest knocked out a lot of her breath and set her head spinning.

Like a cornered animal, she staggered to her feet, her breath almost as rapid as her heartbeat. She could hear the crackle of brush as Ski Mask ran closer. The ragged walls of the wash were more than five feet tall. Too high for a fast escape.

And a fast way out was the only thing that would keep her alive.

To her left a long, pale ribbon of rocks and sand slanted up to a dry waterfall. A glance told her that the dark rocks of the fall were too far off. Every step of the way she would show up against that light sand like the target she was.

She'd be shot to death before she reached the uncertain cover of the dry fall.

To her right the wash took a hard turn around a rocky outcrop. She was running for it before she consciously made a decision. She didn't know if she would find cover at the bend in the wash, or another long stretch of pale sand. But the crooked stretch of wash was the only hope she had.

She sprinted toward the bend, her breath harsh, burning.

A rock poked out of the darkness, tripping her, sending her flying. She landed facedown and felt black light spin down out of the sky over her. She tried to get up, knowing that the shooter could still see her.

Her body didn't respond.

Fighting to breathe, Jill waited to be shot.

91

Beaver Tail Ranch
September 17
6:42 P.M.

With each step, Zach gained on Ski Mask. Whatever the shooter did for a living, wind sprints weren't on his daily to-do list. As Zach closed in, he could hear the man's breath groaning in and out. Zach couldn't see Jill any longer. Either she'd gone to ground or she'd outrun Ski Mask.

Zach's earphones whispered. "The client vanished. The shooter is—shit, he just dropped into some kind of hole. Watch it, Zach!"

He kept running for a long five count, then skidded to a stop near the edge of the hidden ravine. Against the pale sand of the river bottom he saw a bulky shadow turn toward him.

He dropped to the ground as two shots exploded out of the ravine. The shooter was no more than fifteen feet away.

Zach didn't aim toward the muzzle flash. Instead, he aimed for the thighs.

Bring him down and then finish him off.

His gun kicked.

The shadow cursed and went to his knees.

More shots exploded out of the ravine. Even as Zach registered the fact that one of the shots came from a Colt Woodsman, the muscular shadow in the ravine jerked, driven backward, closer to Zach.

"You're dead, bitch!" the man screamed, raising his pistol to send a hail of bullets toward Jill.

Zach didn't know he was yelling until the shadow turned toward him. He saw the twilight gleam of eyes behind the mask and shot twice, the double tap of death.

The shooter slammed against the far wall of the narrow ravine and bumped down to sprawl in the sand.

Prone, Zach kept his pistol pointed at the space where the man's head should have been.

"Jill, it's Zach," he called. "Stay down until I tell you to move."

Nothing answered him but the echo of shots careening back from the mountains.

"Jill!"

Zach didn't remember jumping into the ravine, but he was there, flashlight in one hand and weapon in the other, kicking Ski Mask's gun away.

Not that it mattered. Even the darkness in the bottom of the dry creek couldn't conceal what two bullets at close range had done.

"I'm coming in, Jill. Don't shoot me."

He waited for an answer.

All he heard was the harsh sound of his own breathing and the yammer of ops in his headset, demanding information. He ripped the headset off and let it dangle around his neck as he went toward the darkness at the bend in the streambed.

When he saw Jill sprawled facedown against the pale sand, he went to his knees beside her. Fighting to breathe slowly, he put two fingertips against the pulse point in her neck and prayed like the choirboy he once had been.

Be alive.

Be alive!

His own heart was beating too fast for him to feel if there was a pulse in her neck. He drew in a deep breath and let it out slowly.

He felt the heartbeat under his fingertips at the same instant she groaned.

"She's alive," he said raggedly, replacing the headset. "Now shut up until I find out how bad she's hurt."

Faroe's snarled order stopped all communication.

"Jill," Zach said gently. Then more firmly. "Jill!"

Dazed eyes opened, looking very green in the cone of the flashlight's glare. She breathed with the gasps of someone who has had her breath knocked out. "I thought—you said—shut up."

"Them, not you." He kissed her sweaty, sandy cheek. "Where do you hurt?"

She rolled over, gasped as pain shot through her right arm, sat up, and said, "Pretty much everywhere, but it all still works after a fashion. You okay?"

He gathered her close. "I am now."

92

Beaver Tail Ranch
September 17
6:46 P.M.

Flashlight beams danced through the brush and finally came to the edge of the dry creek.

"We're coming in," a male voice said through Zach's headset.

"Just don't fall on us," Zach said.

Two St. Kilda operators jumped down the bank and landed in the sand like paratroopers.

"Anybody need a medic?" the female op asked.

"No," Jill said.

"Yes," Zach said.

"You told me you were okay," Jill said instantly, running her hands over him, searching for hidden injury.

"Not me," he said, kissing her gritty forehead. "You."

"Nothing wrong with me that soap and water won't cure."

Zach winced and touched his earphones. "Faroe wants me to be sure. Or it could be Lane. Their voices are getting more alike every day."

She leaned over the tiny mike that rested along Zach's jaw. "I'm okay. Dirty, tired, scuffed up some, but nothing dangerous."

"Where's the shooter?" one of the ops asked.

"About forty feet up the draw," Zach asked.

"Dead?"

"Oh yeah," Zach said.

"Know him?" the op asked.

"No. We'll need fingerprints. He was wearing full body armor."

"Gotcha. Photo ID won't help." The op turned and started up the dry wash.

"Why will it take fingerprints?" Jill said.

"Are you sure you want to know?" Zach asked.

The sound of Velcro being stripped open told Zach that the op had found the shooter and was removing body armor.

"That man killed Modesty," Jill said flatly. "I have a right to know."

"I shot him twice in the face at pretty close range."

She drew a ragged breath. "Okay. A photo ID wouldn't be much good right now. Do we know who the well-dressed dude was?"

The remaining op switched channels, talked quietly, and turned to Jill. "The ID we ran on the DOA makes him as a Carson City lawyer."

Jill blinked. "What was he doing here?"

"Good question," the op said. "We don't have an answer. Yet."

The female op's voice carried through the darkness. "Well, hello, Harry."

"You recognize the shooter?" Zach called.

"Not by his beautiful face, that's for sure," the op called back. "He's got a tatt on his left pec. Susie. That was his third wife's name."

"You know him?"

"I worked for Harry 'Score' Glammis while I went to college. He was private eye to Hollywood's rich and corrupt. I quit after Harry beat his wife's lover to death and got away with it. Still has the scars on his knuckles. It wasn't the first time he killed someone. Always in self-defense, of course."

"A real sweetheart," Zach said.

"Word was he had anger-management issues," the female op said dryly, "aka 'roid rage. Looks like you solved his problem the old-fashioned way."

Zach let go of Jill and came to his feet.

"Can you stand up?" he asked her.

Wincing, she pushed to her feet, then swayed a bit.

"You okay?" he said quickly, stepping close, ready to catch her.

"As long as I don't have to do another two-thousand-yard dash over broken country, I'm good." She accepted his arm and leaned into him. "Not great. Just good enough."

"You're way better than that." Zach brushed a kiss over her bleeding lip. "Ready?"

She started to say something, then stopped, remembering. "Have you searched all the cabins? Ski Mask—Score—said something about taking the paintings to be authenticated. I don't think the lawyer was the art expert."

Zach looked at the remaining op.

"We're checking the cabins one by one," the op said.

"Find anyone?" Zach asked when the op switched back.

"So far, two men. Their ID says they're Ken and Lee Dunstan, son and father."

"What's their excuse for being here?"

"They say that they were working for the dead lawyer," the op said. "The old man came here to look at some paintings for the lawyer's client, who claims he was being extorted by one Jillian Breck. Ken Dunstan came along to keep his father company in—and I quote—'a stressful situation.'"

Zach said something bleak under his breath.

"Now what?" Jill asked, looking at him.

"The story is just plausible enough to close the case right here."

"I didn't extort anyone! You know that!"

"Yes, I know." *For all the good that does,* Zach thought tiredly. "But with Glammis and that lawyer dead, we don't have anywhere to go."

"What do you mean?"

"It's over."

"But whoever hired Glammis is at least an accessory to murder," Jill said.

"Glammis is dead. All the dude paying the bills has to say is that Glammis exceeded his orders. Hell, it could even be true."

"You mean the son of a bitch who hired my great-aunt's killer can't be touched?" Jill demanded, her eyes narrow.

"Legally, no. And St. Kilda doesn't do illegal."

Jill just stared at him, her eyes dark.

He pulled her close and held her, rocking slowly. "I'm sorry. Sometimes a little revenge is all you get."

"It's not good enough," she said against his chest.

"I know. But it's all we have."

Sirens wailed in the distance. Someone had called the sheriff.

"Can St. Kilda keep us out of jail?" Jill asked.

"The sheriff won't like it, but yes. Self-defense is a fact."

Jill took a deep breath. "Good. I have an idea."

93

Las Vegas
September 18
2:00 P.M.

The conference room that the Golden Fleece had turned over to St. Kilda for the afternoon looked like an important high-end business center in L.A., Boston, Houston, or Manhattan. Gleaming table, automatic digital and sound recording, computers for everyone attending, pen and paper for those who felt more in control that way, and lush leather chairs for the comfort of the important high-end assets attending the meeting.

Twelve beautifully framed, unsigned landscape paintings stood on easels at the front of the room. Only Ramsey Worthington looked at them. Fascination and dismay fought for control of his expression.

Grace paused in the hallway outside the open door and asked Faroe in a soft voice, "Any word yet?"

"Incoming," he murmured, tapping his Bluetooth earpiece.

"With or without?" she asked.

"With."

Grace's smile was the kind that made Faroe glad she was on his side. She stepped through the open door into the room, where impatience and importance seethed. The air-filtration system was having a hard time blanking out the smell of stale bourbon that Lee Dunstan sweated with every heartbeat. His face looked like he'd slept in it for a long time.

"I was just going to advise my clients to leave," Carter Jenson said, looking at his ten-thousand-dollar watch.

"They would have regretted it," Grace said.

She didn't sit down. Instead she stood at the front of the table, dressed in a silk blouse, low heels, and well-cut slacks, a woman comfortable in her own power. She placed a folder within easy reach on the table.

Faroe leaned against the wall by the doorway with the relaxed readiness of a predator. He purely loved watching Grace downsize swollen egos.

"Do I need to summarize the events of yesterday?" Grace asked, looking around the table.

Caitlin Crawford's suit was much more expensive than her husband's, but she wasn't nearly as relaxed. She was humming like a power line.

"I don't see what yesterday has to do with my husband," she said in a voice that was more clipped than gracious.

"My clients and I have been fully briefed about the altercation at the, uh, ranch," Jenson said, slanting Caitlin a look.

"Bordello," Grace corrected. "The word exists for a reason. The only thing that 'ranch' sold was sex."

Caitlin's mouth flattened.

"Is it still your clients' position that none of them hired Harry 'Score' Glammis?" Grace asked Jenson.

"Yes," the lawyer.

"Damn right," Tal said. "Never heard of him until yesterday."

"Same here," Lee Dunstan said.

Worthington just shrugged and shook his head.

Grace raised one eyebrow, looked at the men, and said, "If that's the way you want it."

"That's the way it *is*," Jenson said.

With unpolished nails, Grace tapped on the folder. Then she removed several sheets of paper from the folder. "For fifteen months, Tal Crawford has been trying to reach an agreement with the IRS over a matter of illegal tax shelters."

"Irrelevant," Jenson snapped.

"This isn't a courtroom, but I'm more than happy to provide relevance," Grace said. "The amount to be paid is still being negotiated, but both parties agree that it will end up in the neighborhood of fifty to sixty million, including penalties."

Caitlin gasped and stared at her husband.

He patted her shoulder absently.

"As I'm sure Mr. Crawford's tax attorneys told him," Grace said, "there are two ways to settle that debt. The first is simply to write a check. Unfortunately, Uncle Sam doesn't like checks that bounce. Mr. Crawford's would."

Tal's face set in tight lines.

"Because bankruptcy specifically excludes federal taxes owed," Grace said, setting aside the sheets, "Mr. Crawford can't use bankruptcy to get out from under Uncle Sam. He could attempt to sell assets, but once word went out that Crawford International was in a big cash bind, the financial vultures would descend and pick him clean to the marrow of his corporate bones. Ultimately the government would be paid, but Mr. Crawford would be penniless."

Worthington shook his head, but not in disagreement. More in pity.

Caitlin's hands clenched, peach nails cutting into her palms.

"The only way Mr. Crawford can pay the government is to lower his bottom line," Grace continued. "Wonder of wonders, a senator from the great state of Nevada attached a rider to a popular bill, permitting individuals who met certain criteria to swap regional art for outstanding federal tax debt."

"Perfectly legal," Jenson said impatiently. "It's done all the time."

"It's called pork-barrel politics, and yes, it's done all the time," Grace said. "No one at this table will be surprised to find out that Mr. Crawford just happens to fit the criteria on the special rider on the popular bill that passed into law six months ago."

Worthington relaxed. It looked like his favorite cash cow was going to survive.

Crawford just looked irritated.

Dunstan's expression was bewildered. Or perhaps it was just his hangover muddling his brain.

"Mr. Crawford owns several pieces of modern art that would have more than paid his debt," Grace said, "but various banks are keeping those paintings in their vaults as collateral on various loans."

"Again, perfectly legal," Jenson said.

Faroe shifted just enough to make the lawyer give him a wary look. Unlike Grace, Faroe hadn't dressed up for the meeting. His dark T-shirt, jeans, and weapon harness were almost as intimidating as his eyes. If anyone asked, he was guarding the paintings.

No one had asked.

"Mr. Crawford has a large collection of Western art."

Grace reached into the folder and drew out more papers as she spoke. "But even the mostly friendly art appraiser wouldn't rate it at enough to cover his taxes."

She glanced at Worthington.

He didn't disagree.

"Auctions are notorious for yielding fat prices for the art involved," Grace said. "They call it auction fever for a reason."

"Again, nothing illegal," Jenson said.

Faroe wondered if a tape recording couldn't replace the lawyer.

"Without the Thomas Dunstan paintings," Grace said, "Crawford's Western art collection might raise twelve million dollars if sold quietly over a period of time. If word of a pending bankruptcy got out, the collection would go at fire-sale prices."

The lawyer looked at Worthington, who didn't disagree.

Grace set more papers on the table. "Which brings us to Thomas Dunstan."

"An iconic, very valuable Western artist," Worthington said promptly.

"Yes," she said, picking up another piece of paper. "Mr. Crawford bought one of Dunstan's paintings last year for four million dollars. Lee Dunstan sold it to him, then donated a share of another Dunstan to Carson City's new museum to offset the taxes."

"A bargain," Tal drawled. "It was one of Dunstan's best, and biggest."

Grace lifted a dark eyebrow. "Bargain or not, it raised the value of the rest of your large Dunstans by millions of dollars. But one sale of one painting wasn't enough to convince the IRS that your entire art collection was adequate compensation for your outstanding tax bill. I believe the figure they required was eight million per Dunstan."

"Dunstans are worth it," Tal said.

"That remains to be proved in the marketplace," Grace said.

"It will be proved tomorrow," Tal retorted.

"If you believe the buzz," Grace agreed. "Or if the auction is rigged. That, Mr. Jenson, is not legal."

Worthington started an indignant defense of the auction.

"Save it for the reporters," Grace said in a clear, cutting voice. "My question to you, Mr. Worthington, is what would happen if twelve previously unknown Dunstans came on the market at the same time?"

Dunstan started ranting about "lying Breck bitches."

Jenson leaned over and said something in Dunstan's ear that cut off the rant in midword.

Tal said, "The only new Dunstan I heard about lately was an out-and-out fraud. Some old lady running a con. Lee set her straight."

"I have a copy of a letter telling Modesty Breck that her painting was essentially worthless," Grace said, "and by the way, lost in the mail. Convenient."

"I object to that characterization," Jenson said quickly.

Grace ignored him. "A few weeks after Modesty received the letter, she died in a fire that the county coroner—an elected rather than a medical position, by the way—said was caused when she tried to refuel a hot stove."

Worthington winced.

"Her great-niece, Jillian Breck, inherited," Grace said.

"What does that have to do with us wasting our time here in—" Jenson began.

"When Jill sent JPEGs of three of her paintings to various art houses," Grace said over Jenson, "she didn't receive any responses. Then someone called 'Blanchard' phoned her and offered to buy the paintings. In the end, he didn't buy anything, but he returned the missing painting to her as slashed-up rags, along with a note that told her to go away or die."

Everyone except Jenson shifted uneasily, carefully not looking at each other.

"Jill went to Garland Frost, a very well-known expert on Western art," Grace said. "While she was at Frost's house, Harry 'Score' Glammis shot Frost and burned the shipping crates he thought contained twelve unsigned Dunstan paintings."

"What the hell?" Tal muttered.

Caitlin shut her eyes. Her nails cut deeper into her palm.

"The paintings weren't burned that time, either," Grace said. "Jill discovered that her paintings and Frost's two signed, authenticated Dunstans all had the same thumbprint along the lower edge of the stretcher."

Worthington sat up straighter and looked at the twelve paintings with a combination of lust and horror.

"Jill went to Canyon County to search for a set of Dunstan's fingerprints. She found it. She also found that the thumbprint on her paintings and Frost's wasn't Thomas Dunstan's."

"Told you so," Lee said fiercely. "Lying bitch was—"

"Jill Breck has all of you by the hair your barber doesn't cut," Grace interrupted coldly. "I suggest you shut up and listen."

Lee's jaw sagged open.

Faroe smothered a smile.

"The thumbprint belonged to Jill's grandmother, Justine Breck, who was also an artist," Grace continued smoothly. "Along with the thumbprints on the arrest cards, Jill found a letter in which Justine told Thomas Dunstan that she was through living a lie."

Lee started ranting again, but it was under his breath.

Faroe stepped from the doorway long enough to let Jill

and Zach in. Zach stayed with Faroe, leaning against the wall, wearing pretty much the same clothes as his boss, right down to the weapon harness.

Jenson, who had been taking notes, shoved the tablet away. "All the thumbprints prove is that Justine was with Dunstan when the canvases were painted, a fact that is already well known. She was his muse. He didn't paint without her."

Zach grimaced. The lawyer had been well briefed.

"Dunstan didn't paint without Justine," Jill said, "but she painted without him. I can prove it. Just as I can prove that Thomas Dunstan signed my grandmother's paintings in order to sell them into the macho world of Western art."

"Preposterous," Jenson said flatly.

Grace's smile was as cold as her husband's. She pulled a final piece of paper from the folder. "This is a sworn deposition from Garland Frost, stating that it is his opinion the twelve unsigned canvases were painted by the same artist who produced the known, signed Thomas Dunstans."

"Even if that proves to be correct," Worthington said, "it hardly proves that the artist was a woman!"

Zach straightened, walked to the canvases at the front of the room, and picked up *Indian Springs*. He took it to Worthington.

"It's unusual for Dunstan to—" Worthington began after barely a glance at the canvas.

"—paint buildings into the landscape," Zach finished curtly. "But he did paint a few and you know it."

Reluctantly Worthington nodded.

"Is there anything else about the canvas that makes you question that it's a Dunstan?" Zach asked.

With an uneasy glance at Tal and Lee, Worthington cleared his throat. "I'd have to study it for—"

"Blah blah blah," Zach cut ruthlessly. "We're not in court.

If someone walked in and plopped this on your desk, which artist would you immediately think of?"

Worthington sighed and gave in. He had his own reputation to consider. Anyone but an idiot could see what was in front of his face. "Thomas Dunstan, of course. The brushwork, the unflinching evocation of the land, the raking light . . ." He shrugged. "Dunstan."

"When *Indian Springs* was painted, the gas station had just been built," Jill said, putting a faded photograph next to the canvas. "And Thomas Dunstan had been dead for five years."

94

Las Vegas
September 19
5:00 P.M.

Jill walked into a room that had a well-stocked wet bar, comfortable furniture, and a closed-circuit TV screen that was half the size of the wall. At present, the screen showed a mosaic of twelve pictures, various angles on a crowd of people drinking wine, champagne, beer, and whiskey, eating delicate lamb "lollipops" and clever pastries, chatting, and clutching catalogues.

"Wow," Jill said.

Zach disconnected from his call, put the cell phone in his jeans pocket, and stepped into the room.

"Sports betting is big in Vegas," he said absently, thinking about what he'd just learned. "The Golden Fleece is more than happy to accommodate the high rollers who want a private party. You can watch lots of games at once or you can have live feed of a single game on the whole screen."

"Y-gene central," she said, sitting down on a long, soft leather sofa.

Zach dropped down next to her, putting a dent in the cushion that made her slide toward him. On the low table in front of them there was a bottle of champagne in an ice bucket, an array of savory foods from the auction floor, and a remote controller that had enough buttons to put a satellite in orbit. He picked up the remote and flipped it end for end.

"Welcome to the biggest temporary casino and art bazaar in Las Vegas," Zach said, aiming the remote at the huge screen. "In the next few hours, somewhere between twenty-five and fifty million dollars worth of art will change hands—not counting the Dunstans that have been withdrawn."

"Brecks," Jill said automatically. "They were painted by my grandmother."

Zach hesitated, then shrugged. "That's for the art community to decide."

"But—" She stopped abruptly. Zach was right. She just didn't like it.

So instead of thinking about the tangle that was Justine's heritage, Jill watched the mosaic of screens covering the casino's mammoth ballroom. A stage had been erected across the front of the room, with a podium for the auctioneer and a long bank of phone positions behind. The ballroom floor had been cleared, except for several bartending stations and a dozen banquet tables heavily laden with finger food.

Several hundred people milled around the free food and drink, but even more fanned out to the perimeter of the room, where hundreds of paintings and sculptures were arrayed behind metallic gold ropes.

"It's not too late," Zach said abruptly, putting the controller aside.

"For what?" Jill asked.

"To let Ramsey Worthington, Lee Dunstan, and Tal Crawford make you a multimillionaire."

"I'd rather watch them eat their words about the greatest *masculine* painter of the American West."

"You sure? Worthington is right—it will be some time before the art historians sort out the new status of Thomas Dunstan/Justine Breck."

"Long enough to bankrupt that son of a bitch," Jill said flatly.

"Which one?"

"The one who's been pumping up the price of Dunstans and rigging an auction so that he can trade his Dunstans for a whacking tax debt."

"Tal Crawford," Zach said.

"That's the son of a bitch I had in mind," she agreed.

"By the time he goes bankrupt, your inheritance might be worth thousands, not millions," Zach pointed out. "Western art collectors can be a macho, pigheaded lot."

"All the sweeter," she said with a grim smile.

He hesitated, then decided Jill might as well know what Faroe had just told him. "Even though it was Caitlin, not Tal, who hired Score?"

Jill turned toward him so fast her short hair flew. "What?"

"St. Kilda hacked some phone records," Zach said, tucking a flyaway strand behind Jill's ear. "Caitlin Crawford was the one pulling Score's strings. Paying for it out of her household account, which Tal funded but never asked where it went."

"Some account," Jill muttered.

"The rich are different. Bottom line is that Tal didn't know what his wife was doing."

"Are you sure?"

"He swore he'd take a lie detector test," Zach said. "Faroe believes him. Said the old boy about stroked out when his wife screamed at him that he'd ruined everything, that she'd die poor and it was all his fault because he'd lost his business edge."

Jill didn't say anything.

"Does that change anything for you?" Zach asked.

"Like what?"

"The auction. Your paintings."

Jill's eyes narrowed. Her fingertips tapped a slow rhythm on his thigh.

Zach let her think while he watched the TV. He recognized a surprising number of people from his years with Garland Frost. Men from Texas with beers and bolo ties, women with wineglasses held nipple-high, the better to display their five- and six-carat diamonds. The diamonds were real. Most of the breasts weren't.

One screen showed a Montana art dealer who wore a rodeo cowboy's championship belt buckle—one he'd earned the hard way rather than a pawnshop trophy. Another screen showed a pig farmer from Arkansas who owned the second-largest string of slaughterhouses in the West. His wife was the trophy variety, wearing second-skin designer jeans, a lacy flesh-colored bra, and a black suede vest that had been carefully tailored to barely cover her.

Other screens showed a prematurely bald Hollywood producer with so much vanity he shaved and polished his head. Near him was a pleasantly cutthroat venture capitalist with his intelligent, gracious wife.

"She thought she was helping her husband?" Jill asked finally.

"You mean Caitlin?"

"Yes."

"She was helping herself," Zach said. "She's pathologically afraid of being poor."

Jill let out a long breath. "And I'd rather be poor than play a rich man's game of blue smoke and murder. Let her sink."

Zach shifted suddenly, lifting Jill onto his lap. "I really like that about you."

"What?"

"You know what's real and what isn't."

"Rapids are real," she said, putting her arms around him. "You're real. I'd like to teach you about my favorite rivers."

"Sold," Zach said. "As long as I get to show you my favorite junkyards and teach you about old muscle cars along the way."

"Still looking for that hemi whatever?"

"That's a convertible Hemi-cuda, the Holy Grail of muscle cars."

She laughed and leaned closer. "I suspect you'll learn the rivers real quick, but I have to warn you, I'm not good at the car thing. It could take me a long time to learn."

Zach's arms tightened around her. "I'm counting on it."

Welcome to the World of Elizabeth Lowell

Turn the page for a look

at the other suspenseful titles available from

the celebrated *New York Times* bestselling author

ELIZABETH LOWELL

Innocent as Sin

Kayla Shaw is a private banker in Arizona—smart and capable but underpaid and underappreciated. Rand McCree is a haunted man who paints landscapes in the Pacific Northwest, burning with a need for answers about the terrible event that shattered his world. They are two strangers with nothing in common . . . until their lives entwine—and explode.

On what at first appears to be an ordinary day, everything changes for Kayla, as she barely escapes a kidnapping attempt and finds herself accused of a shocking crime: the illegal laundering of hundreds of millions of dollars. Damned by lies and false "evidence," she is trapped with no place to run.

After five agonizing years, Rand has finally been offered what he desires the most: the name of his twin brother's murderer. Hungry for vengeance, he accepts a job with St. Kilda Consulting that will place him in the killer's orbit . . . and tantalizingly close to Kayla Shaw.

Suspicious of each other, needing each other, they are two against the world—with unknown enemies on all sides and even the government itself suspect—as the violence of the past erupts in the present. And now innocence alone will not be enough to keep Kayla Shaw alive. . . .

The Wrong Hostage

Orphaned at thirteen, Grace Silva clawed her way out of poverty and violence to become one of the most respected judges on the federal bench. Grace believes in the rule of law—lives it, breathes it. She has always been buttoned up and buttoned down.

Except once.

Joe Faroe has learned that laws are made by politicians, and politicians are all too human. He believes in the innocents, the ones getting ground up by governments that are too polarized or too corrupt to protect their own citizens. He's been through the political meat grinder himself. It cost him his career, his freedom, and the woman who still haunts him. Since then Faroe has worked outside the rules and politics of government as a kidnap specialist for St. Kilda Consulting, a Manhattan-based global business that concentrates on the shadow world where governments can't go. He is good at his work—intelligent, confident, ruthless.

Until a friend dies trying to kill him.

Now Faroe is out of the business. Retired. He's through trying to save a world that doesn't want to be saved.

Then Grace comes to him, past and present collide, and Faroe finds himself sucked back into the shadows, tracking a violent killer who holds the life of Grace's son in his bloody hands.

Whirlpool

When an exquisitely crafted, authentic imperial Fabergé egg mysteriously shows up at Laurel Swann's home studio, she knows it can only be from one person—her father, who has drifted in and out of her life for as long as she can remember. But this time Jamie Swann leaves her something too many people will kill for.

Out of her league and desperate, Laurel is forced to accept help from the very man who is trying to ensnare her father in his own web of double crosses. Cruz Rowan can help her stay alive, but will he do the same for her father?

Always Time to Die

Former U.S. Senator Quintrell is dead. His son, New Mexico's governor, is preparing his run for the highest political office in the land. And dark family secrets are about to explode with the devastating force of a Southwestern earthquake.

An eccentric Quintrell aunt has invited genealogist Carolina "Carly" May to their Taos compound to compile a record of the illustrious family. But digging into the past is raising troubling questions about a would-be president's private life . . . and the grisly street crime that left his drug-addicted sister dead. As a dark world of twisted passions and depravity slowly opens up before Carly, there is no one she dares trust—perhaps least of all Dan Duran, a dangerous, haunted enigma who's tied to the Quintrells' history. But she will need an ally to survive the terrible mysteries a father carried to the grave—because following the bloodlines of the powerful can be a bloody business. And some dead secrets can kill.

The Secret Sister

Christy McKenna, the smartest fashion writer in New York, thought she'd escaped her childhood in the impoverished rural West. Then came a call for help from the one person she could not refuse—her sister, the internationally celebrated model known only as Jo.

Jo's plea draws Christy back to the magnificent mountains and mysterious red-rock canyons of the Four Corners country. But she's too late—Jo has disappeared. However, Christy does find an unlikely ally in outlaw archaeologist Aaron Cain, and together they pursue Jo and a fabulous cache of ancient Indian artifacts worth millions.

Christy and Cain clash at every turn, but their antagonism soon turns into partnership—and blazing passion.

The Color of Death

Kate Chandler has accepted a commission that will solidify her reputation as a world-class gem cutter. But during what should have been a simple transfer, seven rare, priceless sapphires vanish without a trace along with their courier, her brother Lee, who now, quite possibly, is dead. And suddenly Kate is on the run, pursued by federal agents who believe she's the criminal mastermind of a cunning bait-and-switch.

Only Kate suspects the terrifying truth: that she's stumbled into a conspiracy of deceit, betrayal, and cold-blooded murder that goes far beyond a simple jewel heist. Getting Sam Groves, the FBI special agent who's her constant shadow, to trust her is a step in the right direction—but it may be too little and too late in a bloody game where terror dictates her every move. Because a ruthless assassin has already received the order that Kate Chandler must die. . .

Die in Plain Sight

When Lacey Quinn inherits the striking landscapes done by her late, much-loved grandfather, she believes they are as good as anything hanging in museums. But the paintings now in her possession are more than the works of a talented master. They are anguished voices from the grave . . . crying murder!

Lacey begins researching her grandfather's past—and is rocked almost immediately by a strange series of violent events. Someone wants to steal her inheritance, to reduce the paintings to unrecognizable ashes in a suspicious blaze. Someone wants to prevent Lacey from examining her grandfather's work too closely . . . by any means necessary.

Ian Lapstrake, a security specialist, has taken an interest in Lacey's inheritance . . . and in her. Troubled by what he sees, he becomes Lacey's shadow, as her search for answers leads them both down an ever-darkening road paved with lies, blood, and devastating secrets.

Running Scared

In the scorching heat of the Southwestern desert, a frightened old man knows his time is quickly running out . . . as the lethal secret he protects can be hidden no longer.

Risa Sheridan knows everything about gold—its mysteries, its allure, its perils. Her boss, Shane Tannahill—owner of the ultra-successful Las Vegas gambling mecca the Golden Fleece—is addicted to the stuff. Now an ancient Celtic piece is being offered to Shane for his collection, with the promise of more to come, and the casino owner is hooked. But though she shares Shane's enthusiasm, Risa is wary—because something about this particular artifact is mysterious and troubling, something that says "stay away." It is a voice that should be heeded, because soon people are dying all around them. And whether it's an ancient curse that has taken hold of their lives or the simple, murderous greed of unscrupulous adversaries, there is suddenly no place in the surreal, blinding glitter of Vegas for Risa and Shane to hide . . .

Moving Target

The troubling message from Serena Charters's late grandmother appears in a package containing four pages of a centuries-old illuminated manuscript—a strange inheritance that hides many secrets . . . and has already cost many lives. Seeking answers, Serena turns to Erik North of Rarities Unlimited, a reclusive manuscript appraiser with a passion for the past. Without warning, they are thrust together into the center of a lethal firestorm that rages between two worlds—one long dead, yet living on in an ancient text, the other chillingly alive and fraught with peril. In the blink of an eye, Serena and Erik have become targets of an unseen and determined stalker as they get closer to shocking revelations about Serena's legacy, the cold murder of an eccentric old woman in the heat of the Mojave Desert . . . and just how far a remorseless killer is willing to go. And now their only slim hope of survival is to keep moving.

THE DONOVAN SERIES
Amber Beach

Donovan International is a power to be reckoned with in the dazzling and cutthroat worldwide gem trade—and is therefore a target for the murderous greed of unscrupulous competitors. Though a shrewd businesswoman, Honor Donovan has been effectively shut out of the dangerous family enterprise by the Donovan males—until her favorite brother, Kyle, mysteriously vanishes along with a fortune in stolen amber.

Now, linking up with "fishing guide" Jake Mallory—whose previous association with the Donovans has bred mistrust and suspicion—Honor sets out for the Pacific Northwest in search of answers. But old wars and new politics have lured ruthless, high-stakes players from around the globe into a deadly game. And suddenly, elusive trust can be the only salvation—and death the penalty for deceit—if Honor and Jake hope to survive the perilous intrigues surrounding a breathtaking lost Czarist treasure known as the Amber Room. . .

THE DONOVAN SERIES
Jade Island

Wild and restless, Kyle Donovan has freed himself from the constraints of his family's high-powered gem-trading empire to rove the world as a treasure hunter. Now the president of Donovan International has given Kyle an assignment with explosive ramifications. A case he must take.

When one of China's legendary cultural treasures is stolen, Lianne Blakely, a mysterious and beautiful jade expert, is accused of the theft. It's Kyle's job to get to the bottom of what could be a potential disaster for the Donovans as well as for Lianne.

But Kyle finds himself irresistibly drawn to the exotic beauty and captivated by her fierce claim of innocence. Soon they are in dangerous pursuit of the real thief, drawn deeper into the perils of spiraling power plays, and linked by a passion as powerful as the lore of the ancient culture and as enduring as the splendor of the treasured jade.

THE DONOVAN SERIES
Pearl Cove

Surrounded by potential enemies, Hannah McGarry faces the mystery of her husband's suspicious death, the prospect of bankruptcy . . . and the disappearance of the fabulous Black Trinity necklace that was to be her financial security. Desperate, she calls Archer Donovan, a silent partner in Pearl Cove, her late husband's pearl farm venture. He might help her . . . if the price is right.

Archer Donovan would rather forget he'd ever heard of Pearl Cove . . . its memories of living on the dark side, the soul-numbing certainty that there was no law, no justice, no mercy, just hunters and the hunted. That life taught him to trust no one but family. But when Hannah McGarry calls in an old debt Archer is back in the game. And at his side in pursuit of the stolen fortune is a woman he shouldn't want, yet cannot resist . . . a woman who may know more than she's telling about her husband's death . . . and more than is safe to know about the dark and elusive black pearls. With deadly competitors tailing them, Archer and Hannah race through uncharted waters in search of the fabulous Black Trinity. And the closer they come to finding the coveted pearls, the closer they come to danger and death . . . and to each other.

THE DONOVAN SERIES
Midnight in Ruby Bayou

Faith Donovan is famous for crafting exquisite jewelry studded with fabulous gems. But the dangerous task of acquiring the rare rubies she needs for her art has taught Faith to be wary of anyone outside her own family—especially someone like Owen Walker, an adventurer with an intimate knowledge of the ruby trade and man's murderous greed. But now necessity has thrown them together, as they venture into the shadowy world of the wealthy and mysterious Montegeaus in search of quality stones. A powerful Georgia clan descended from pirates, the Montegeaus are said to possess a staggering fortune in gems, hidden for generations in the legendary Blessing Chest. In the living shadows of historic Ruby Bayou, Faith and Walker are soon drawn into a terrifying web of corruption and betrayal, and haunted by the dark, unfolding secrets of Montegeaus past and present. For there are those who would kill for the contents of the Blessing Chest. And now two outsiders who have learned too much stand in the way . . .

Breathtaking passion and suspense from
New York Times bestselling author

ELIZABETH
LOWELL

THE COLOR OF DEATH
978-0-06-050414-4

DEATH IS FOREVER
978-0-06-051109-8

DIE IN PLAIN SIGHT
978-0-06-050411-3

THIS TIME LOVE
978-0-380-78994-8

RUNNING SCARED
978-0-06-103108-3

EDEN BURNING
978-0-380-78995-5

MOVING TARGET
978-0-06-103107-6